THE BREAKAWAYS

Cathy G. Johnson

Colors by Kevin Czap

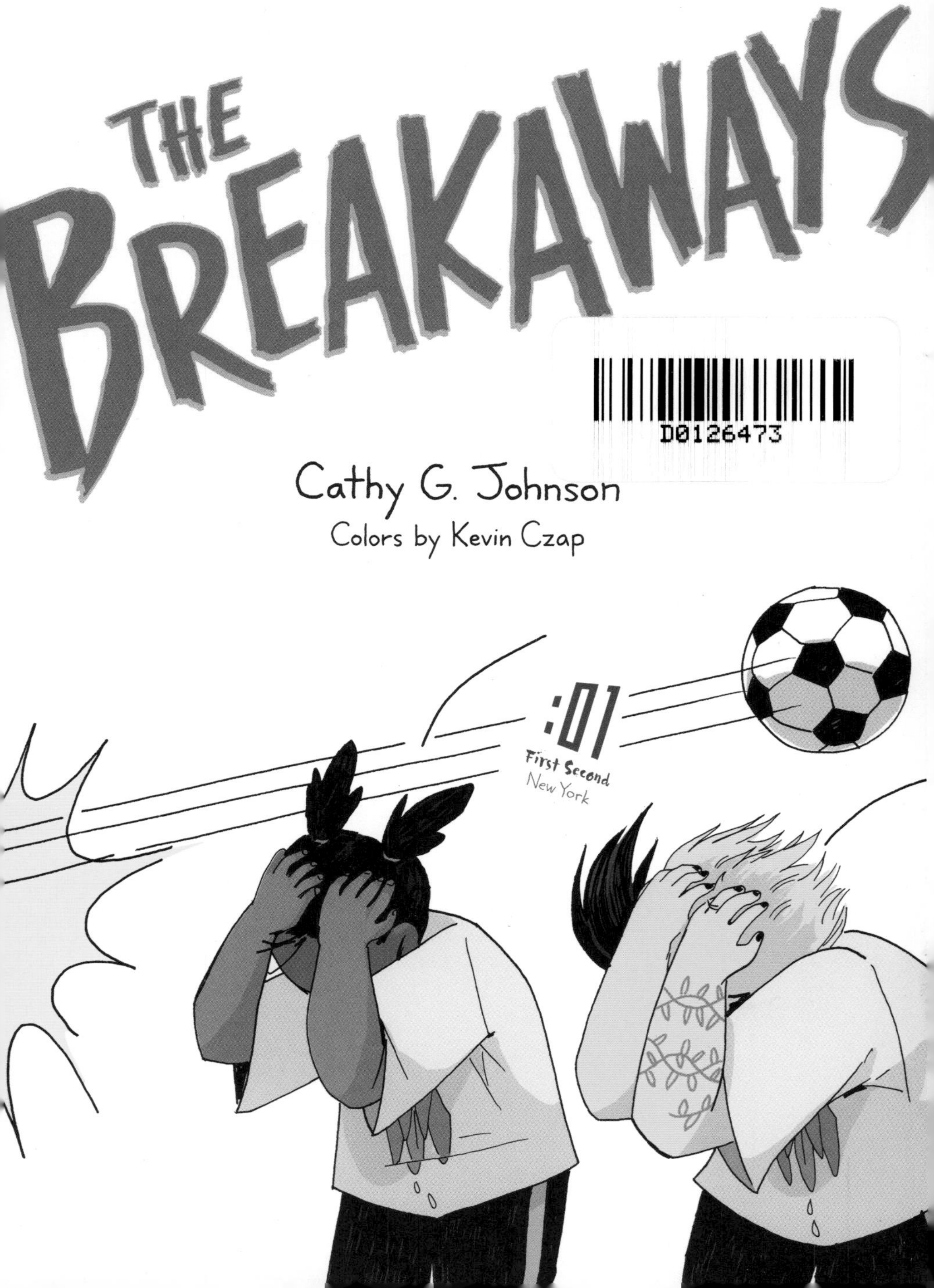

:01 First Second
New York

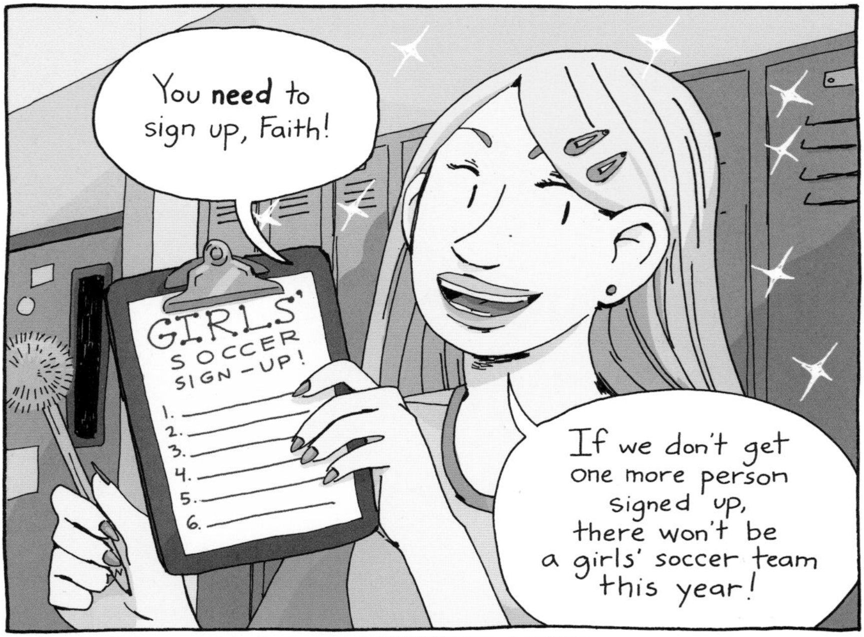
You **need** to sign up, Faith!
GIRLS' SOCCER SIGN-UP!
1.
2.
3.
4.
5.
6.
If we don't get one more person signed up, there won't be a girls' soccer team this year!

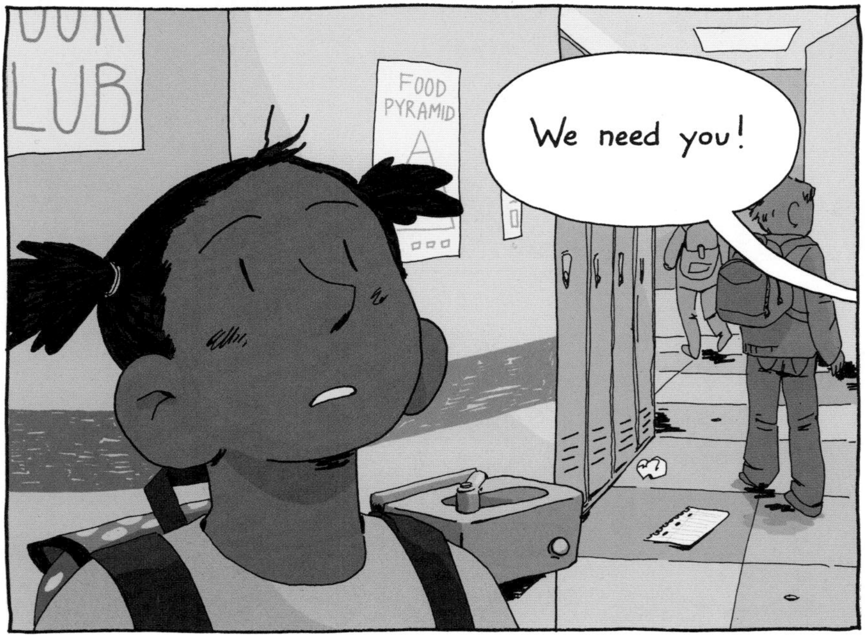
LUB
FOOD PYRAMID
We need you!

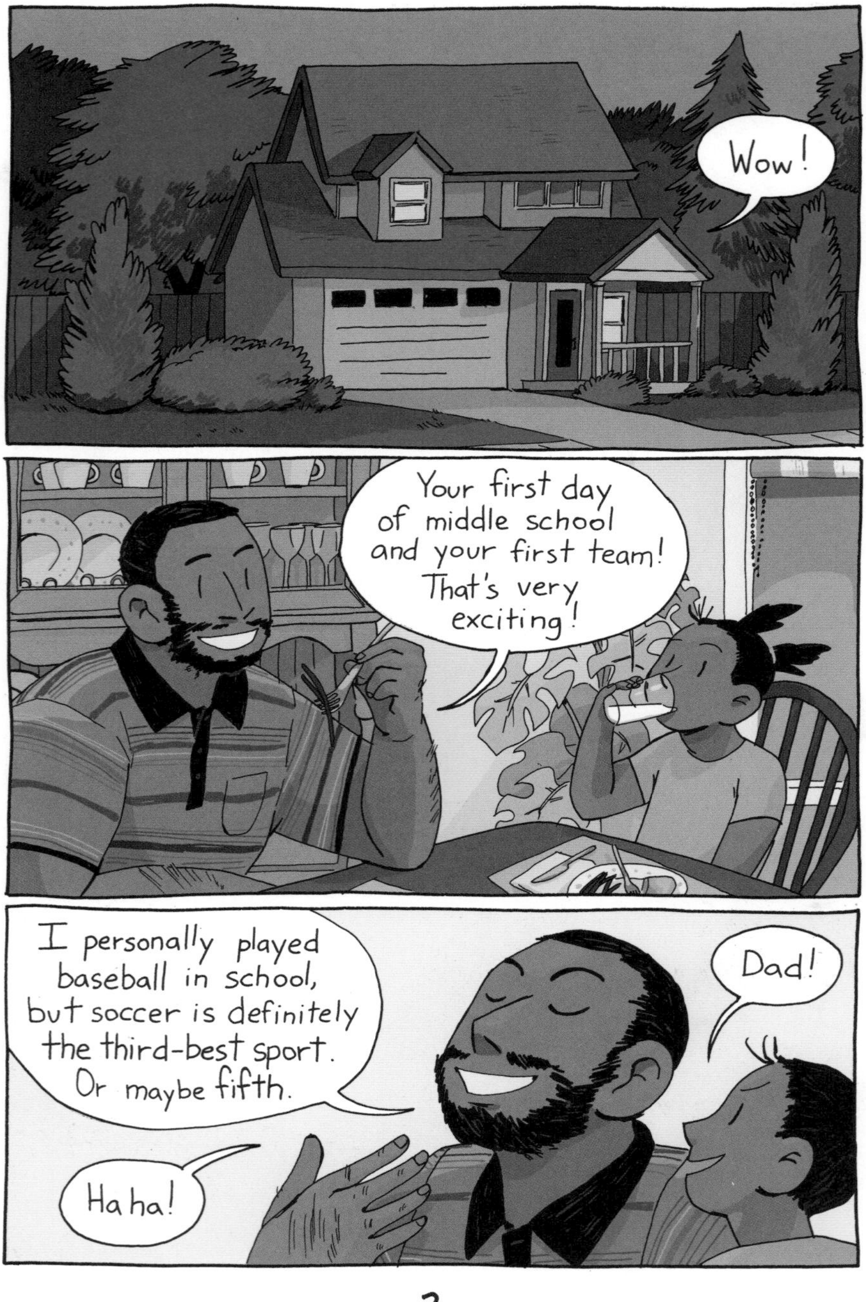
Wow!
Your first day of middle school and your first team! That's very exciting!
I personally played baseball in school, but soccer is definitely the third-best sport. Or maybe fifth.
Dad!
Ha ha!

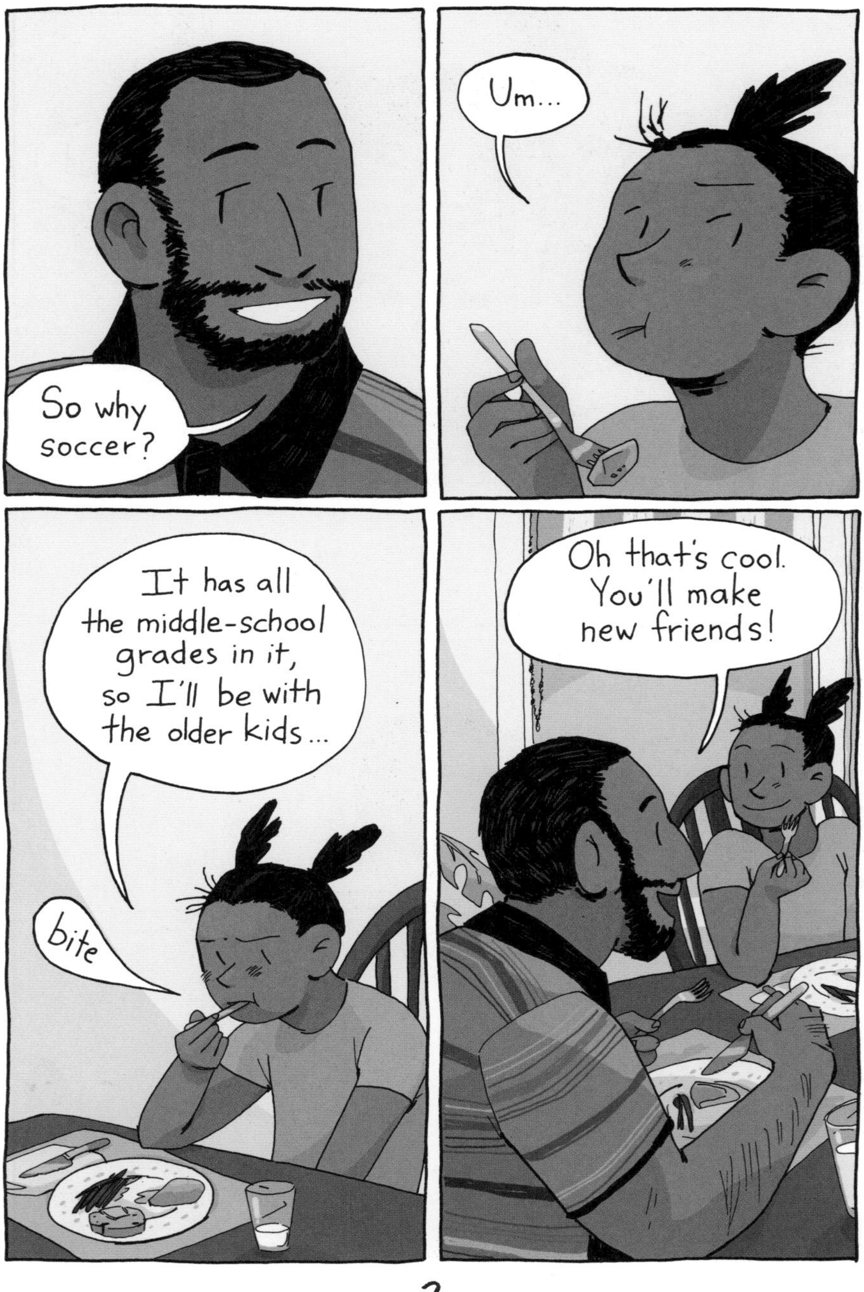
So why soccer?
Um...
It has all the middle-school grades in it, so I'll be with the older kids...
bite
Oh that's cool. You'll make new friends!

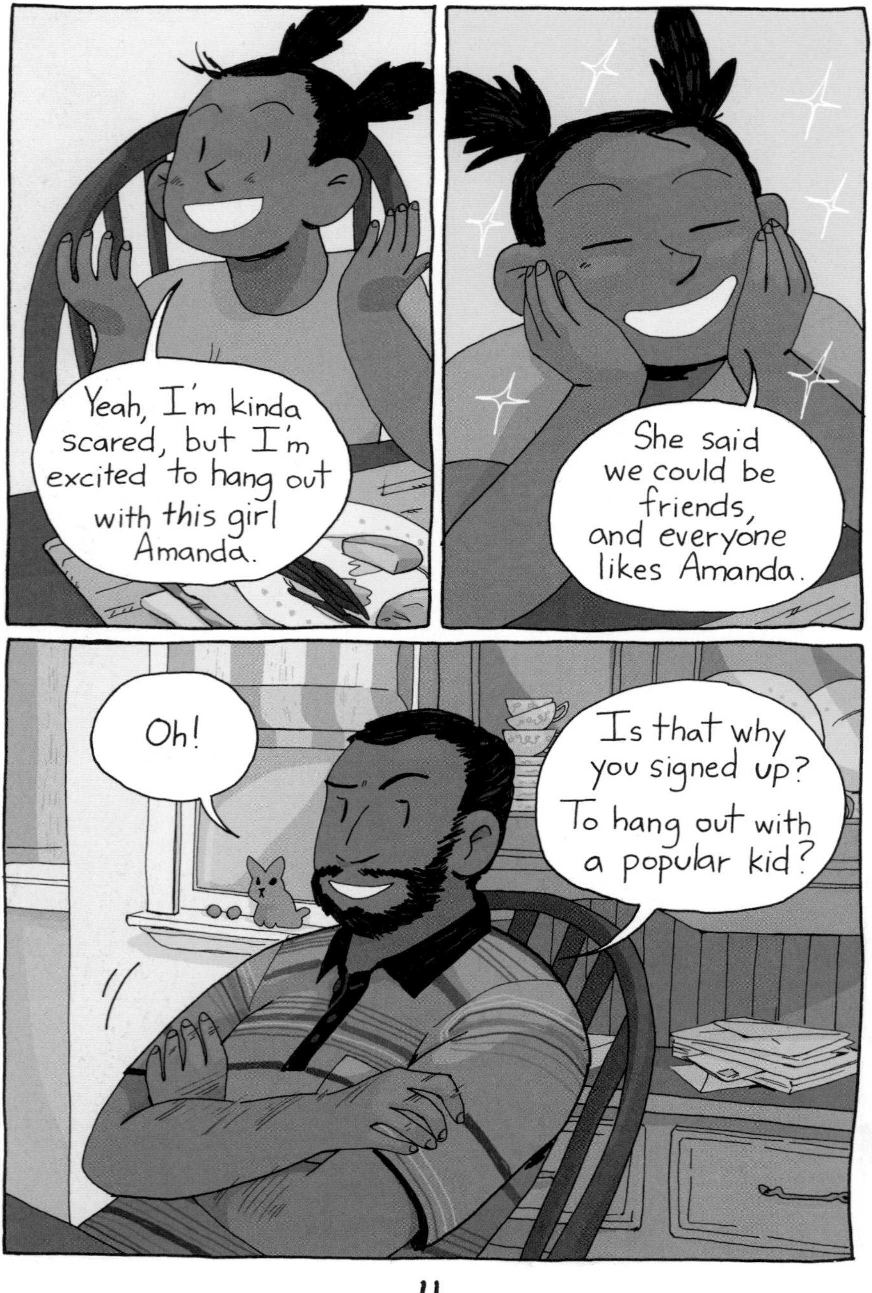
Yeah, I'm kinda scared, but I'm excited to hang out with this girl Amanda.
She said we could be friends, and everyone likes Amanda.
Oh!
Is that why you signed up? To hang out with a popular kid?

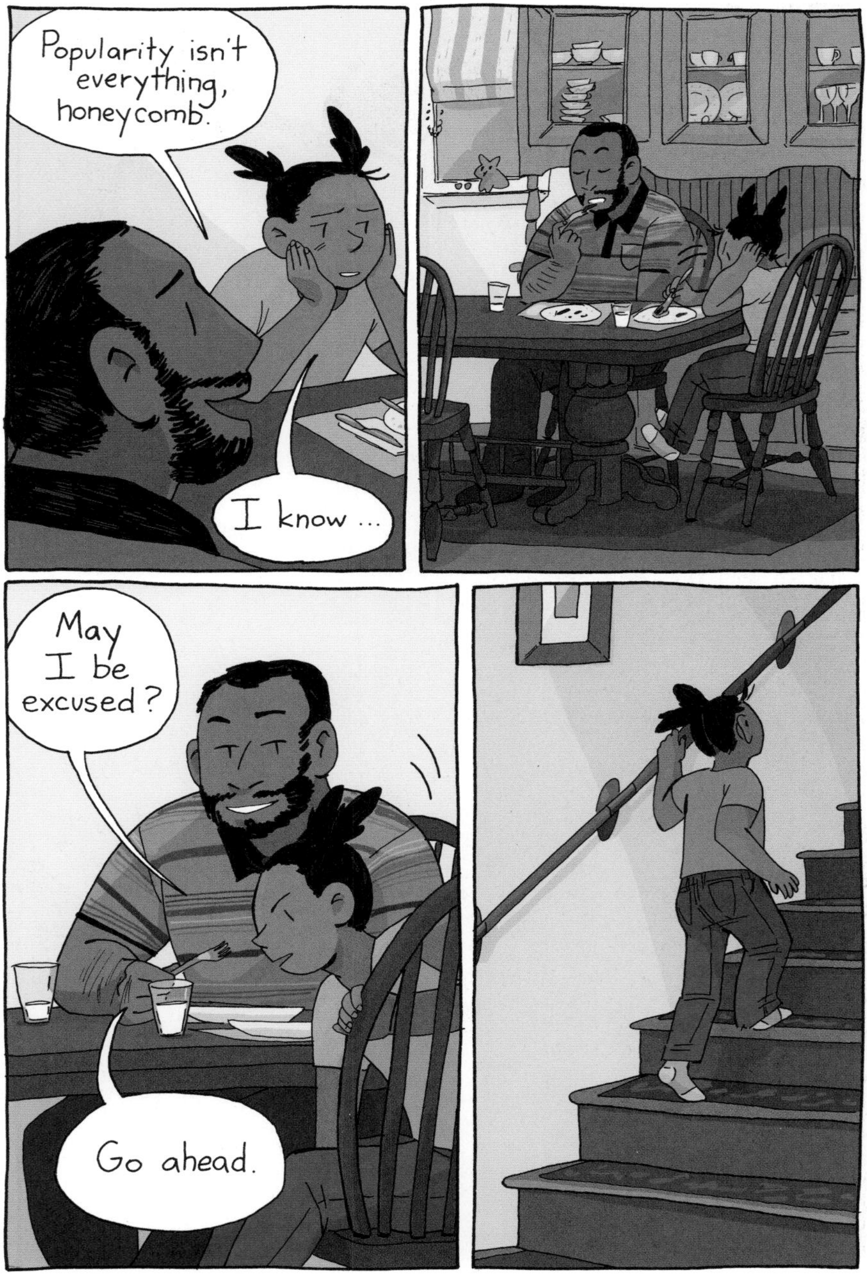

Popularity isn't everything, honeycomb.
I know ...
May I be excused?
Go ahead.

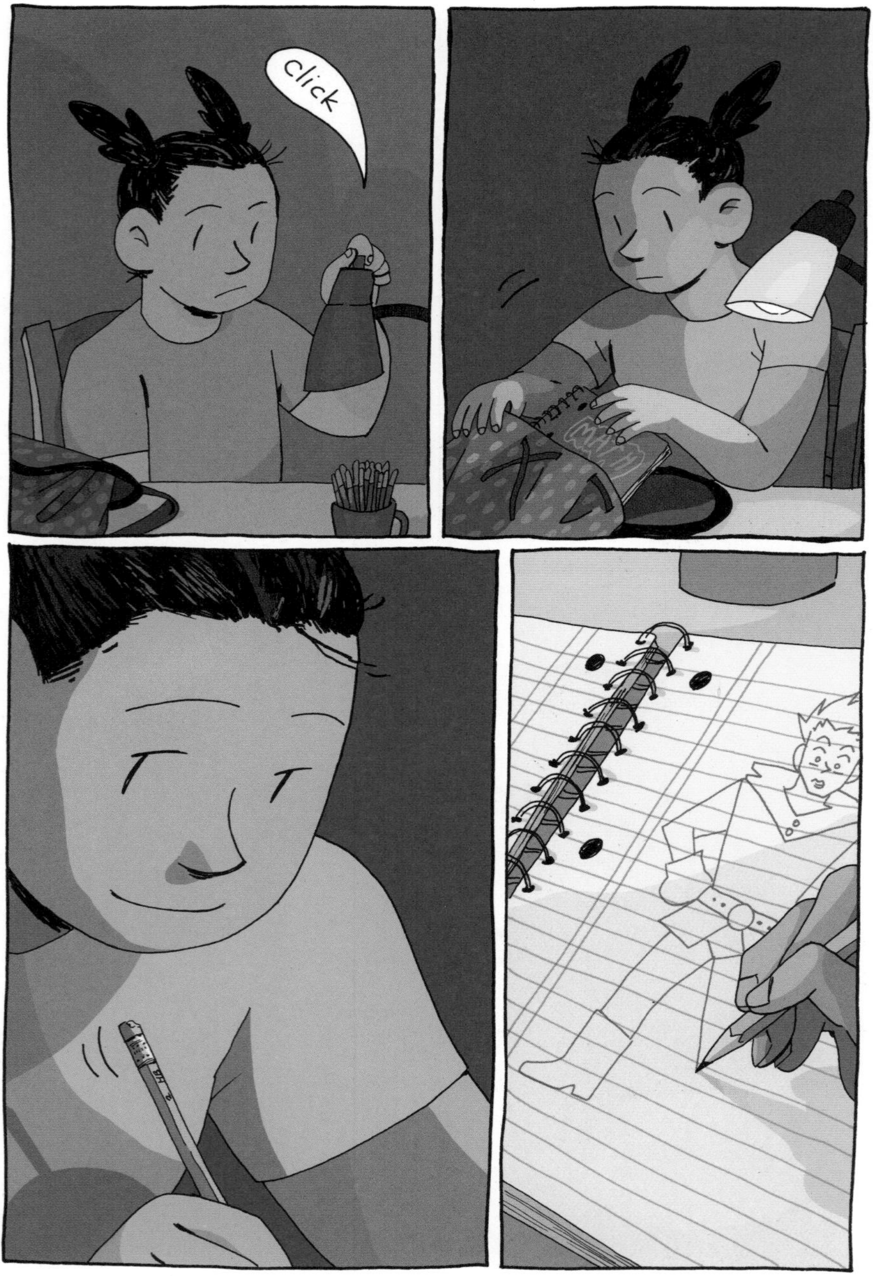
click

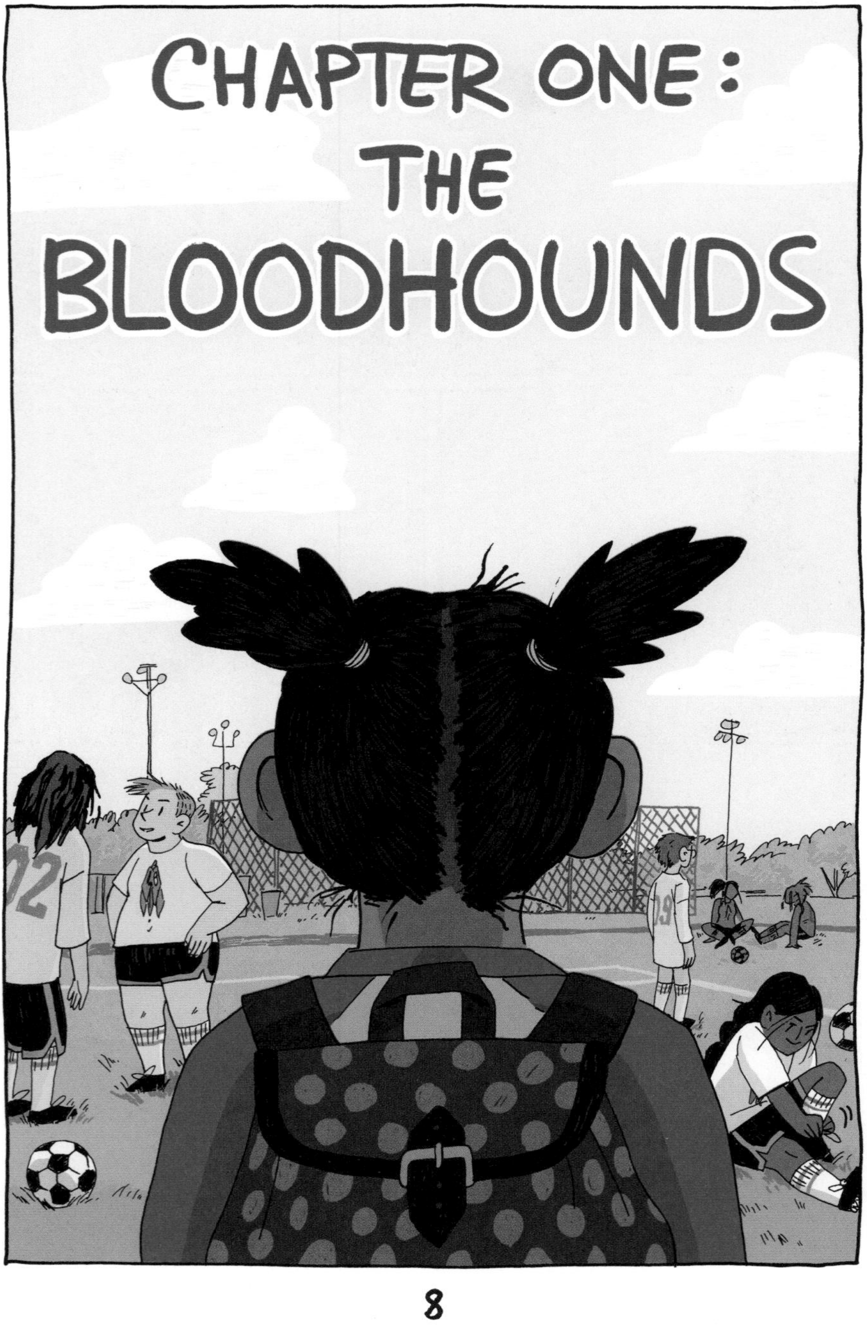
CHAPTER ONE:
THE
BLOODHOUNDS

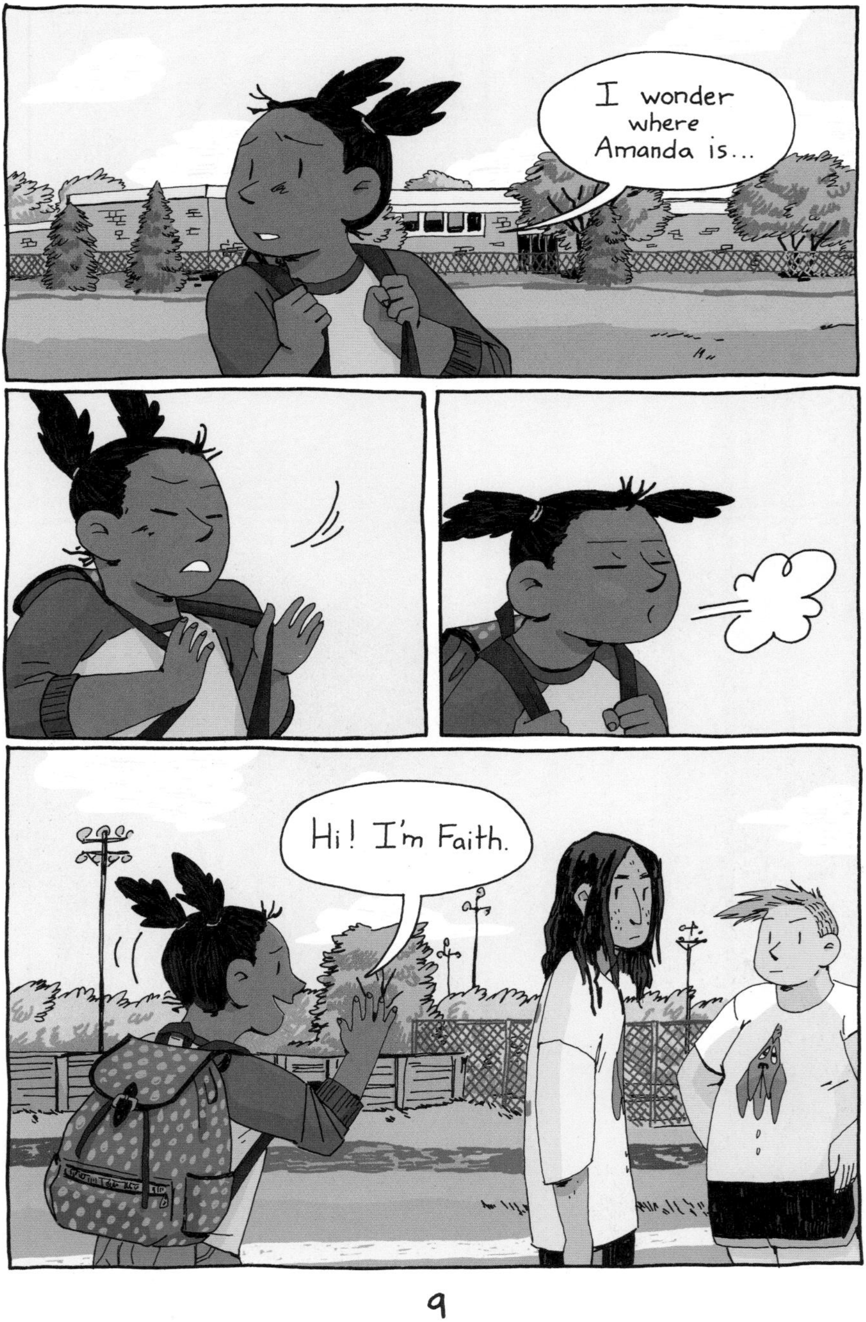
I wonder where Amanda is...
Hi! I'm Faith.

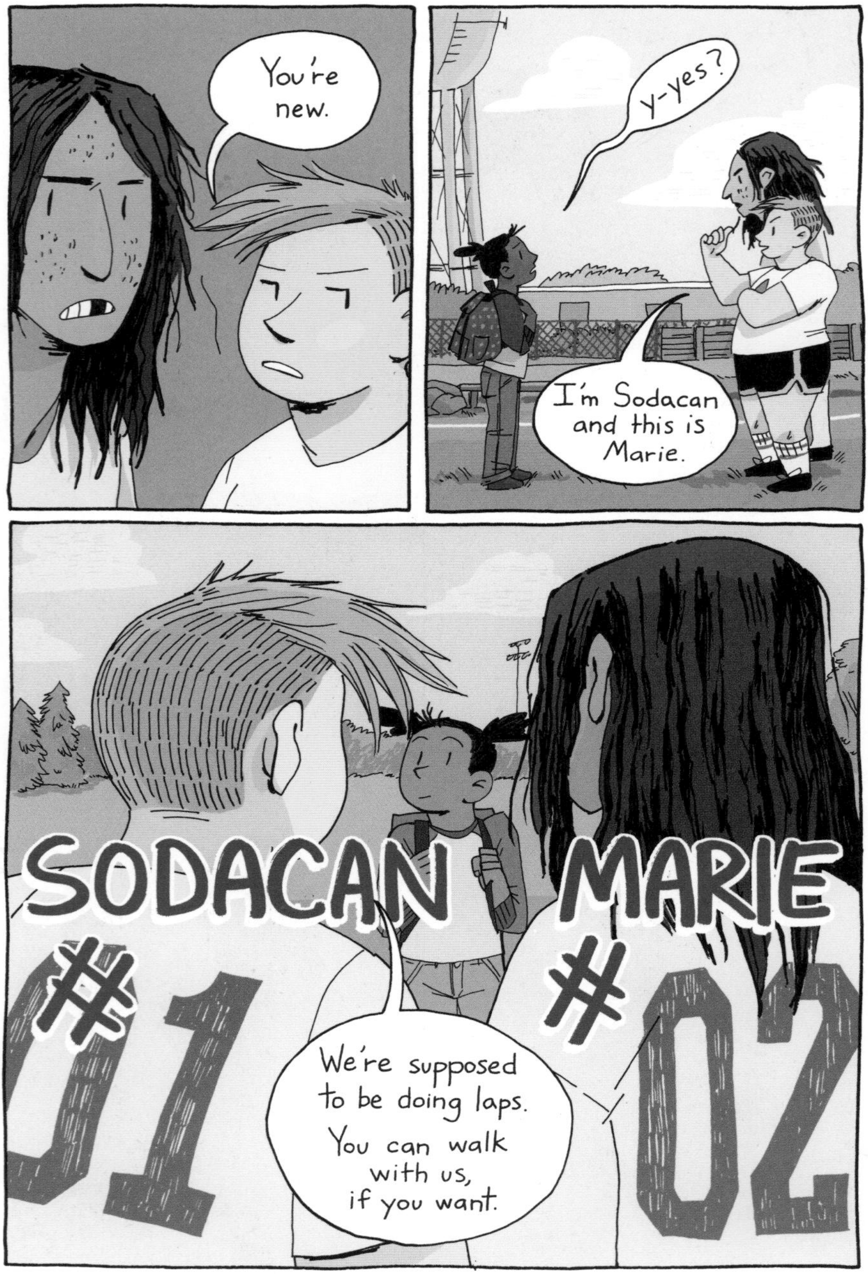
You're new.
y-yes?
I'm Sodacan and this is Marie.
SODACAN
#01
MARIE
#02
We're supposed to be doing laps.
You can walk with us, if you want.

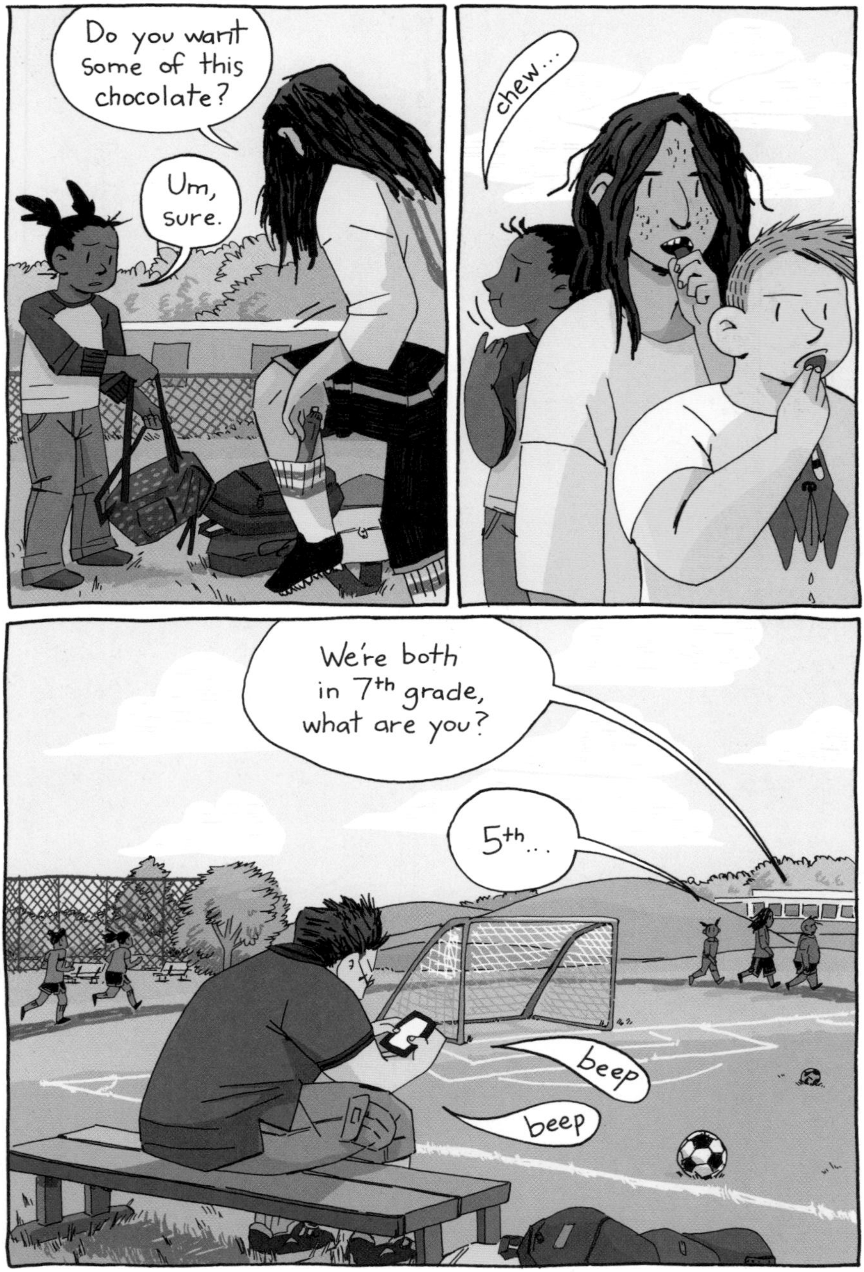
Do you want some of this chocolate?
Um, sure.
chew...
We're both in 7th grade, what are you?
5th...
beep
beep

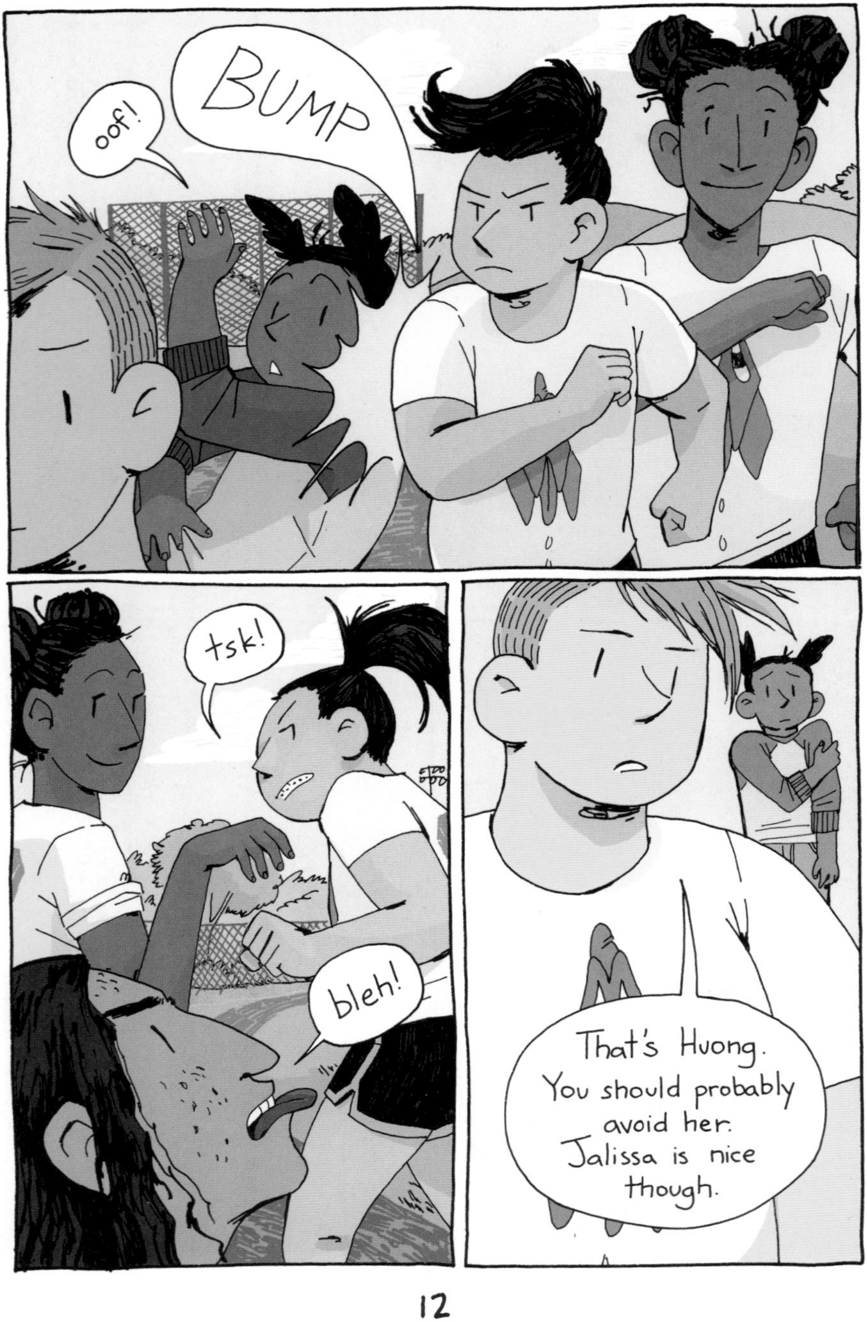
oof!
BUMP
tsk!
bleh!
That's Huong. You should probably avoid her. Jalissa is nice though.

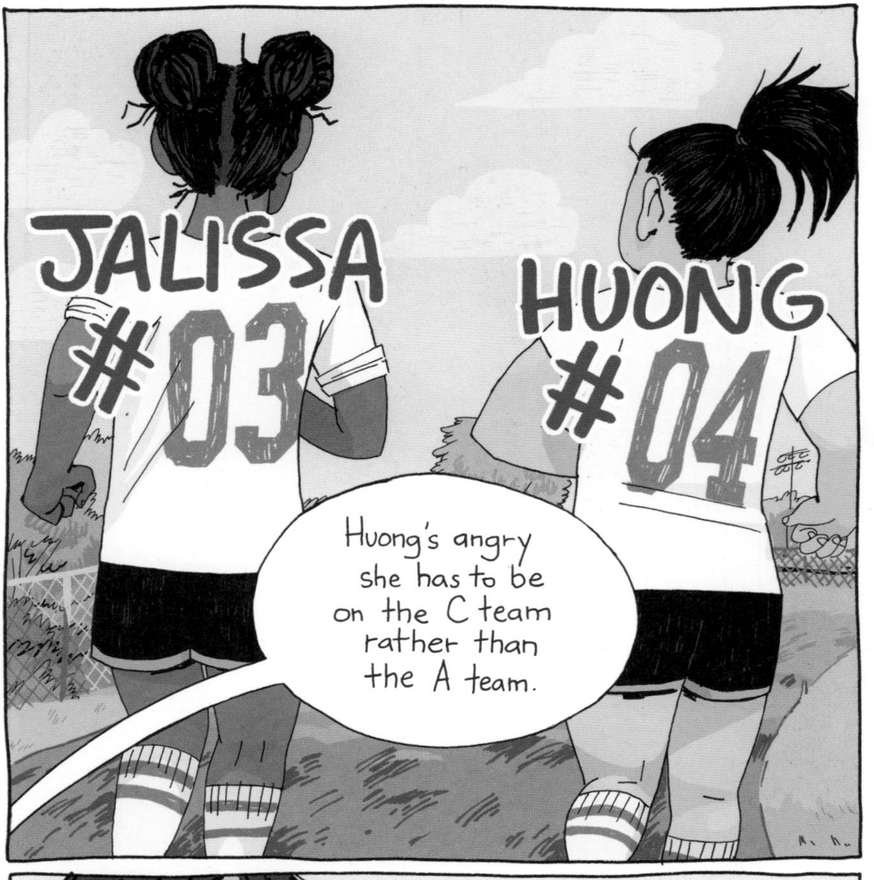
JALISSA #03
HUONG #04
Huong's angry she has to be on the C team rather than the A team.

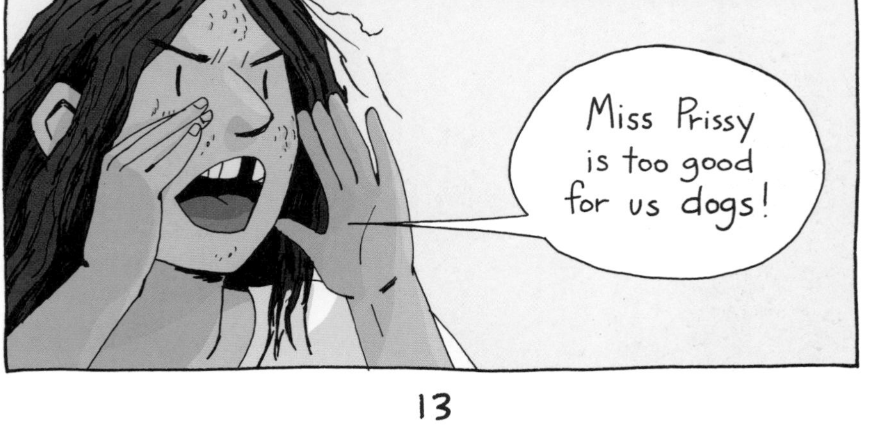
Miss Prissy is too good for us dogs!

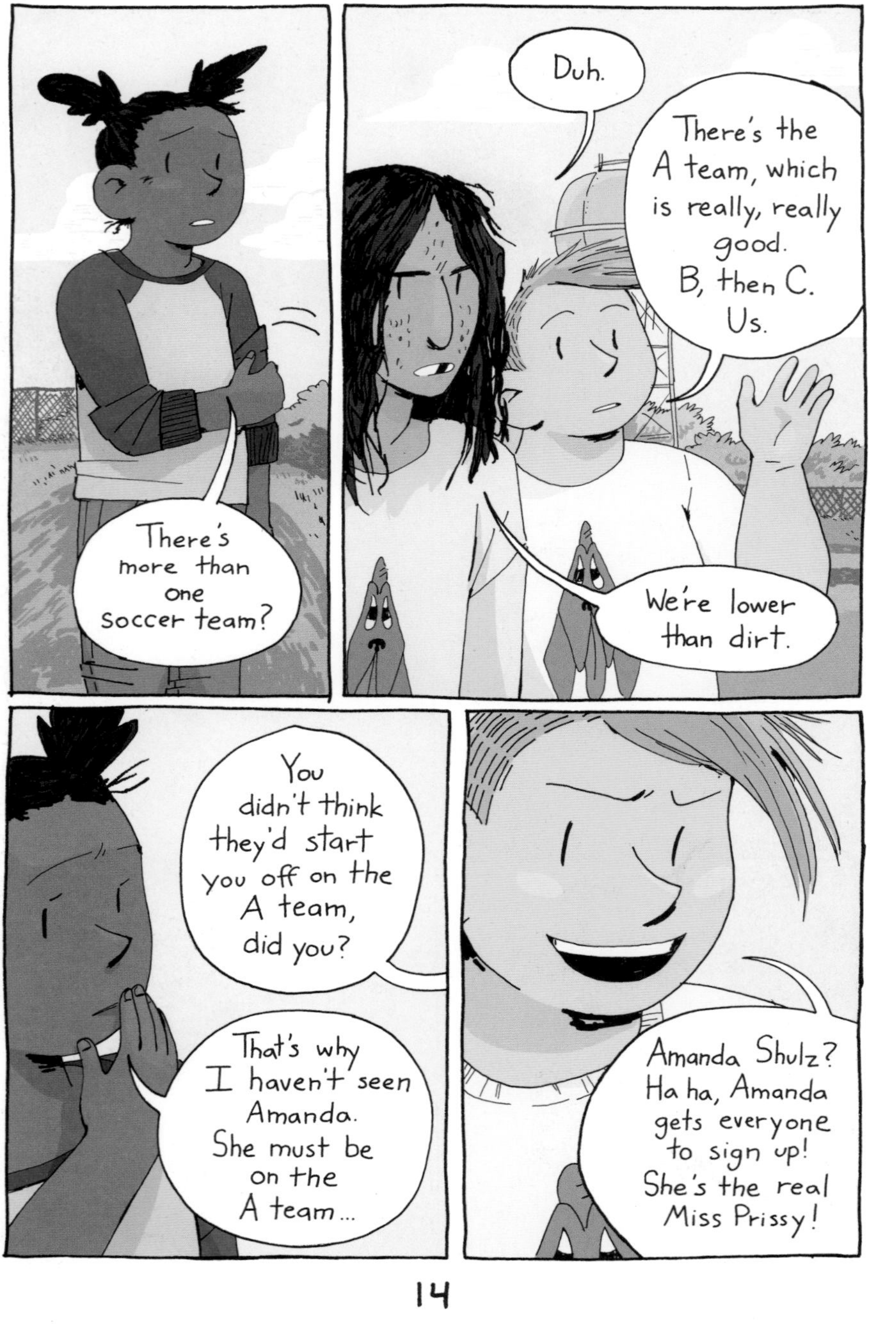
There's more than one soccer team?
Duh.
There's the A team, which is really, really good. B, then C. Us.
We're lower than dirt.
You didn't think they'd start you off on the A team, did you?
That's why I haven't seen Amanda. She must be on the A team...
Amanda Shulz? Ha ha, Amanda gets everyone to sign up! She's the real Miss Prissy!

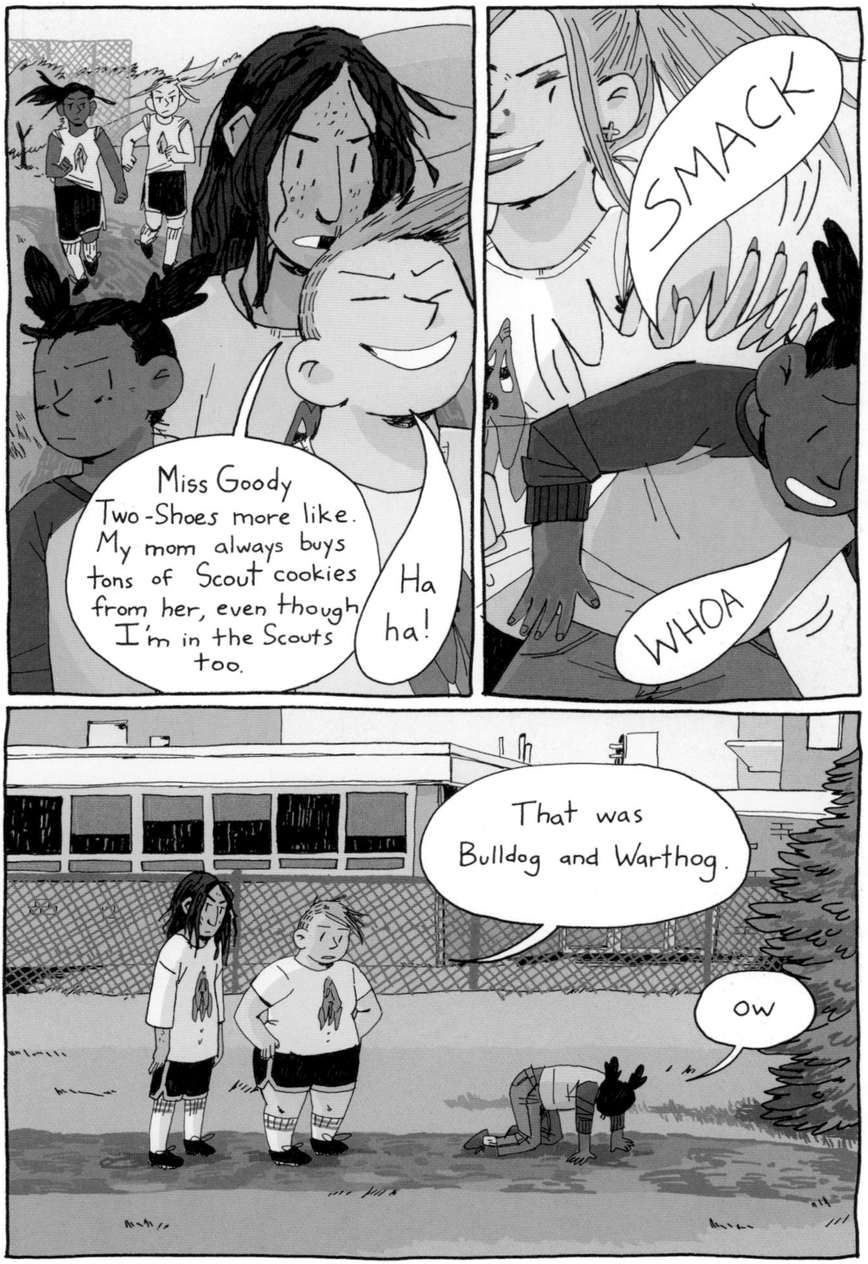
Miss Goody Two-Shoes more like. My mom always buys tons of Scout cookies from her, even though I'm in the Scouts too.
Ha ha!
SMACK
WHOA
That was Bulldog and Warthog.
OW

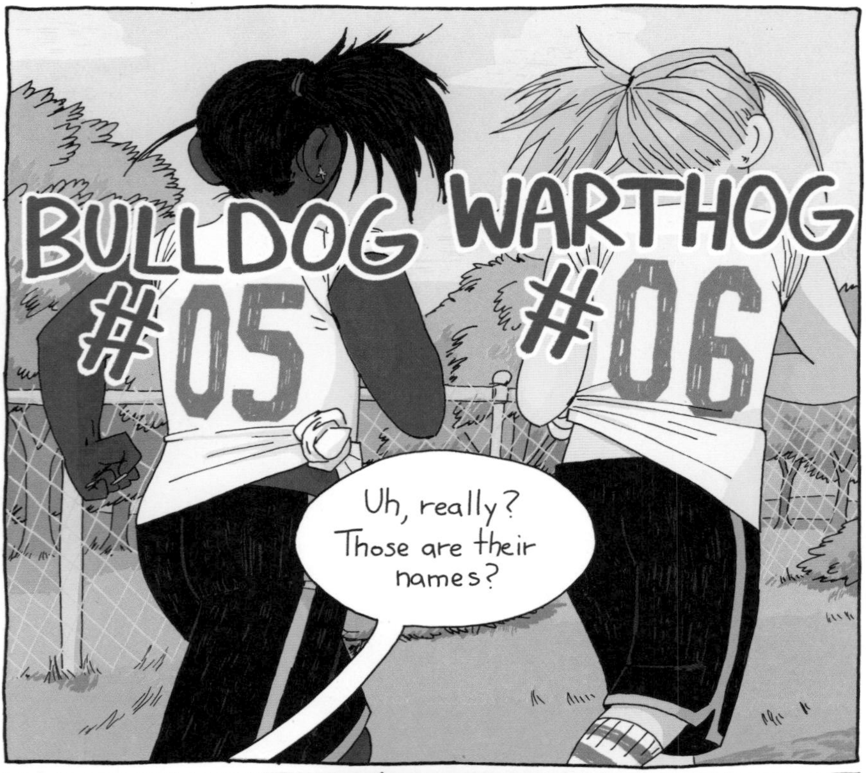
BULLDOG #05
WARTHOG #06
Uh, really? Those are their names?

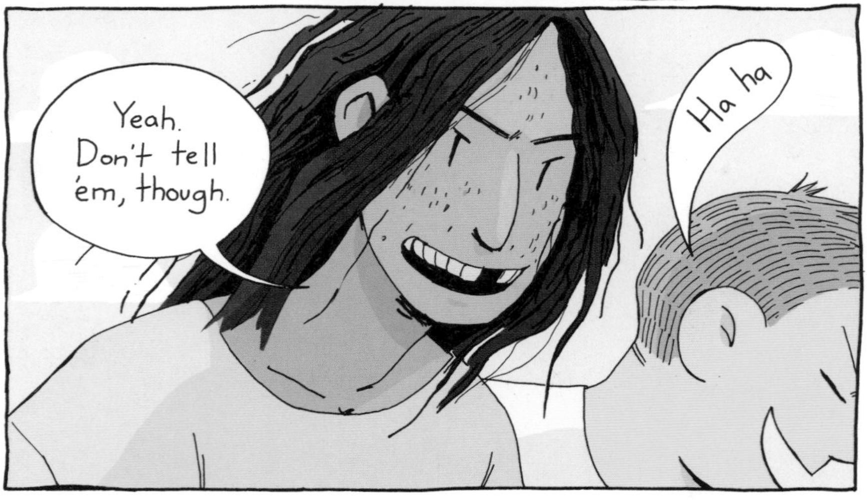
Yeah. Don't tell 'em, though.
Ha ha

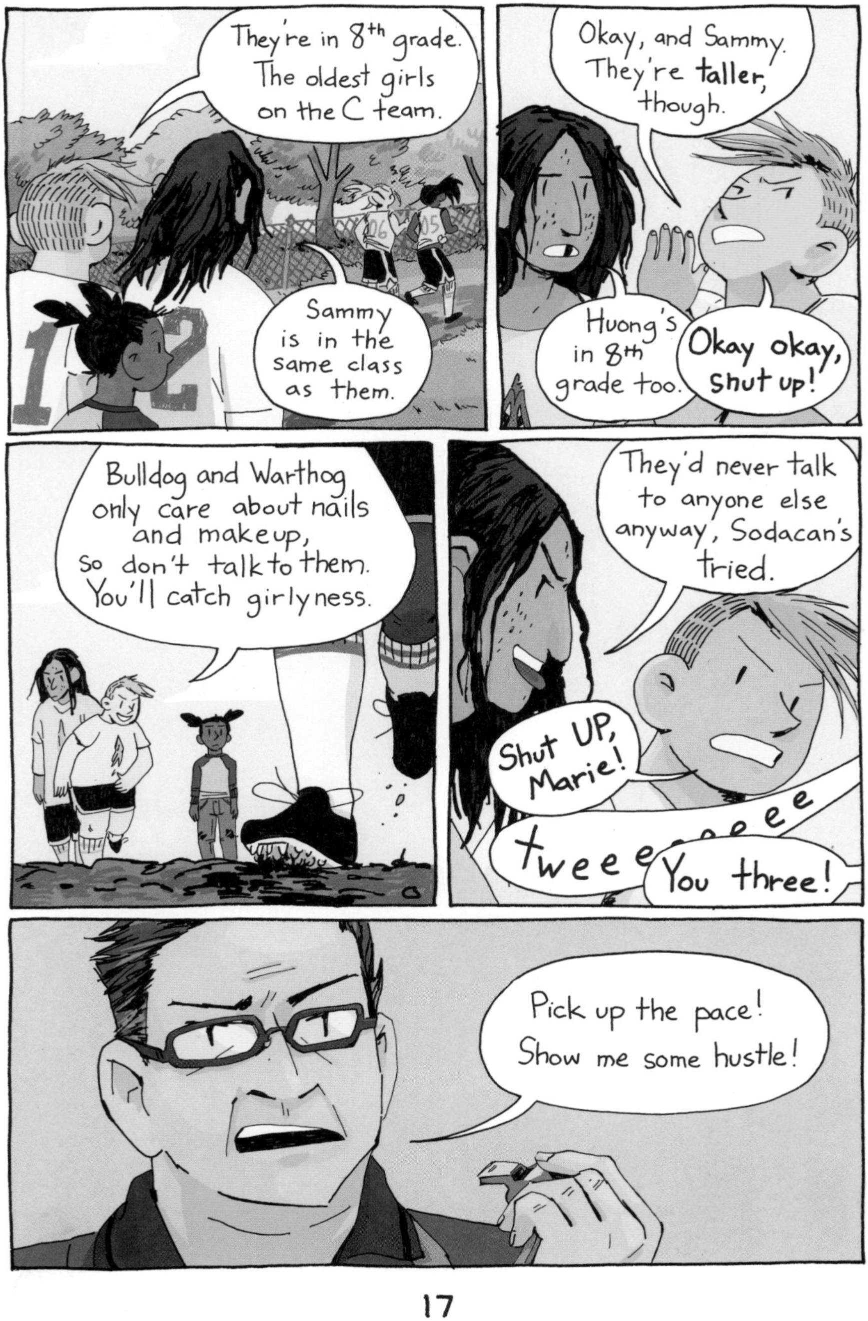
They're in 8th grade. The oldest girls on the C team.
Sammy is in the same class as them.
Okay, and Sammy. They're **taller**, though.
Huong's in 8th grade too.
Okay okay, shut up!
Bulldog and Warthog only care about nails and makeup, so don't talk to them. You'll catch girlyness.
They'd never talk to anyone else anyway, Sodacan's tried.
Shut UP, Marie!
tweeeeeeeee
You three!
Pick up the pace! Show me some hustle!

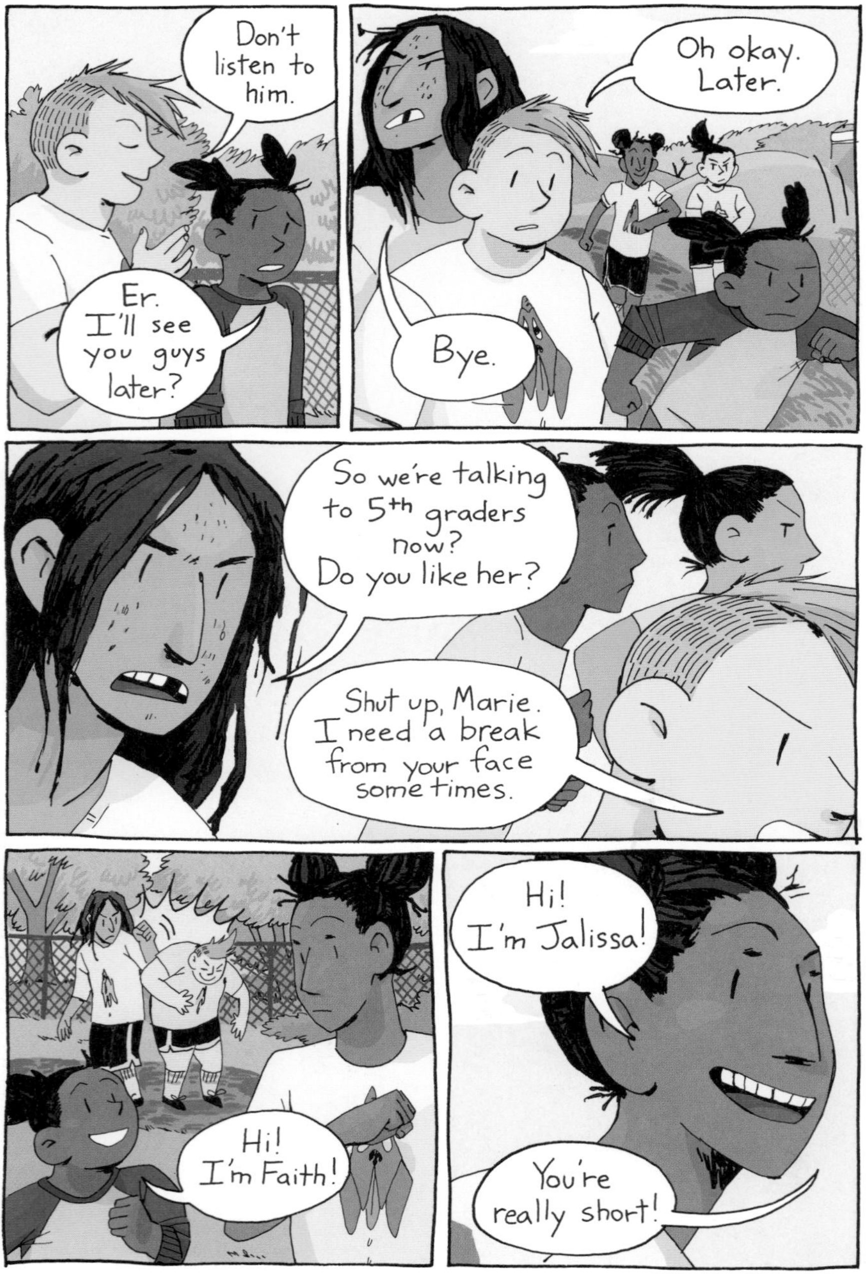
Don't listen to him.
Er. I'll see you guys later?
Oh okay. Later.
Bye.
So we're talking to 5th graders now? Do you like her?
Shut up, Marie. I need a break from your face some times.
Hi! I'm Faith!
Hi! I'm Jalissa!
You're really short!

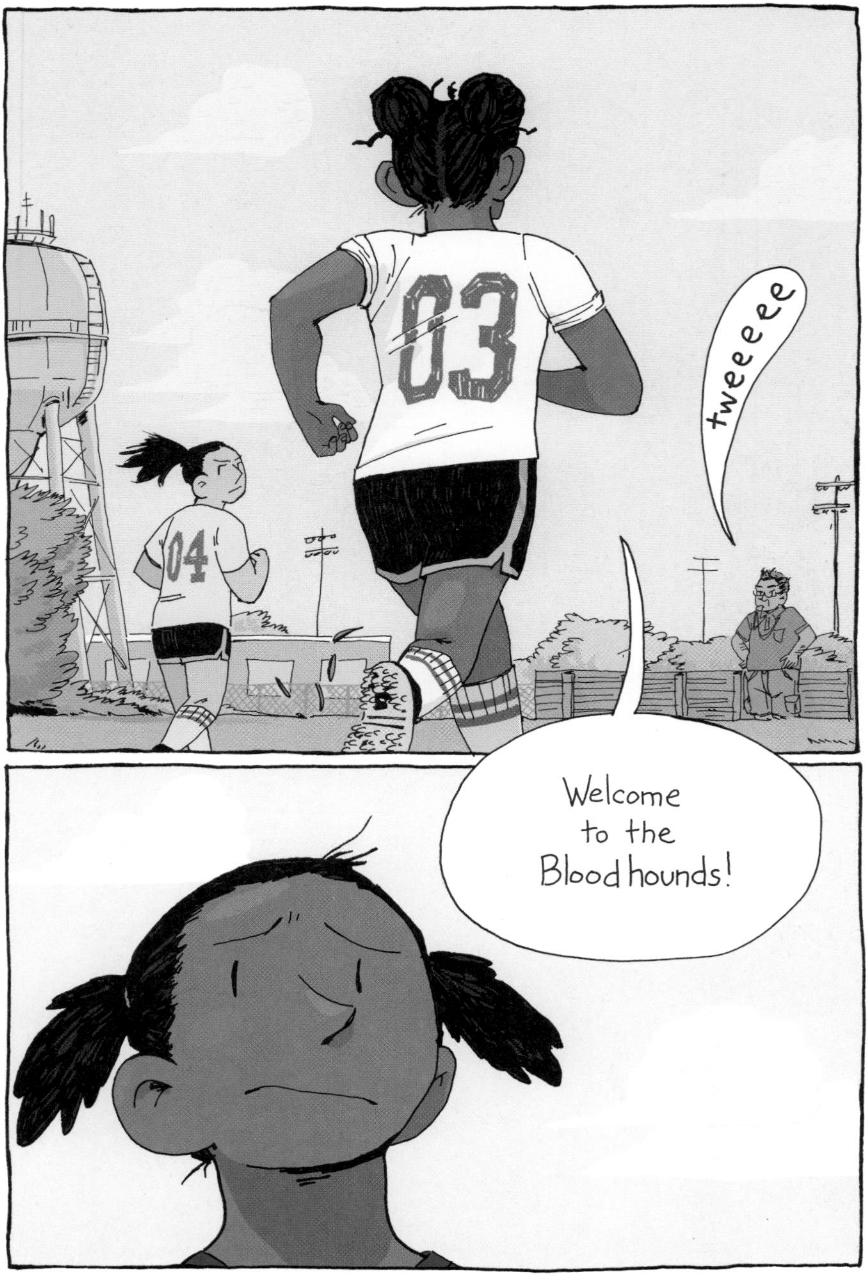
tweeee
Welcome to the Bloodhounds!

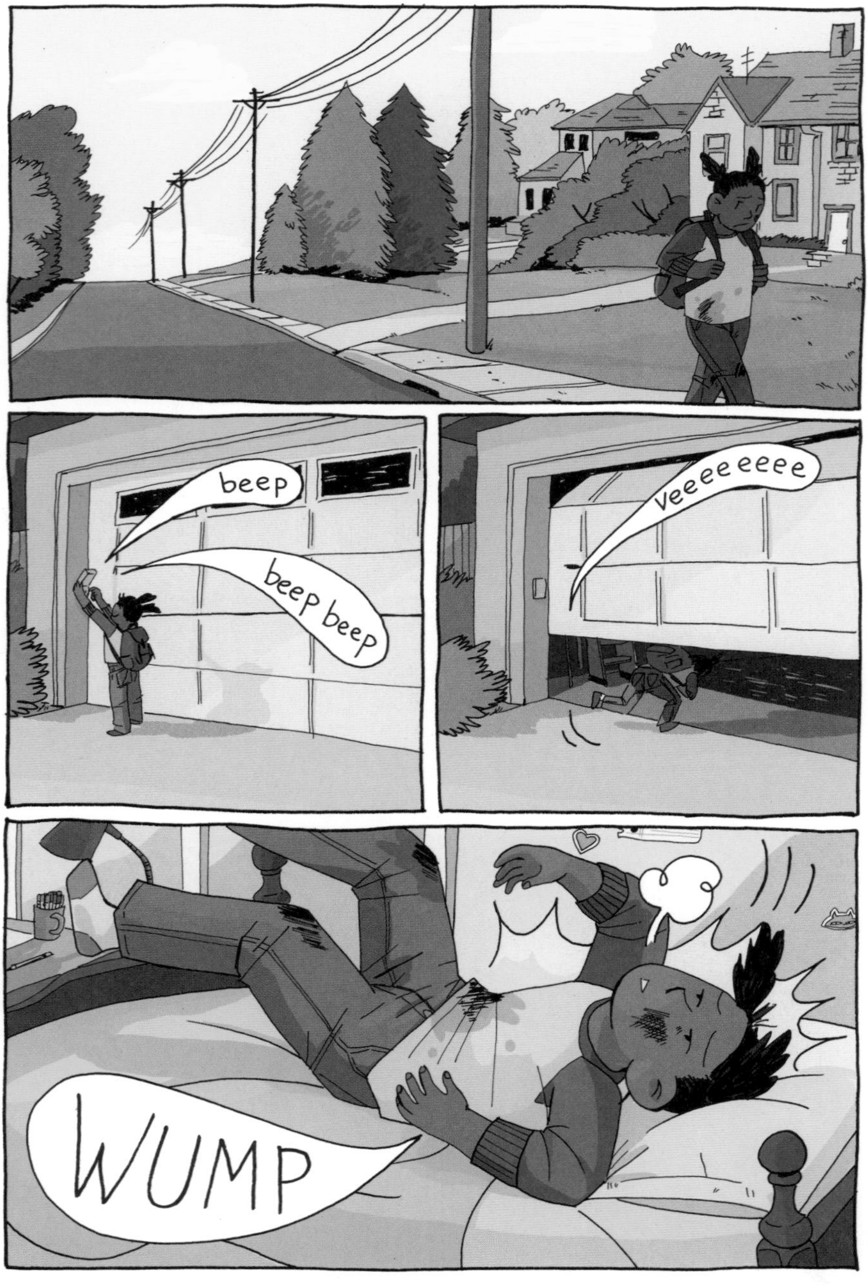
beep
beep beep
veeeeeeee
WUMP

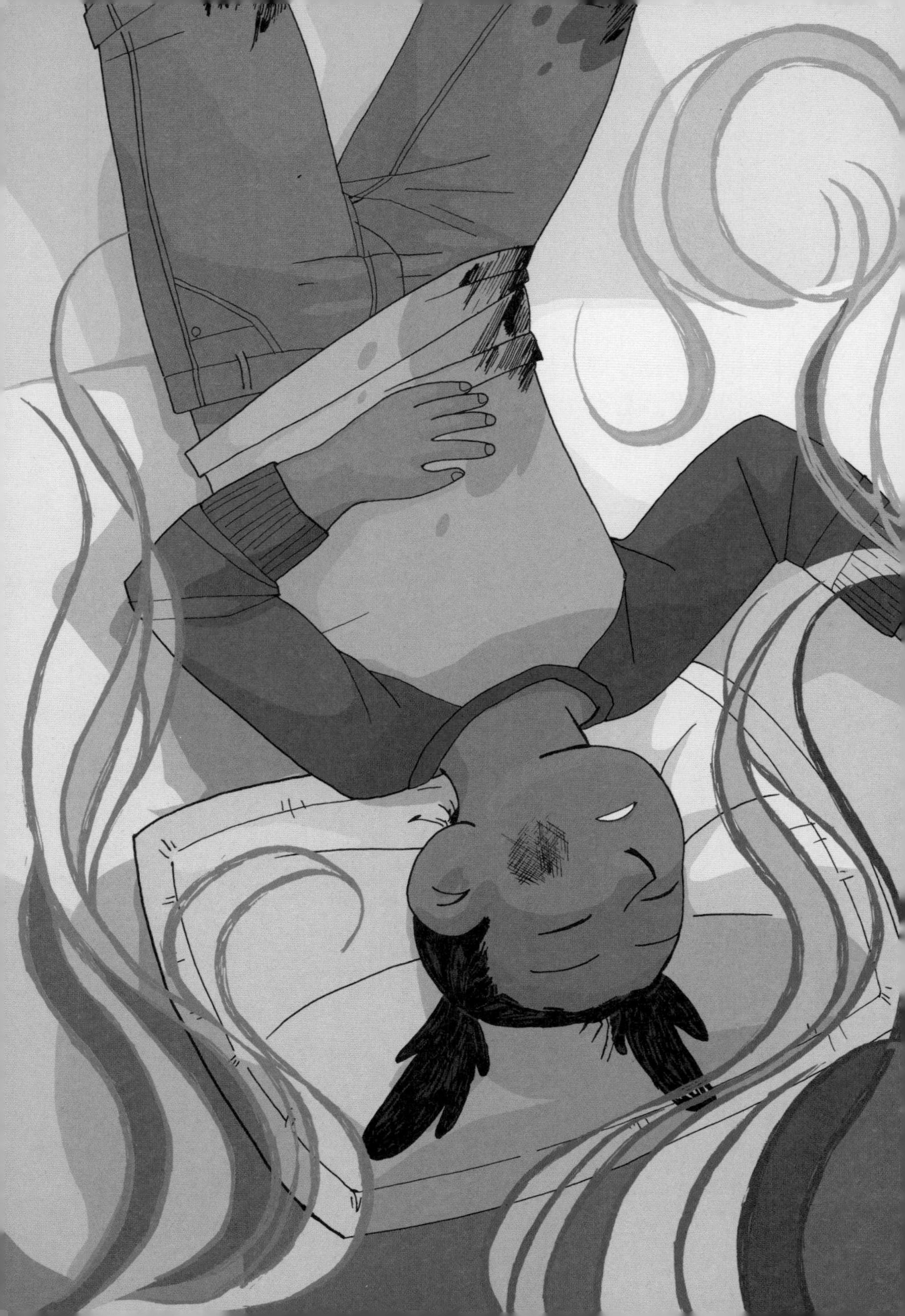

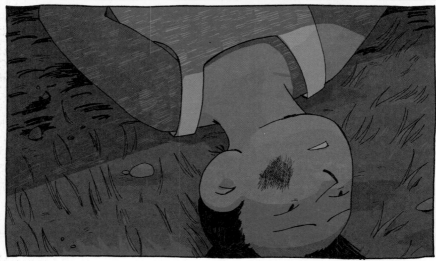

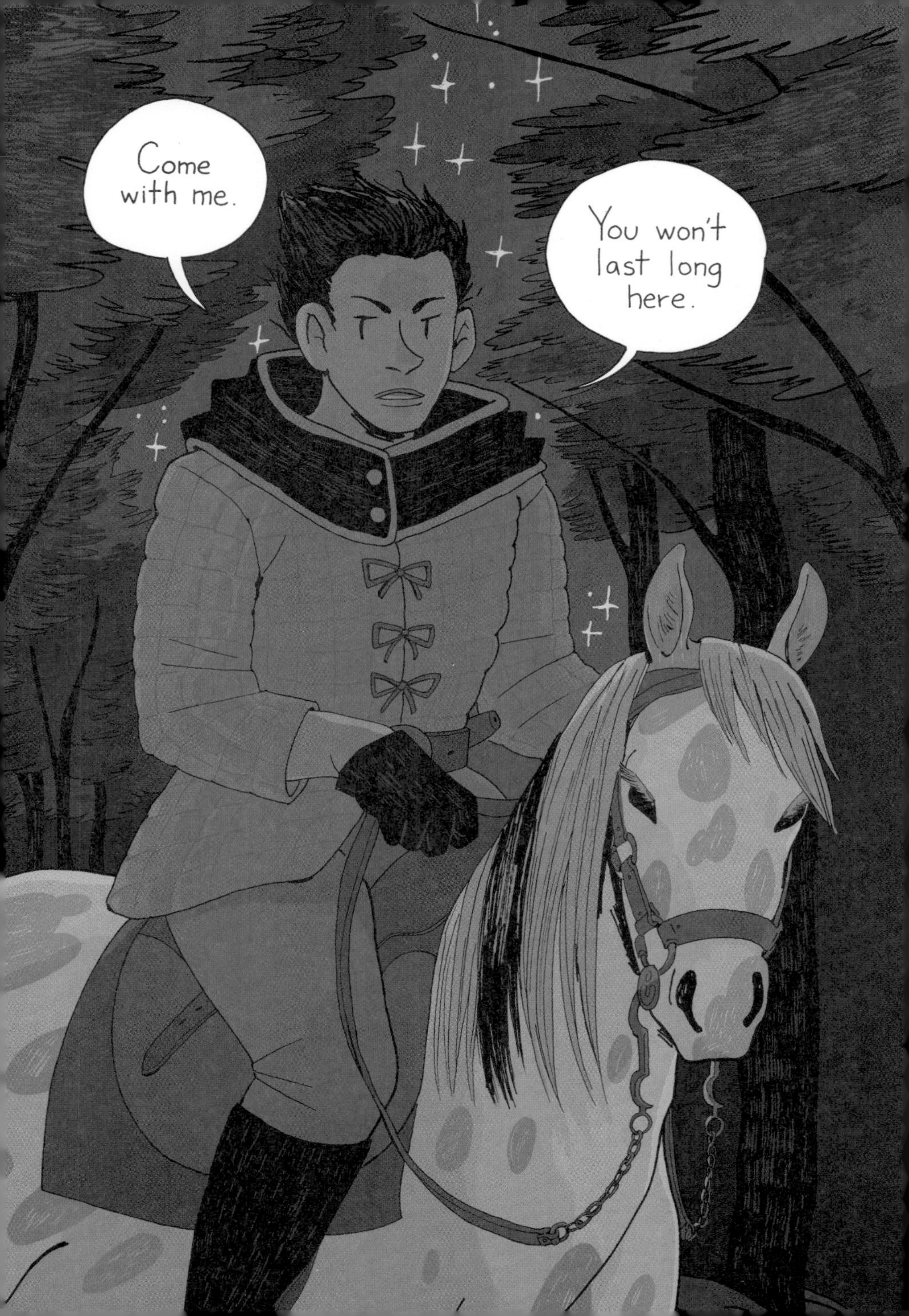
Come with me.
You won't last long here.

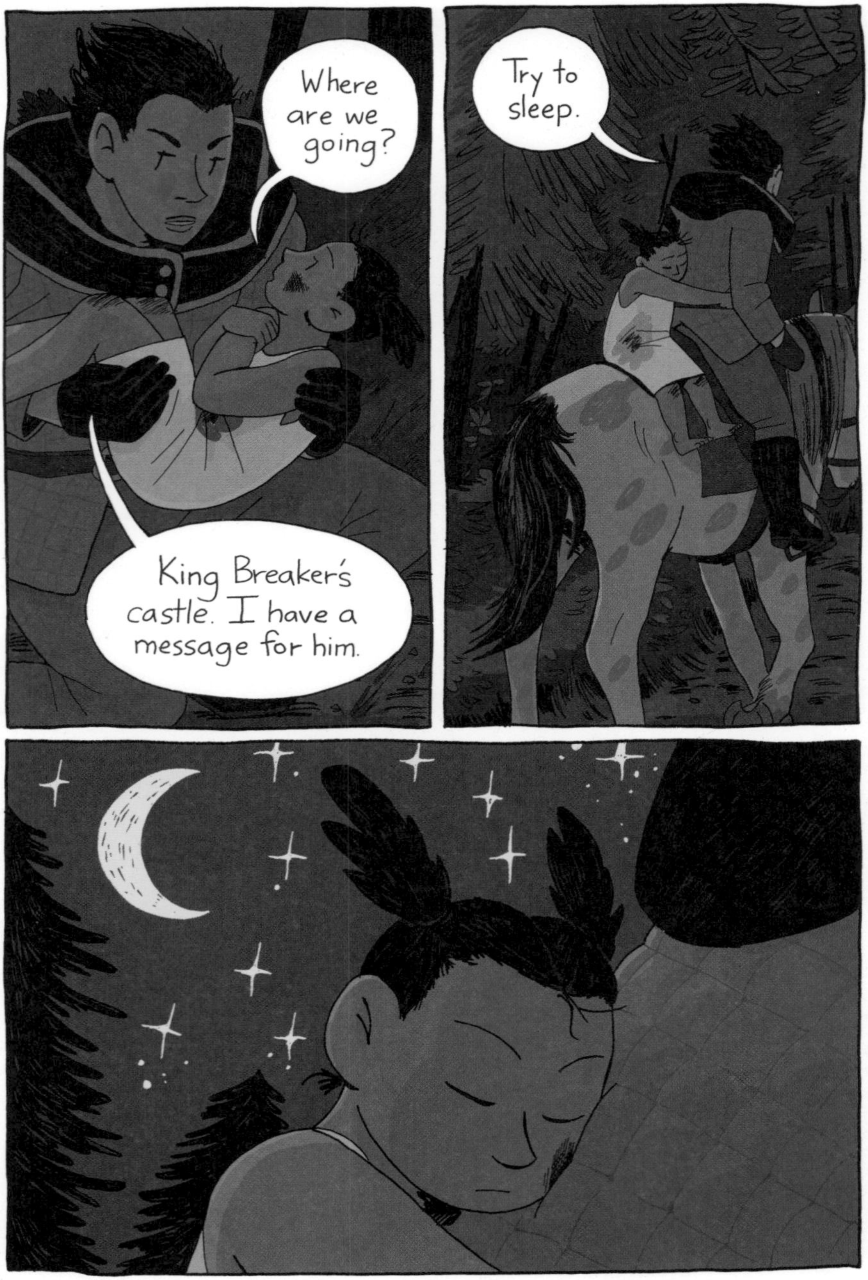
Where are we going?
King Breaker's castle. I have a message for him.
Try to sleep.

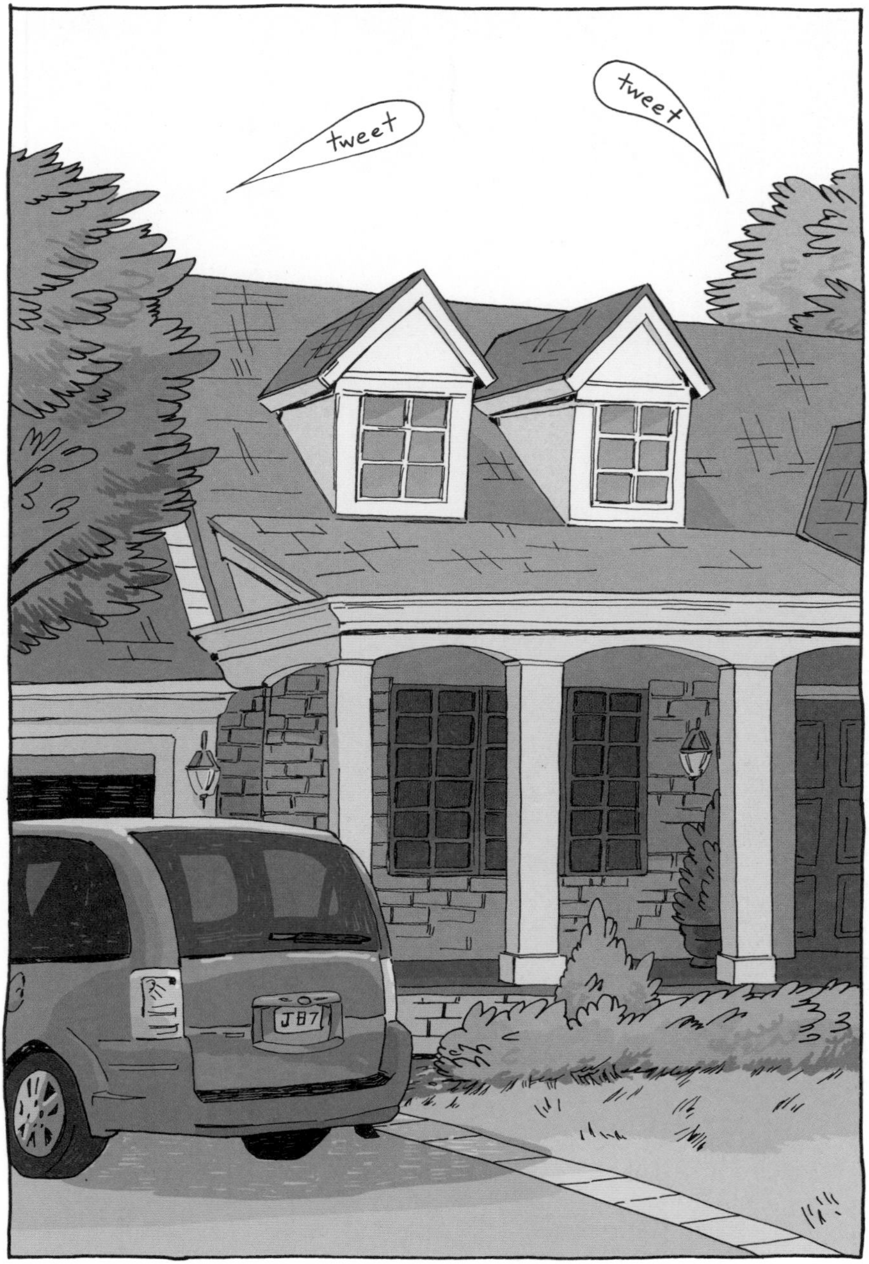
tweet
tweet
JB7

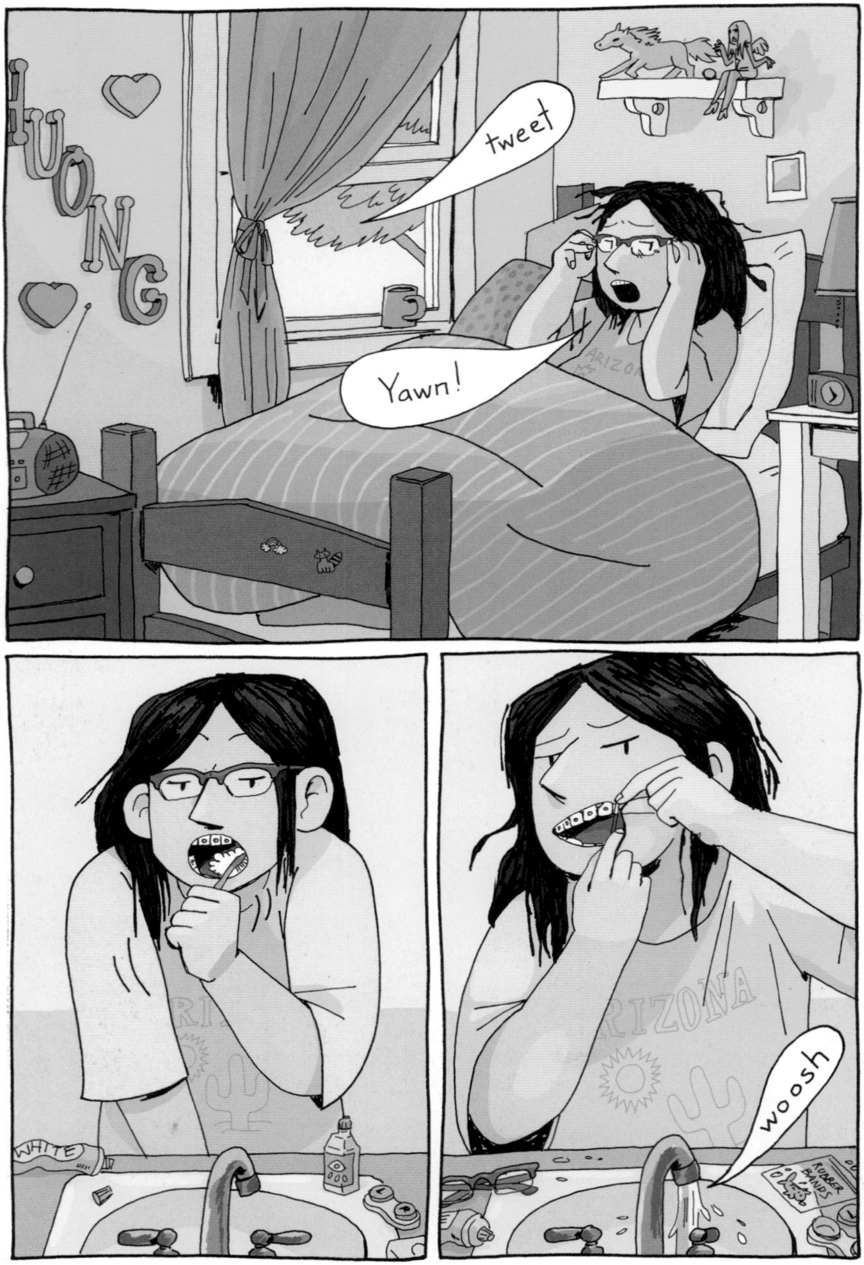
HUONG
tweet
Yawn!
WHITE
ARIZONA
RUBBER BANDS
woosh

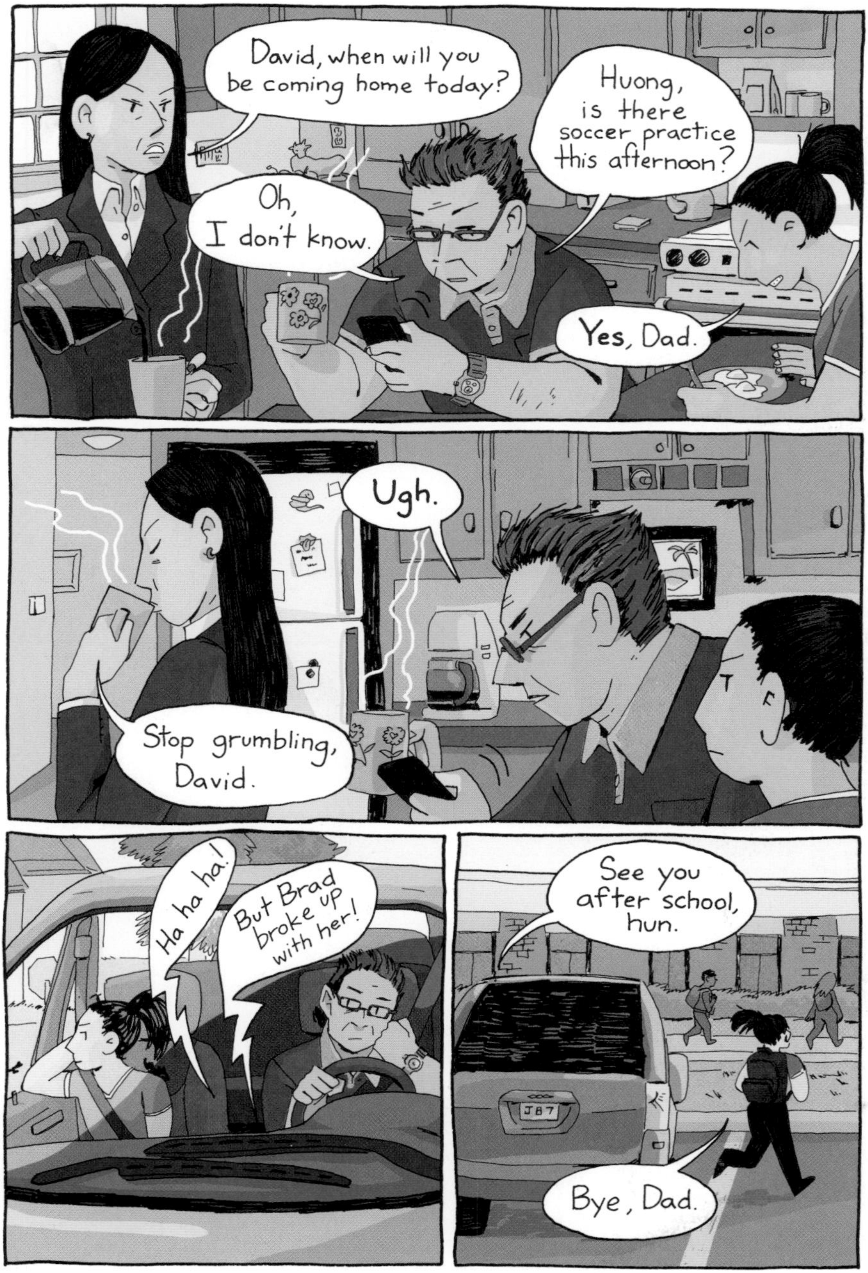
David, when will you be coming home today?
Oh, I don't know.
Huong, is there soccer practice this afternoon?
Yes, Dad.
Ugh.
Stop grumbling, David.
Ha ha ha!
But Brad broke up with her!
See you after school, hun.
Bye, Dad.

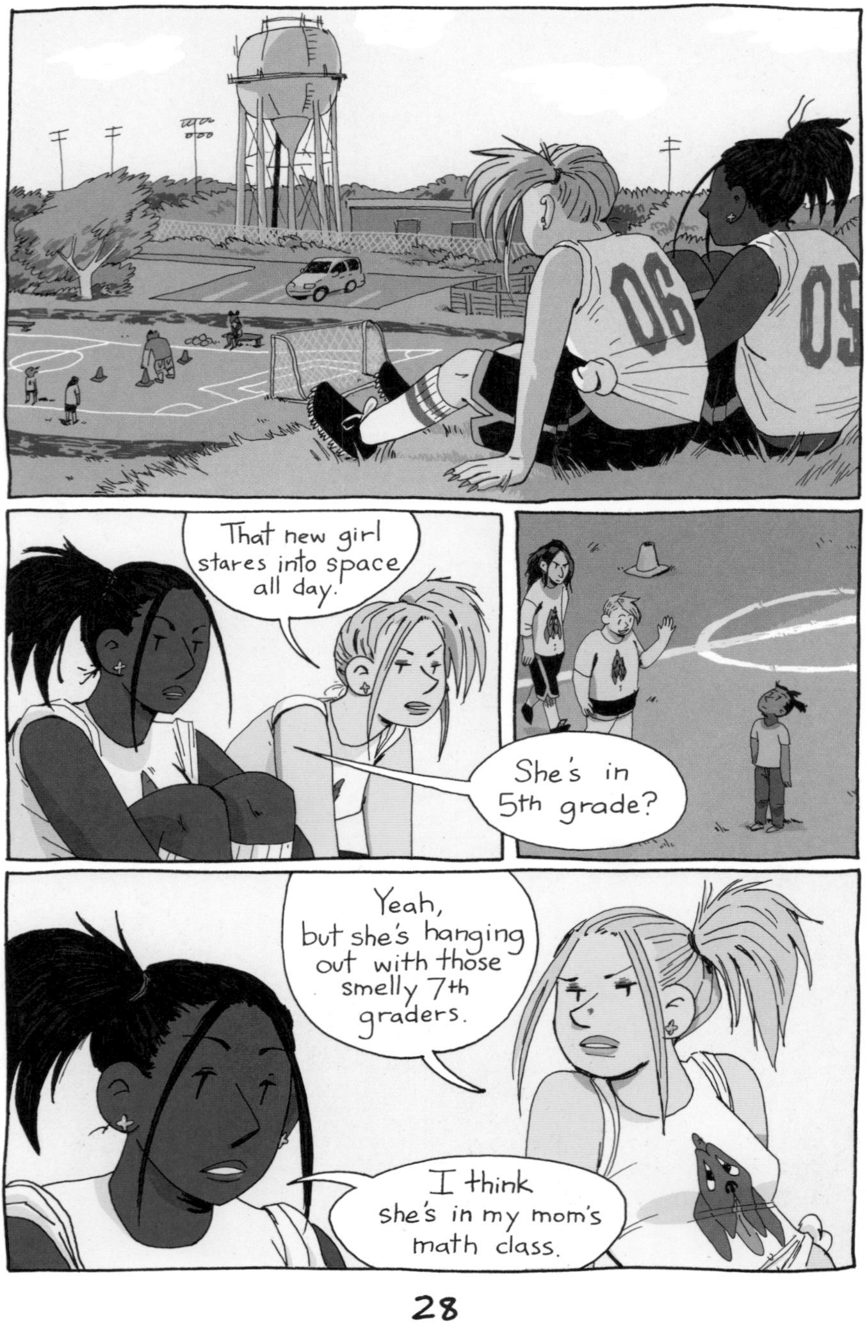
06
05
That new girl stares into space all day.
She's in 5th grade?
Yeah, but she's hanging out with those smelly 7th graders.
I think she's in my mom's math class.

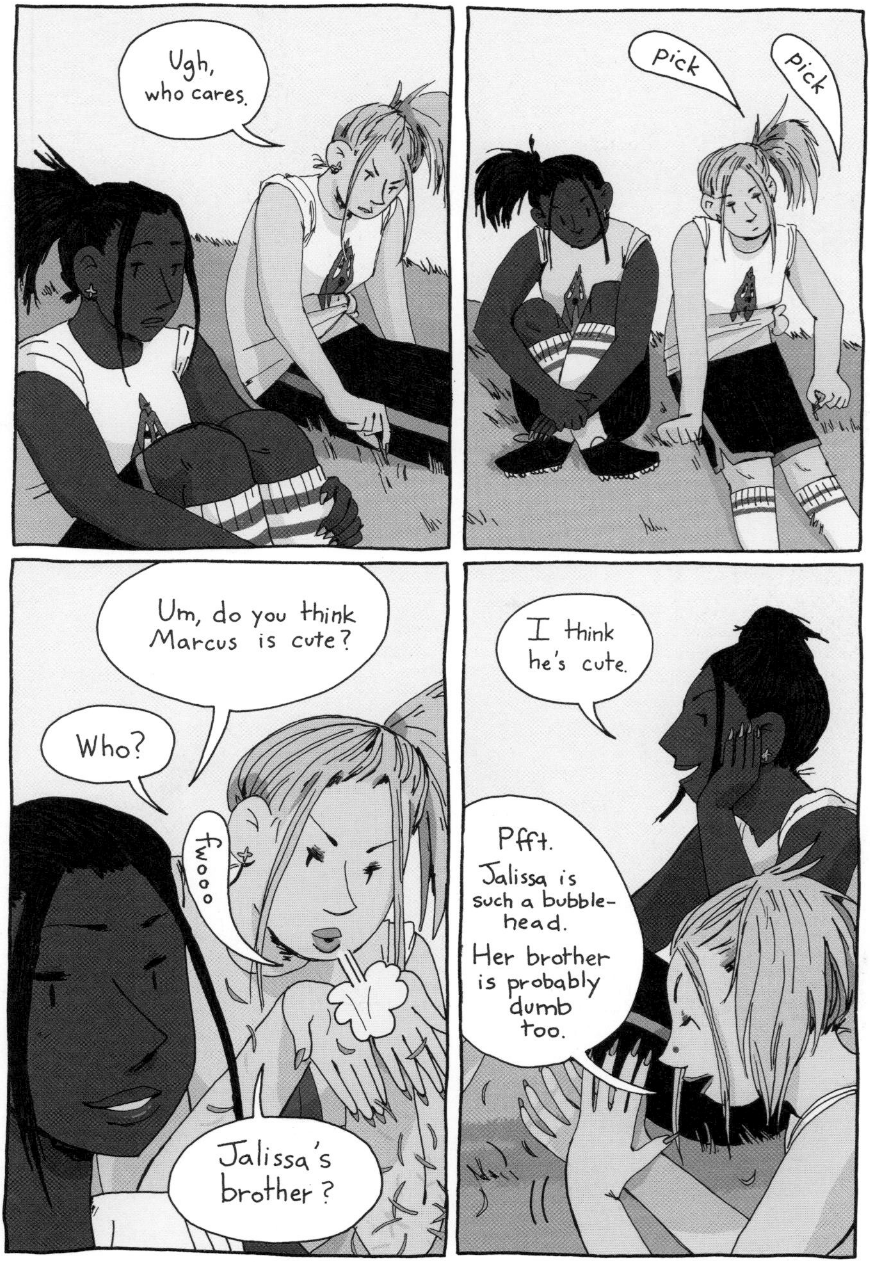
Ugh, who cares.
pick
pick
Um, do you think Marcus is cute?
Who?
fwooo
Jalissa's brother?
I think he's cute.
Pfft.
Jalissa is such a bubble-head.
Her brother is probably dumb too.

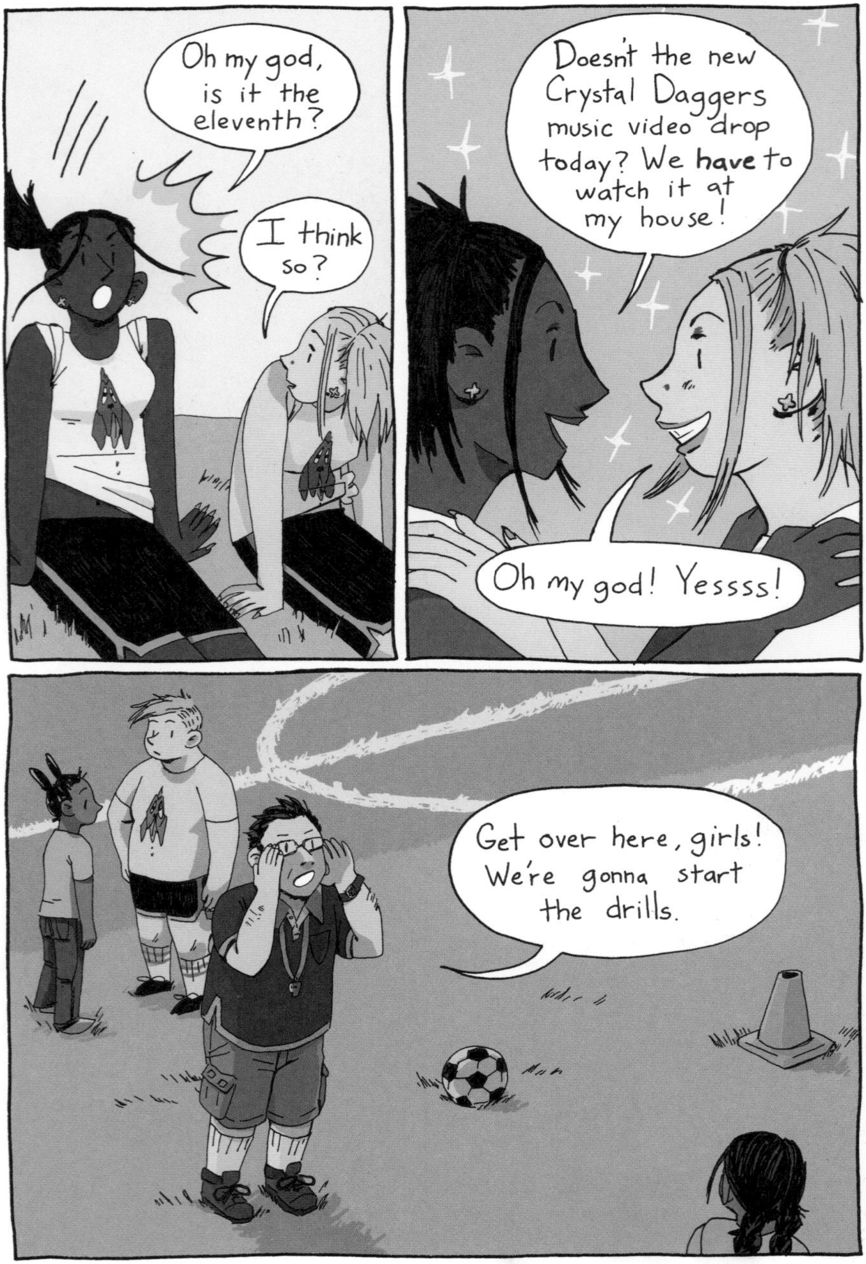
Oh my god, is it the eleventh?
I think so?
Doesn't the new Crystal Daggers music video drop today? We **have** to watch it at my house!
Oh my god! Yessss!
Get over here, girls! We're gonna start the drills.

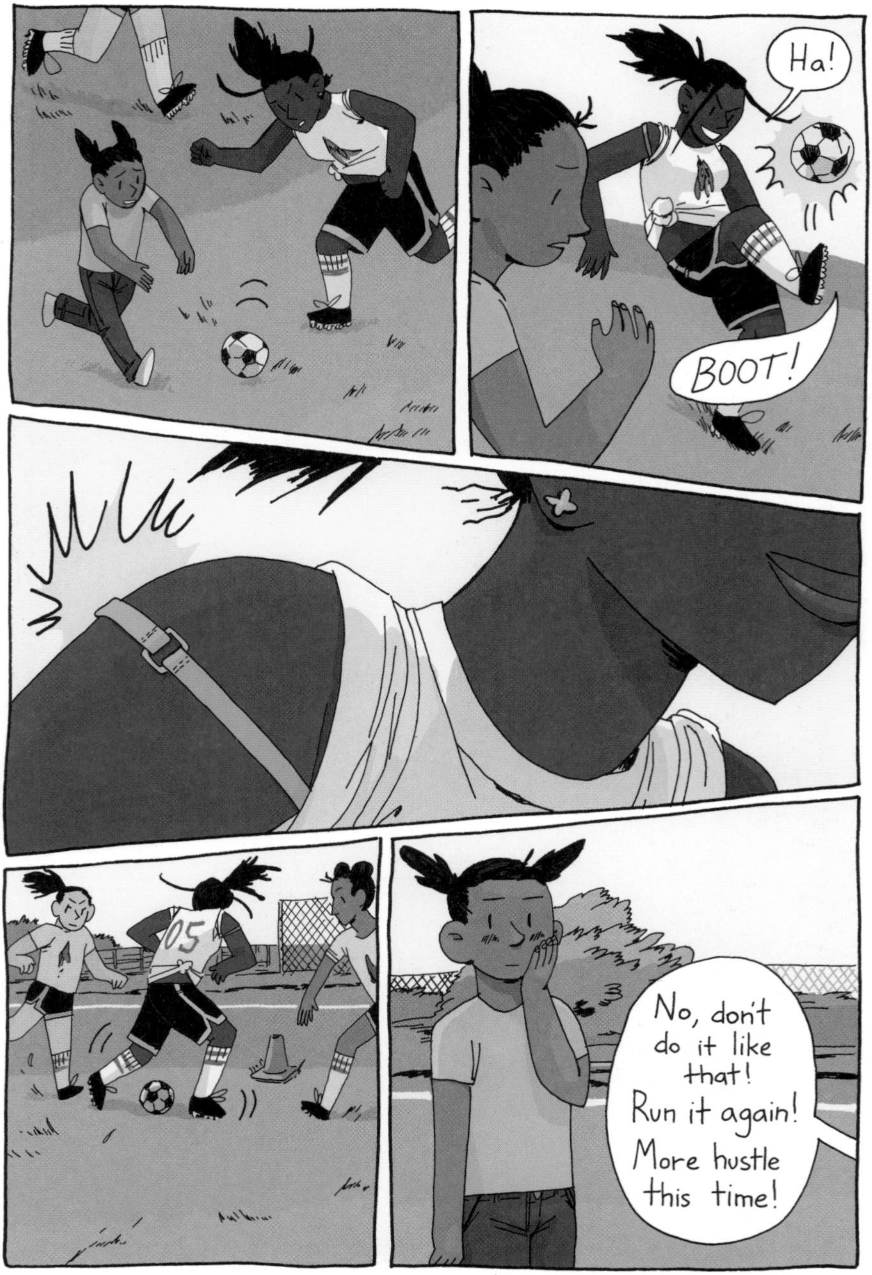
Ha!
BOOT!
No, don't do it like that! Run it again! More hustle this time!

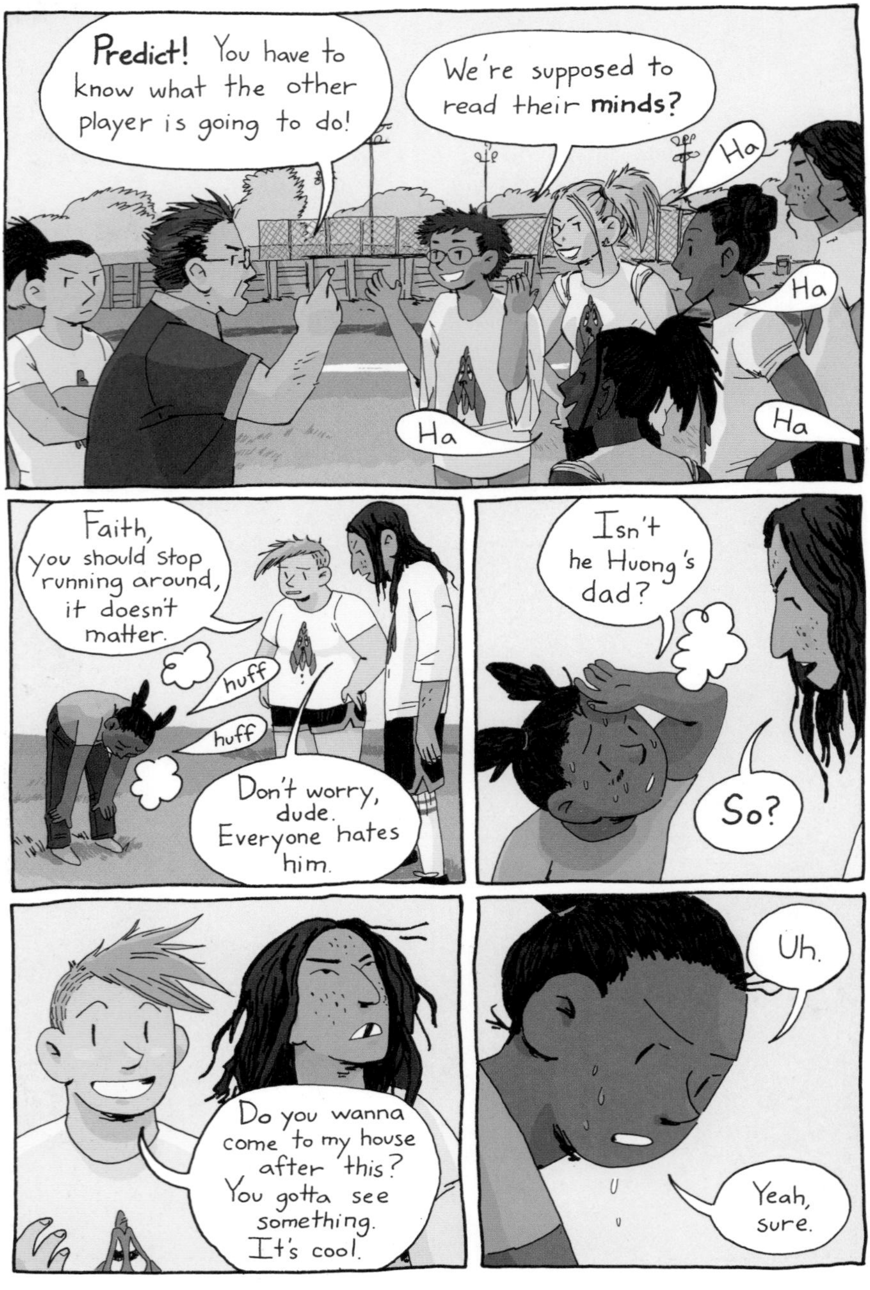

Predict! You have to know what the other player is going to do!
We're supposed to read their minds?
Ha
Ha
Ha
Ha
Faith, you should stop running around, it doesn't matter.
huff
huff
Don't worry, dude. Everyone hates him.
Isn't he Huong's dad?
So?
Do you wanna come to my house after this? You gotta see something. It's cool.
Uh.
Yeah, sure.

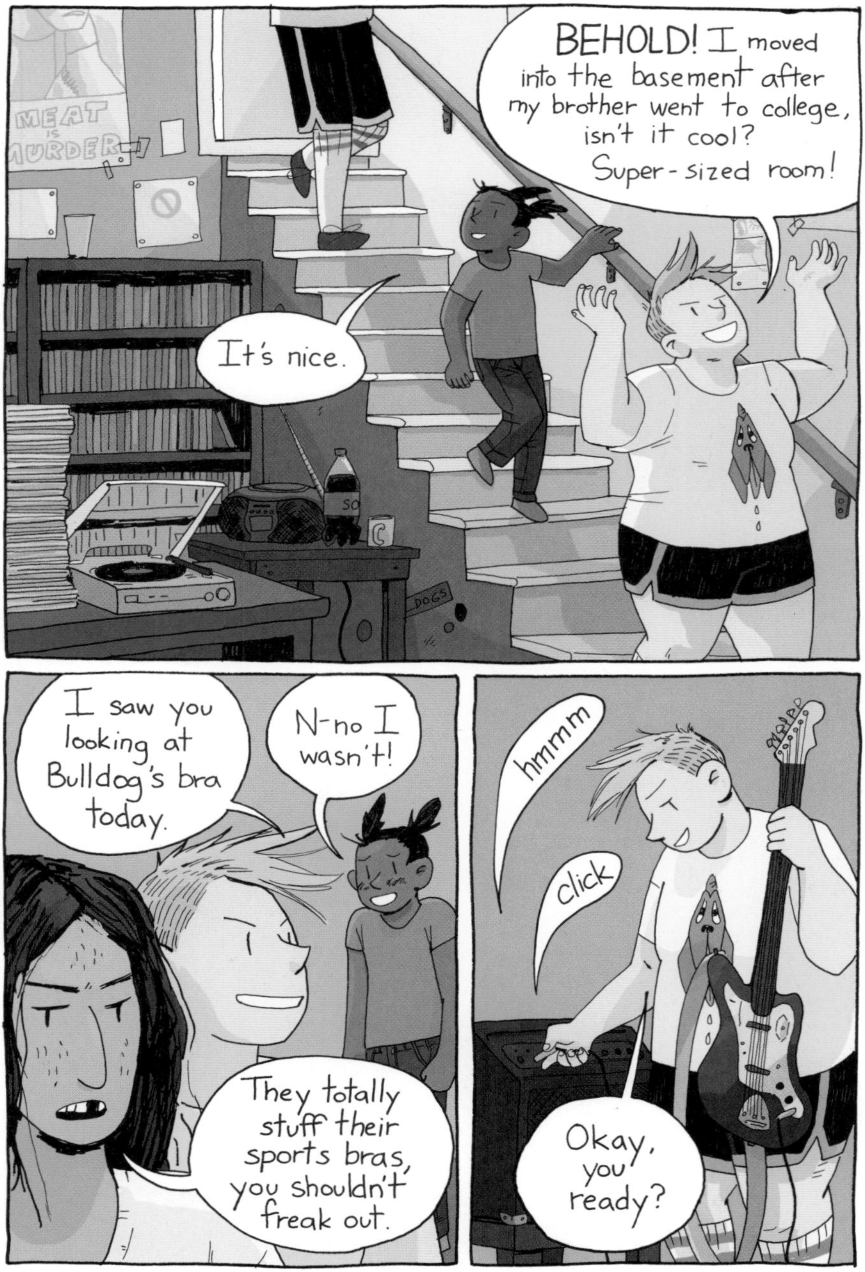
BEHOLD! I moved into the basement after my brother went to college, isn't it cool? Super-sized room!
It's nice.
MEAT IS MURDER
SO
C
DOGS
I saw you looking at Bulldog's bra today.
N-no I wasn't!
They totally stuff their sports bras, you shouldn't freak out.
hmmm
click
Okay, you ready?

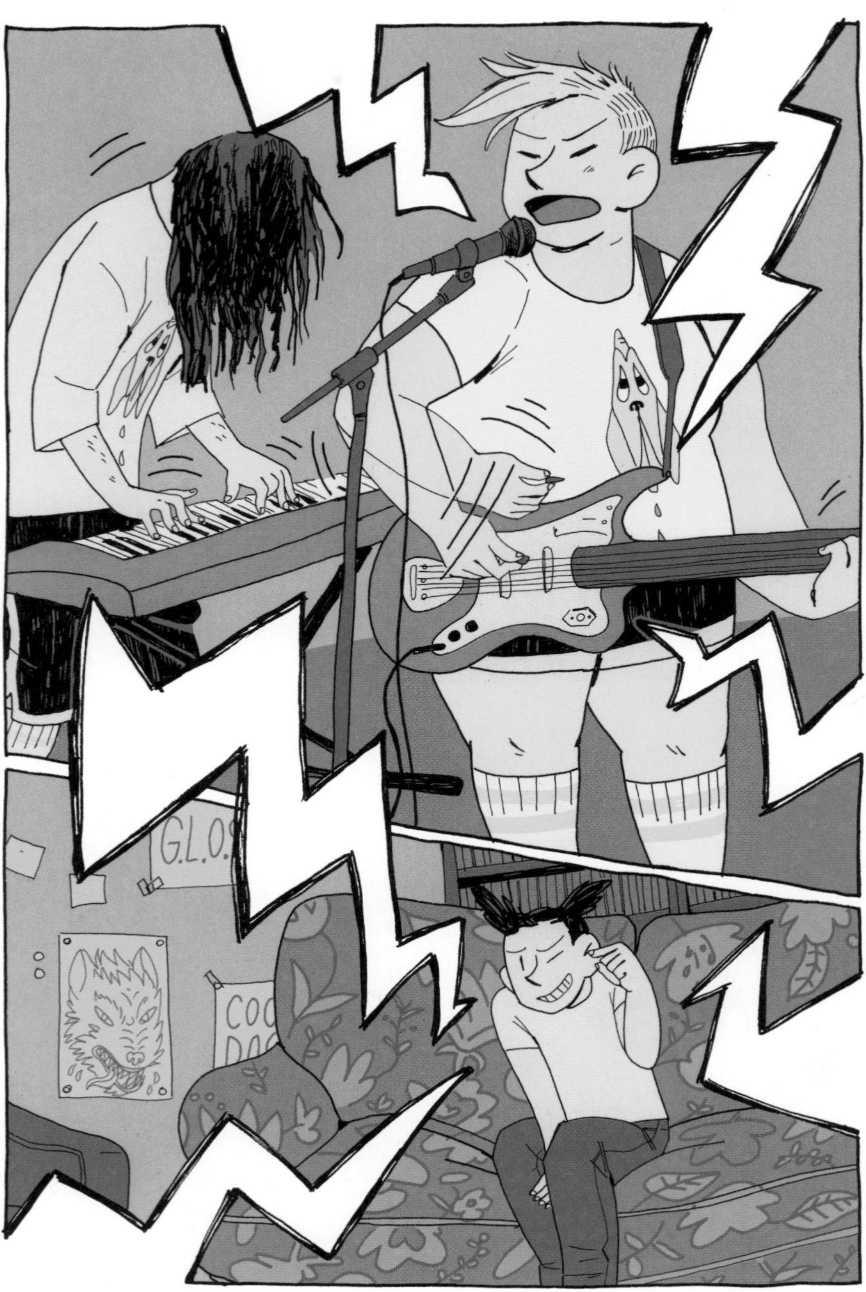

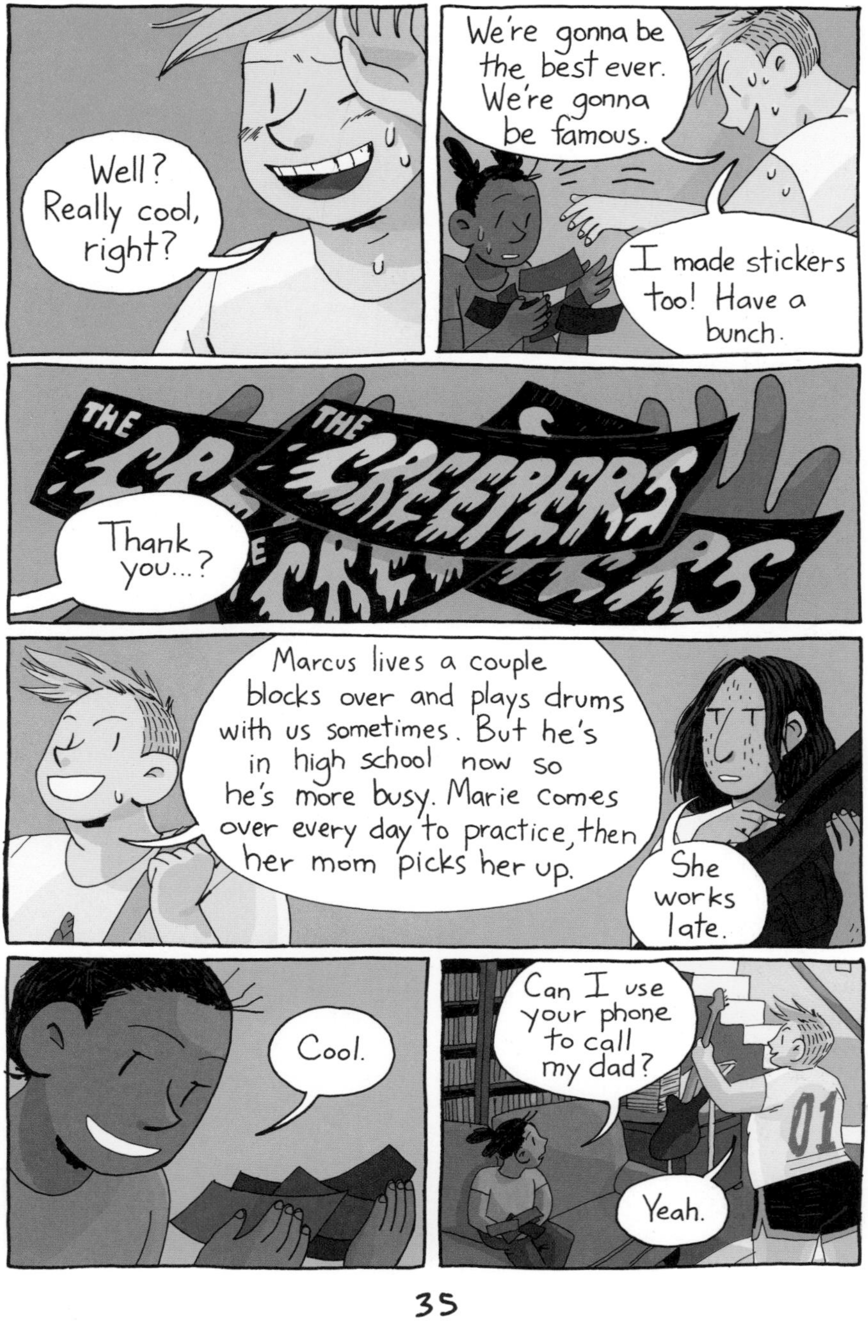
Well? Really cool, right?
We're gonna be the best ever. We're gonna be famous.
I made stickers too! Have a bunch.
THE CREEPERS
Thank you...?
Marcus lives a couple blocks over and plays drums with us sometimes. But he's in high school now so he's more busy. Marie comes over every day to practice, then her mom picks her up.
She works late.
Cool.
Can I use your phone to call my dad?
Yeah.

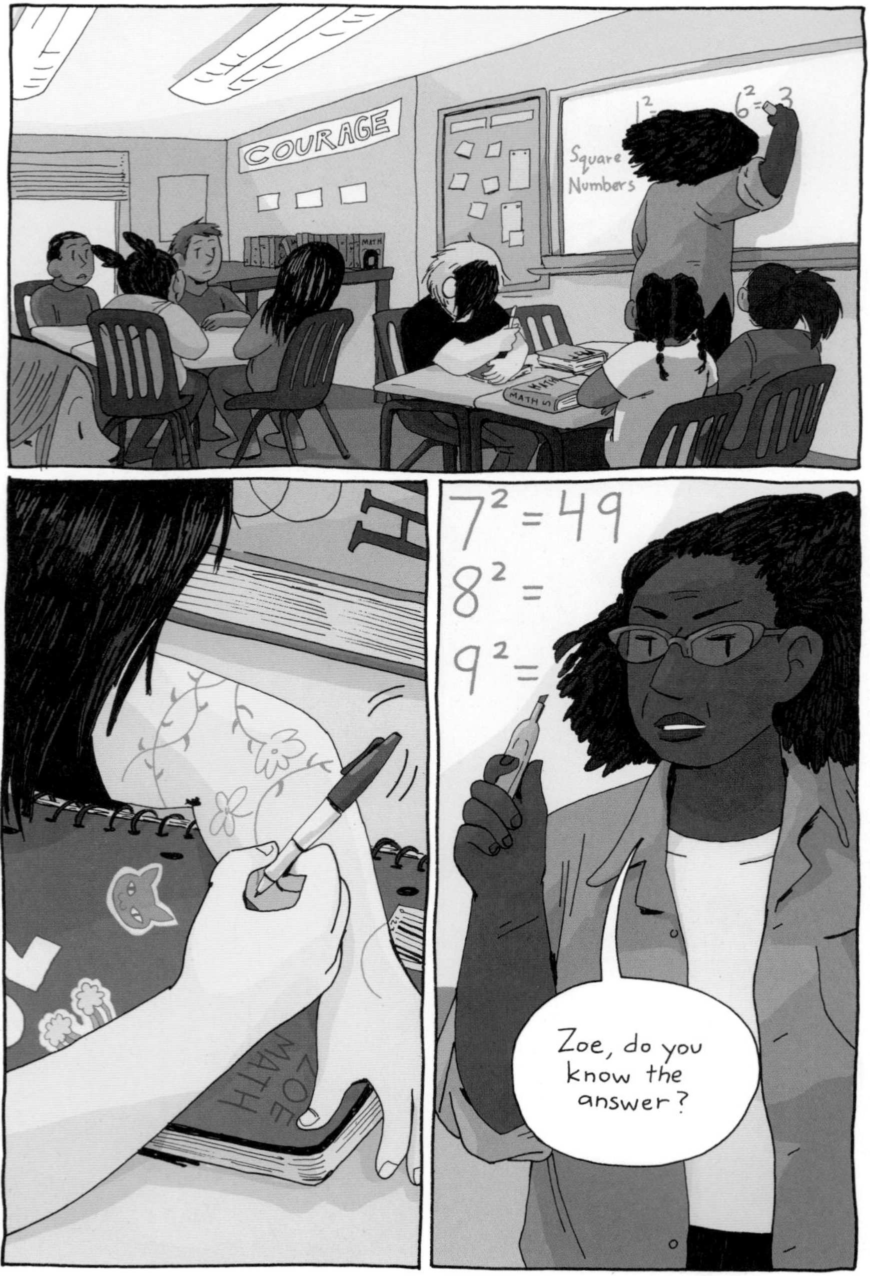
COURAGE
Square Numbers
$6^2 = 3$
MATH
$7^2 = 49$
$8^2 =$
$9^2 =$
ZOE MATH
Zoe, do you know the answer?

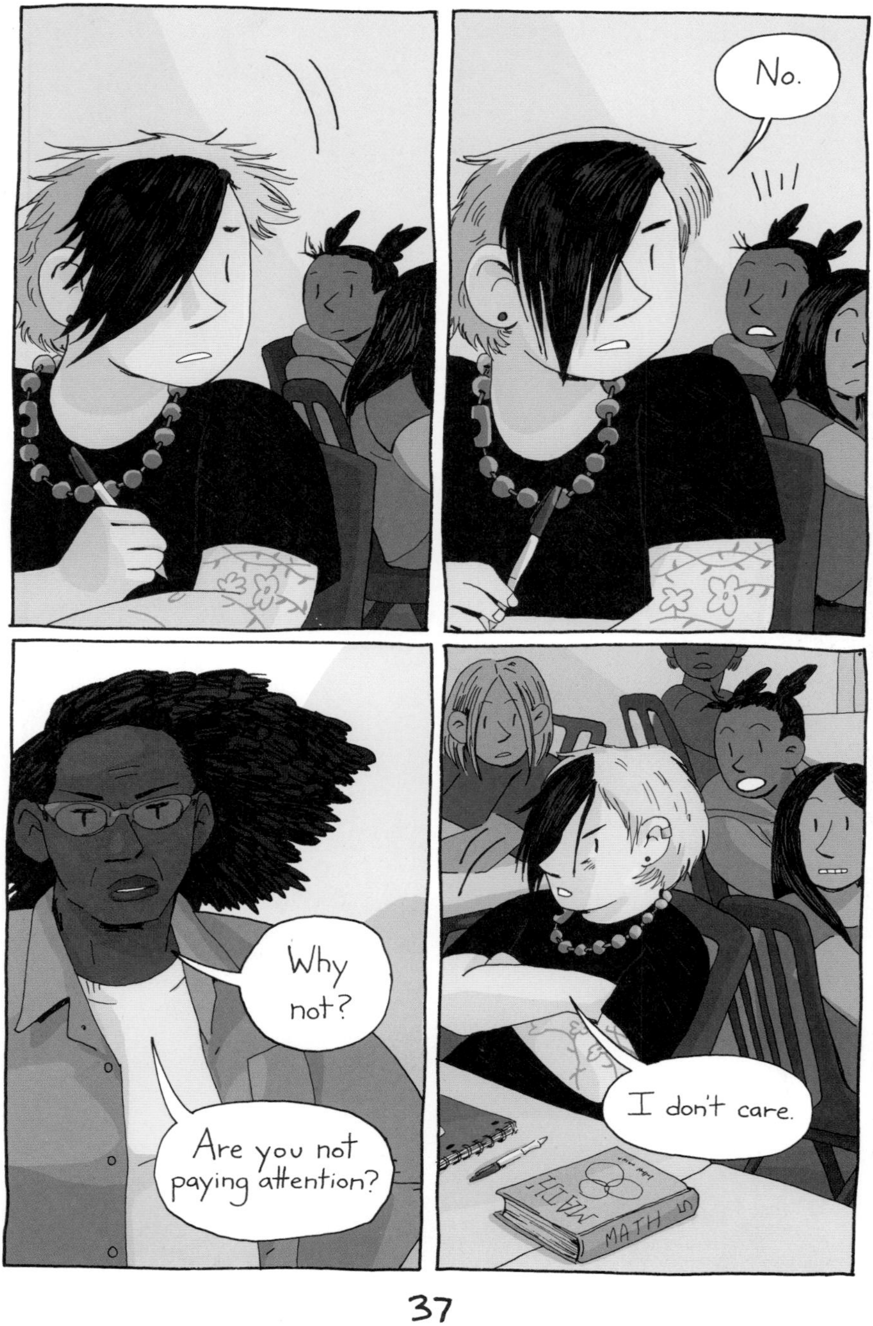
No.
Why not?
Are you not paying attention?
I don't care.
MATH
MATH 5

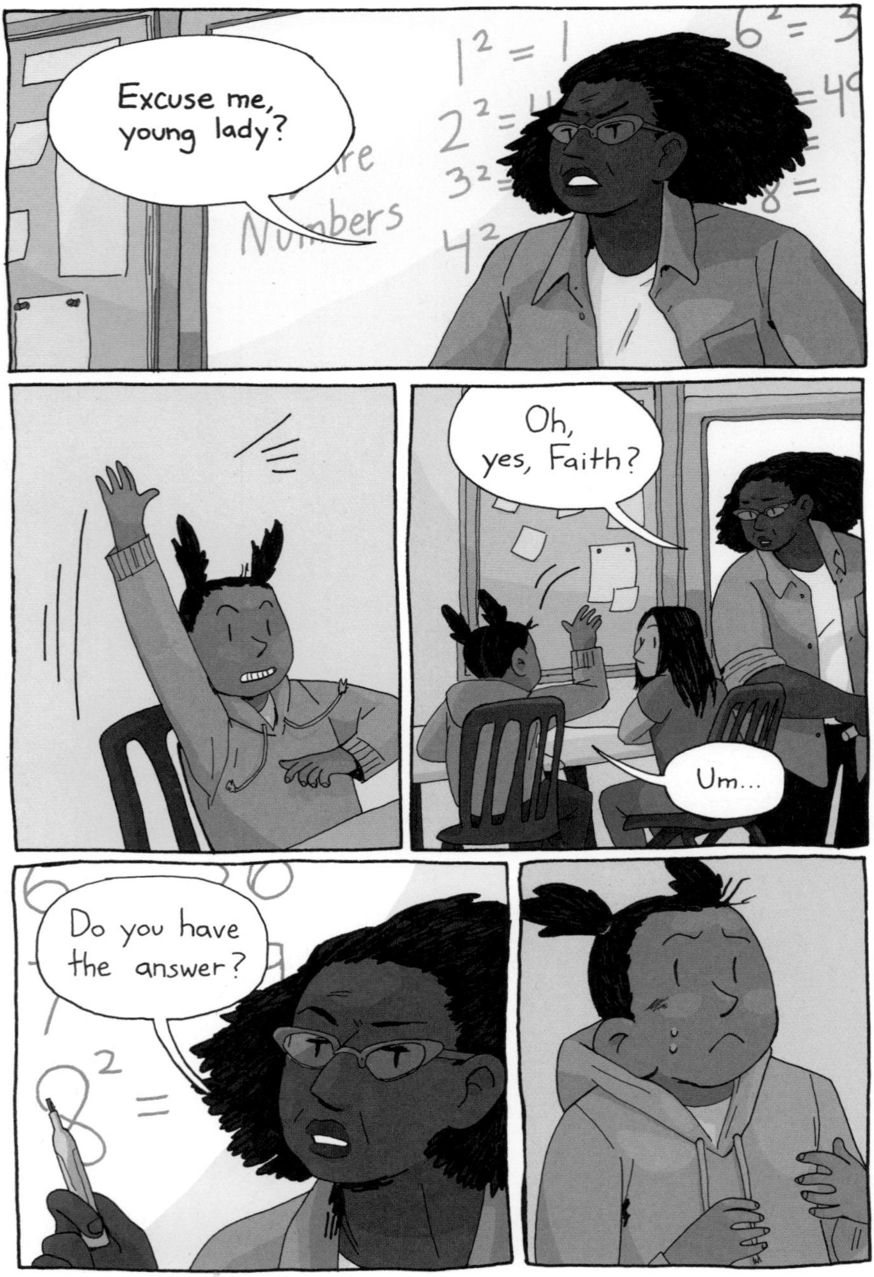
Excuse me, young lady?
Oh, yes, Faith?
Um...
Do you have the answer?

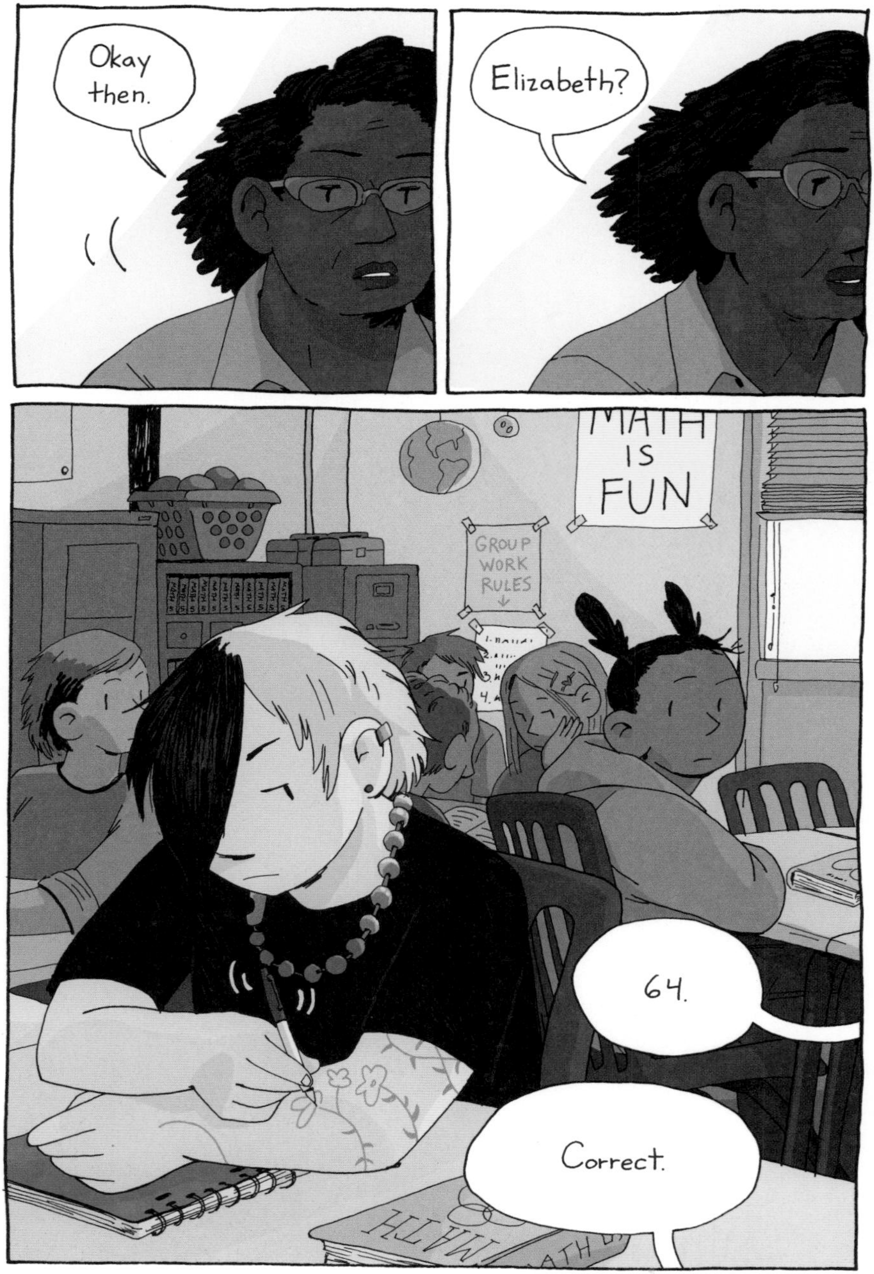
Okay then.
Elizabeth?
MATH IS FUN
GROUP WORK RULES
64.
Correct.

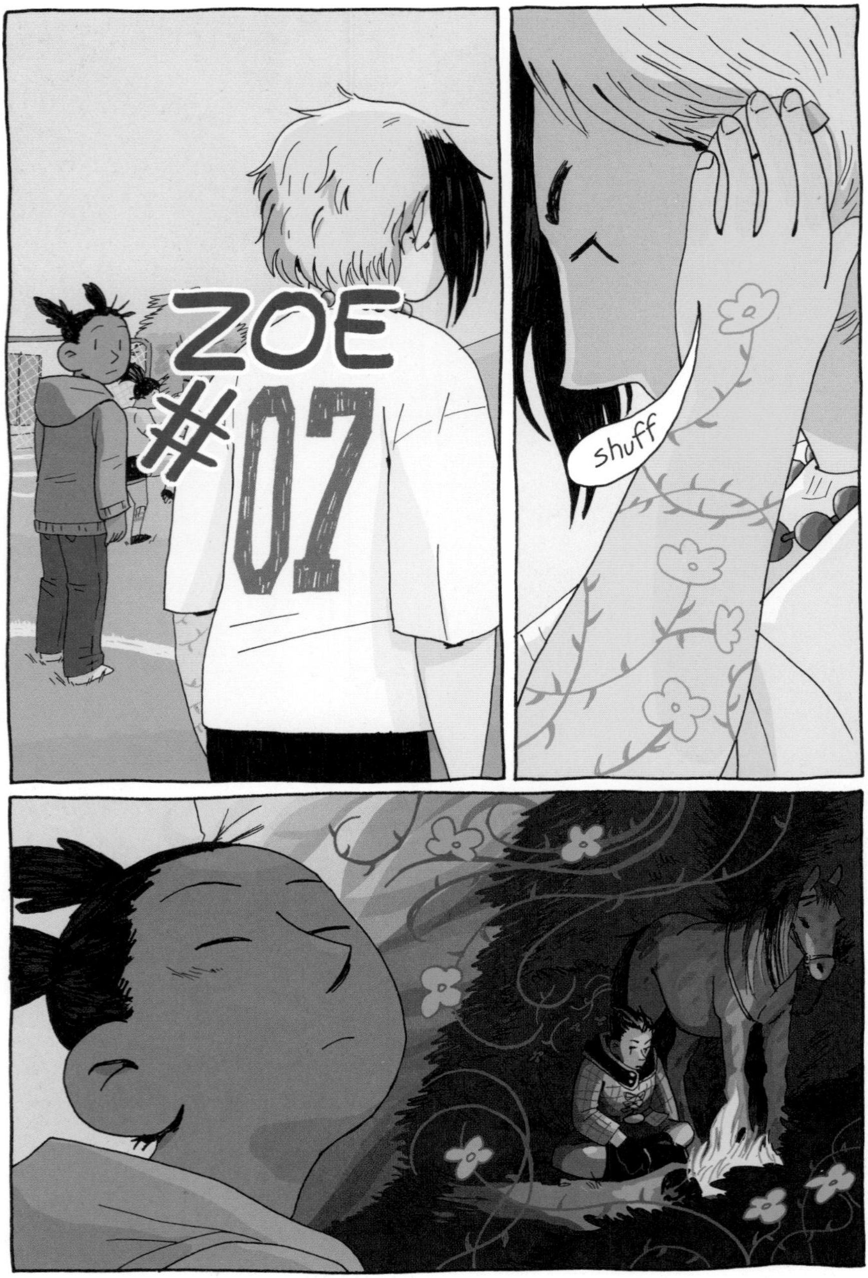
ZOE
#07
shuff

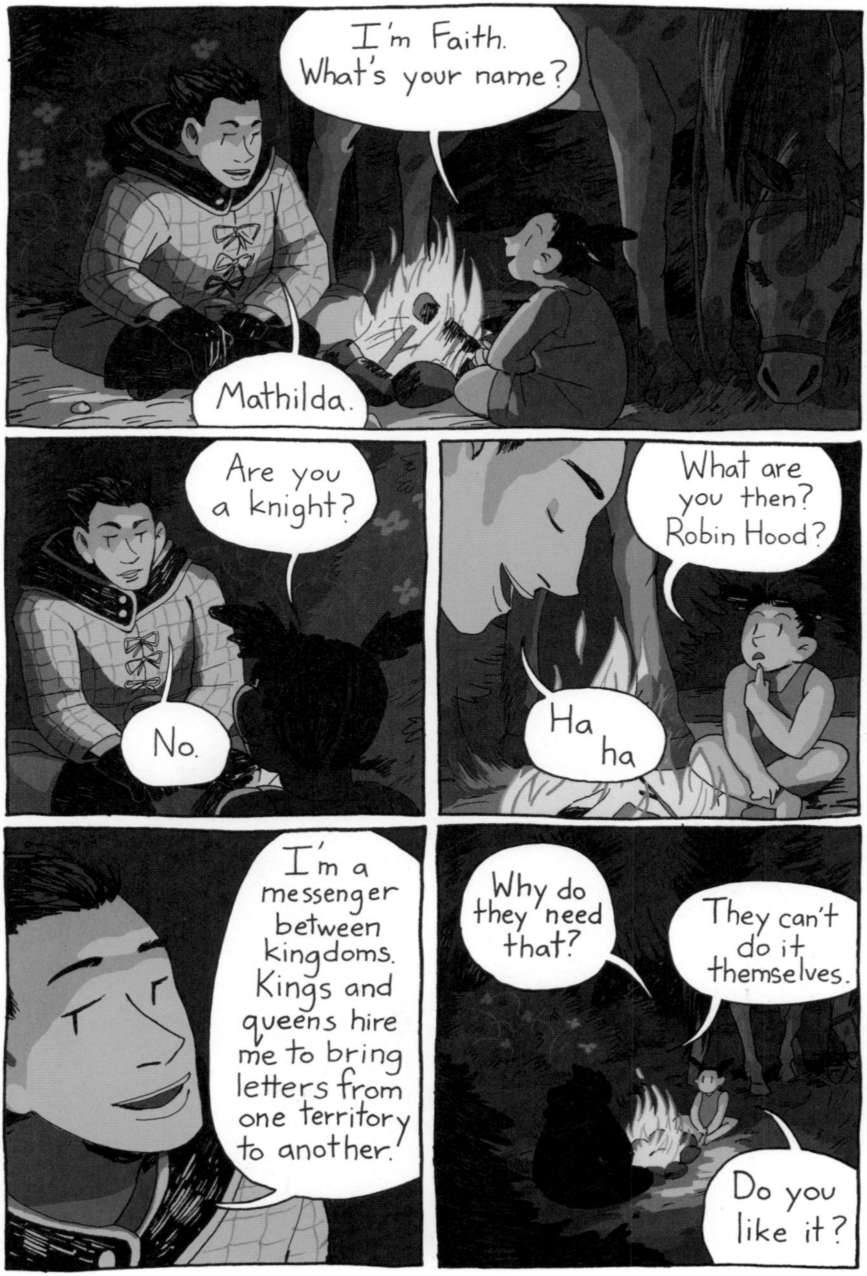
I'm Faith. What's your name?
Mathilda.
Are you a knight?
No.
What are you then? Robin Hood?
Ha ha
I'm a messenger between kingdoms. Kings and queens hire me to bring letters from one territory to another.
Why do they need that?
They can't do it themselves.
Do you like it?

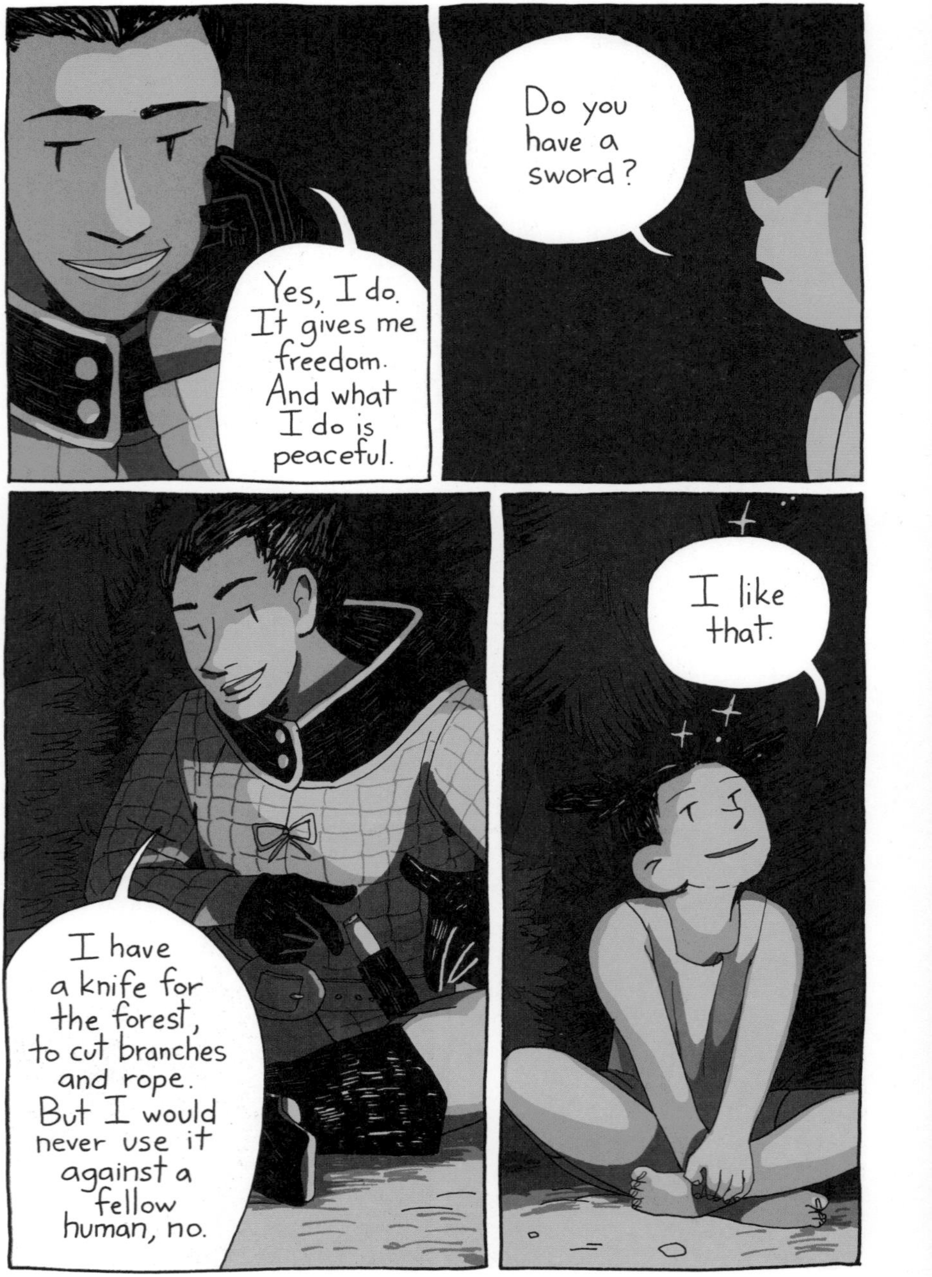
Yes, I do. It gives me freedom. And what I do is peaceful.
Do you have a sword?
I have a knife for the forest, to cut branches and rope. But I would never use it against a fellow human, no.
I like that.

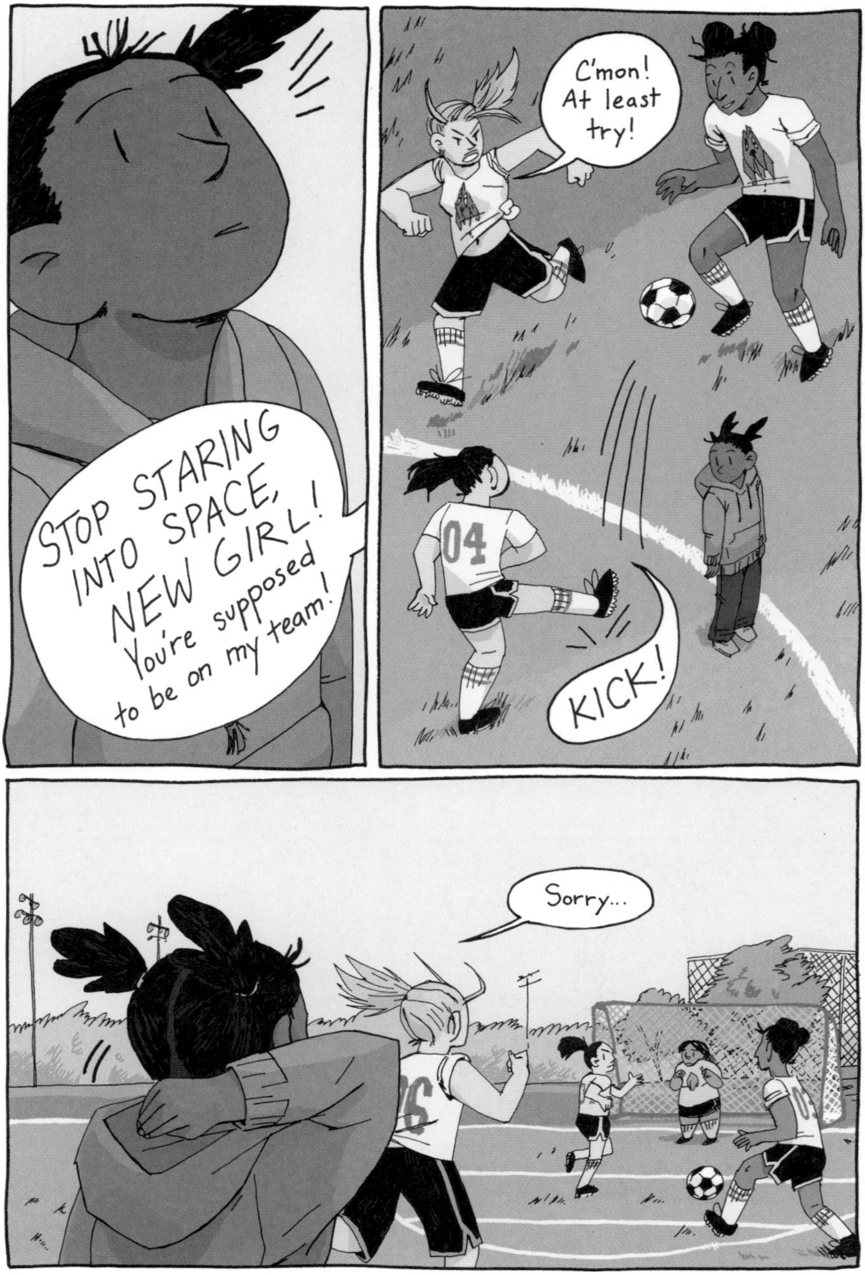
STOP STARING INTO SPACE, NEW GIRL! You're supposed to be on my team!
C'mon! At least try!
KICK!
Sorry...

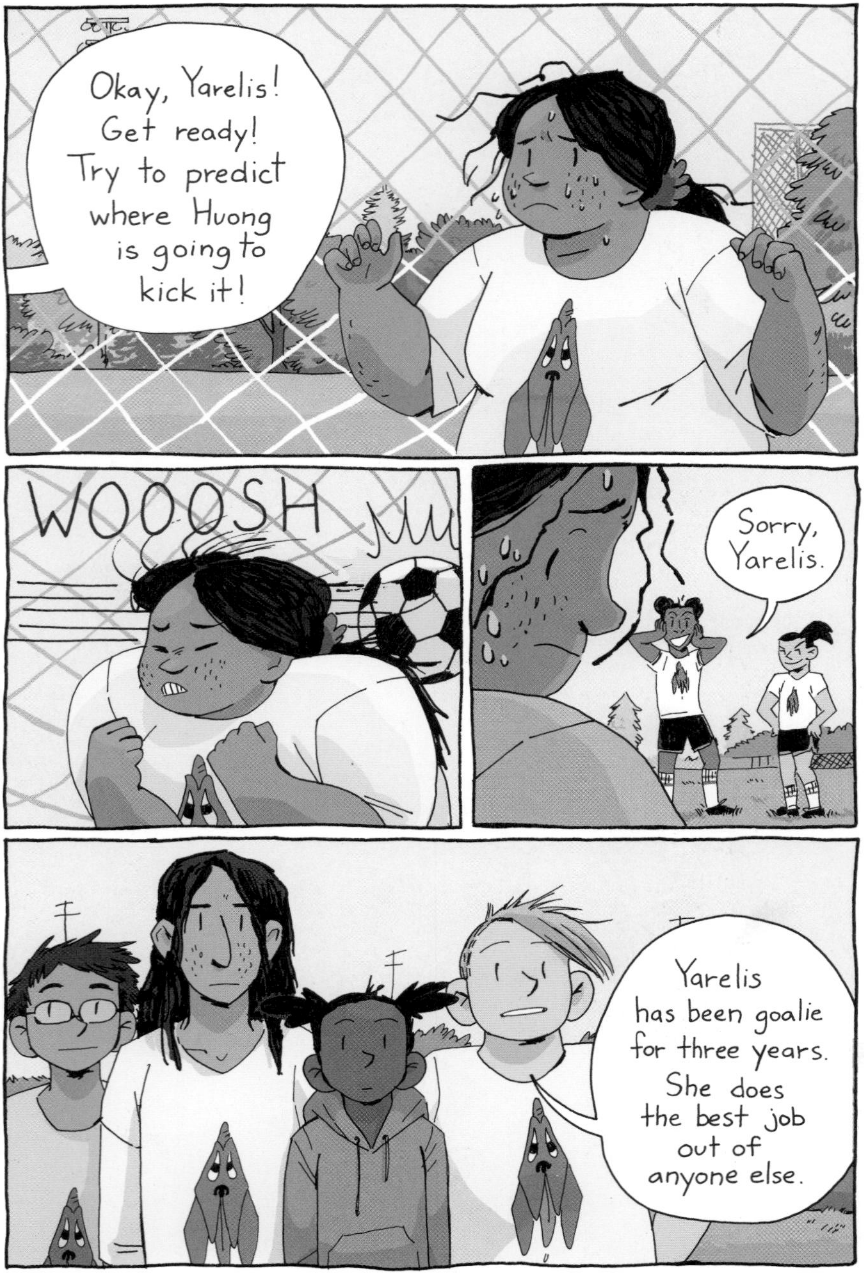
Okay, Yarelis! Get ready! Try to predict where Huong is going to kick it!
WOOOSH
Sorry, Yarelis.
Yarelis has been goalie for three years. She does the best job out of anyone else.

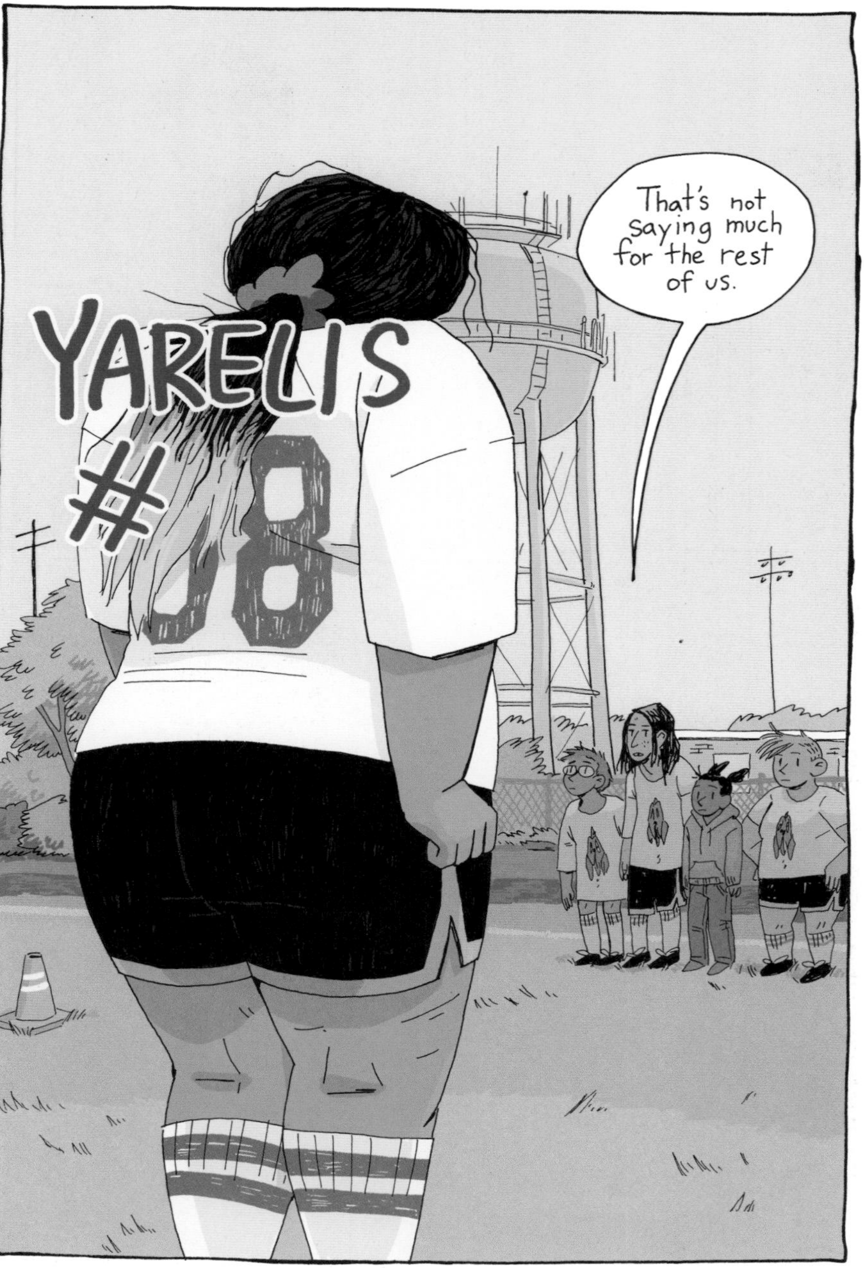
YARELIS
#08
That's not saying much for the rest of us.

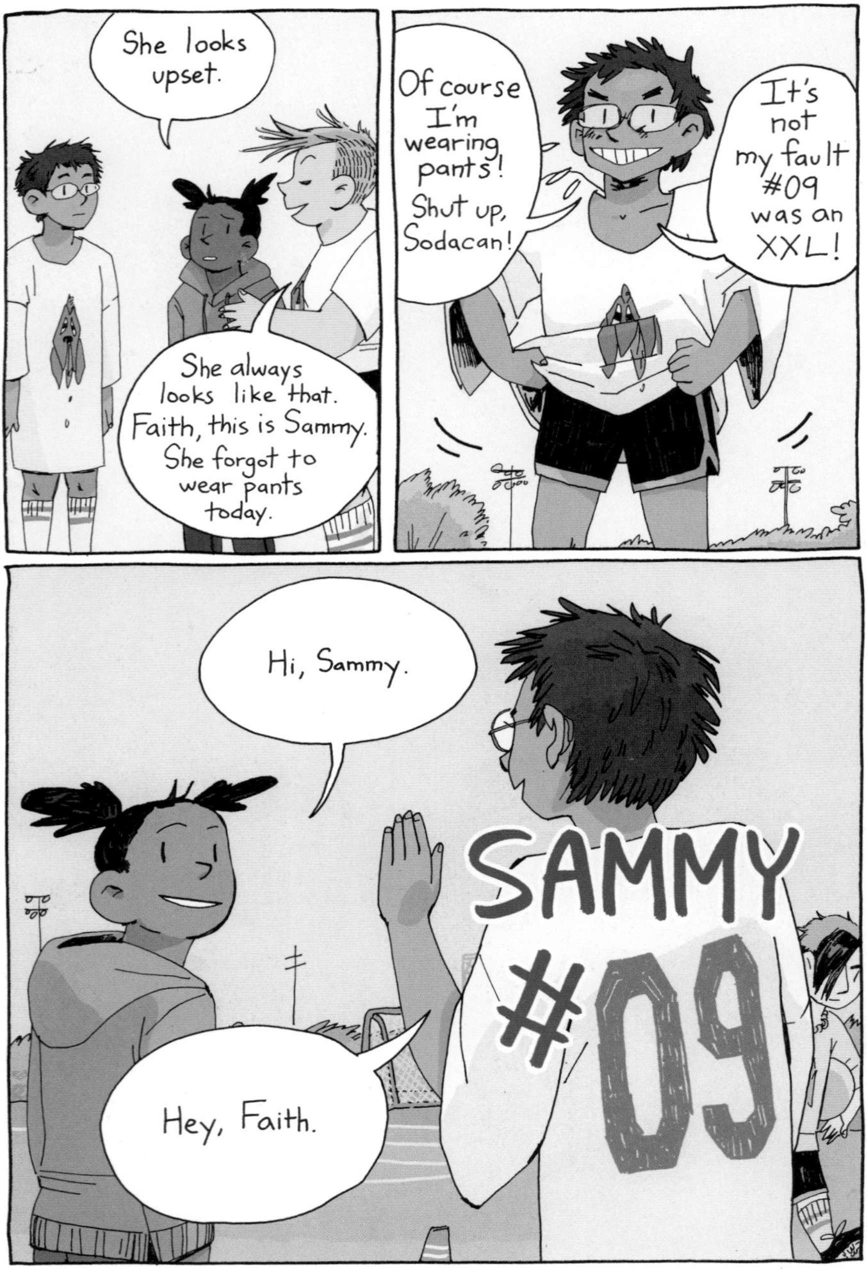
She looks upset.
She always looks like that. Faith, this is Sammy. She forgot to wear pants today.
Of course I'm wearing pants! Shut up, Sodacan!
It's not my fault #09 was an XXL!
Hi, Sammy.
SAMMY #09
Hey, Faith.

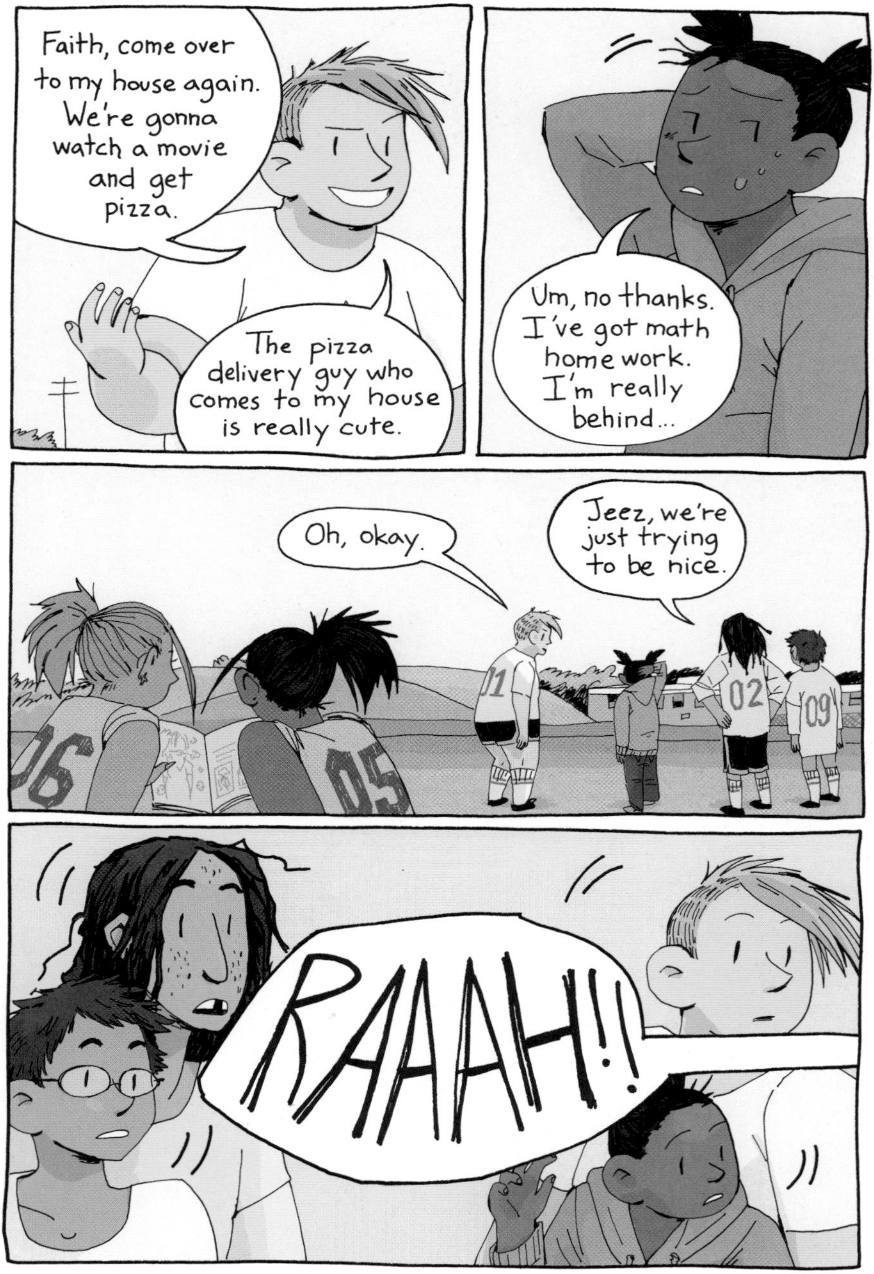
Faith, come over to my house again. We're gonna watch a movie and get pizza.
The pizza delivery guy who comes to my house is really cute.
Um, no thanks. I've got math home work. I'm really behind...
Oh, okay.
Jeez, we're just trying to be nice.
01
02
09
06
05
RAAAH!!

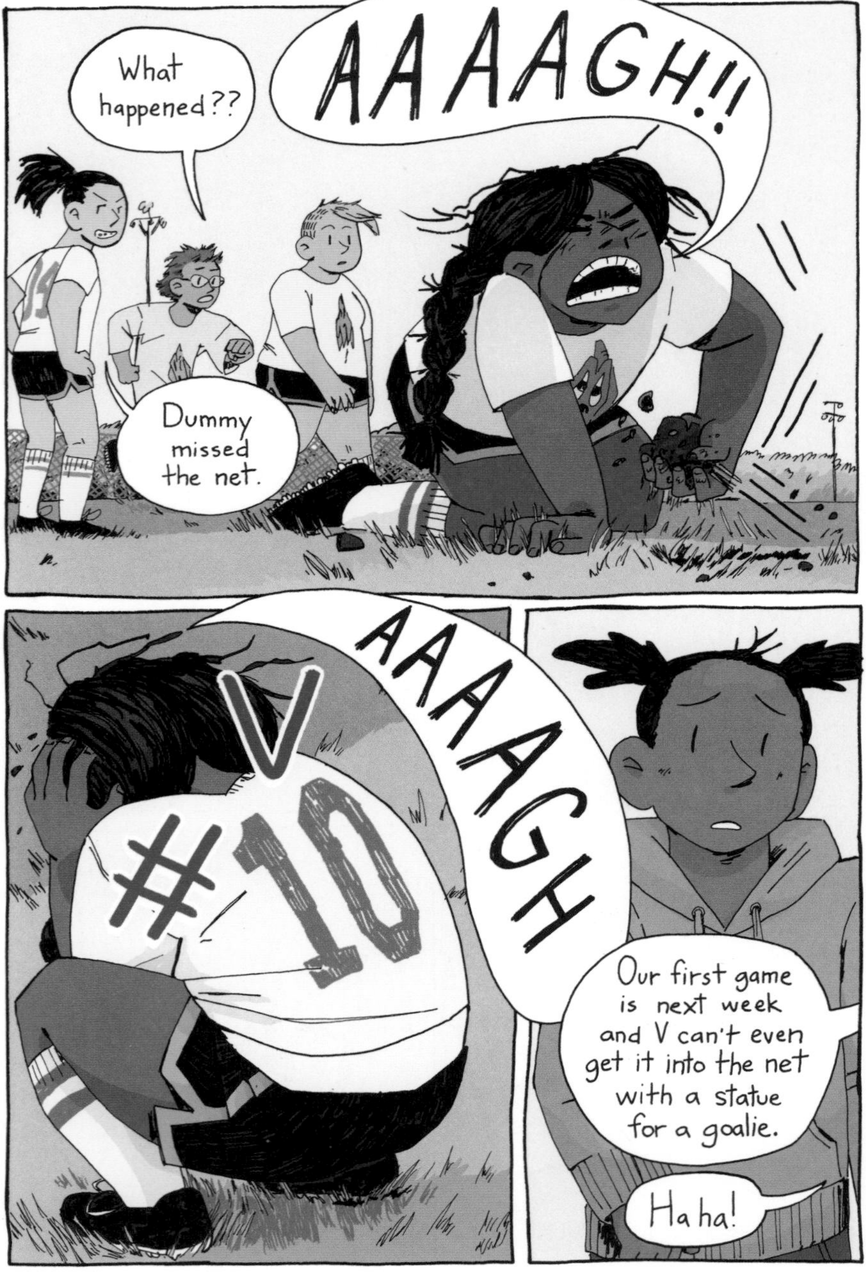
What happened??
AAAAGH!!
Dummy missed the net.
AAAAGH
V
#10
Our first game is next week and V can't even get it into the net with a statue for a goalie.
Ha ha!

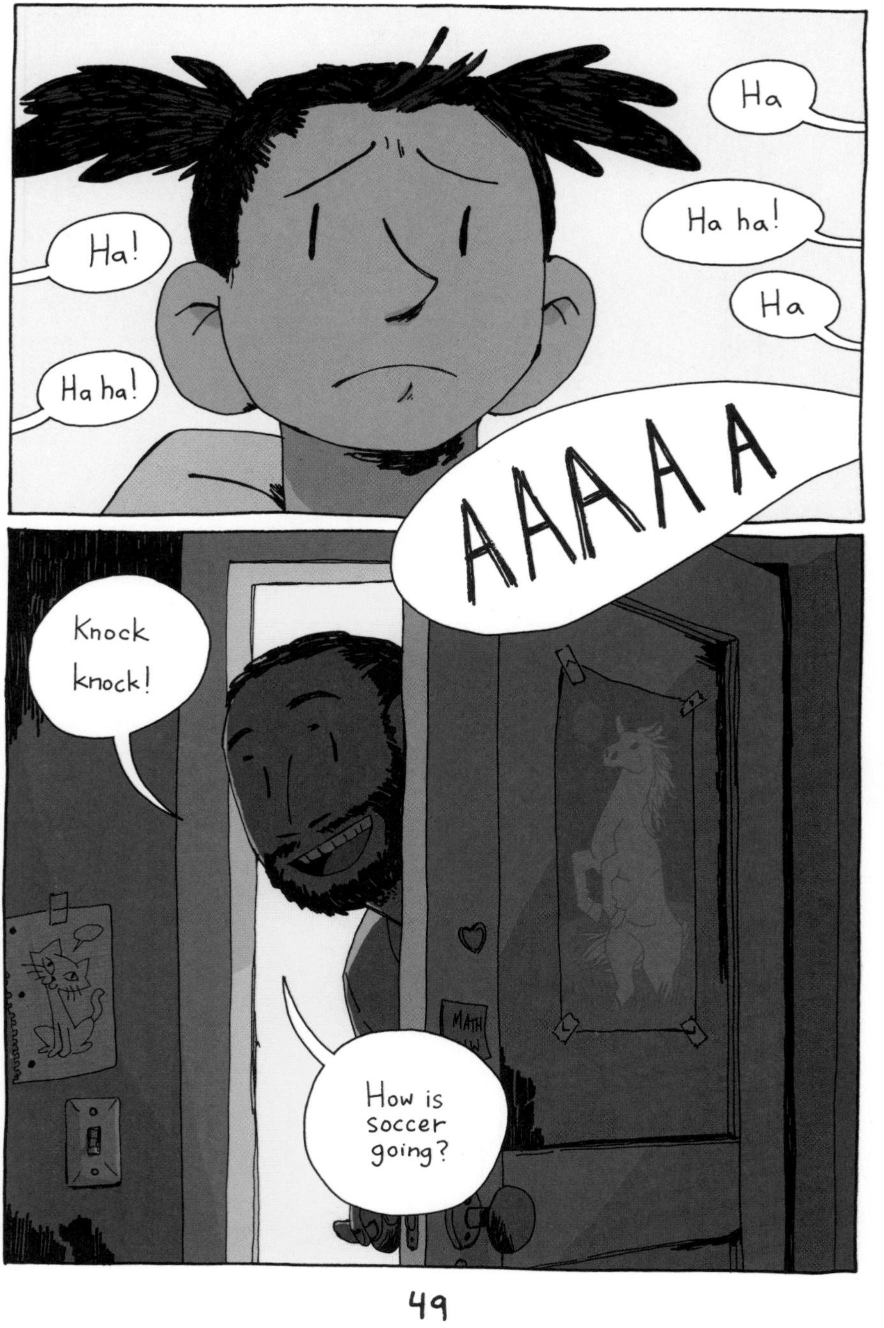
Ha
Ha ha!
Ha!
Ha
Ha ha!
AAAAA
Knock knock!
MATH
How is soccer going?

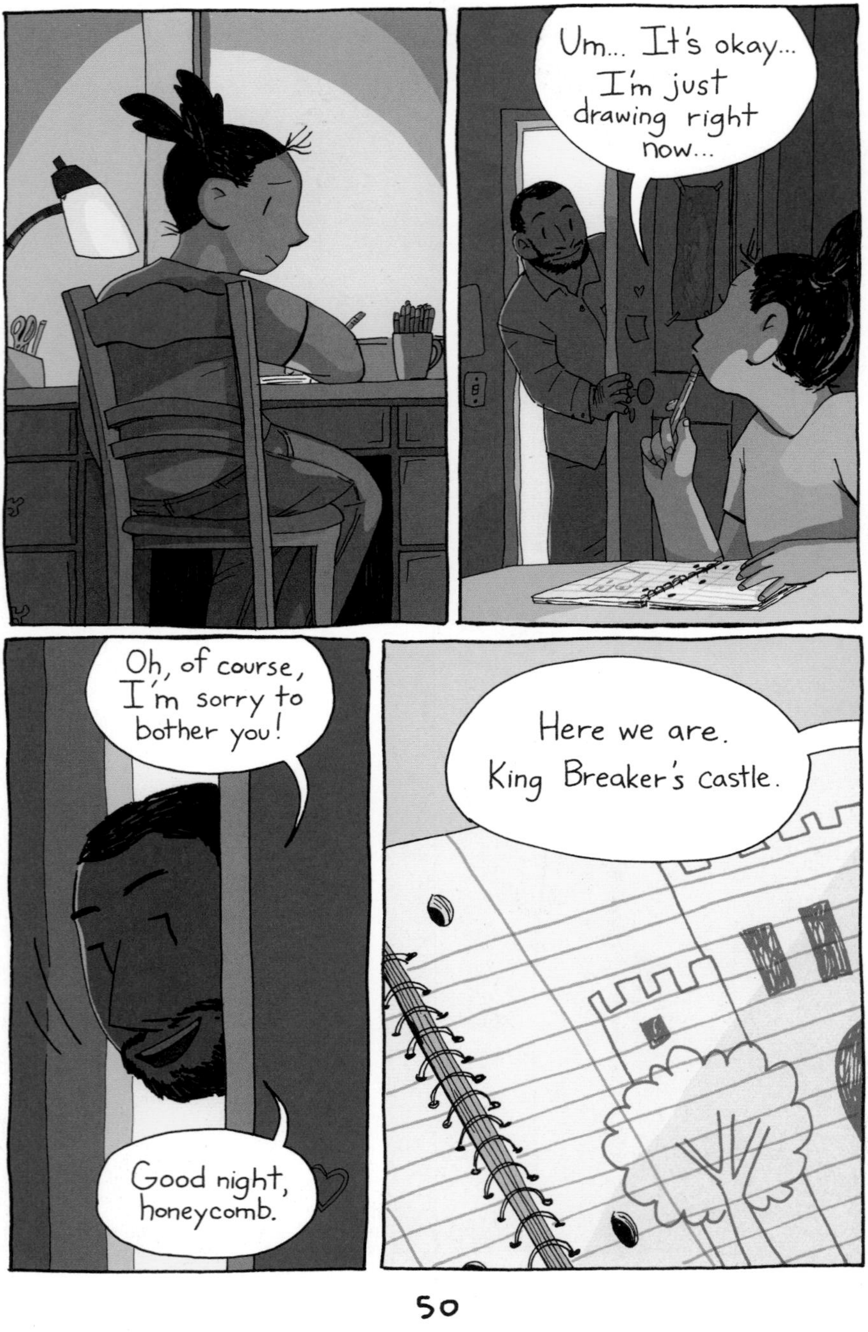

Um... It's okay... I'm just drawing right now...
Oh, of course, I'm sorry to bother you!
Good night, honeycomb.
Here we are. King Breaker's castle.

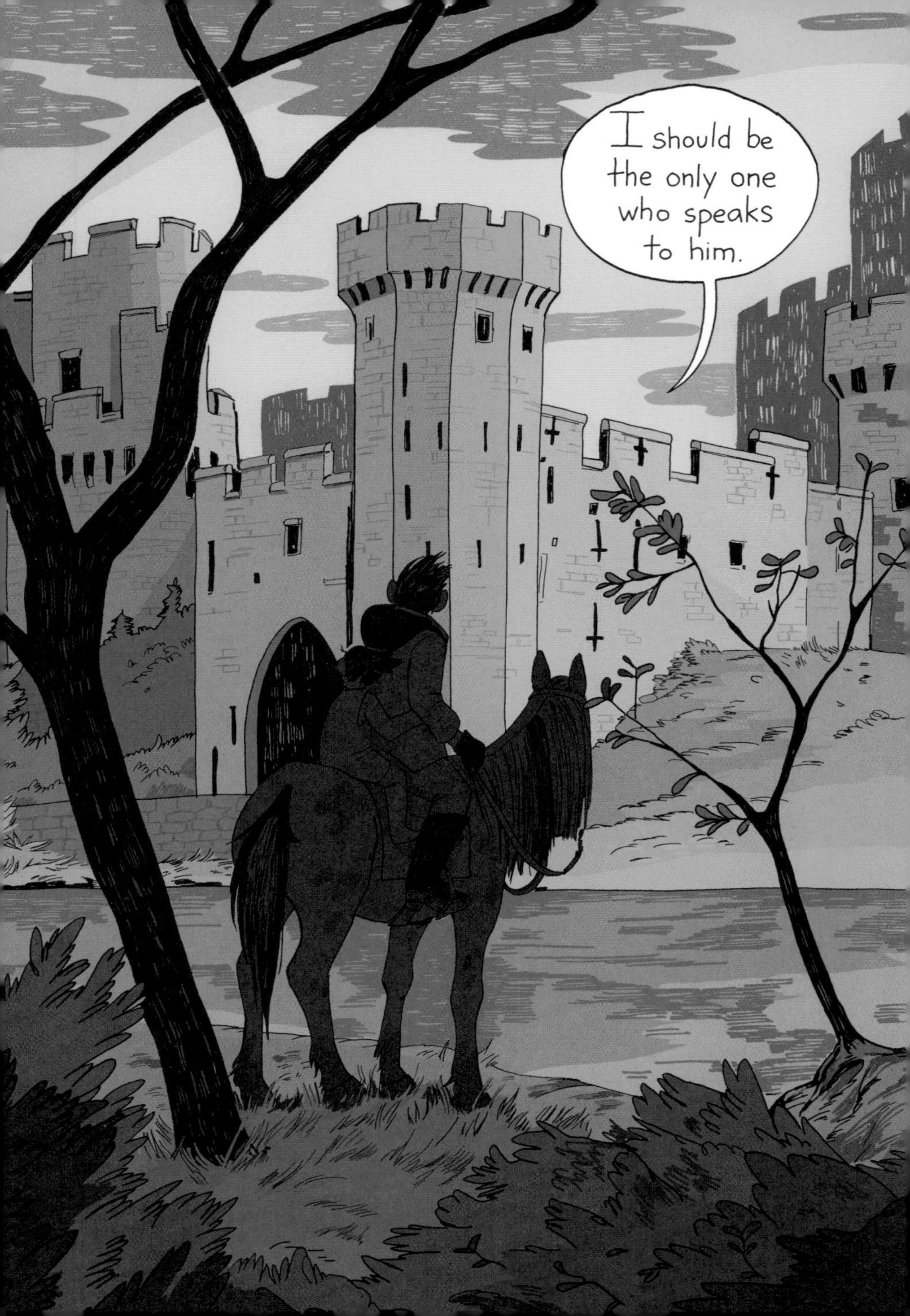
I should be the only one who speaks to him.

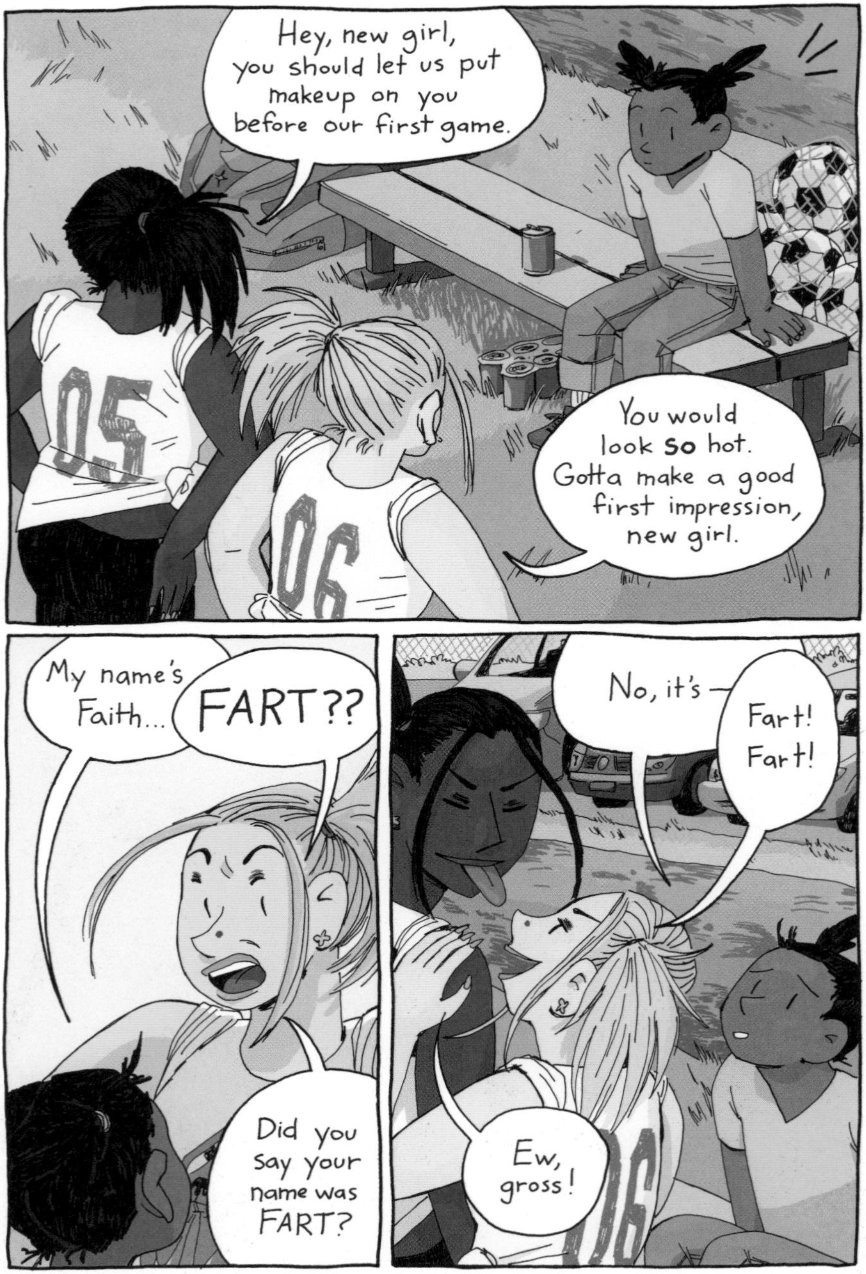
Hey, new girl, you should let us put makeup on you before our first game.
You would look **so** hot. Gotta make a good first impression, new girl.
My name's Faith...
FART??
Did you say your name was FART?
No, it's—
Fart! Fart!
Ew, gross!

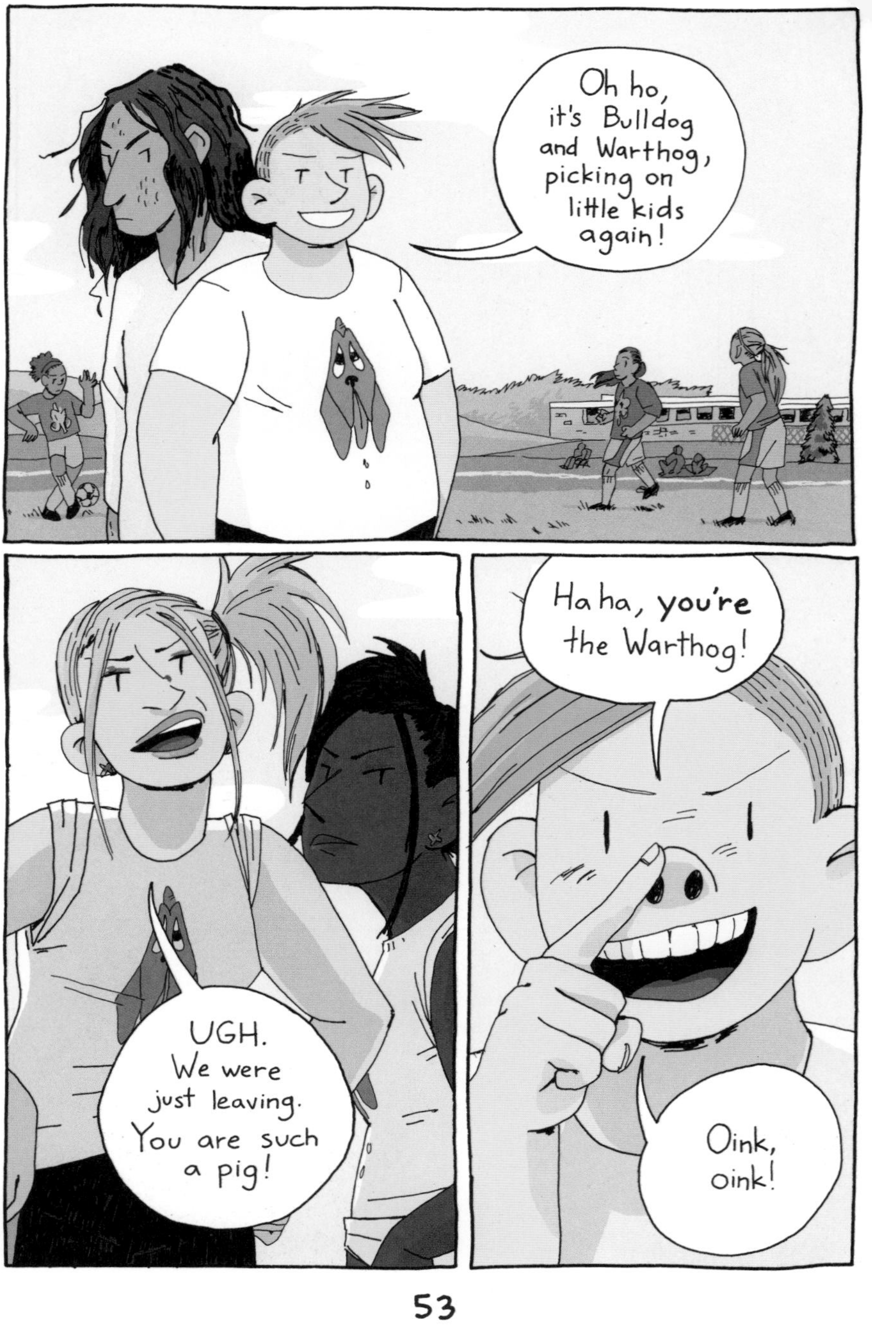
Oh ho, it's Bulldog and Warthog, picking on little kids again!
UGH. We were just leaving. You are such a pig!
Ha ha, **you're** the Warthog!
Oink, oink!

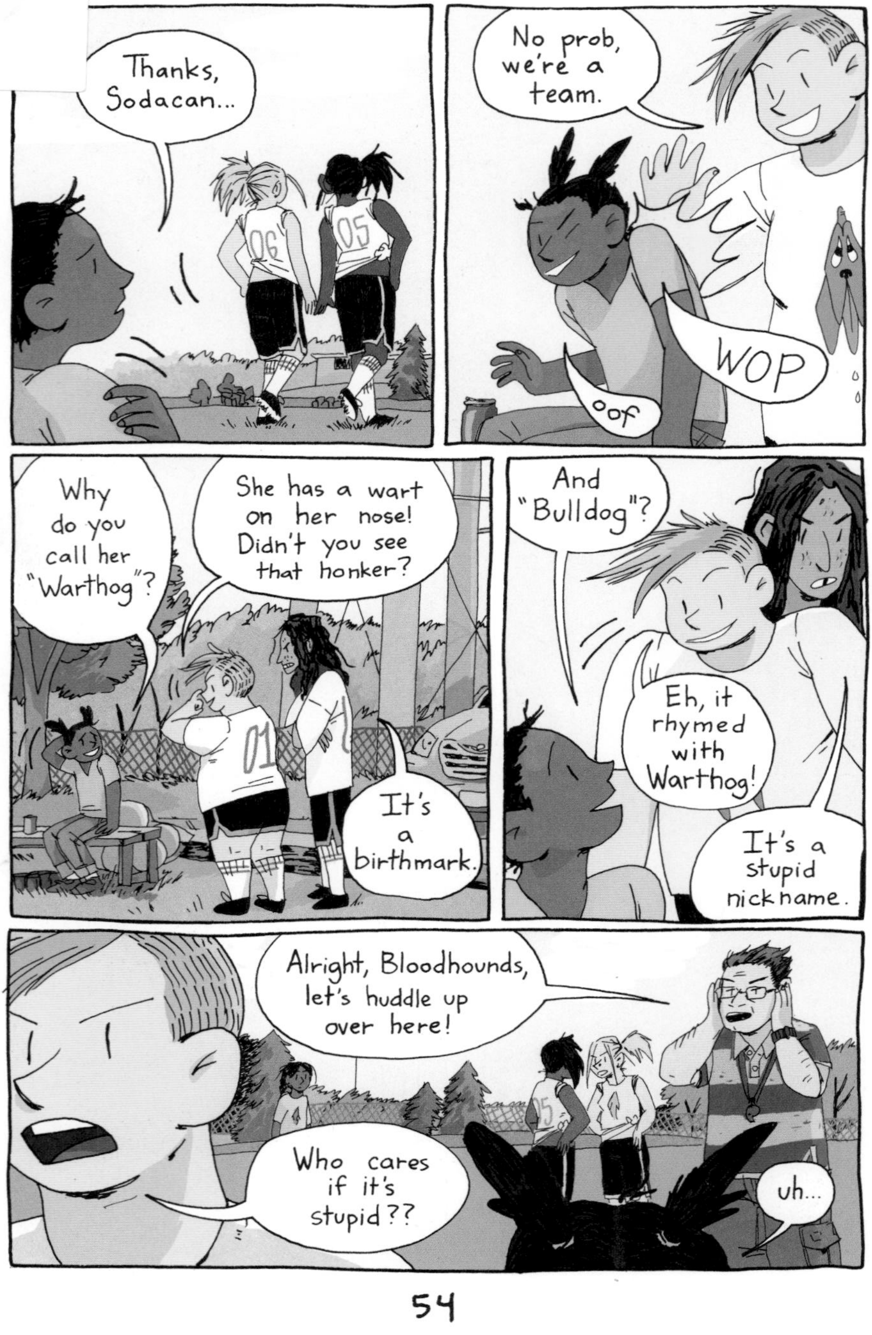
Thanks, Sodacan...
No prob, we're a team.
WOP
oof
Why do you call her "Warthog"?
She has a wart on her nose! Didn't you see that honker?
It's a birthmark.
And "Bulldog"?
Eh, it rhymed with Warthog!
It's a stupid nickname.
Alright, Bloodhounds, let's huddle up over here!
Who cares if it's stupid??
uh...

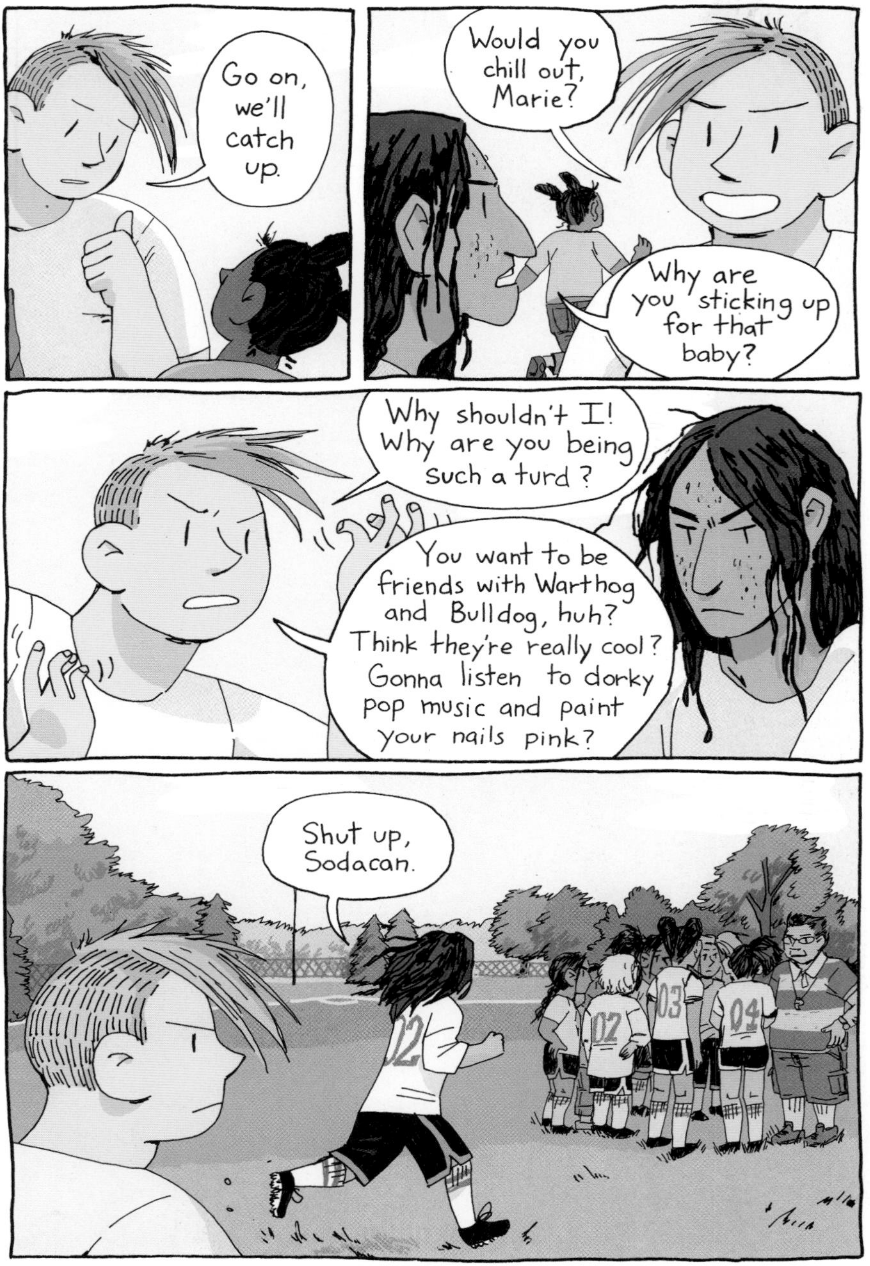

Go on, we'll catch up.
Would you chill out, Marie?
Why are you sticking up for that baby?
Why shouldn't I! Why are you being such a turd?
You want to be friends with Warthog and Bulldog, huh? Think they're really cool? Gonna listen to dorky pop music and paint your nails pink?
Shut up, Sodacan.
02
02
03
04

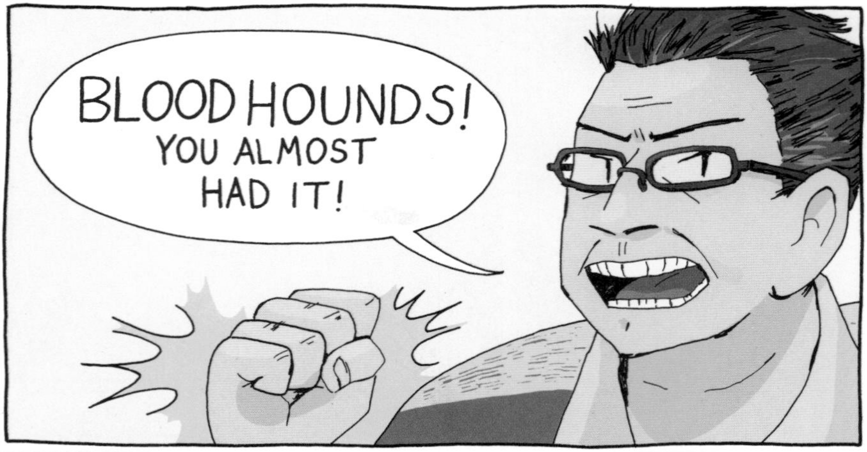
BLOODHOUNDS! YOU ALMOST HAD IT!

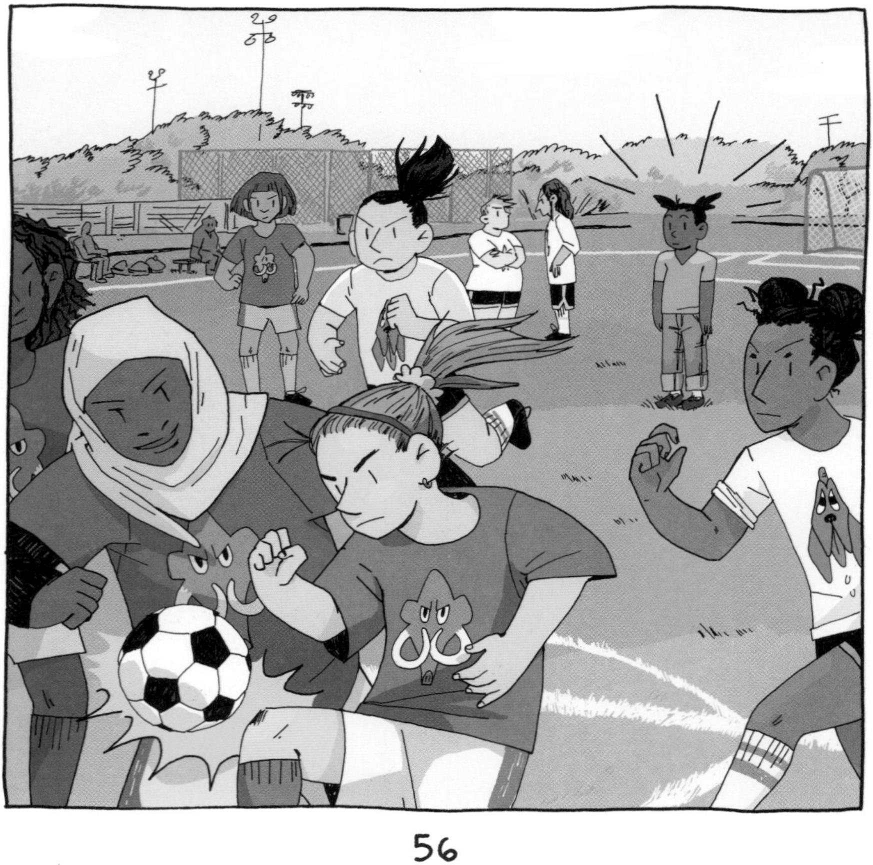

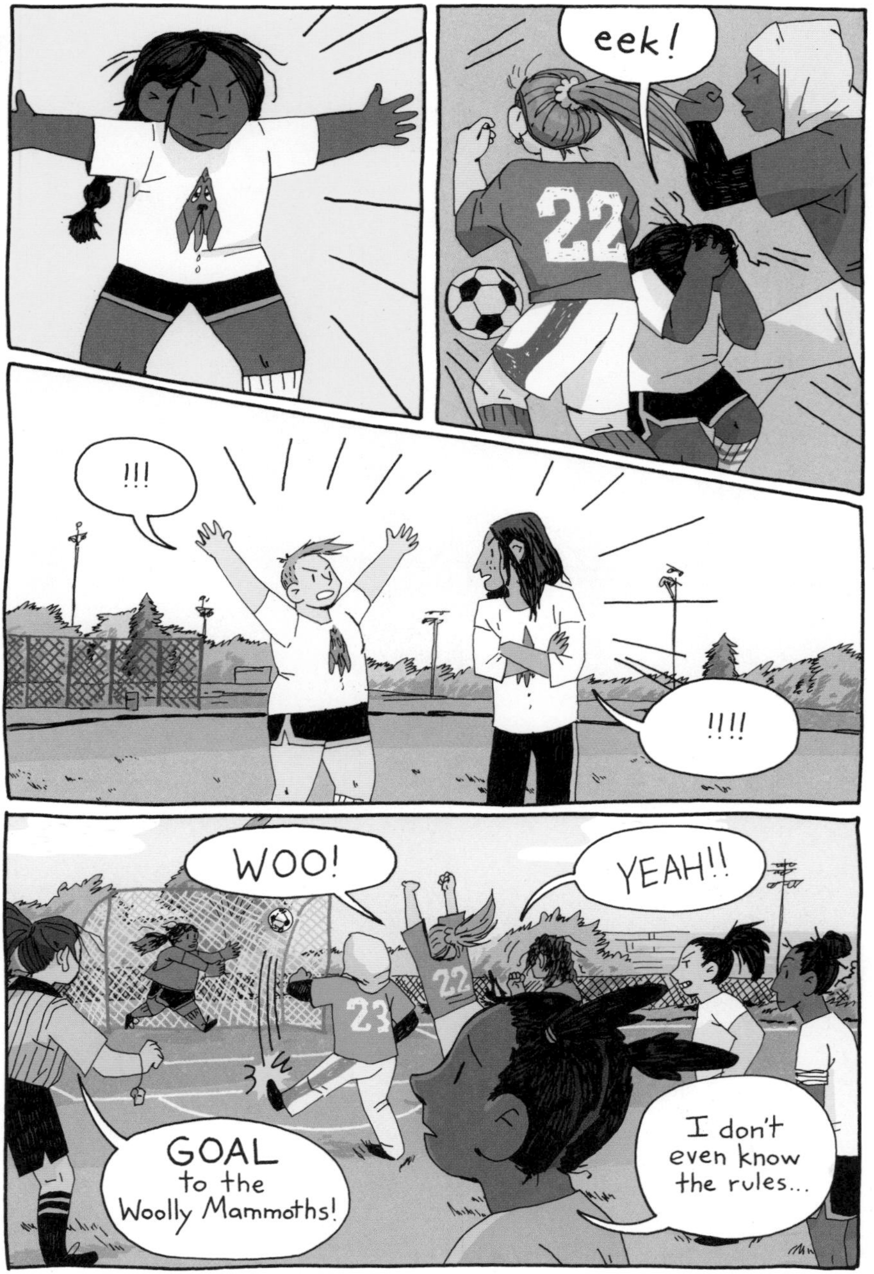
eek!
!!!
!!!!
WOO!
YEAH!!
GOAL
to the
Woolly Mammoths!
I don't
even know
the rules...

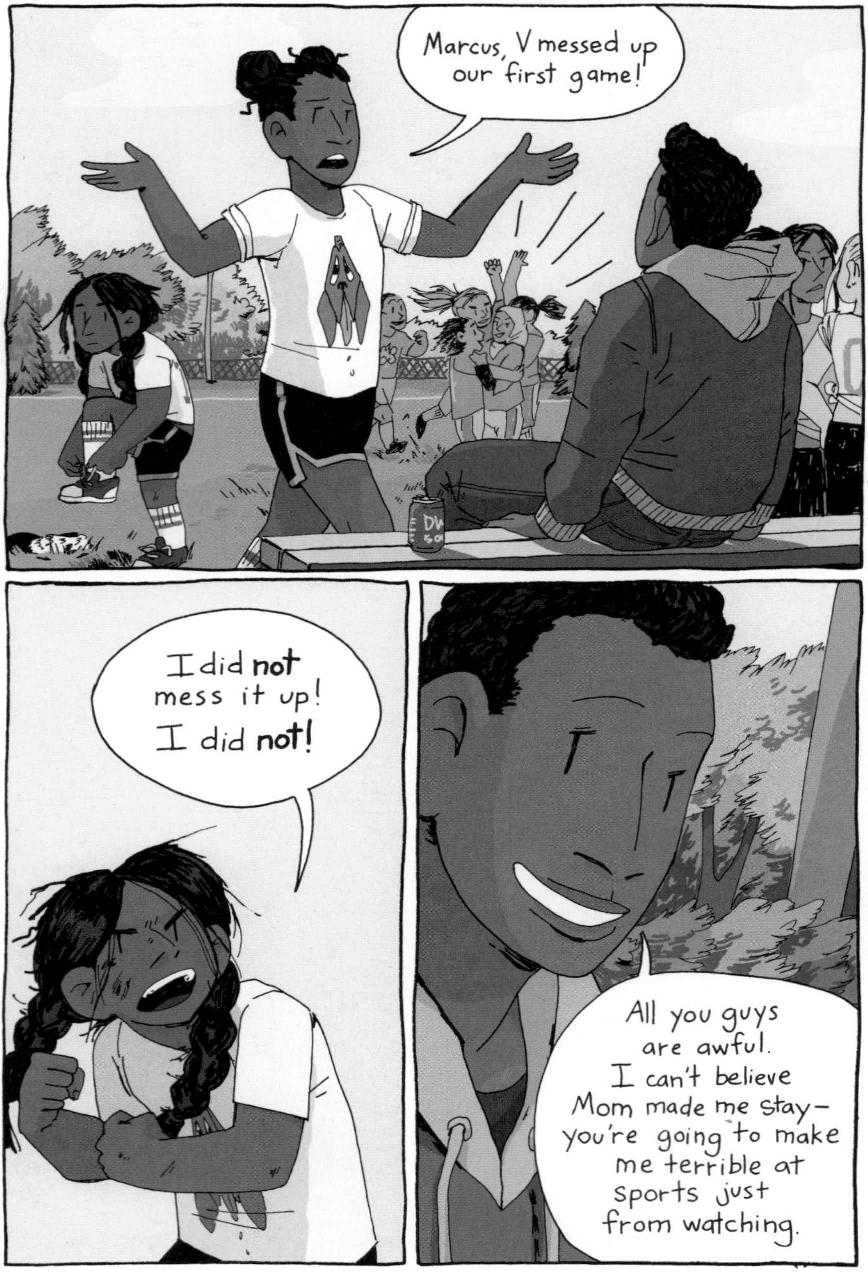
Marcus, V messed up our first game!
I did **not** mess it up! I did **not**!
All you guys are awful. I can't believe Mom made me stay— you're going to make me terrible at sports just from watching.

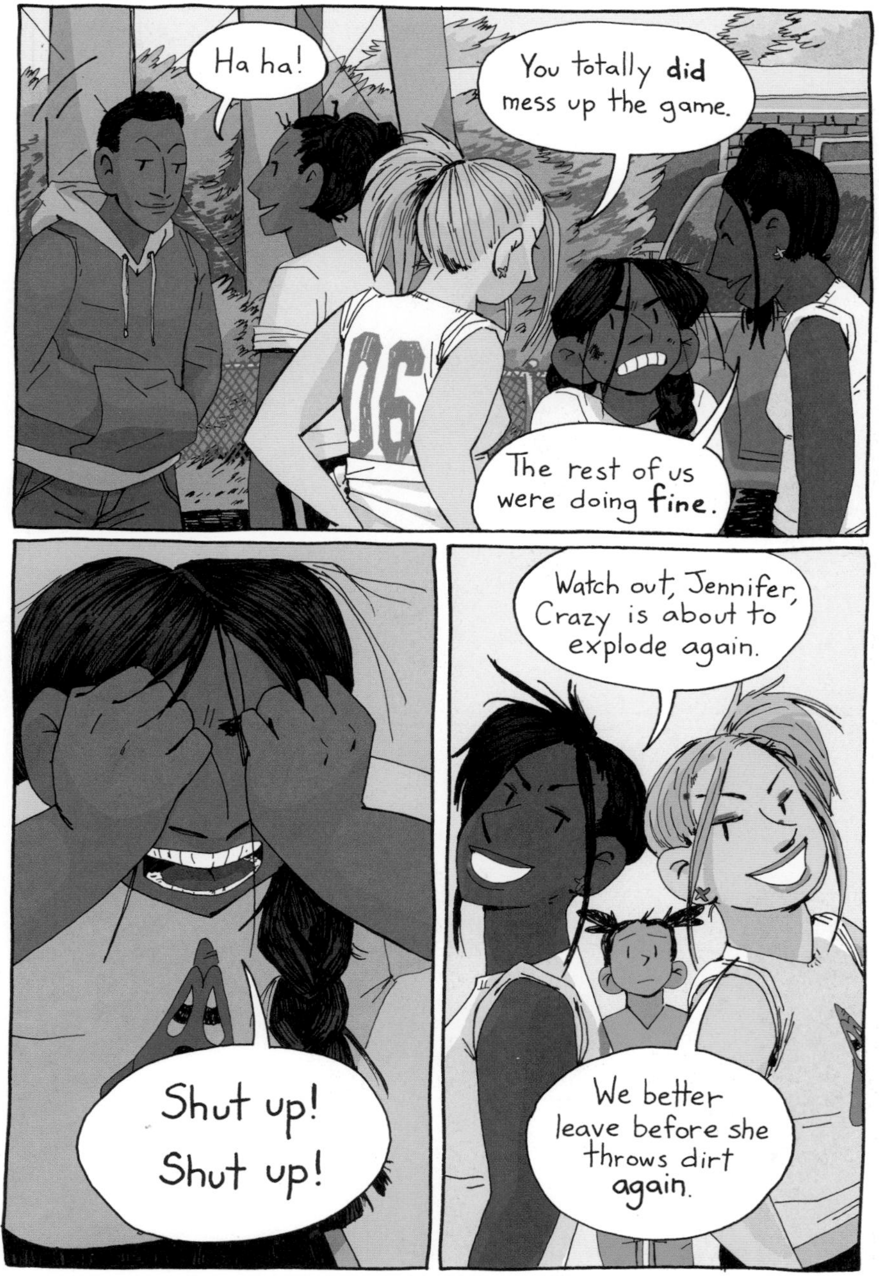
Ha ha!
You totally **did** mess up the game.
The rest of us were doing **fine**.
Shut up! Shut up!
Watch out, Jennifer, Crazy is about to explode again.
We better leave before she throws dirt **again**.

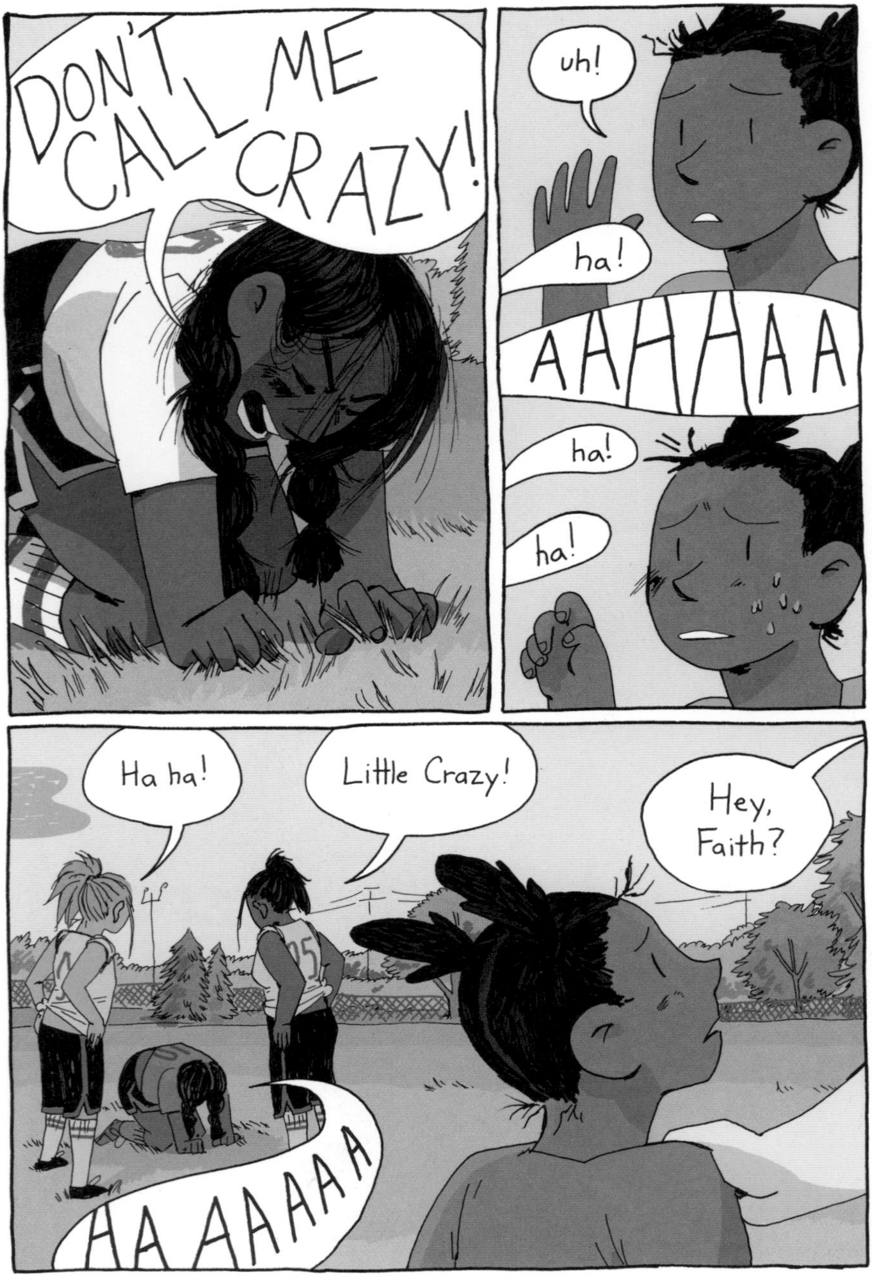
DON'T CALL ME CRAZY!
uh!
ha!
AAHHAAA
ha!
ha!
Ha ha!
Little Crazy!
Hey, Faith?
HAAAAAA

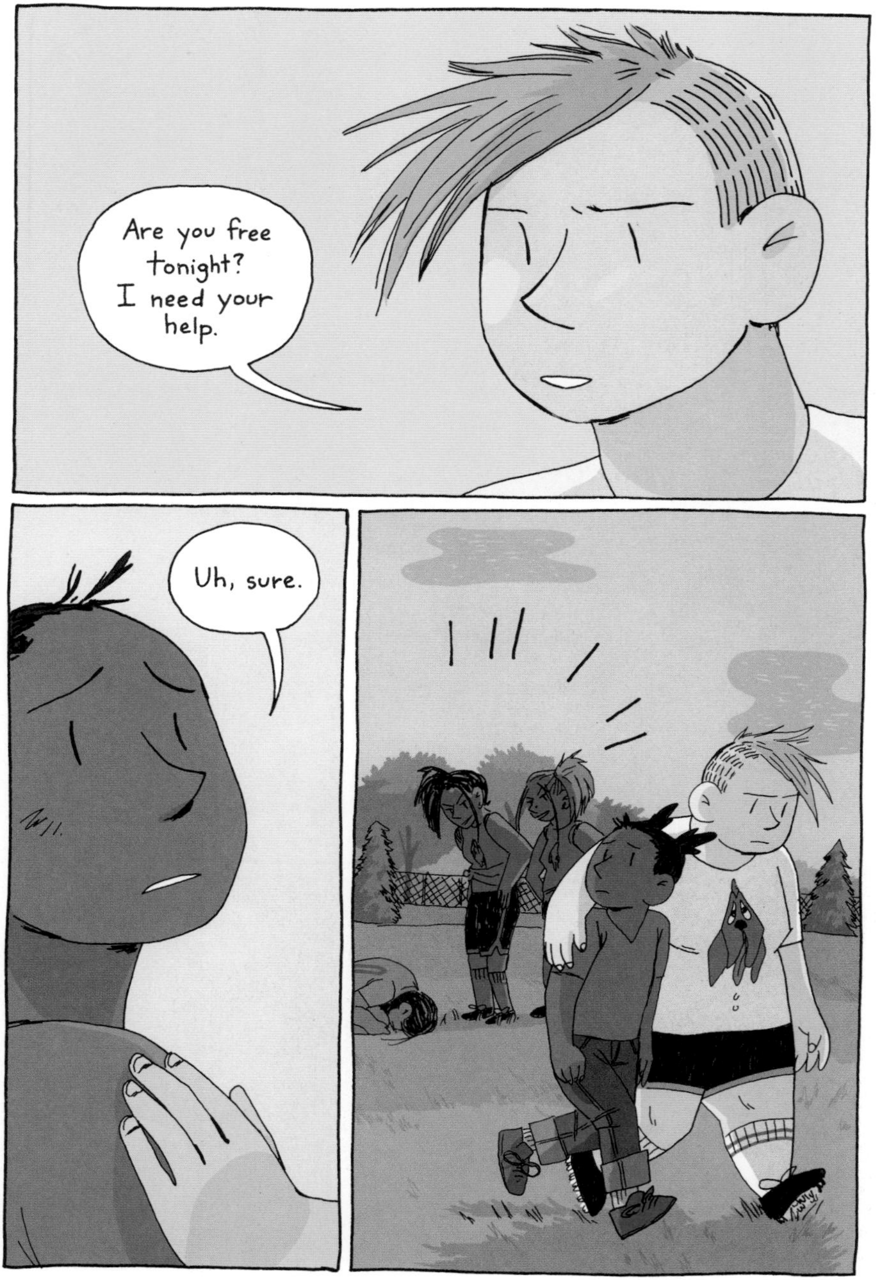
Are you free tonight? I need your help.
Uh, sure.

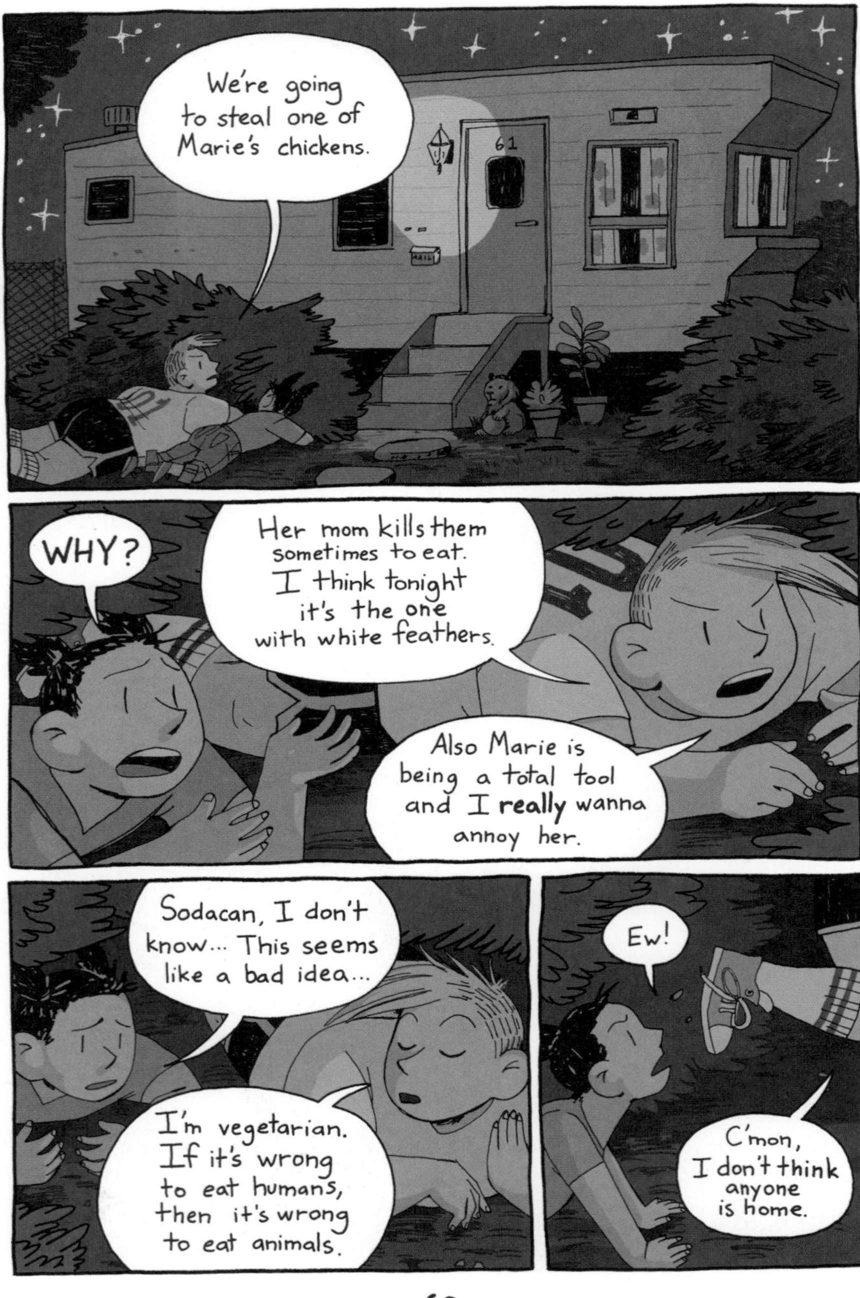
We're going to steal one of Marie's chickens.
61
MAIL
WHY?
Her mom kills them sometimes to eat. I think tonight it's the one with white feathers.
Also Marie is being a total tool and I **really** wanna annoy her.
Sodacan, I don't know... This seems like a bad idea...
I'm vegetarian. If it's wrong to eat humans, then it's wrong to eat animals.
Ew!
C'mon, I don't think anyone is home.

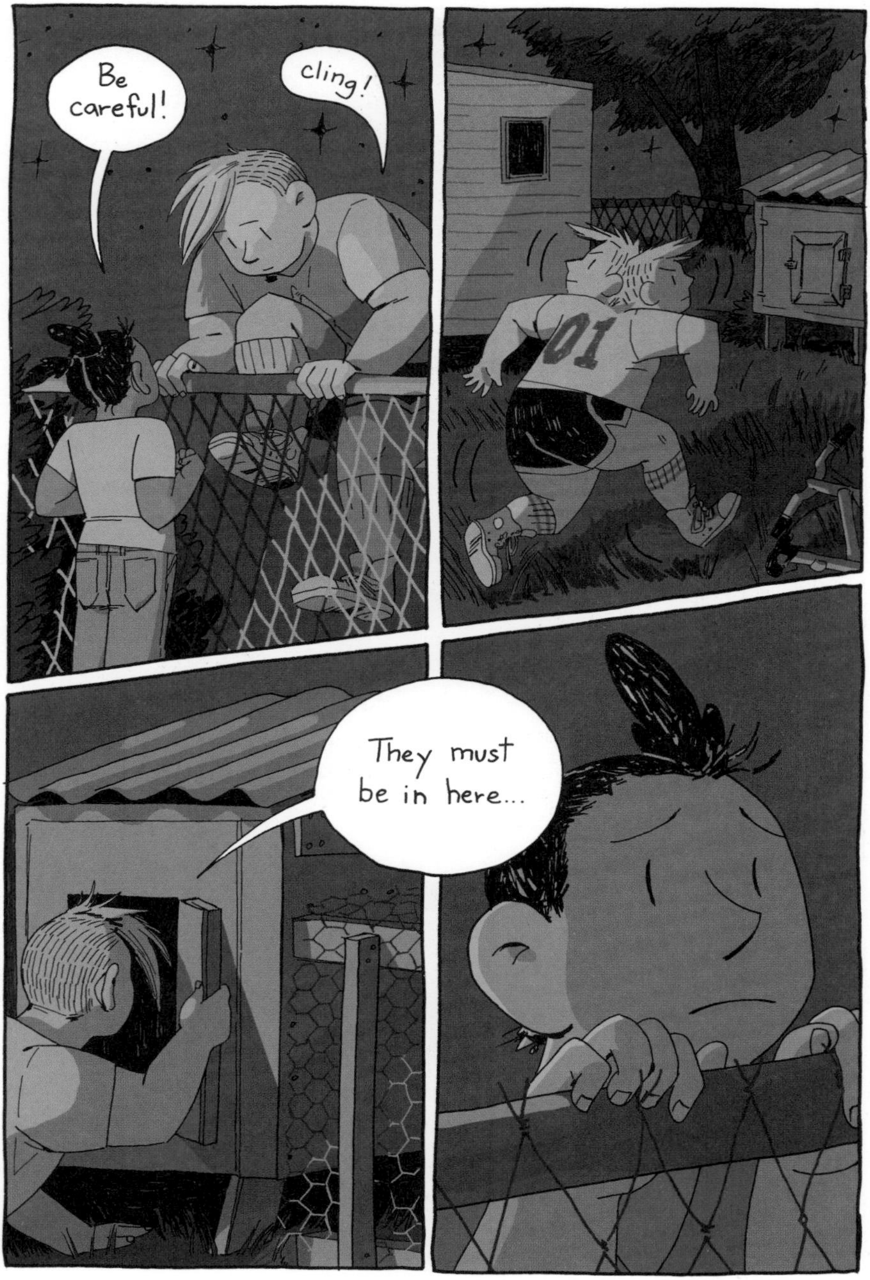
Be careful!
cling!
01
They must be in here...

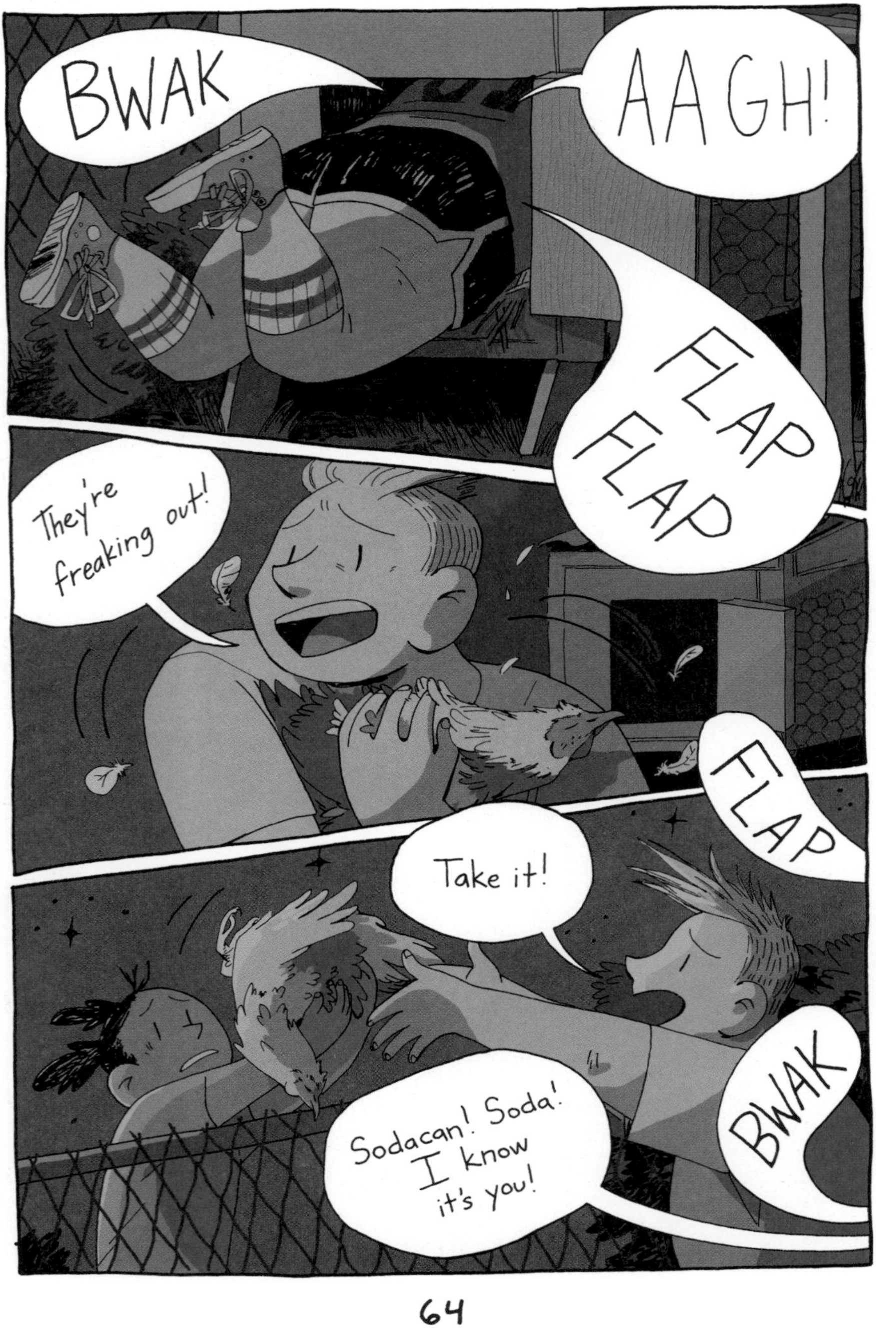
BWAK
AAGH!
FLAP FLAP
They're freaking out!
FLAP
Take it!
BWAK
Sodacan! Soda! I know it's you!

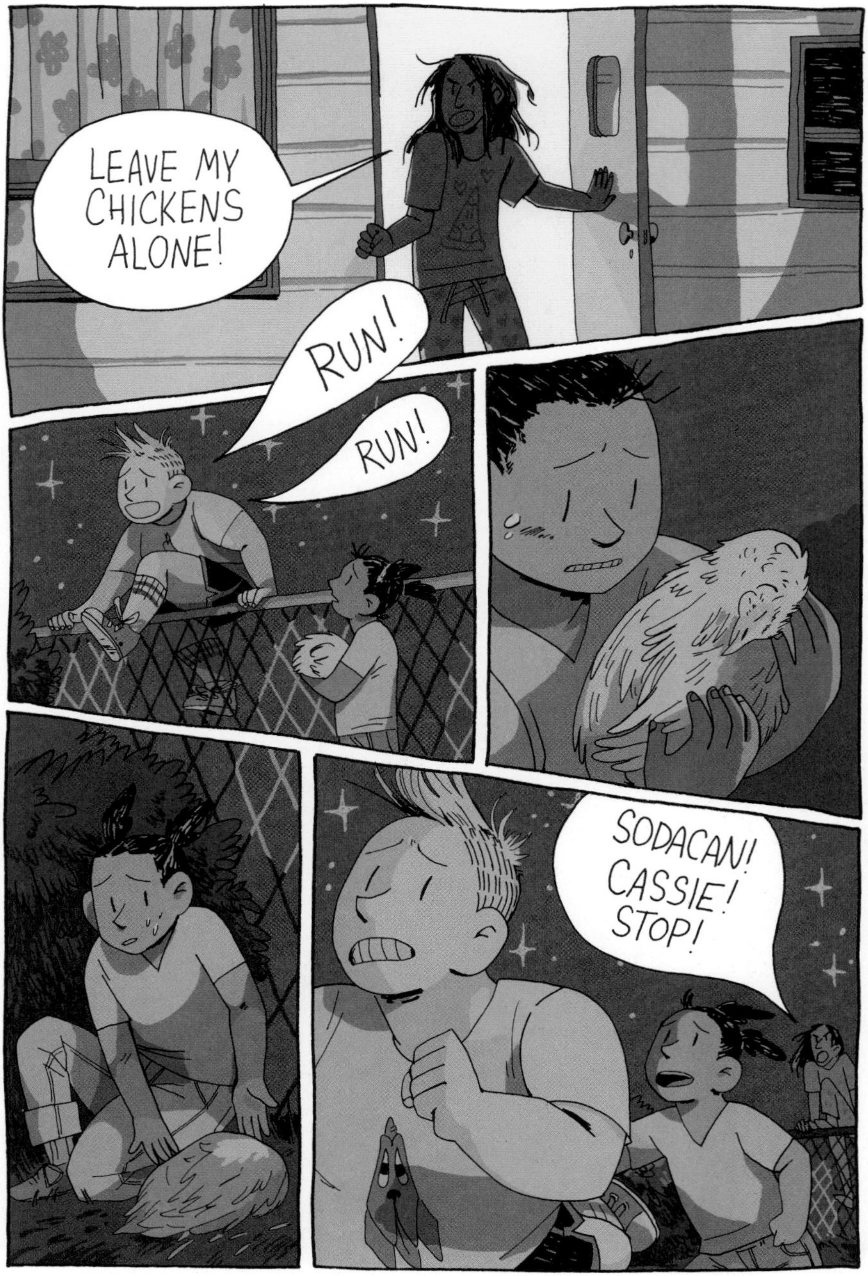
LEAVE MY CHICKENS ALONE!
RUN!
RUN!
SODACAN! CASSIE! STOP!

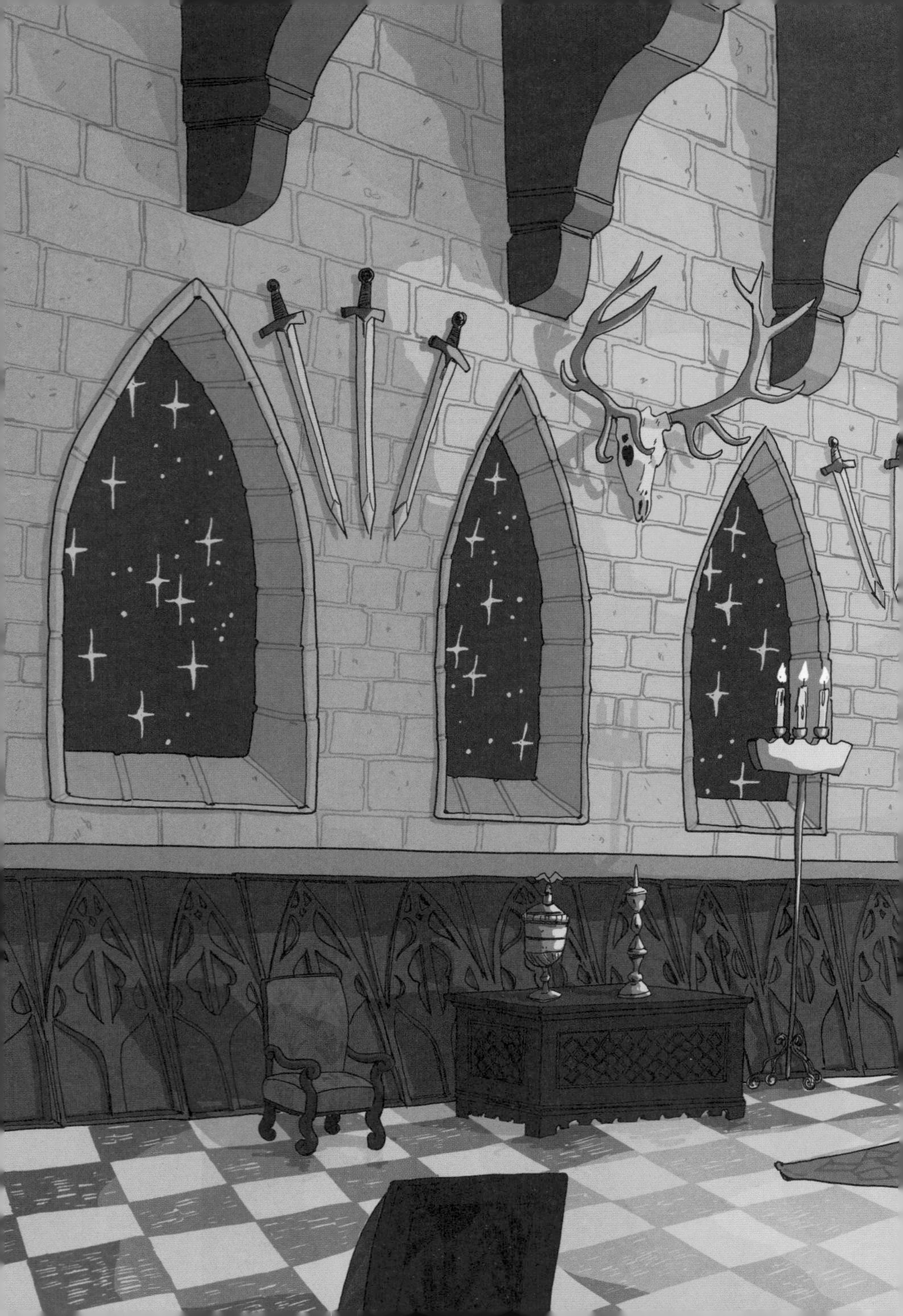

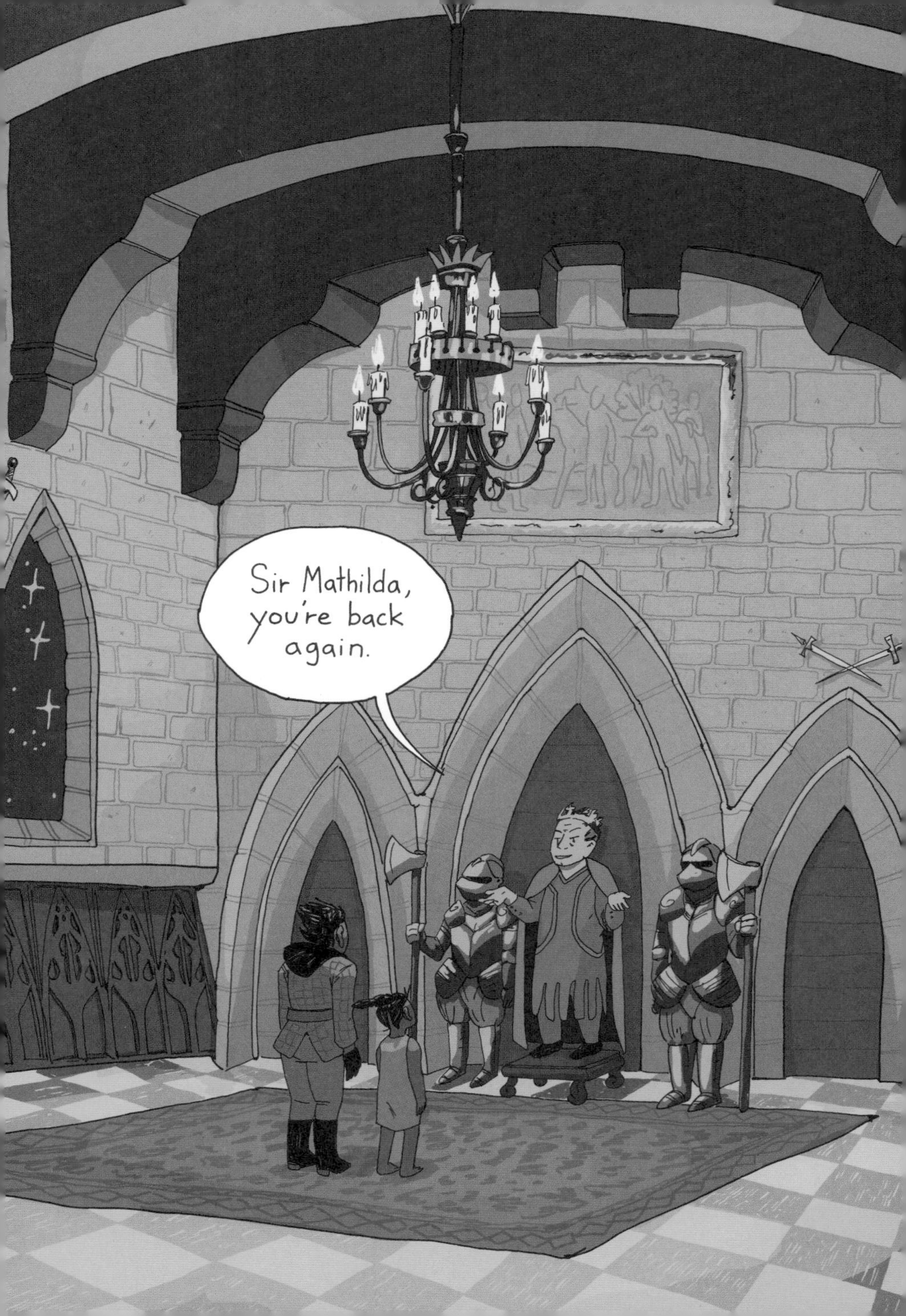
Sir Mathilda, you're back again.

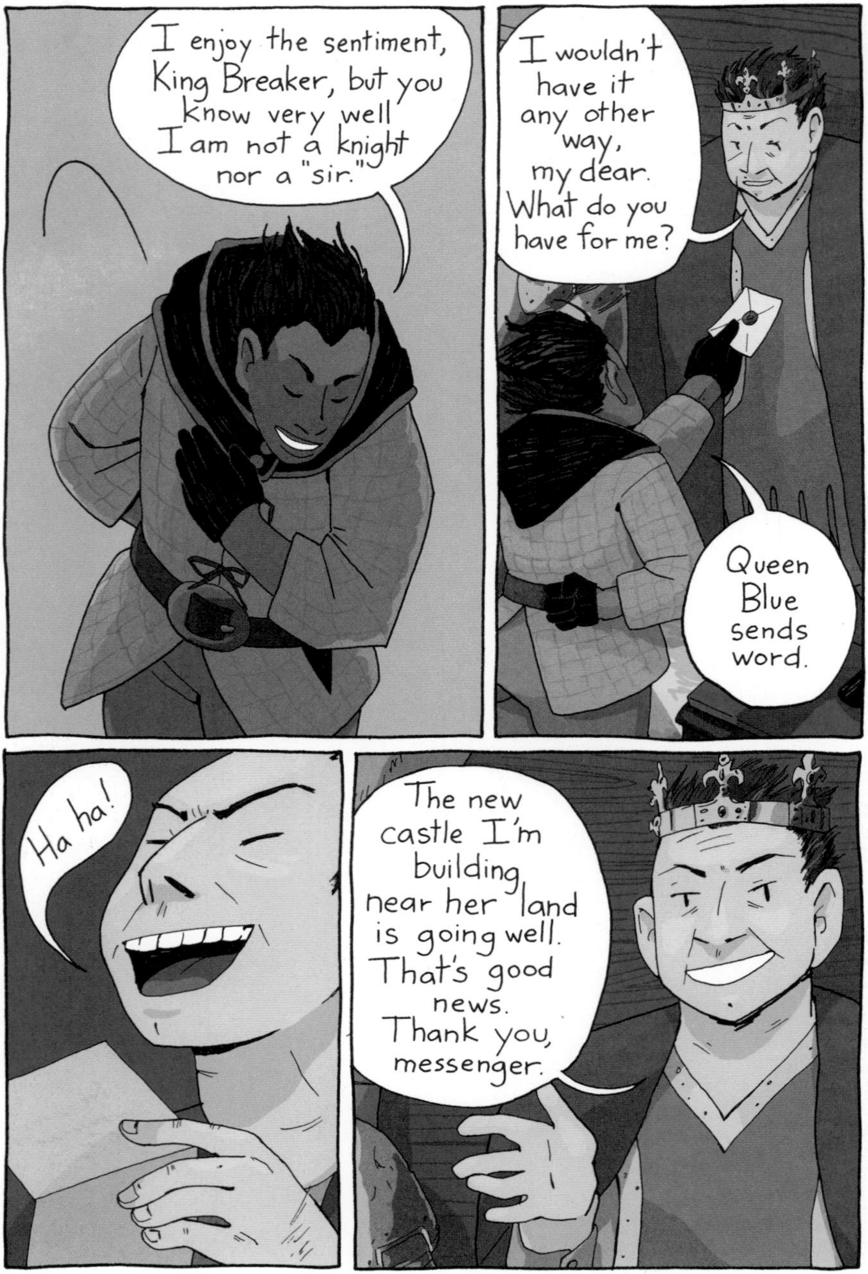

I enjoy the sentiment, King Breaker, but you know very well I am not a knight nor a "sir."
I wouldn't have it any other way, my dear. What do you have for me?
Queen Blue sends word.
Ha ha!
The new castle I'm building near her land is going well. That's good news. Thank you, messenger.

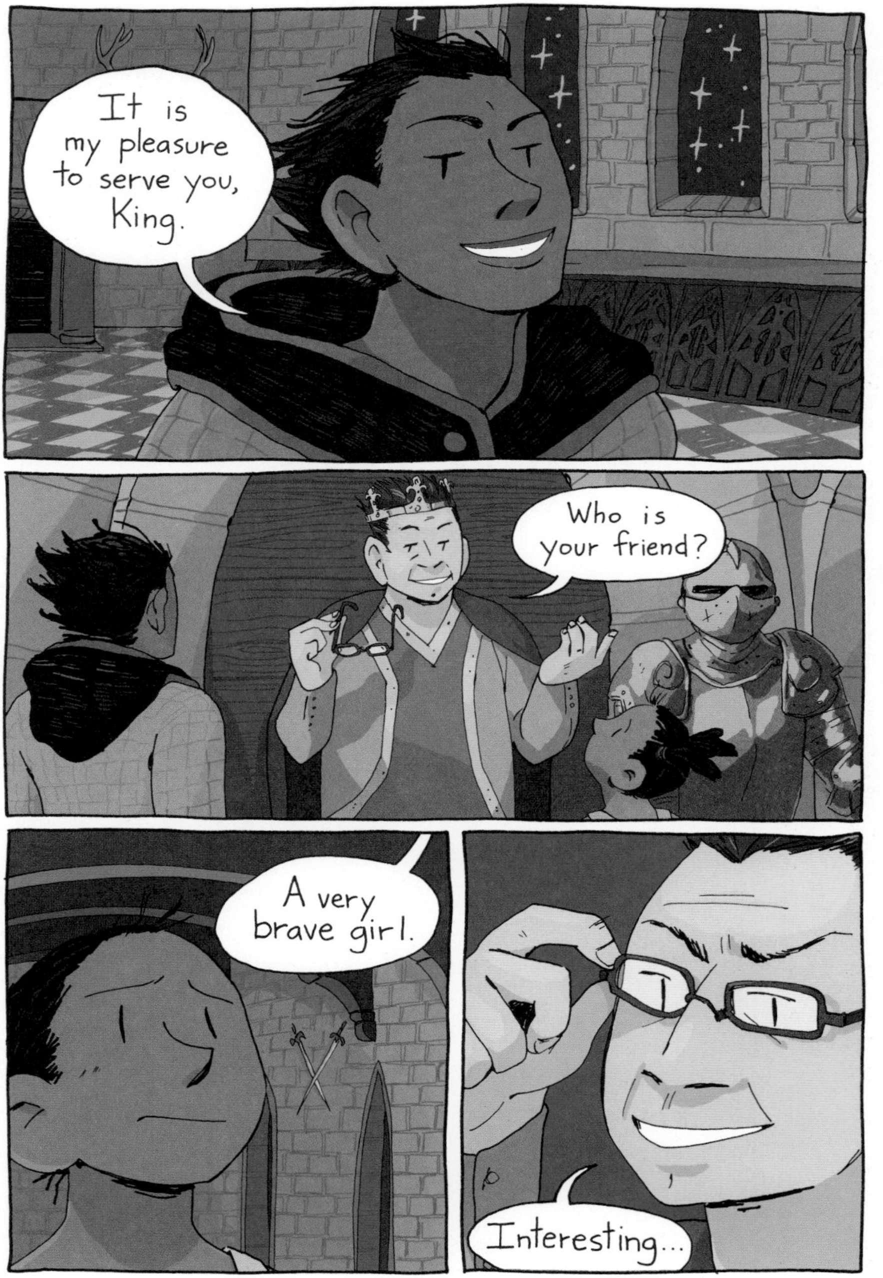
It is my pleasure to serve you, King.
Who is your friend?
A very brave girl.
Interesting...

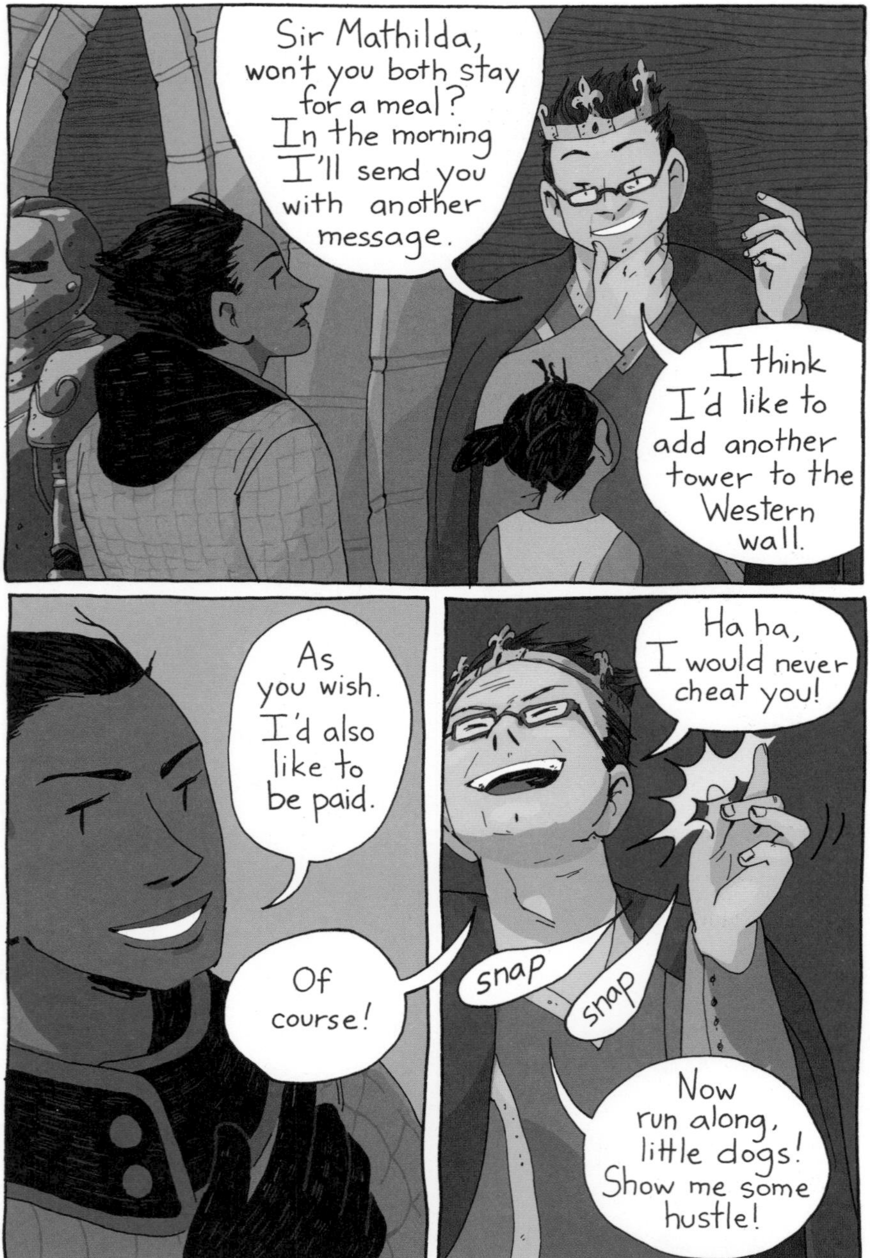
Sir Mathilda, won't you both stay for a meal? In the morning I'll send you with another message.
I think I'd like to add another tower to the Western wall.
As you wish. I'd also like to be paid.
Of course!
Ha ha, I would never cheat you!
snap
snap
Now run along, little dogs! Show me some hustle!

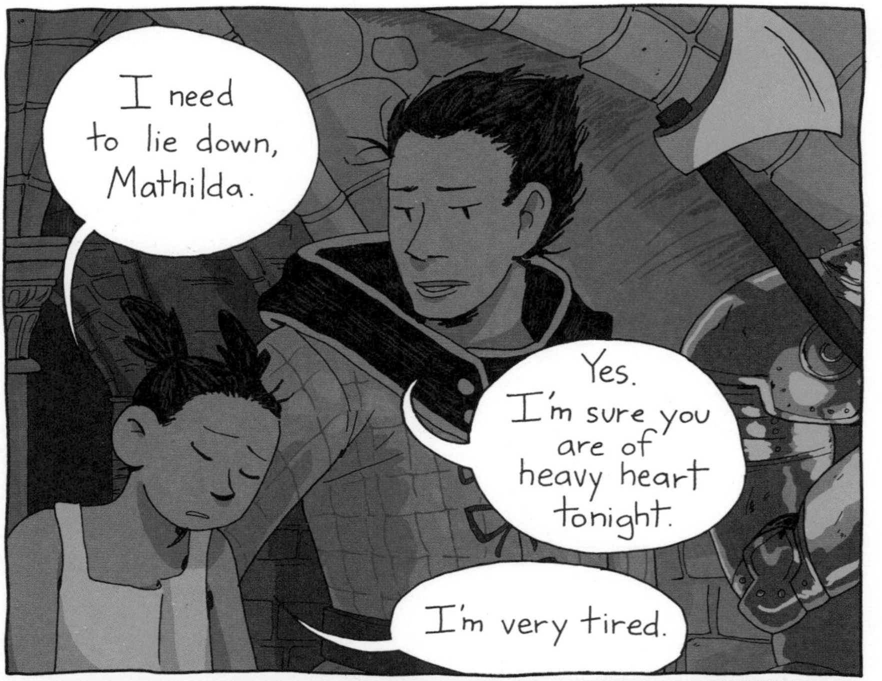
I need to lie down, Mathilda.
Yes. I'm sure you are of heavy heart tonight.
I'm very tired.

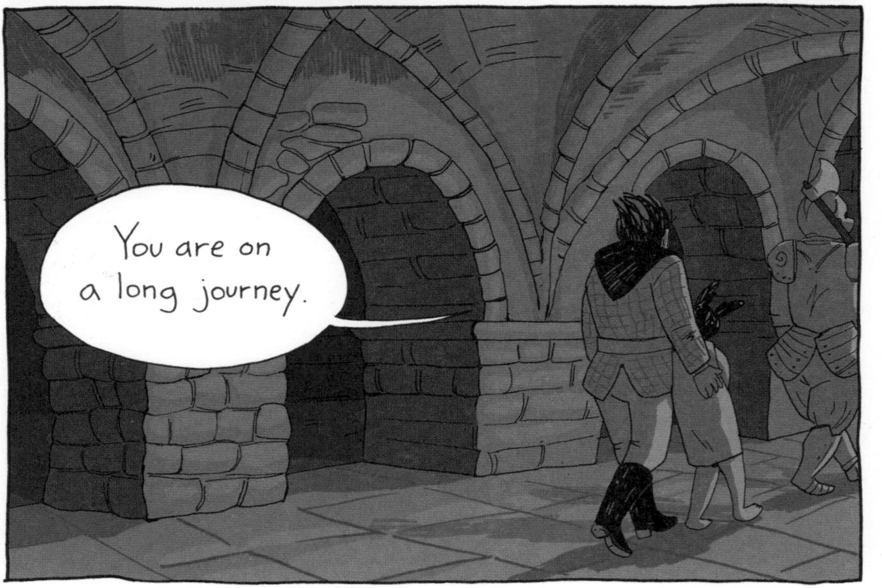
You are on a long journey.

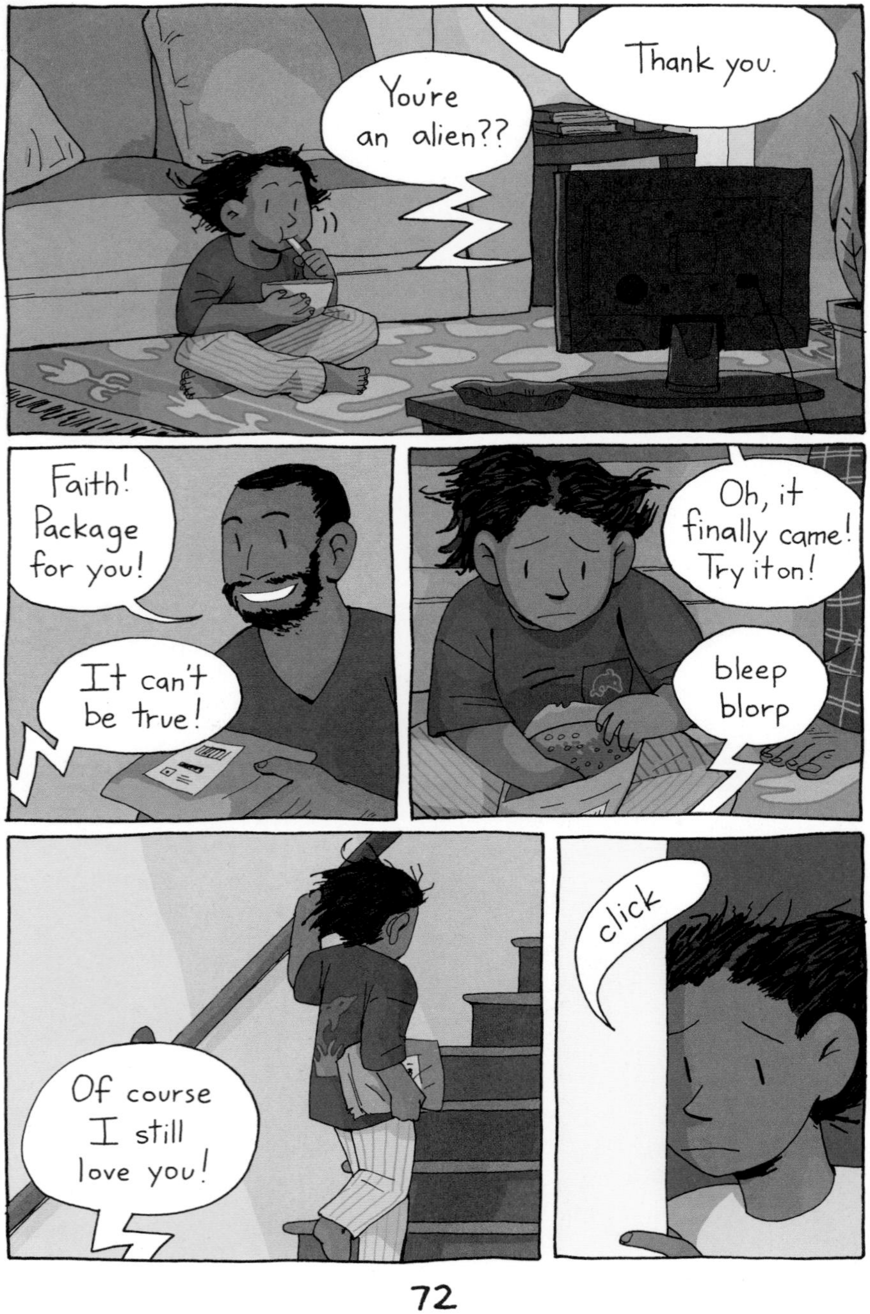
You're an alien??
Thank you.
Faith! Package for you!
It can't be true!
Oh, it finally came! Try it on!
bleep blorp
Of course I still love you!
click

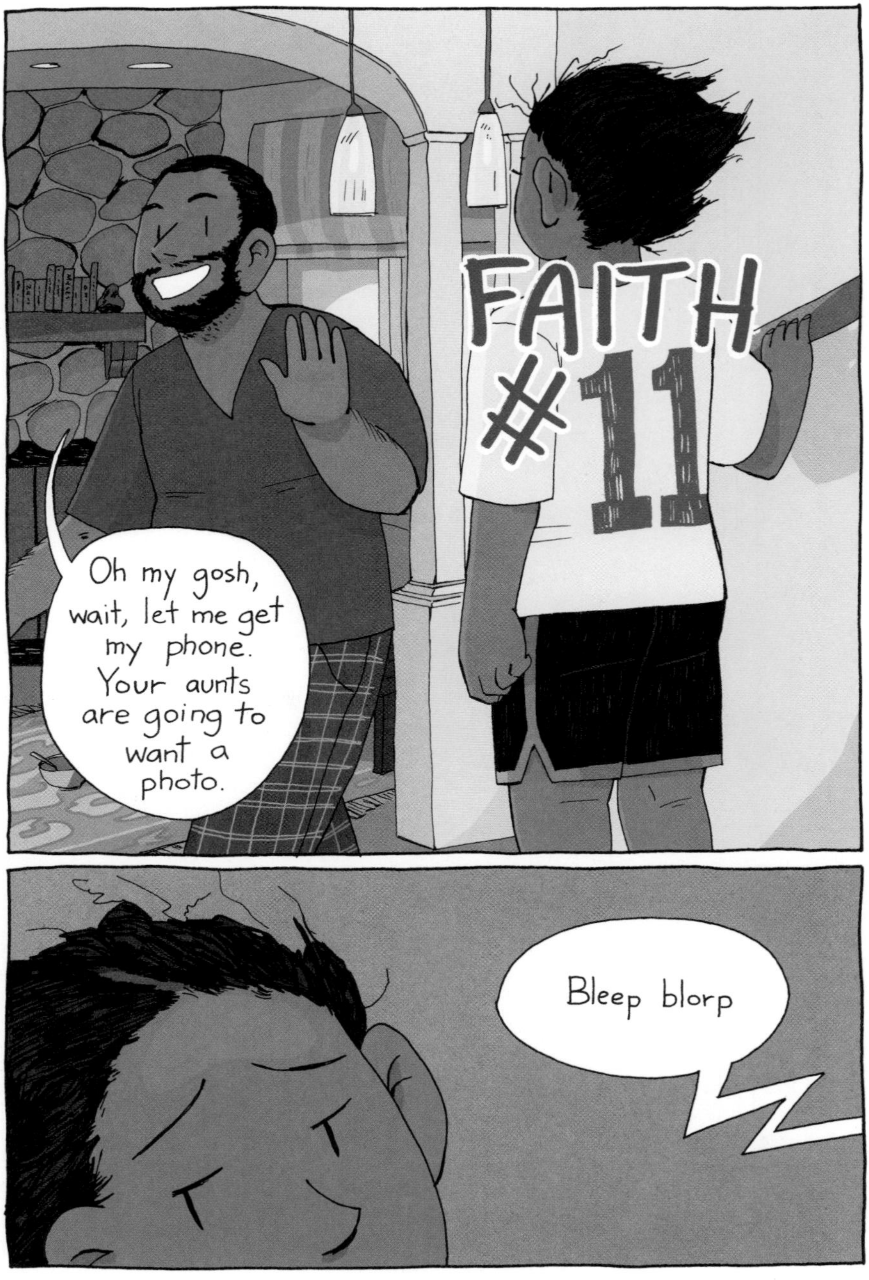
FAITH
#11
Oh my gosh, wait, let me get my phone. Your aunts are going to want a photo.
Bleep blorp

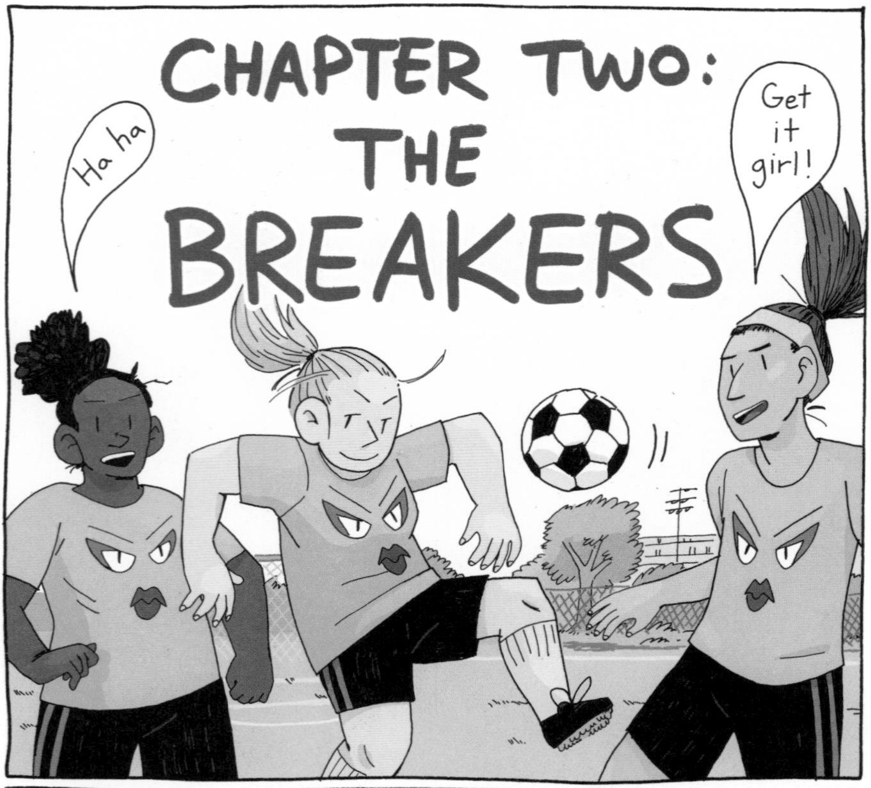
CHAPTER TWO:
THE
BREAKERS
Ha ha
Get it girl!

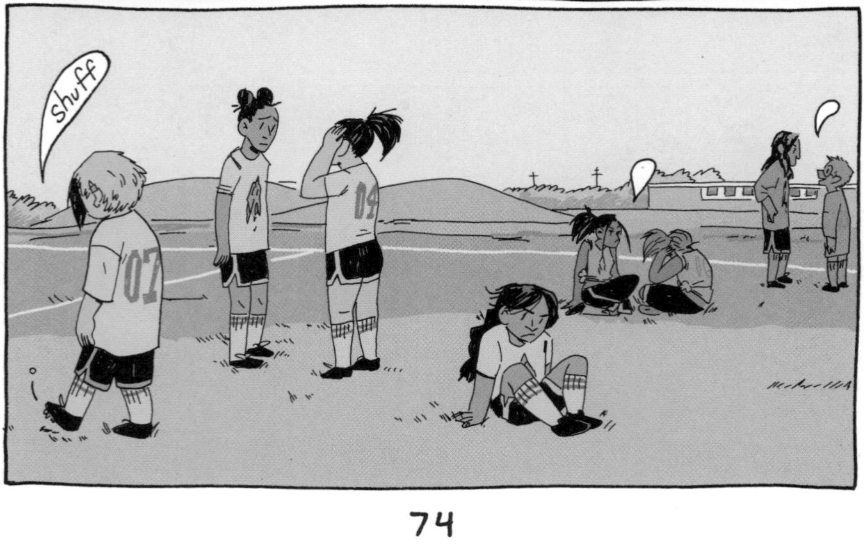
shuff

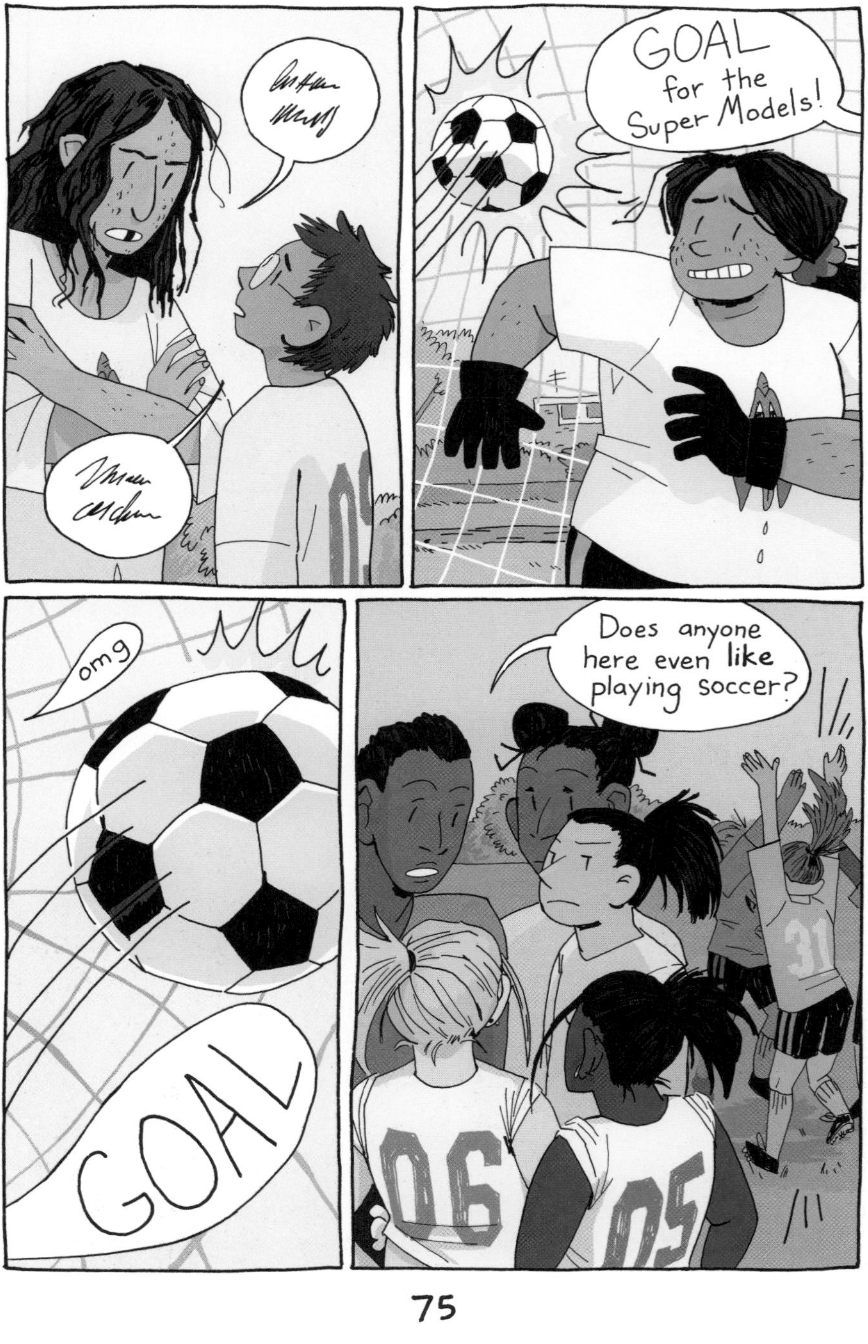
GOAL
for the Super Models!
omg
GOAL
Does anyone here even like playing soccer?

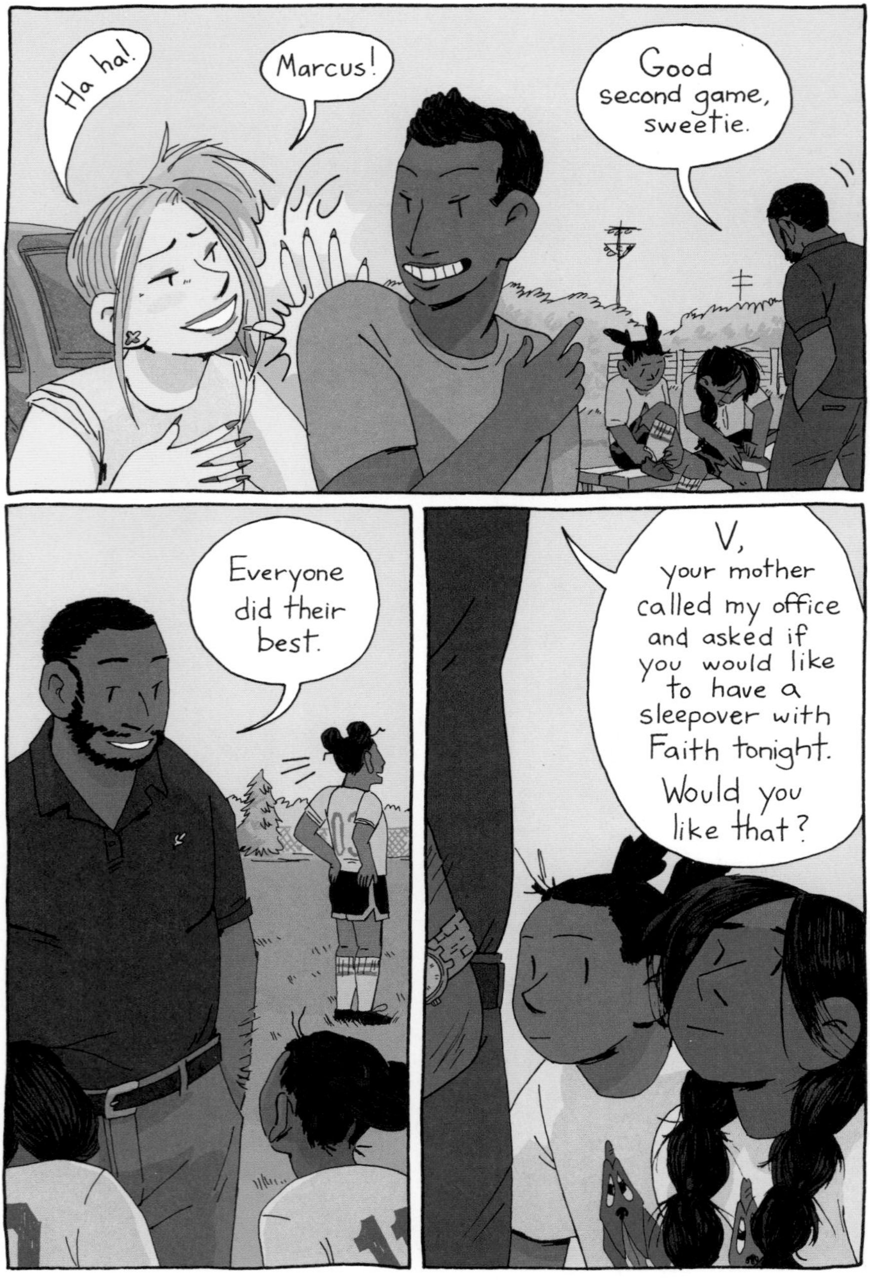
Ha ha!
Marcus!
Good second game, sweetie.
Everyone did their best.
V, your mother called my office and asked if you would like to have a sleepover with Faith tonight.
Would you like that?

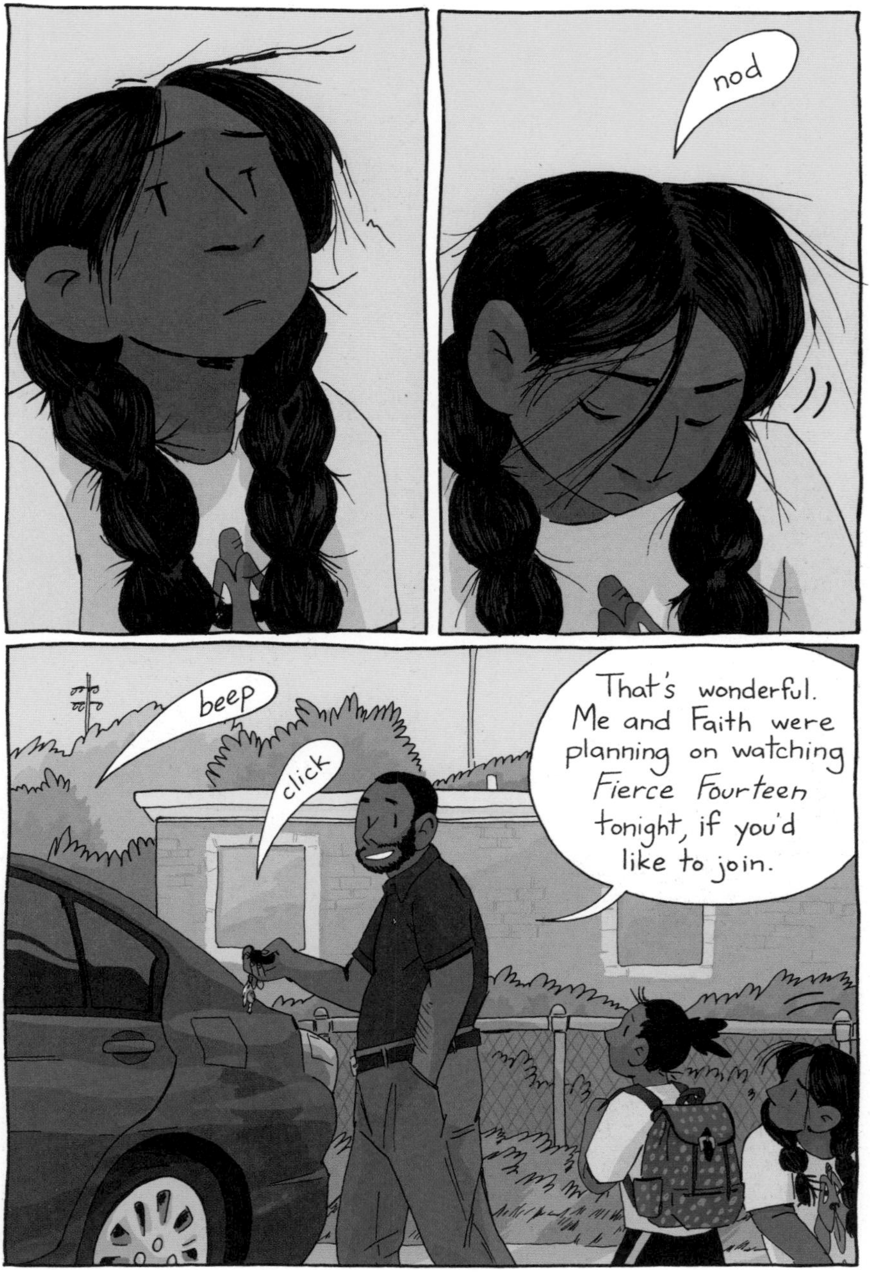
nod
beep
click
That's wonderful. Me and Faith were planning on watching *Fierce Fourteen* tonight, if you'd like to join.

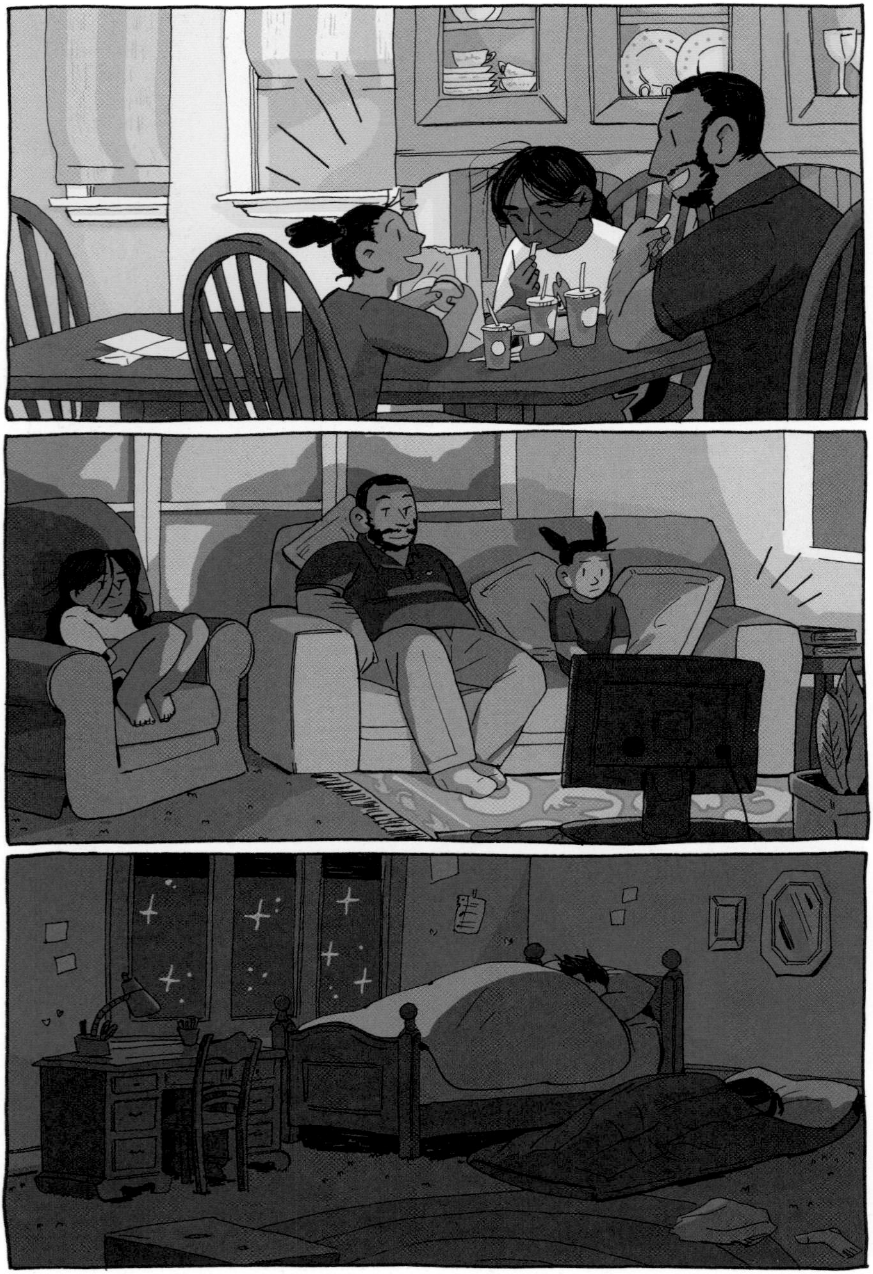

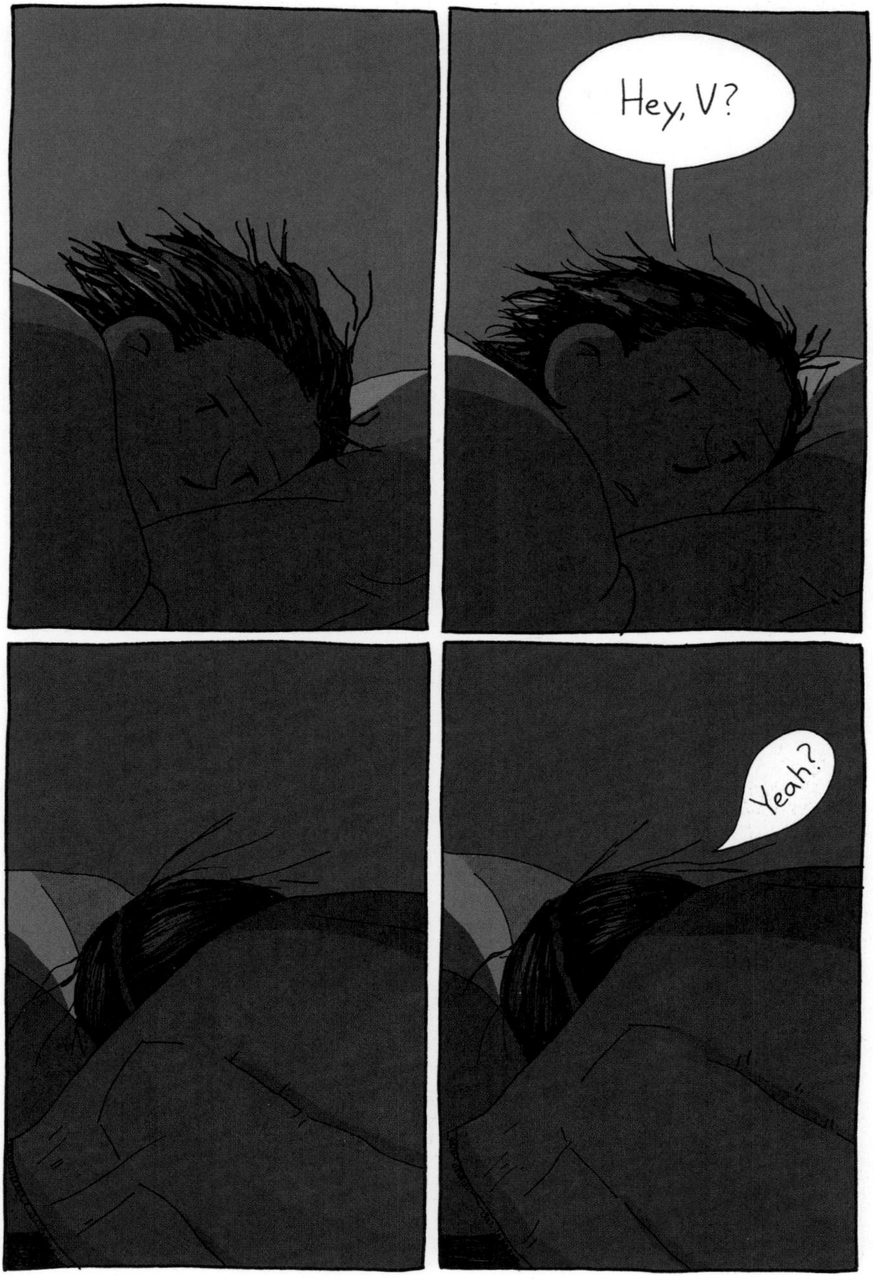
Hey, V?
Yeah?

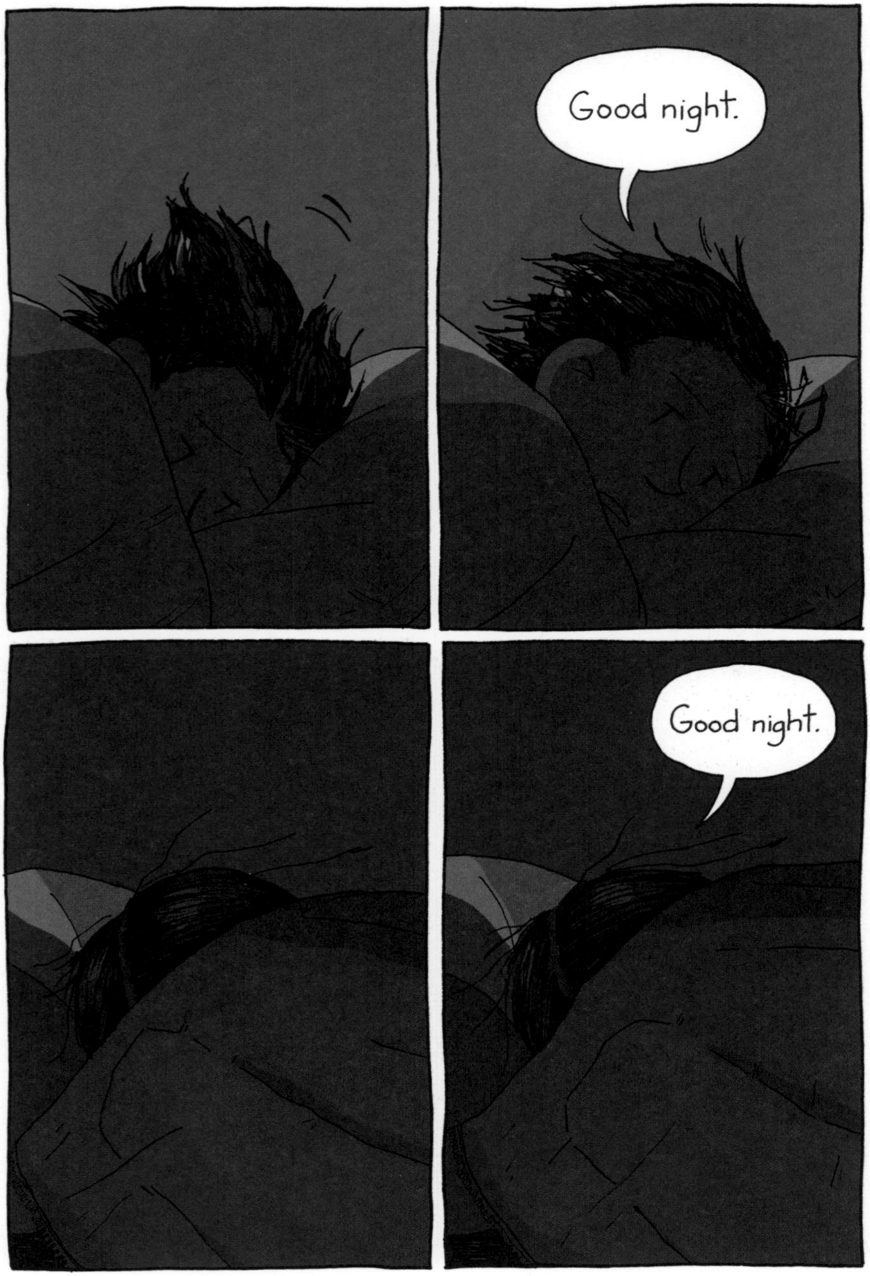
Good night.
Good night.

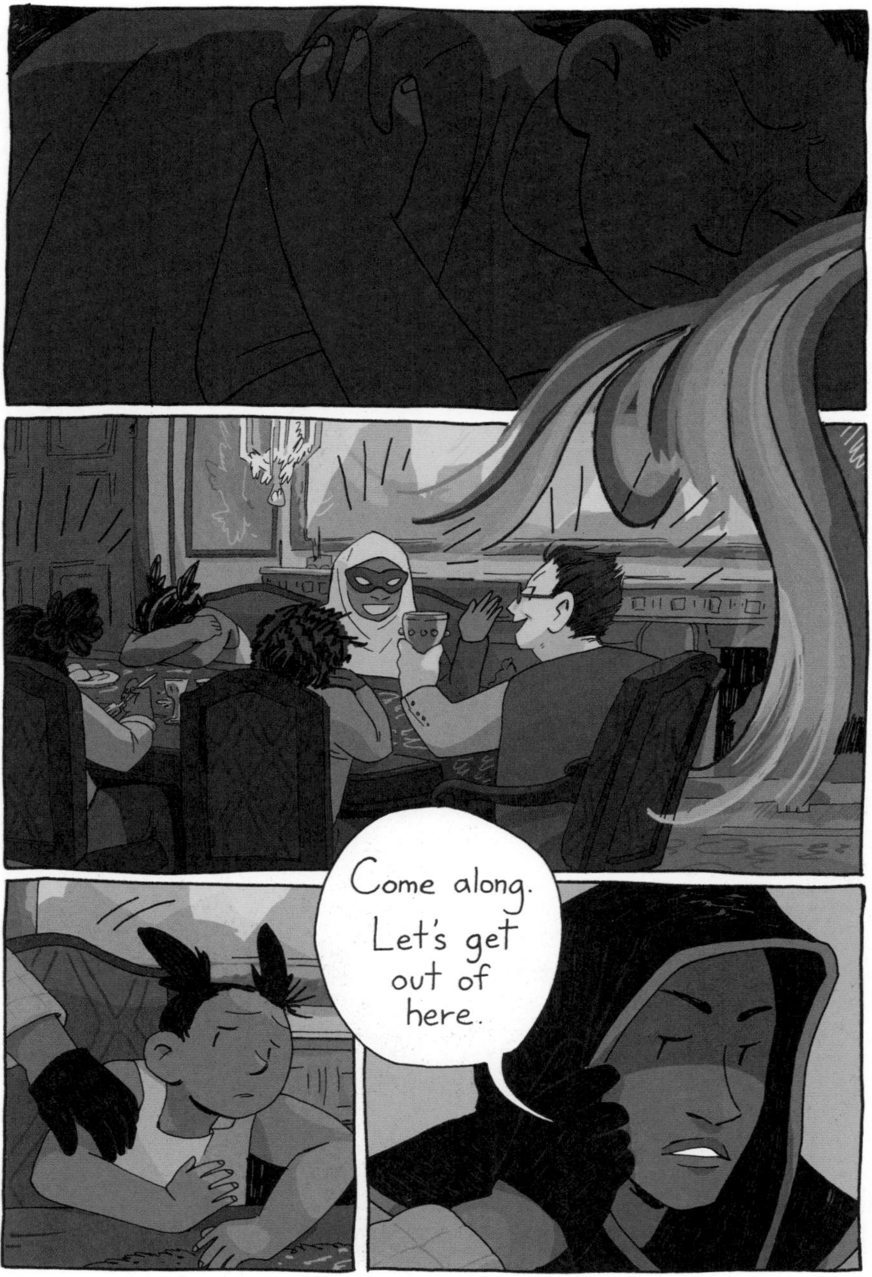
Come along. Let's get out of here.

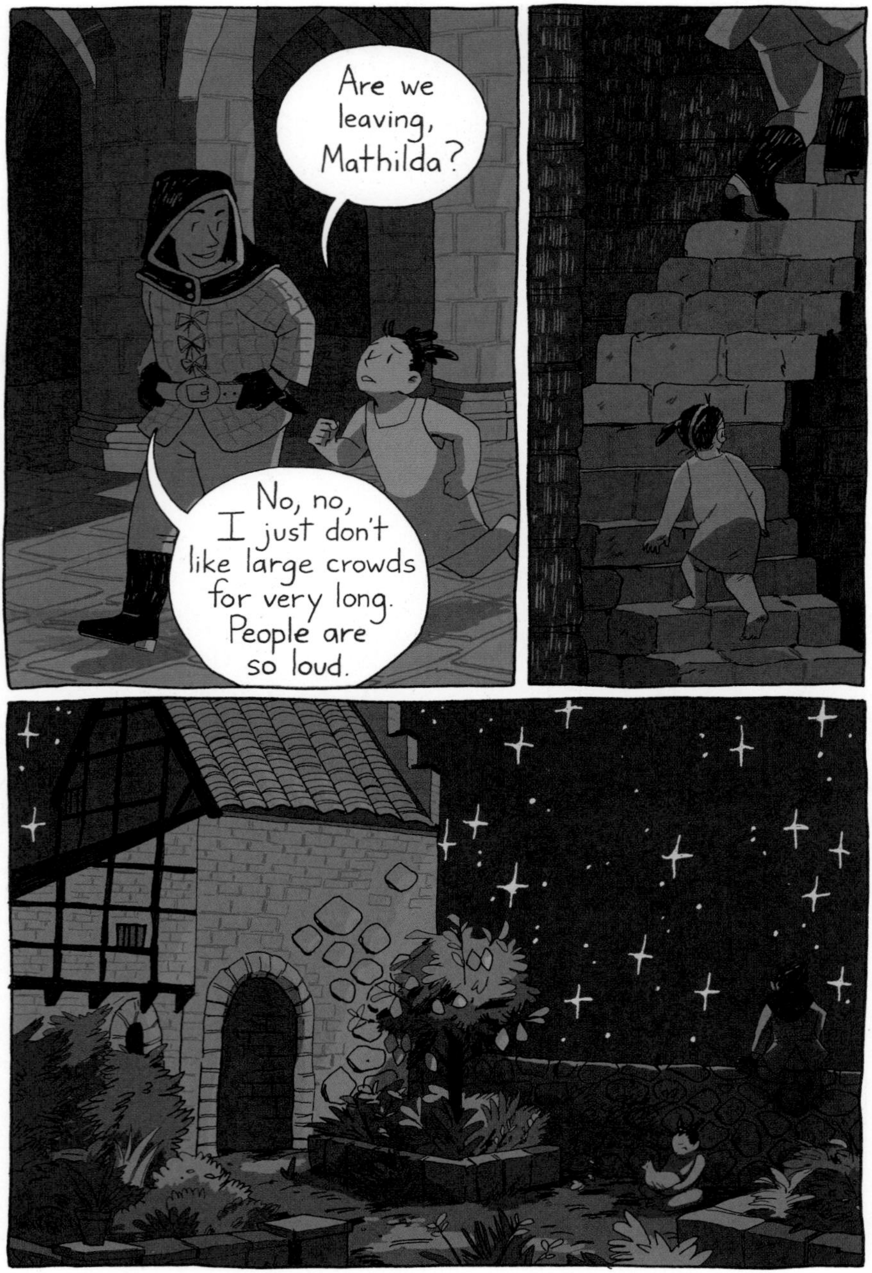
Are we leaving, Mathilda?
No, no, I just don't like large crowds for very long. People are so loud.

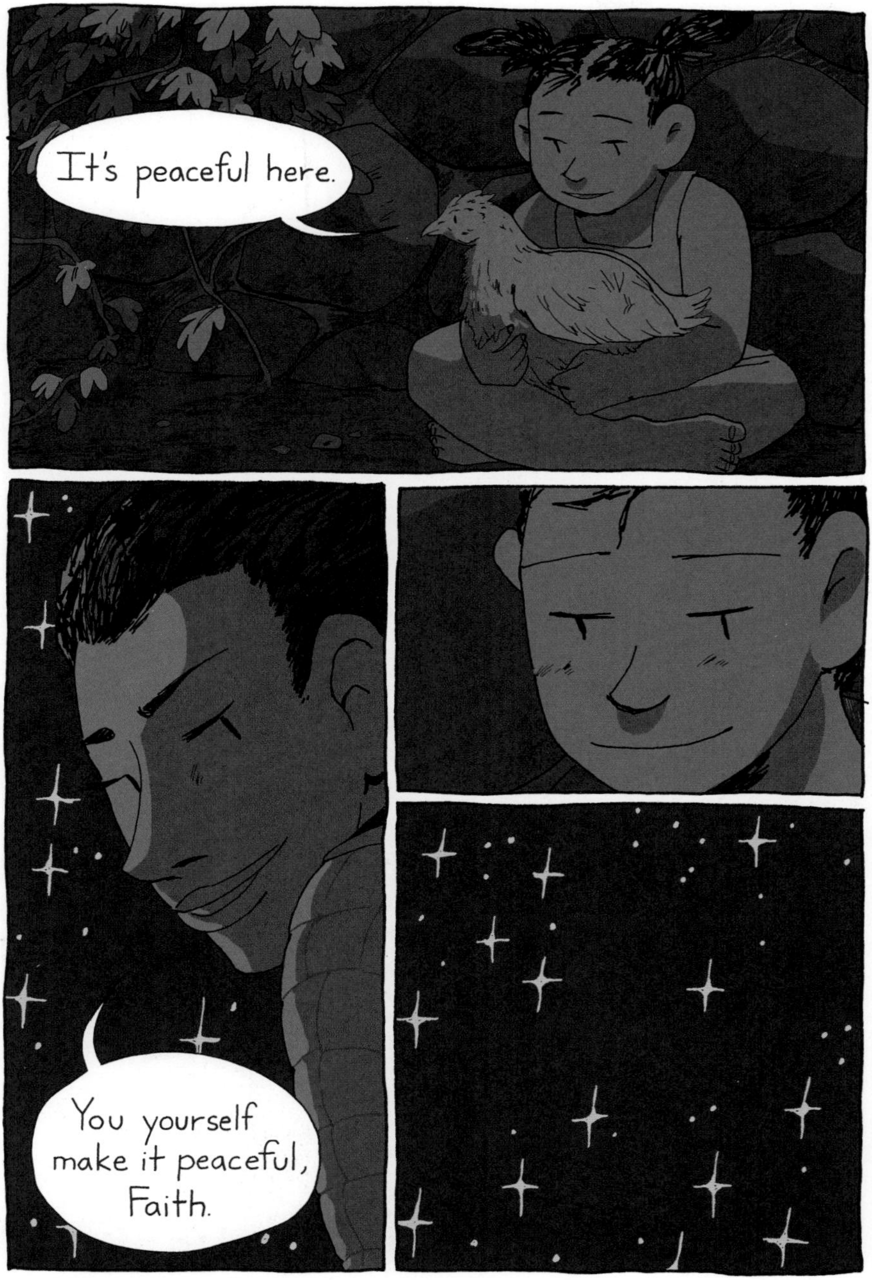
It's peaceful here.
You yourself make it peaceful, Faith.

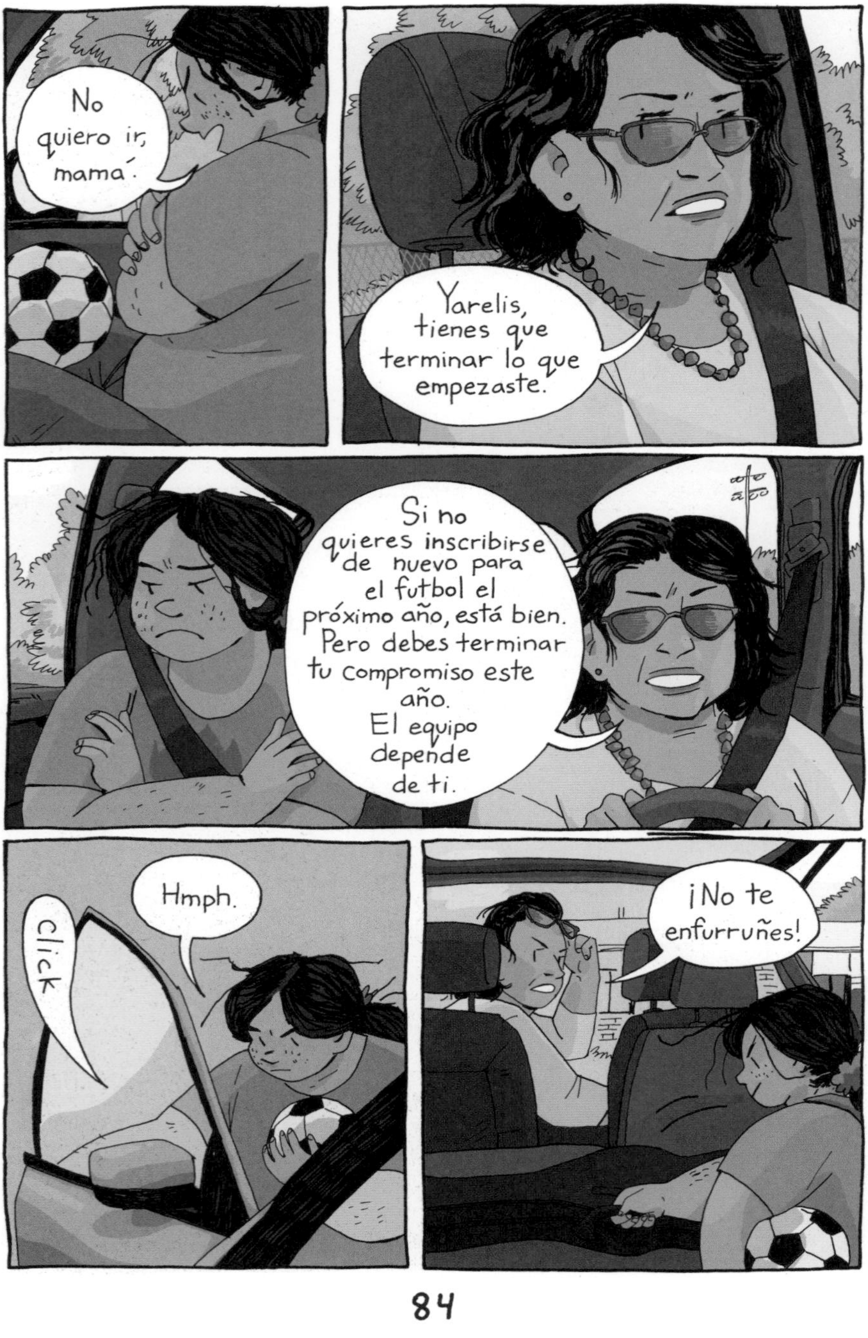
No quiero ir, mamá.
Yarelis, tienes que terminar lo que empezaste.
Si no quieres inscribirse de nuevo para el futbol el próximo año, está bien. Pero debes terminar tu compromiso este año. El equipo depende de ti.
Hmph.
Click
¡No te enfurruñes!

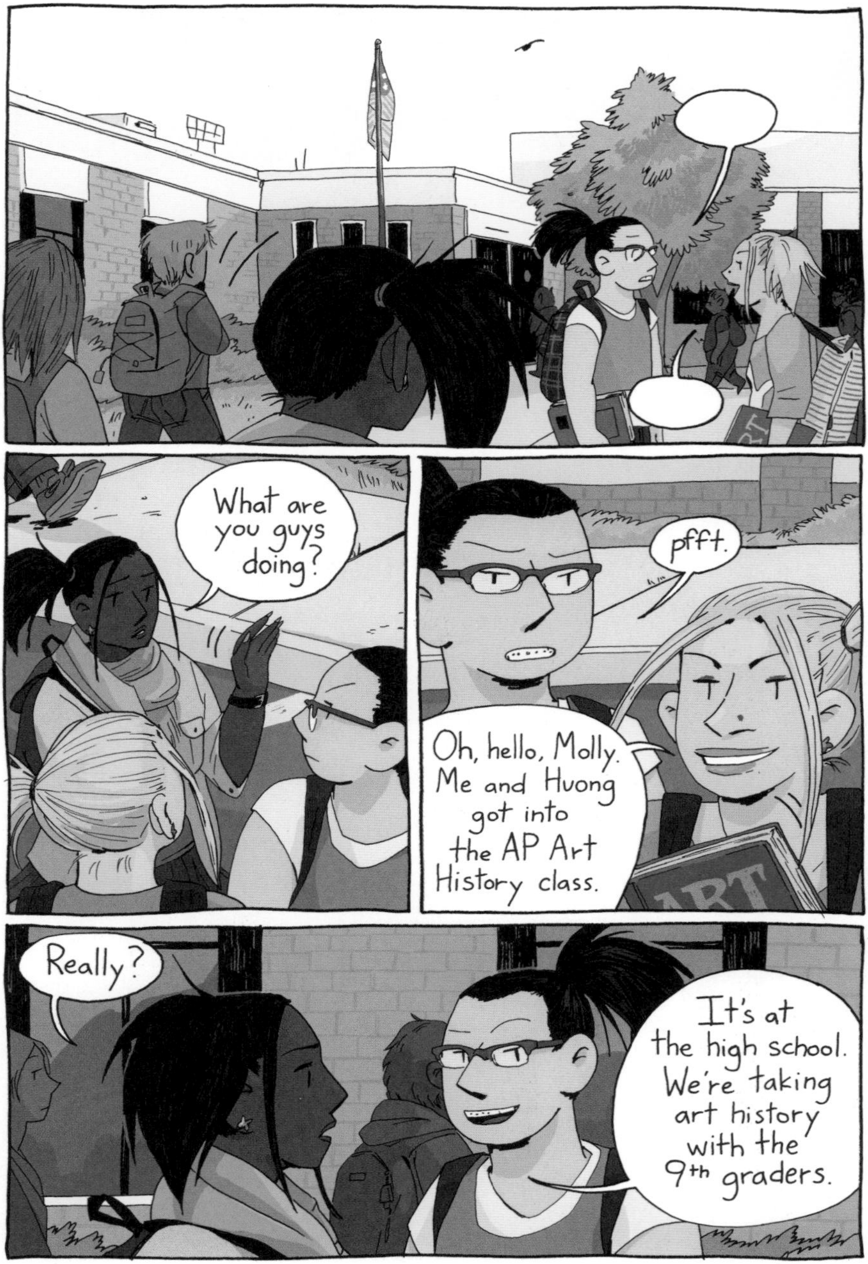
What are you guys doing?
pfft.
Oh, hello, Molly. Me and Huong got into the AP Art History class.
ART
Really?
It's at the high school. We're taking art history with the 9th graders.

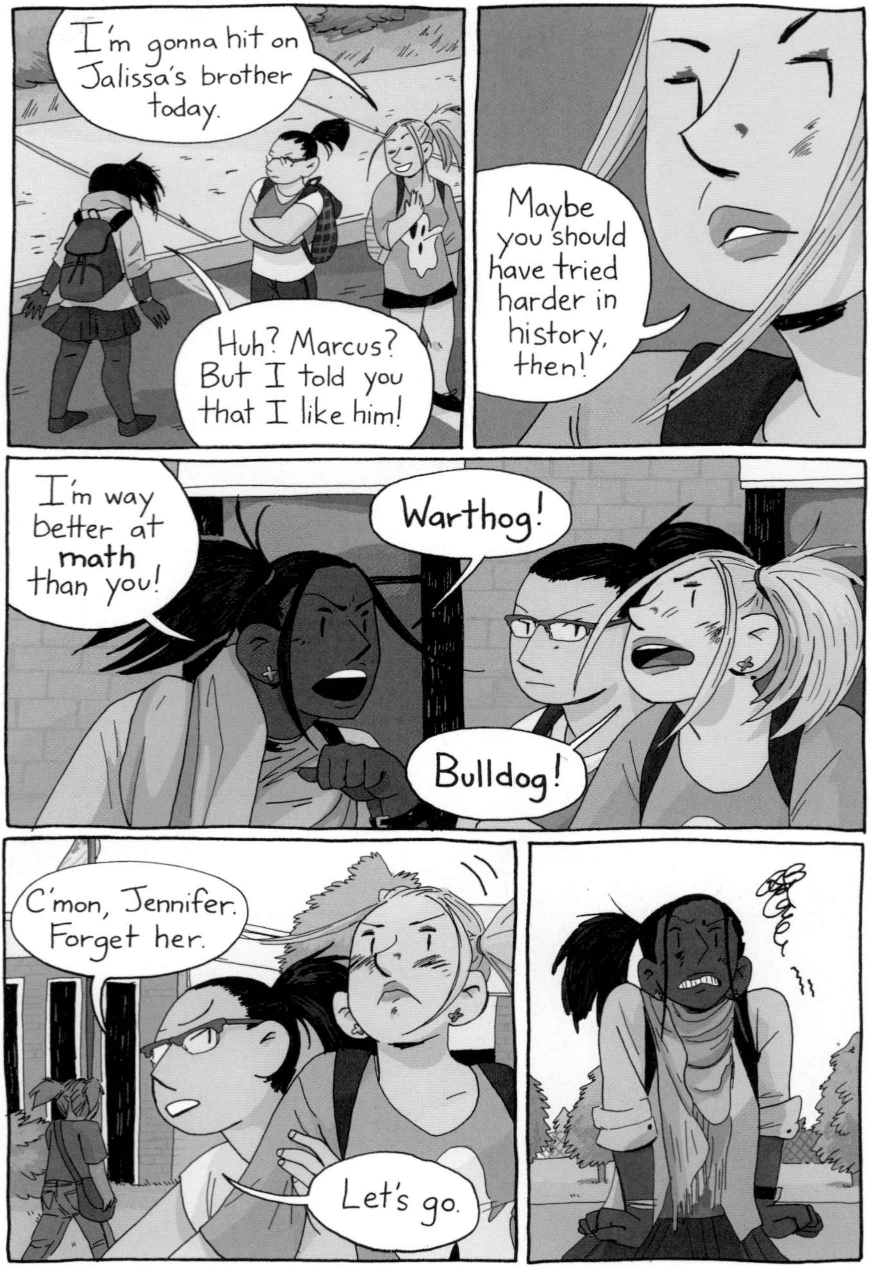
I'm gonna hit on Jalissa's brother today.
Huh? Marcus? But I told you that I like him!
Maybe you should have tried harder in history, then!
I'm way better at **math** than you!
Warthog!
Bulldog!
C'mon, Jennifer. Forget her.
Let's go.

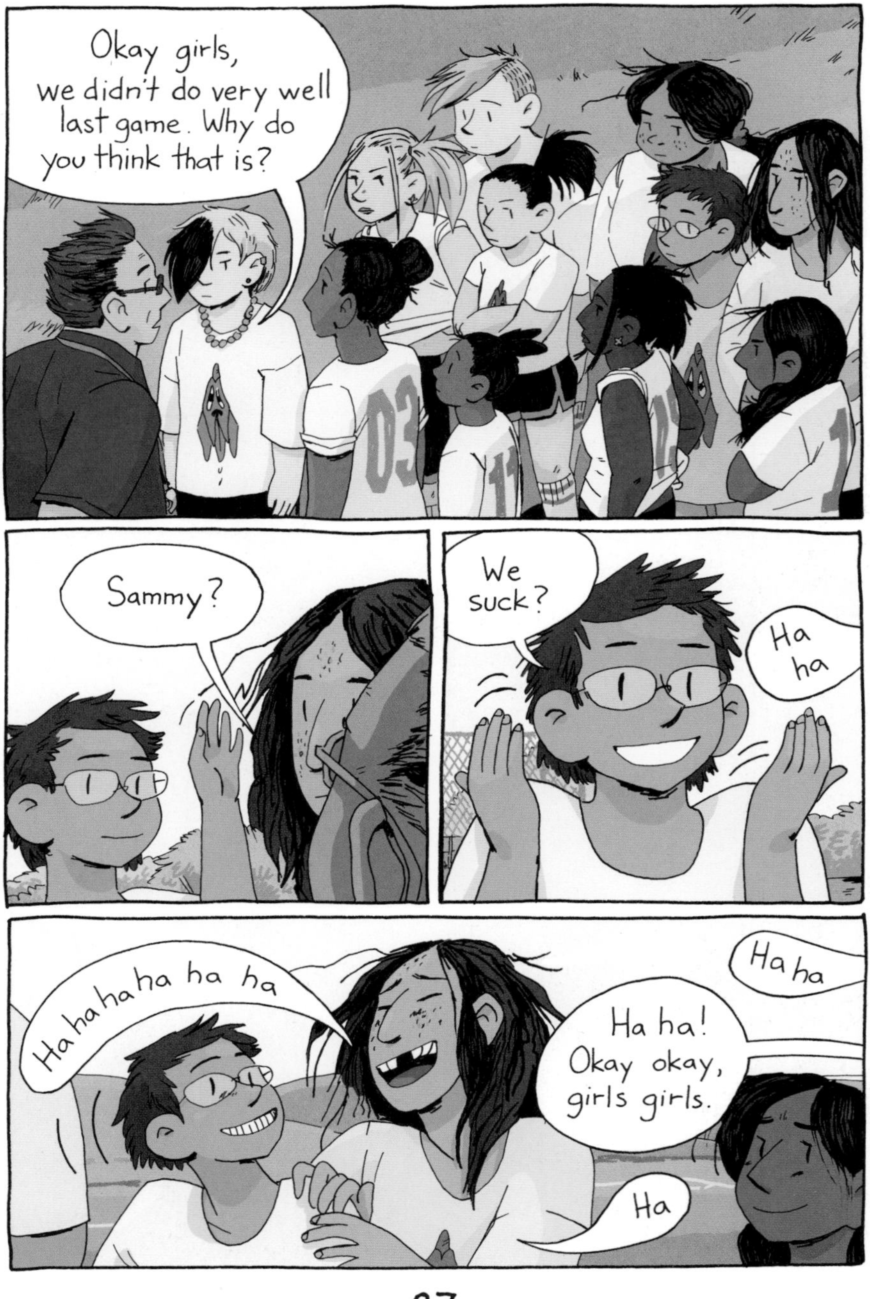
Okay girls, we didn't do very well last game. Why do you think that is?
Sammy?
We suck?
Ha ha
Hahahahaha ha ha
Ha ha
Ha ha! Okay okay, girls girls.
Ha

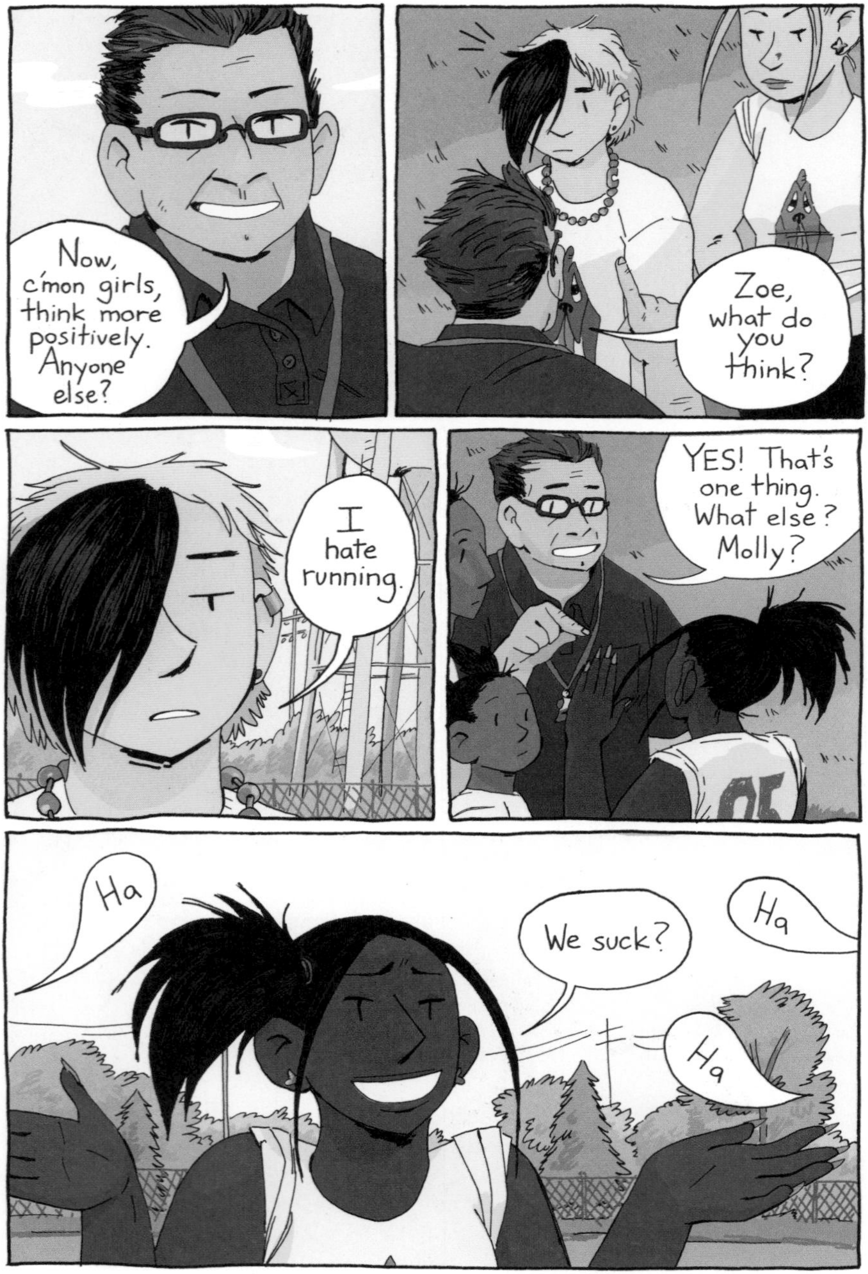
Now, c'mon girls, think more positively. Anyone else?
Zoe, what do you think?
I hate running.
YES! That's one thing. What else? Molly?
Ha
We suck?
Ha
Ha

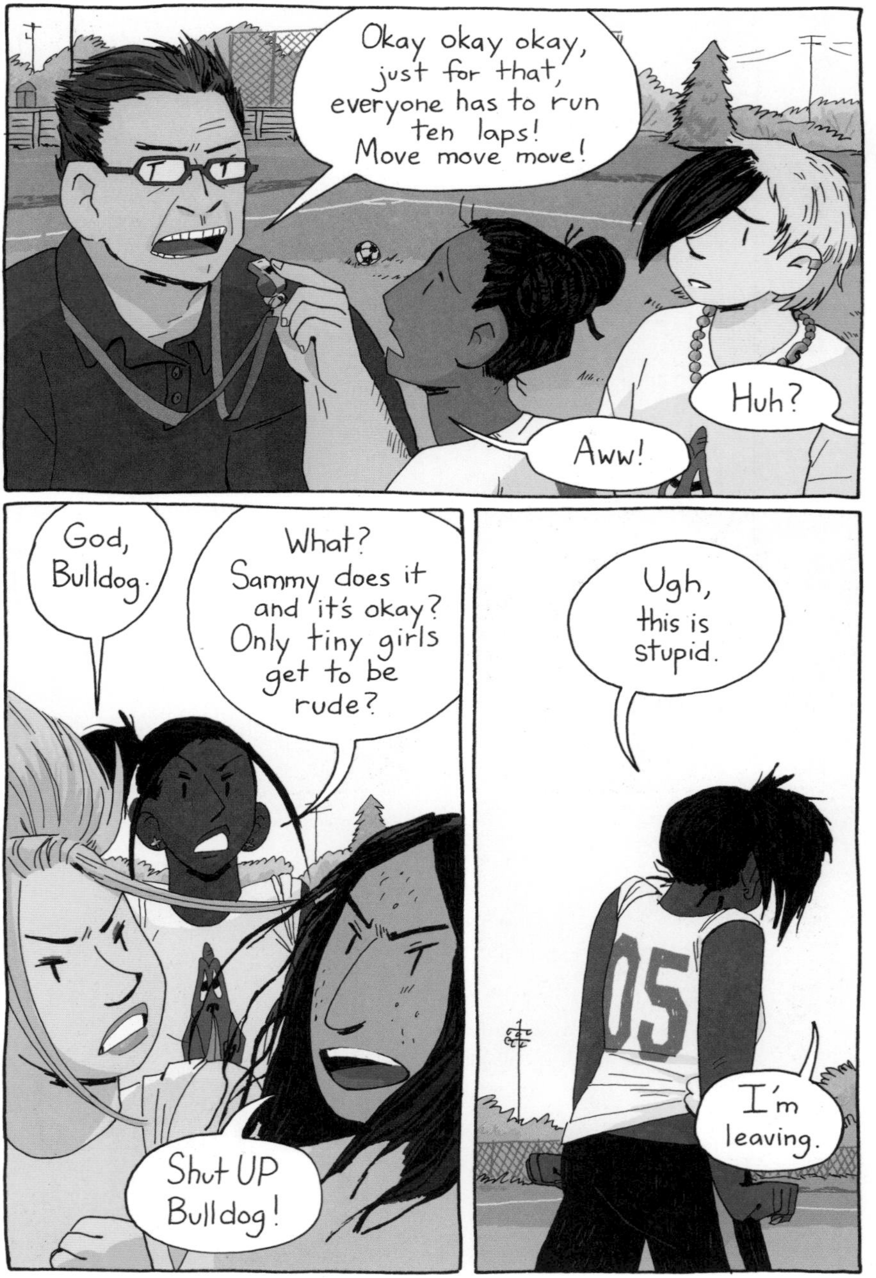
Okay okay okay, just for that, everyone has to run ten laps! Move move move!
Huh?
Aww!
God, Bulldog.
What? Sammy does it and it's okay? Only tiny girls get to be rude?
Shut UP Bulldog!
Ugh, this is stupid.
I'm leaving.

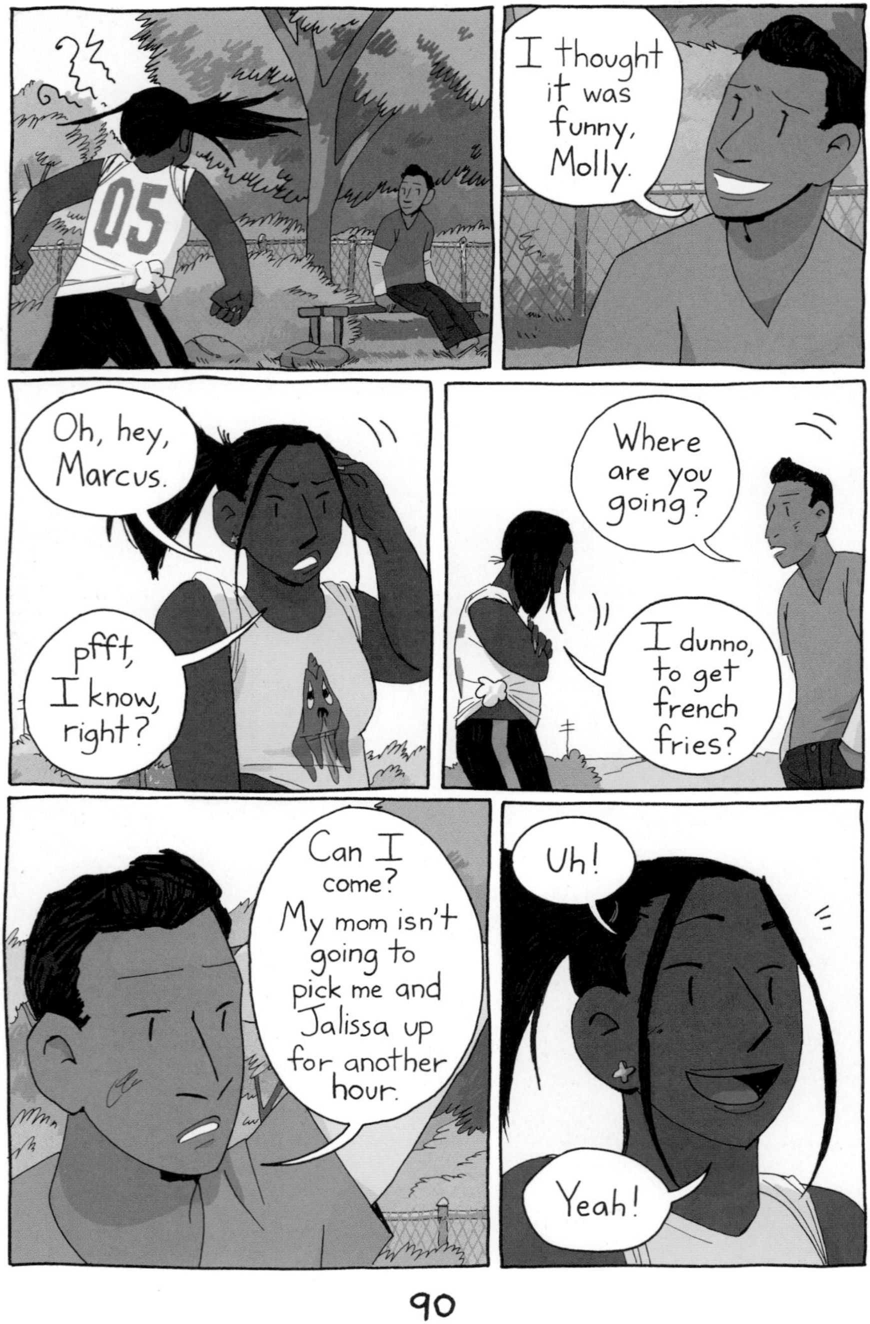
I thought it was funny, Molly.
Oh, hey, Marcus.
pfft, I know, right?
Where are you going?
I dunno, to get french fries?
Can I come? My mom isn't going to pick me and Jalissa up for another hour.
Uh!
Yeah!

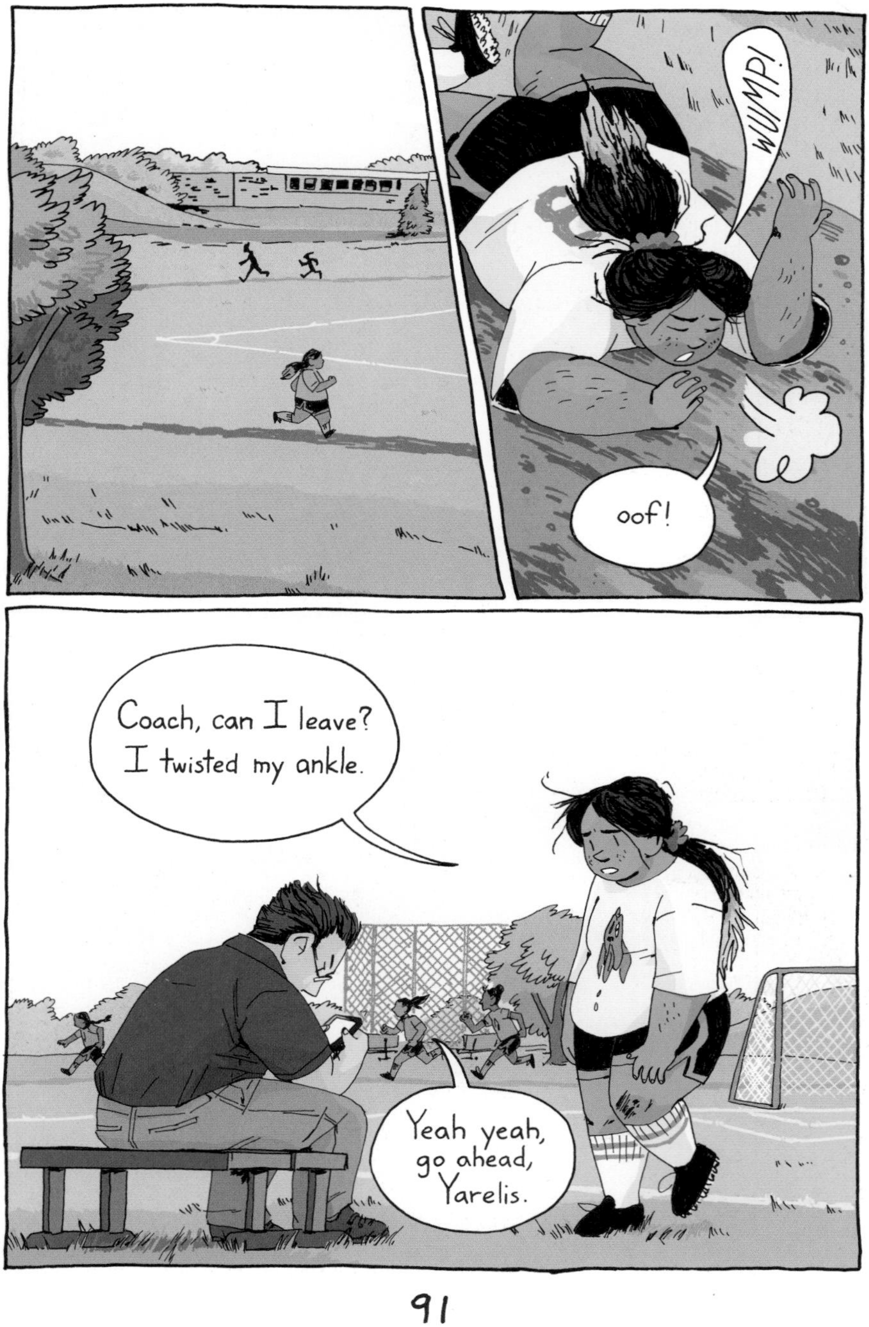
WUMP!
oof!
Coach, can I leave? I twisted my ankle.
Yeah yeah, go ahead, Yarelis.

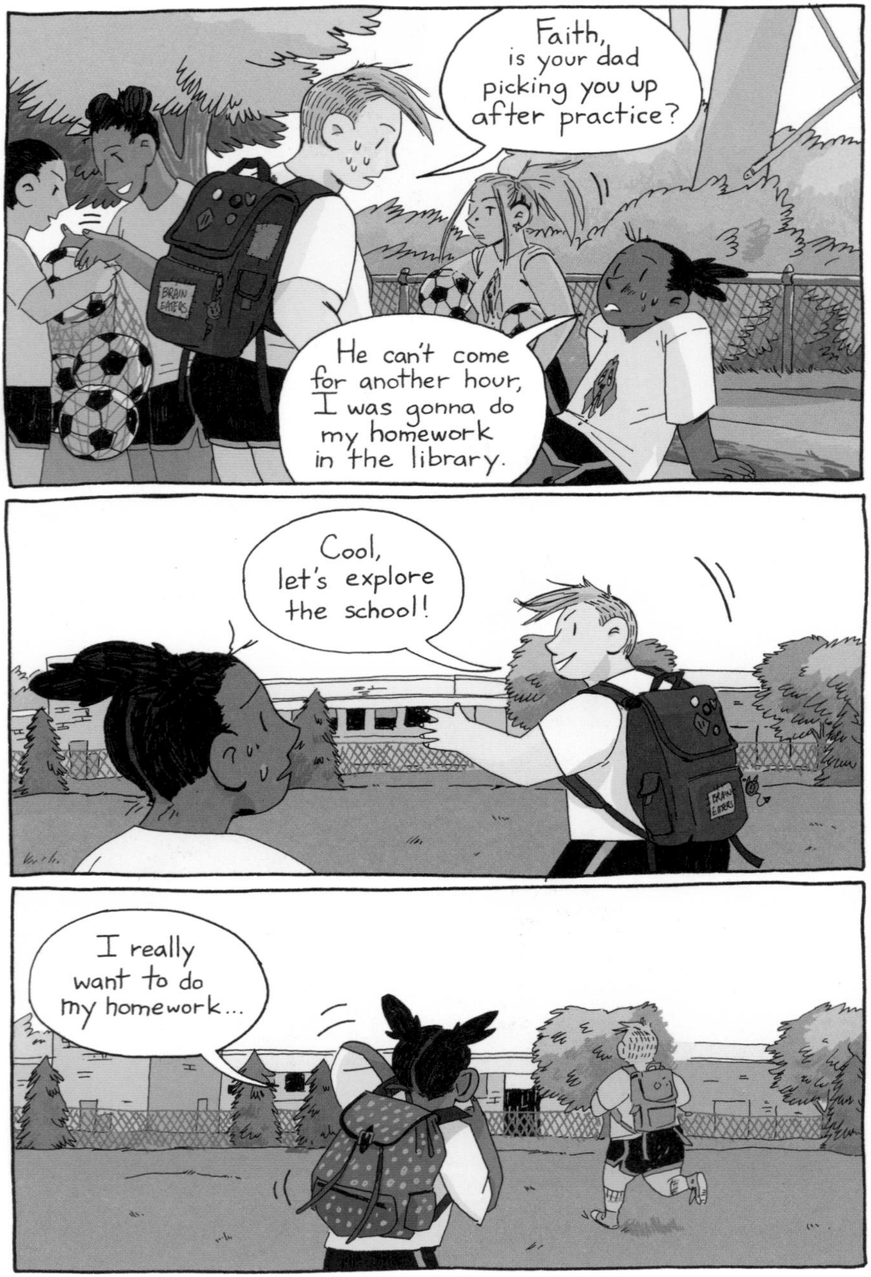
Faith, is your dad picking you up after practice?
He can't come for another hour, I was gonna do my homework in the library.
Cool, let's explore the school!
I really want to do my homework...

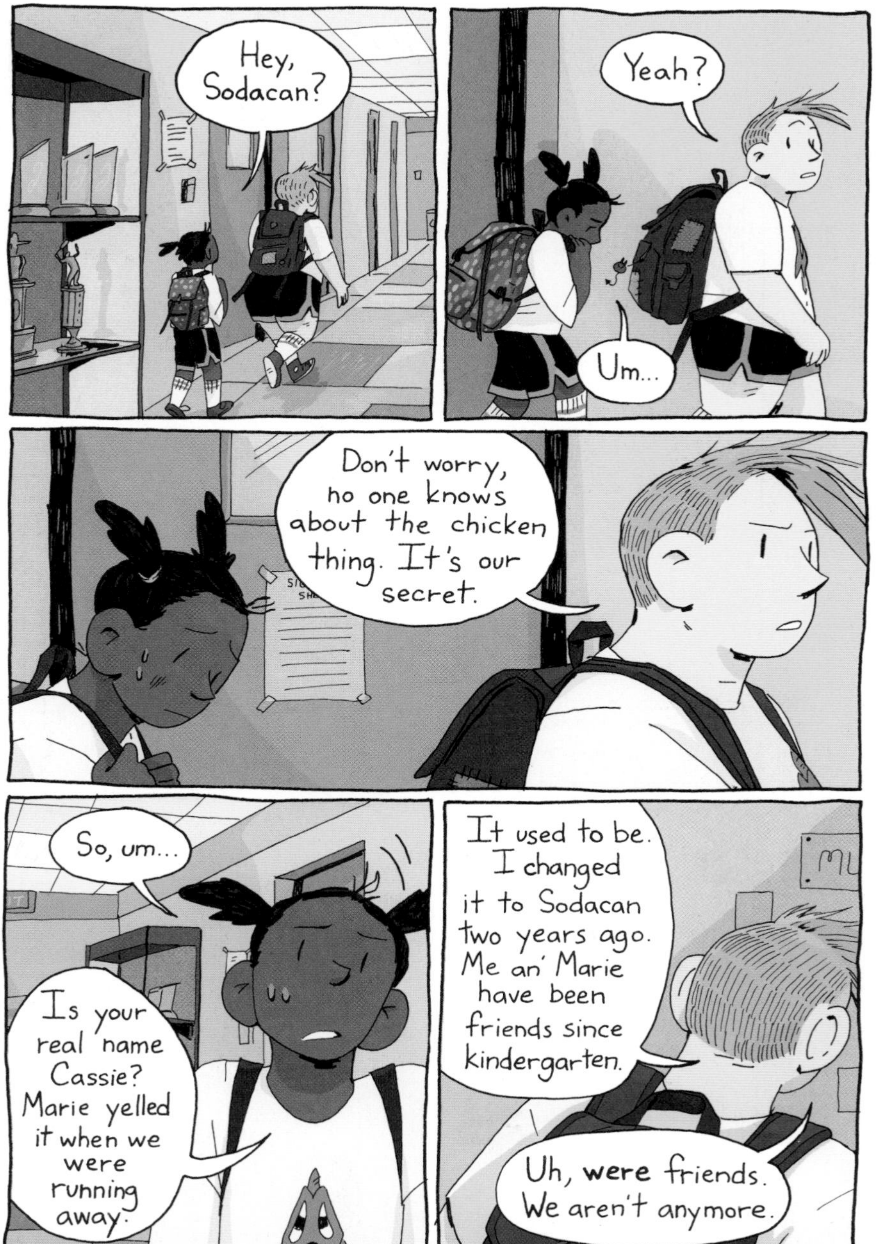
Hey, Sodacan?
Yeah?
Um...
Don't worry, no one knows about the chicken thing. It's our secret.
So, um...
Is your real name Cassie? Marie yelled it when we were running away.
It used to be. I changed it to Sodacan two years ago. Me an' Marie have been friends since kindergarten.
Uh, **were** friends. We aren't anymore.

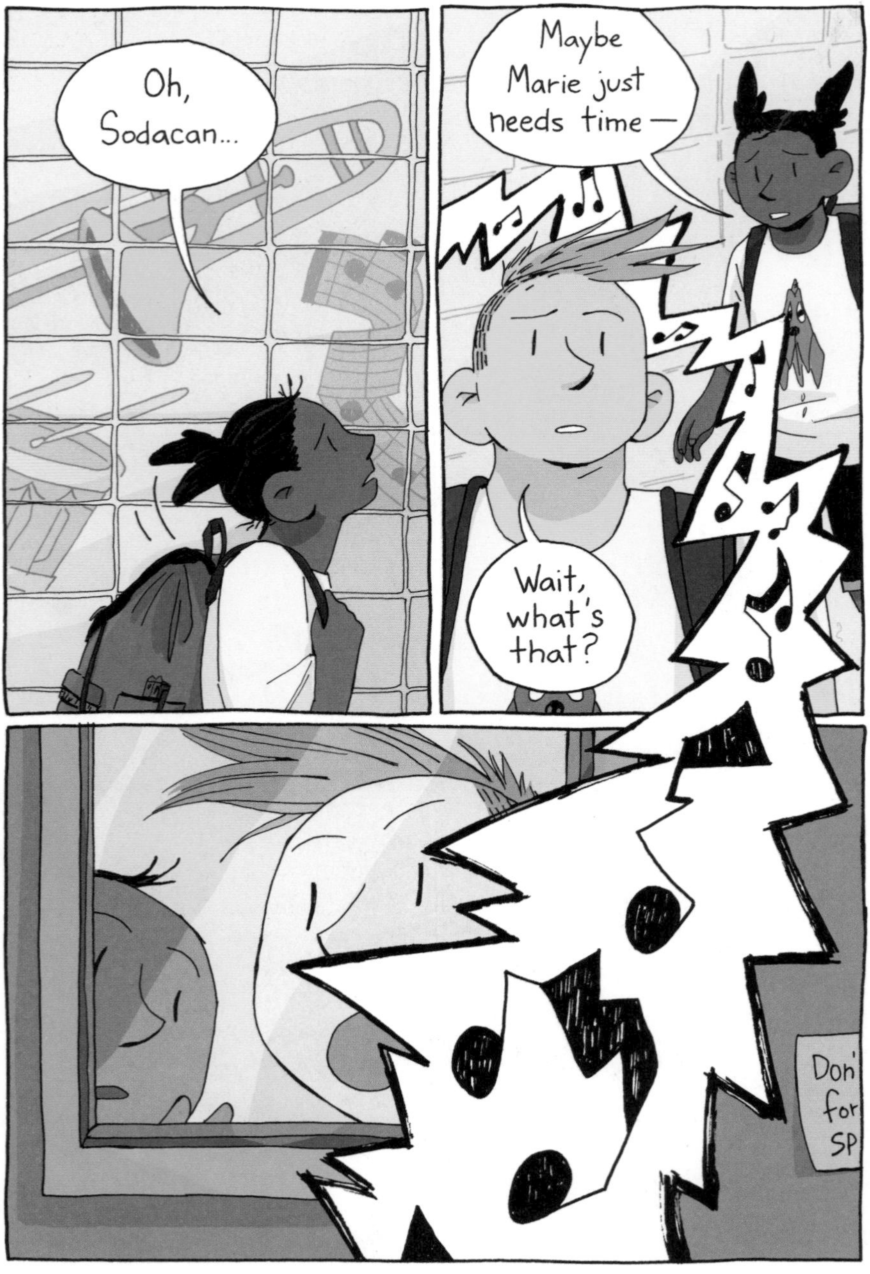
Oh, Sodacan...
Maybe Marie just needs time—
Wait, what's that?
Don' for SP

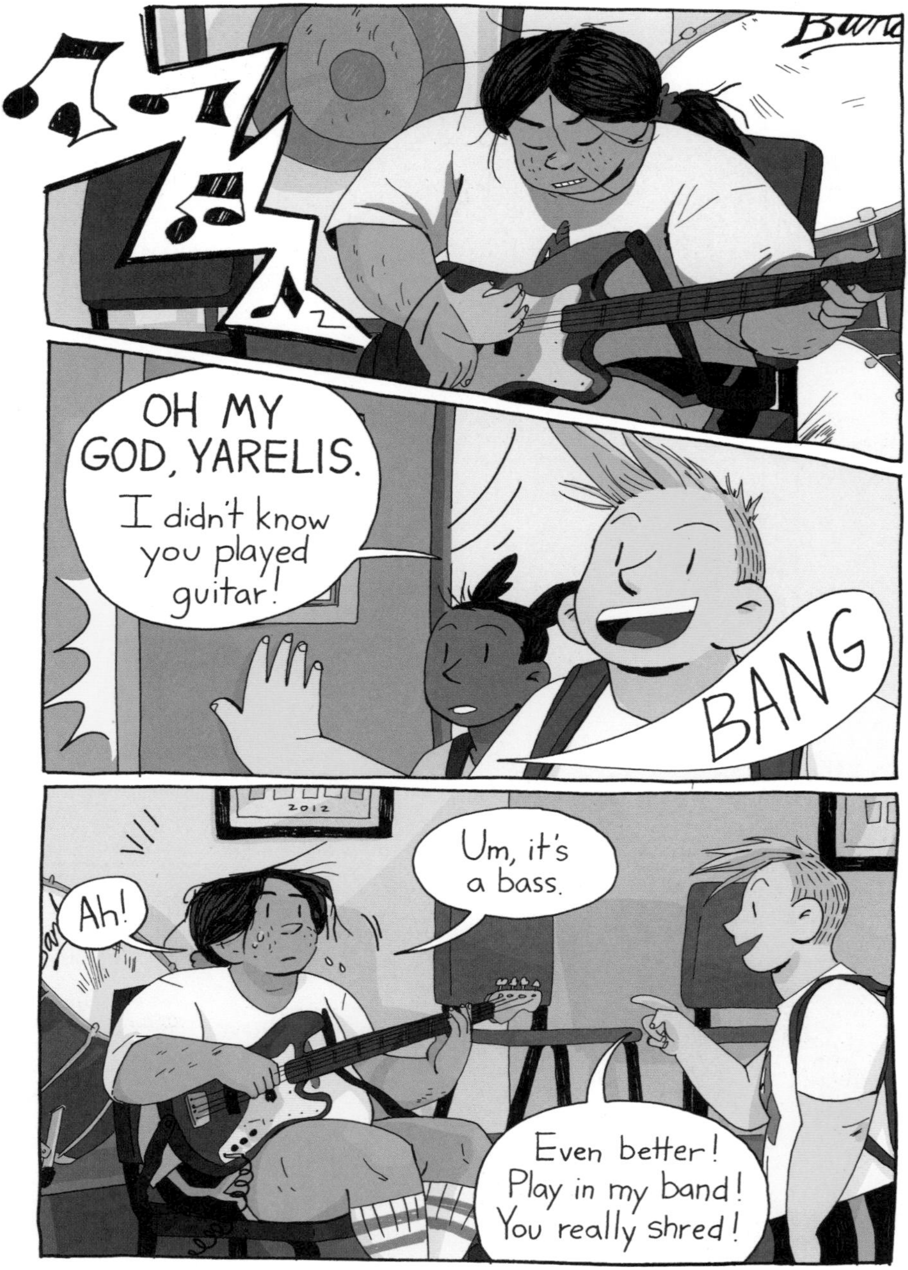
OH MY GOD, YARELIS.
I didn't know you played guitar!
BANG
Ah!
Um, it's a bass.
Even better! Play in my band! You really shred!

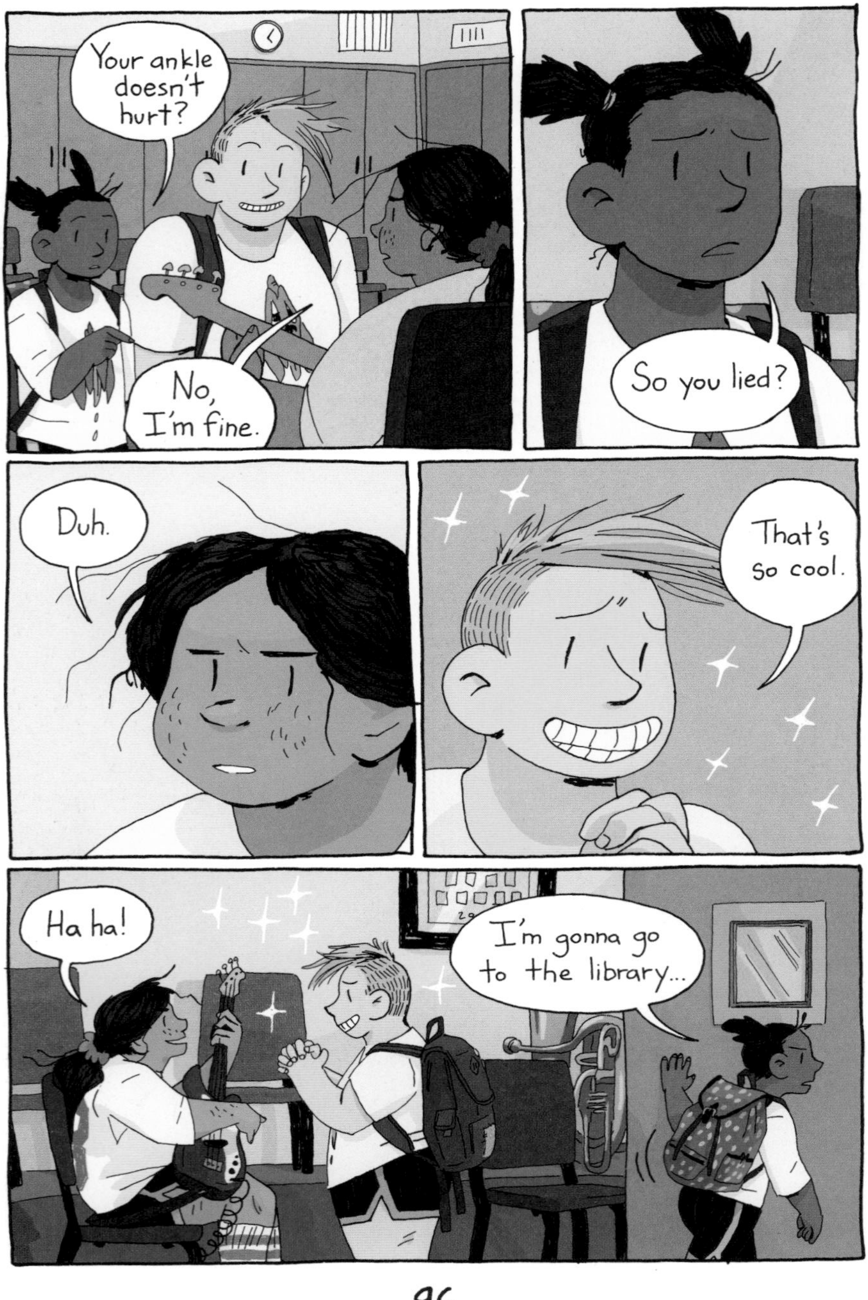
Your ankle doesn't hurt?
No, I'm fine.
So you lied?
Duh.
That's so cool.
Ha ha!
I'm gonna go to the library...

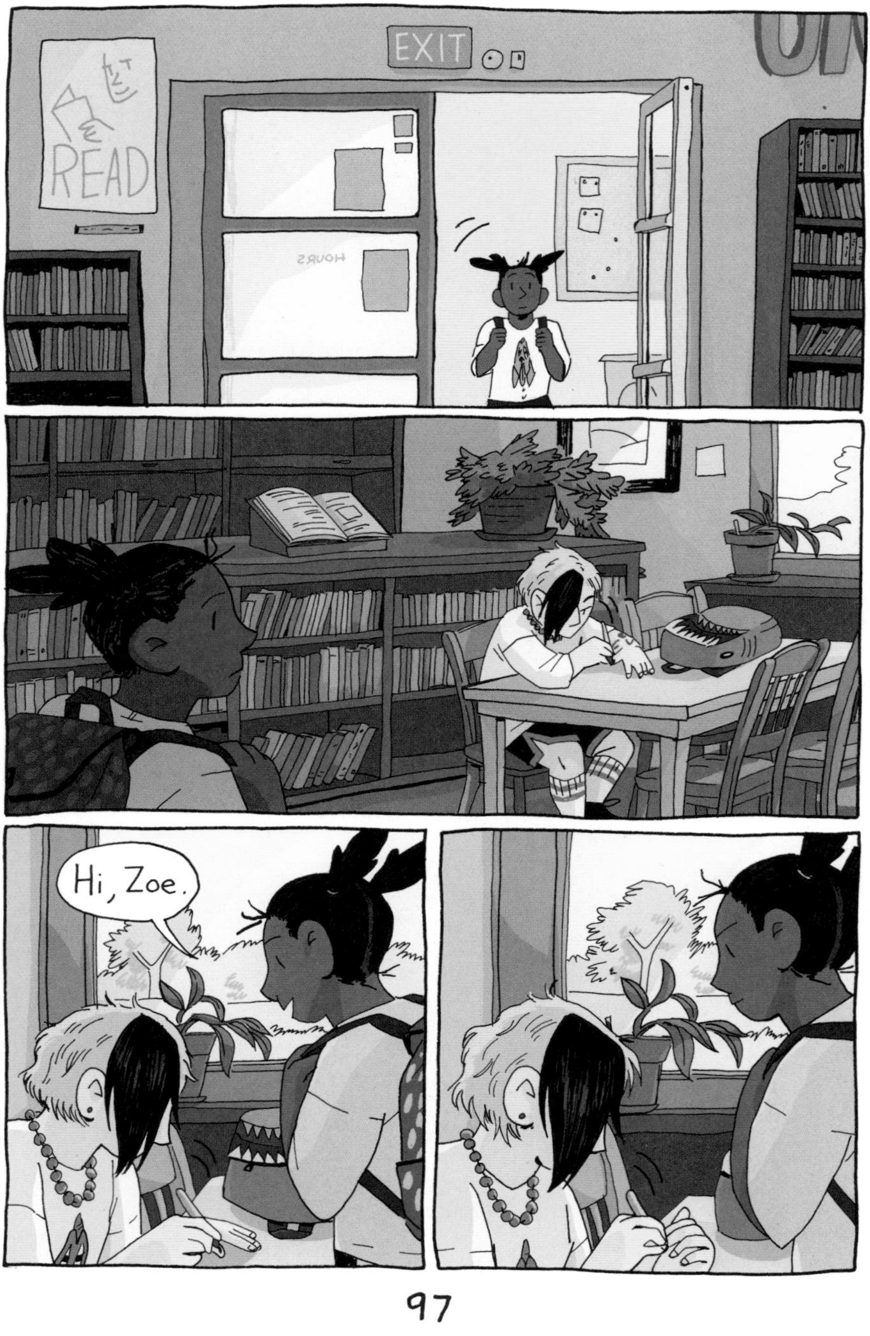
EXIT
READ
HOURS
Hi, Zoe.

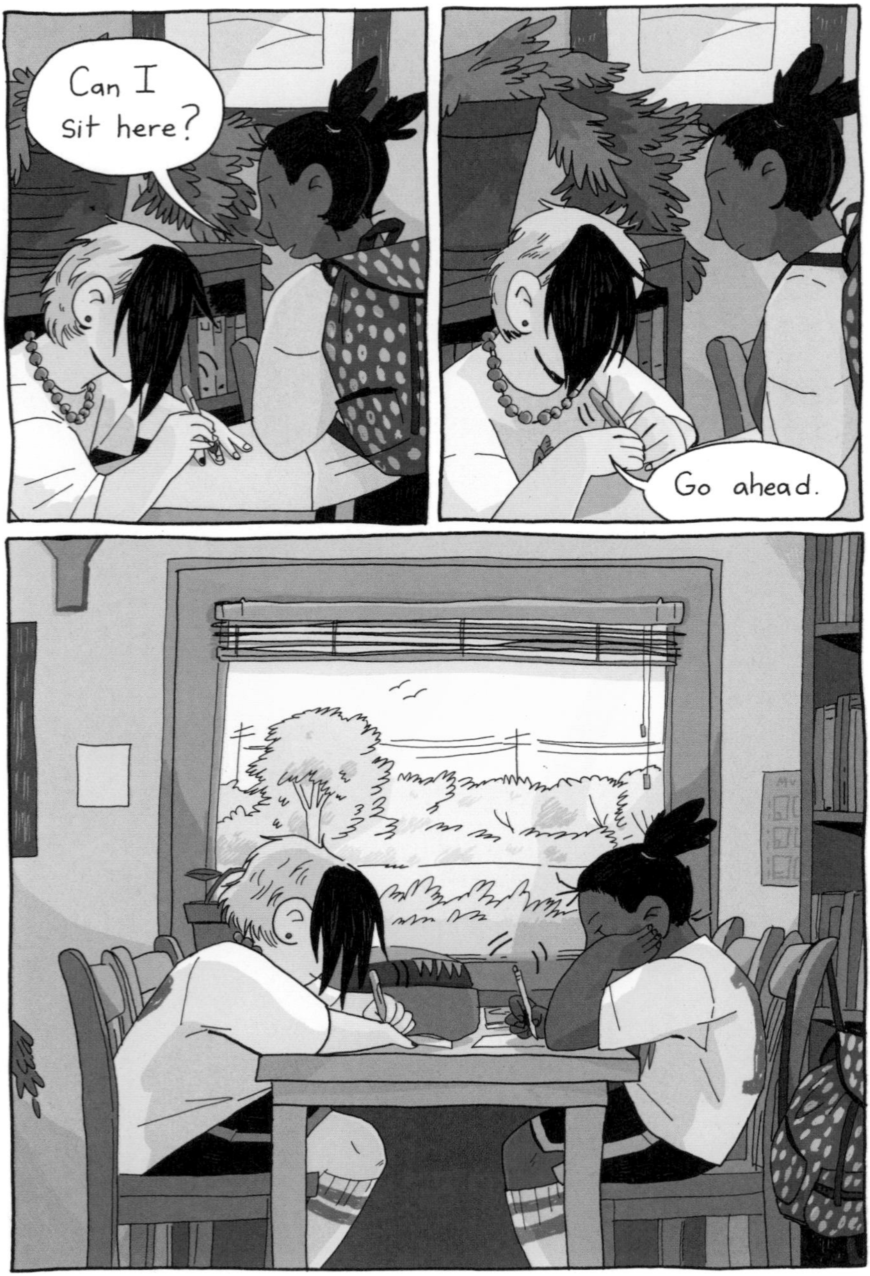
Can I sit here?
Go ahead.

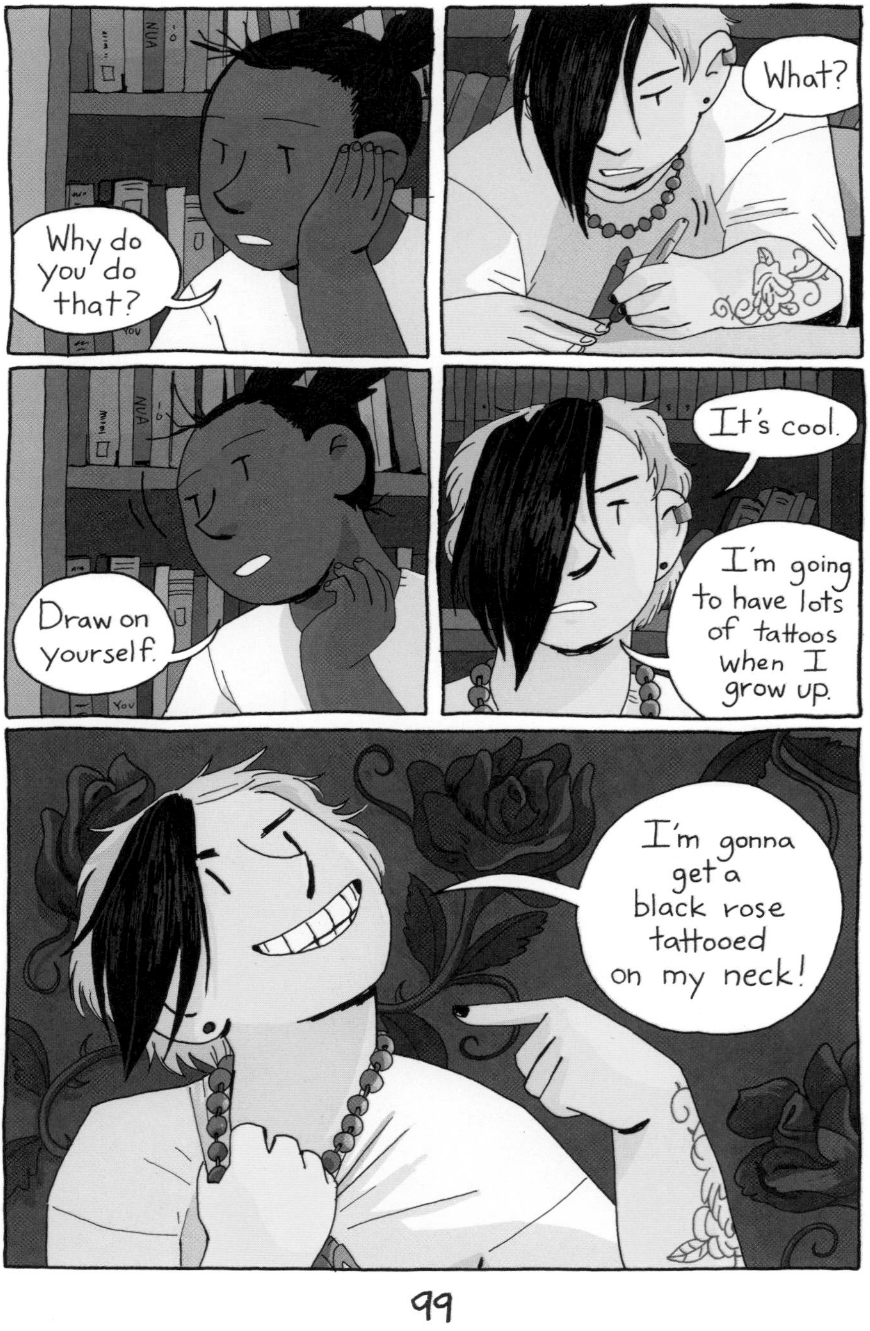
Why do you do that?
What?
Draw on yourself.
It's cool.
I'm going to have lots of tattoos when I grow up.
I'm gonna get a black rose tattooed on my neck!

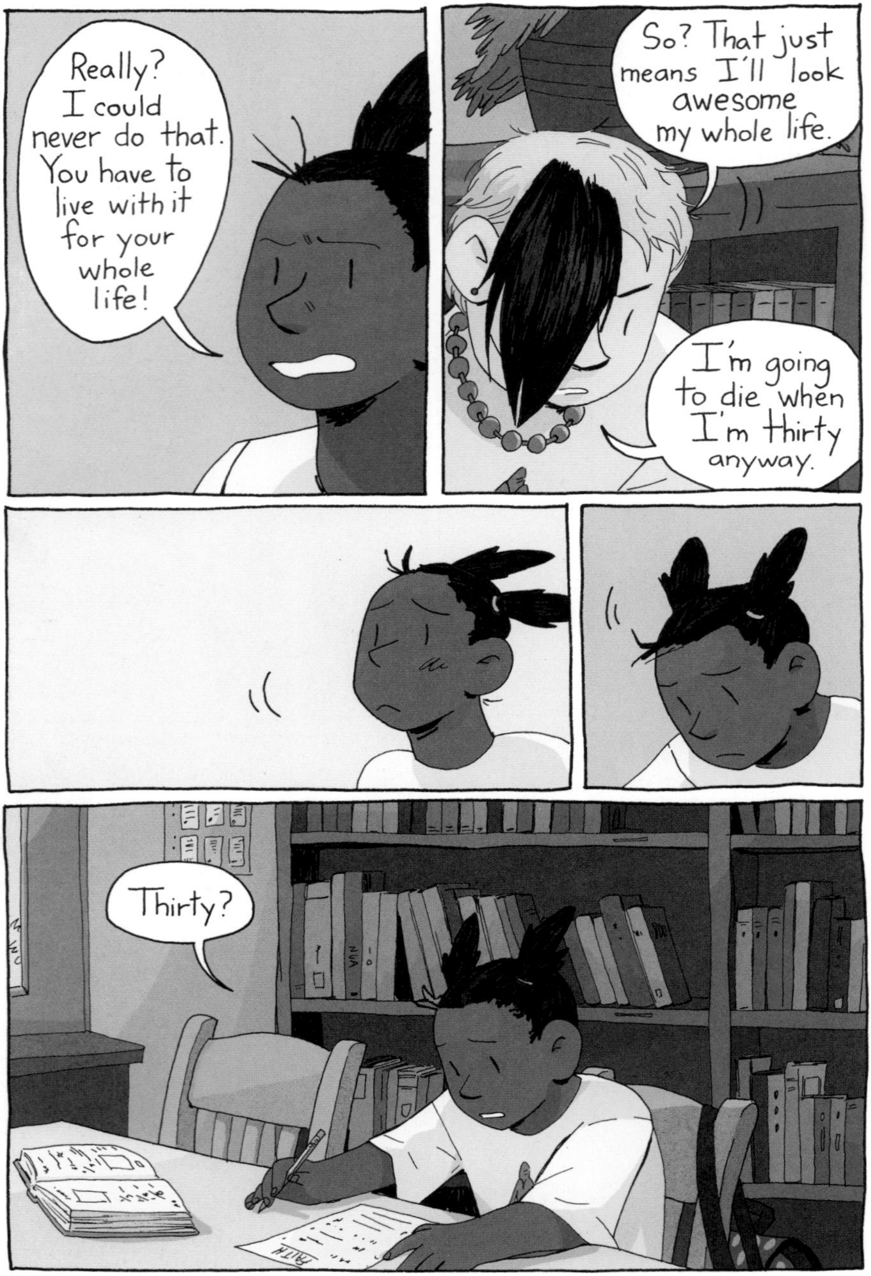
Really? I could never do that. You have to live with it for your whole life!
So? That just means I'll look awesome my whole life.
I'm going to die when I'm thirty anyway.
Thirty?

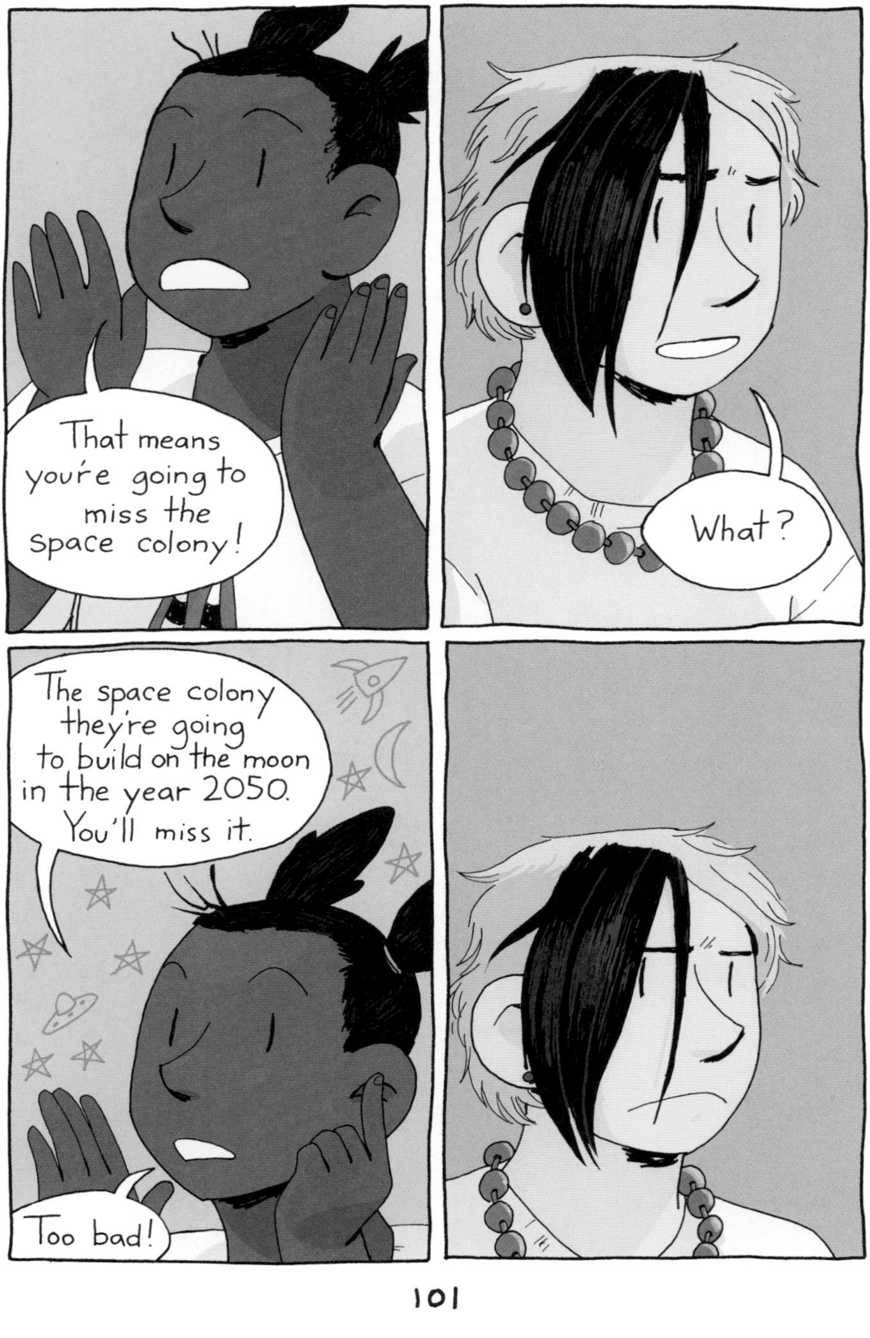
That means you're going to miss the space colony!
What?
The space colony they're going to build on the moon in the year 2050. You'll miss it.
Too bad!

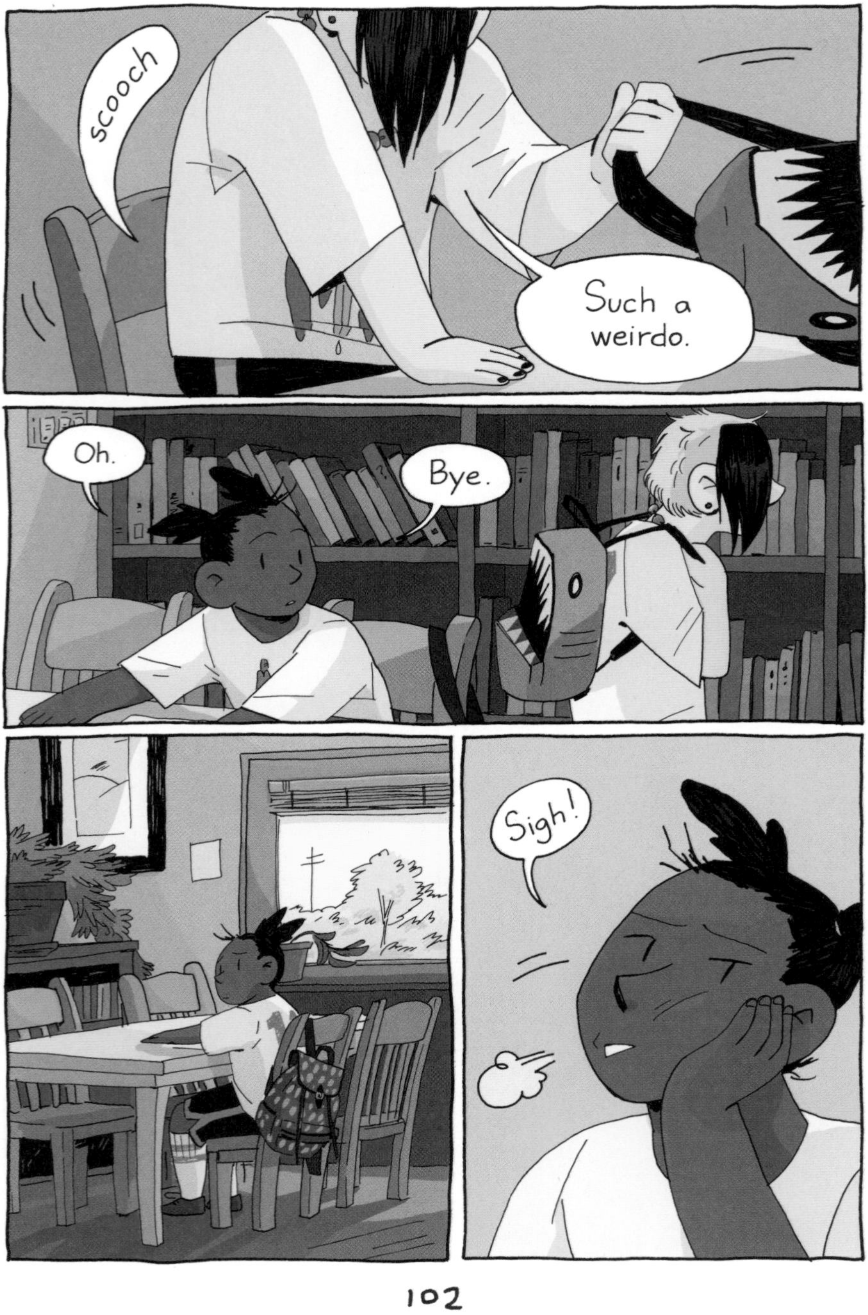
scooch
Such a weirdo.
Oh.
Bye.
Sigh!

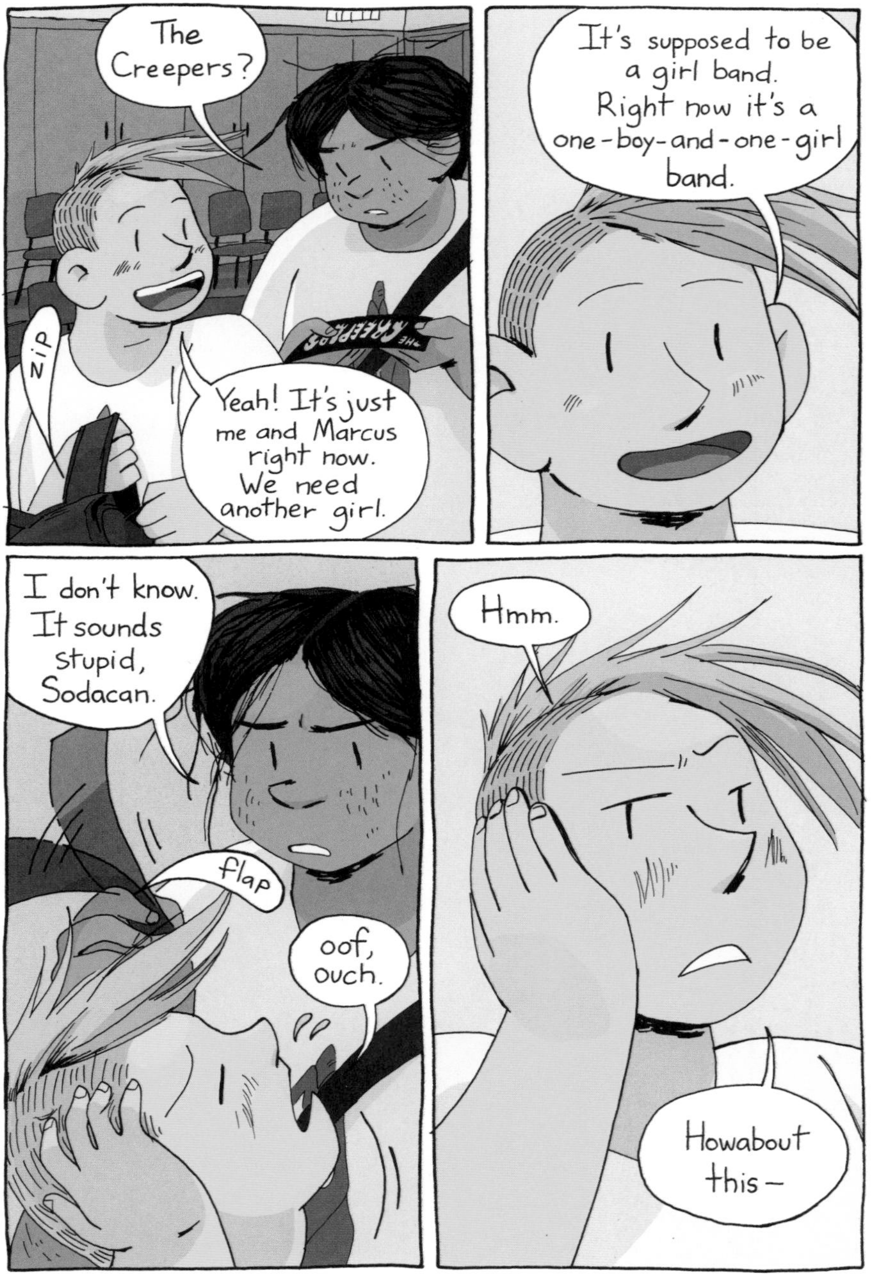
The Creepers?
zip
Yeah! It's just me and Marcus right now. We need another girl.
It's supposed to be a girl band. Right now it's a one-boy-and-one-girl band.
I don't know. It sounds stupid, Sodacan.
flap
oof, ouch.
Hmm.
Howabout this—

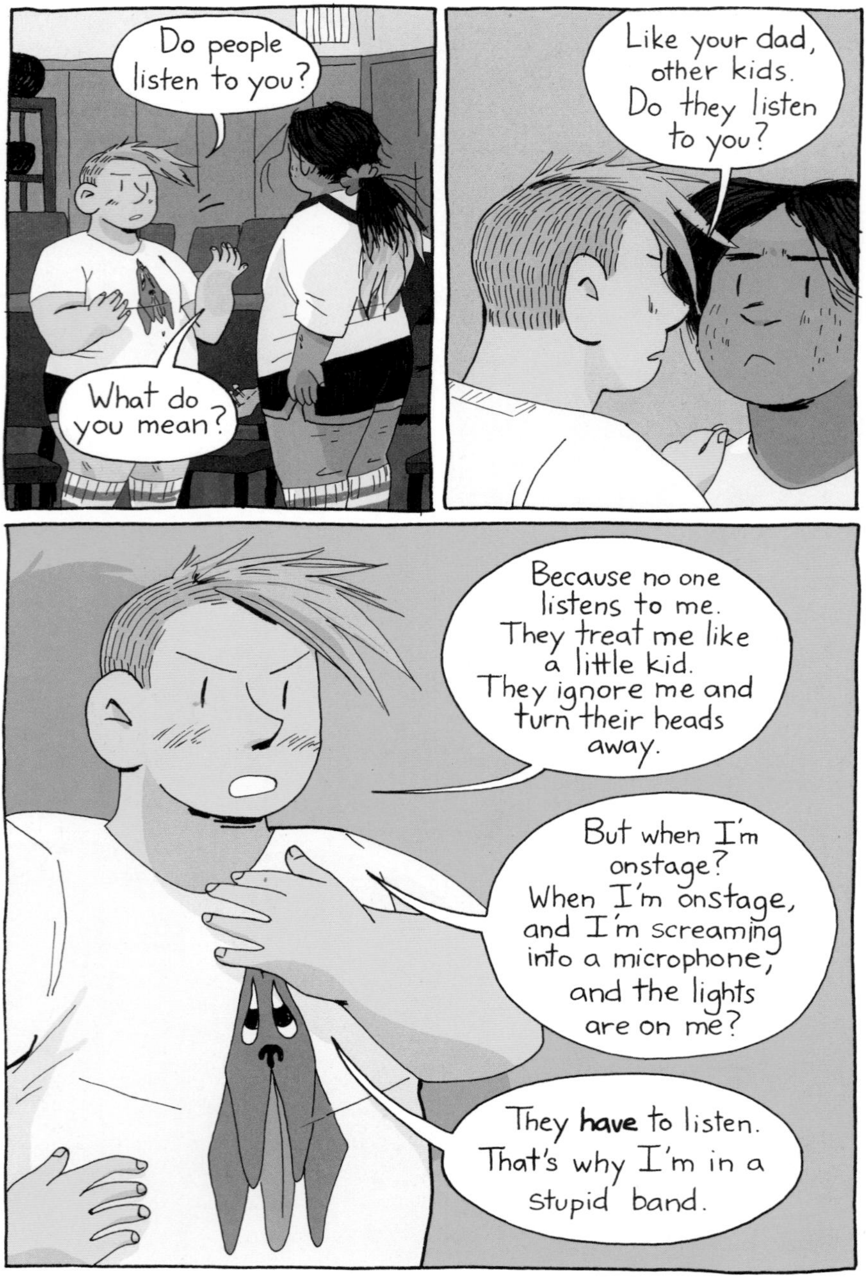
Do people listen to you?
What do you mean?
Like your dad, other kids. Do they listen to you?
Because no one listens to me. They treat me like a little kid. They ignore me and turn their heads away.
But when I'm onstage? When I'm onstage, and I'm screaming into a microphone, and the lights are on me?
They **have** to listen. That's why I'm in a stupid band.

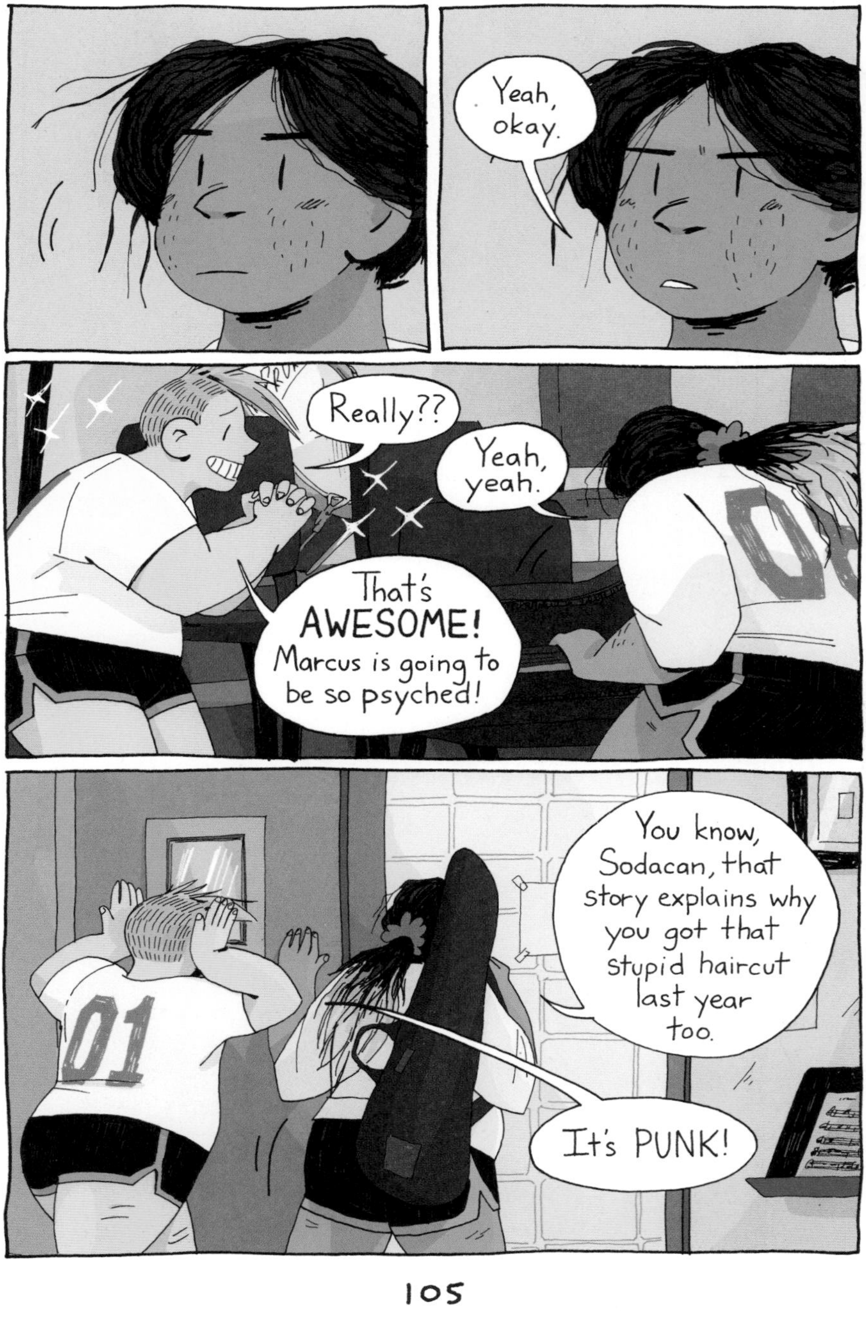
Yeah, okay.
Really??
Yeah, yeah.
That's AWESOME! Marcus is going to be so psyched!
You know, Sodacan, that story explains why you got that stupid haircut last year too.
It's PUNK!

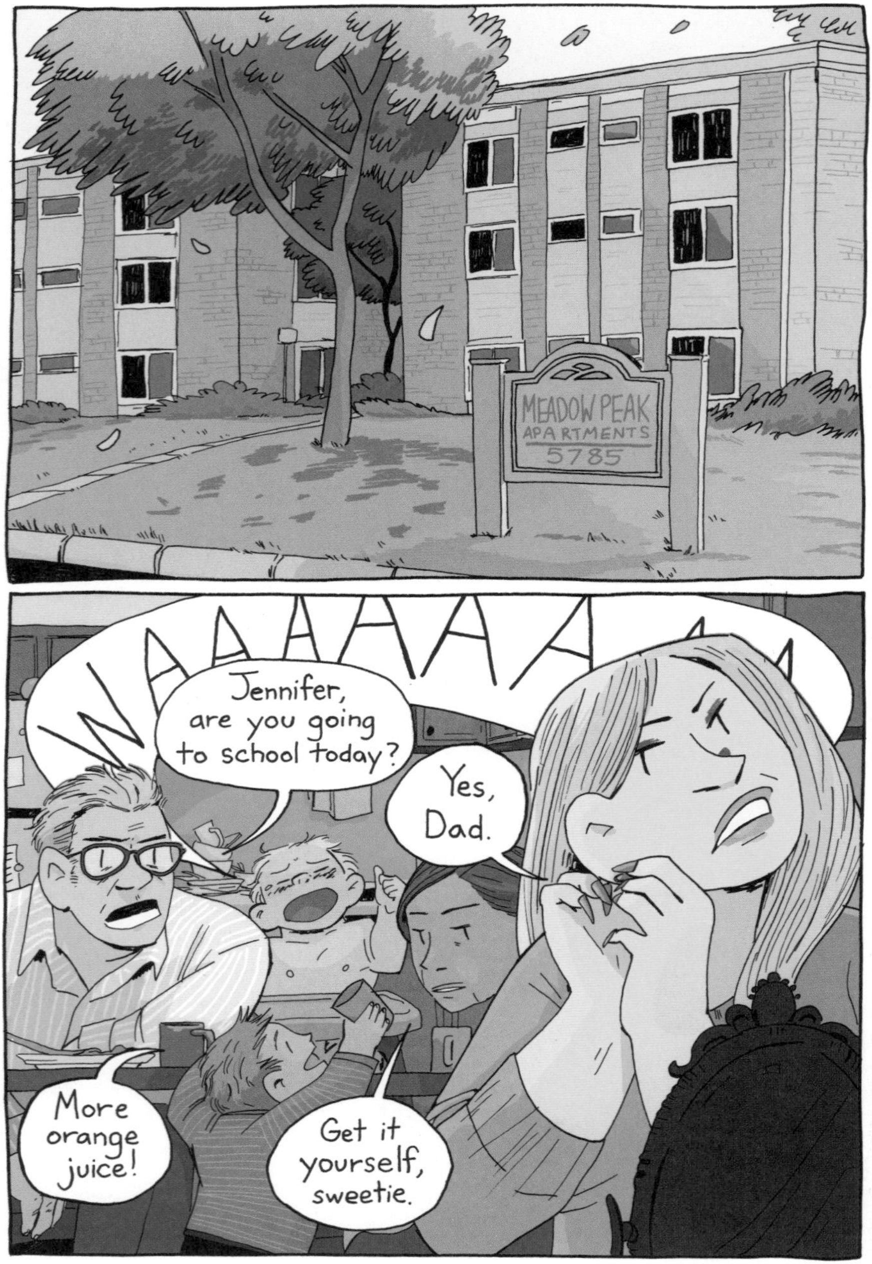
MEADOW PEAK
APARTMENTS
5785
NAAAAAAAA
Jennifer, are you going to school today?
Yes, Dad.
More orange juice!
Get it yourself, sweetie.

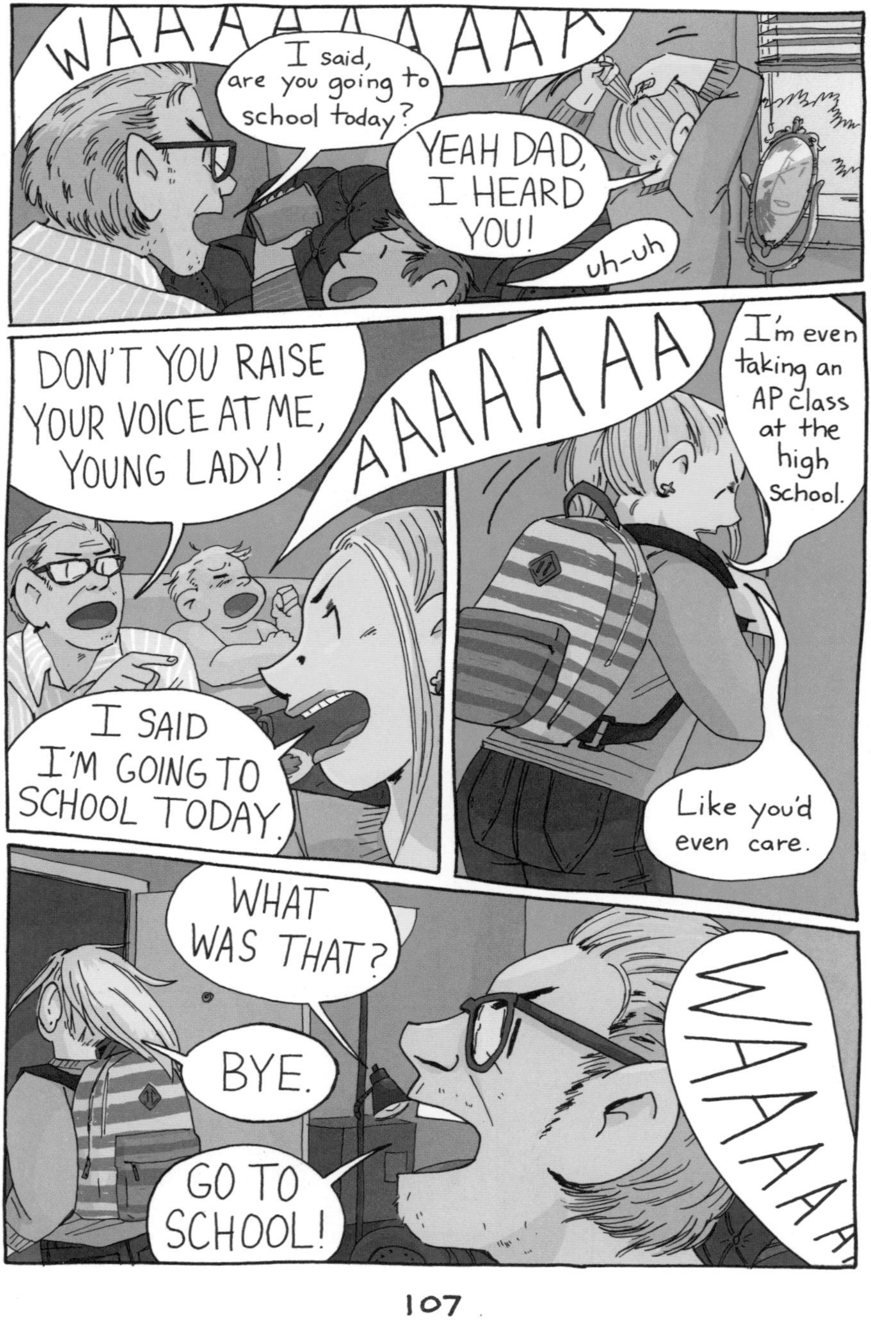
WAAAAAAAAA
I said, are you going to school today?
YEAH DAD, I HEARD YOU!
uh-uh
DON'T YOU RAISE YOUR VOICE AT ME, YOUNG LADY!
AAAAAAA
I SAID I'M GOING TO SCHOOL TODAY.
I'm even taking an AP class at the high school.
Like you'd even care.
WHAT WAS THAT?
BYE.
GO TO SCHOOL!
WAAAAA

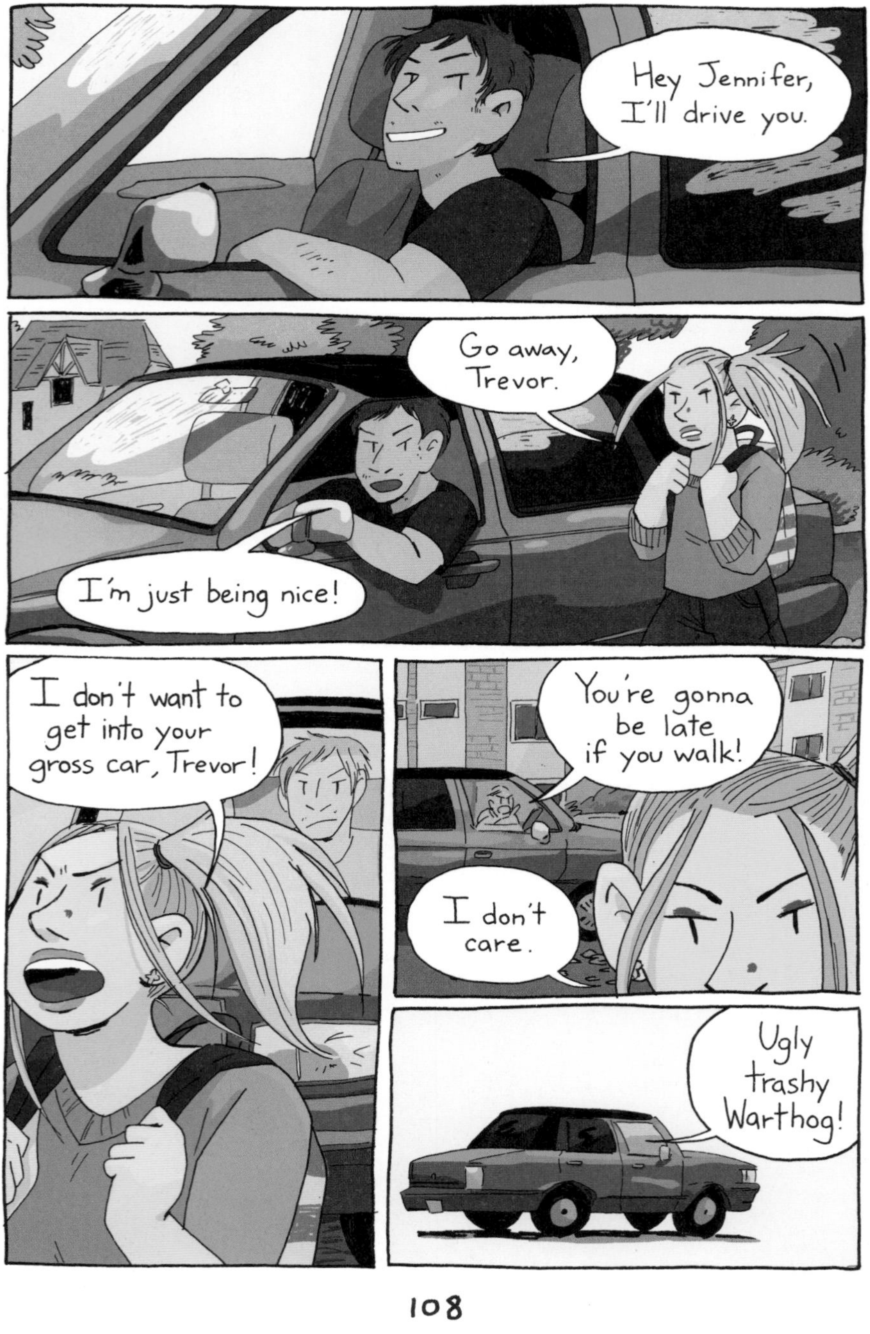
Hey Jennifer, I'll drive you.
Go away, Trevor.
I'm just being nice!
I don't want to get into your gross car, Trevor!
You're gonna be late if you walk!
I don't care.
Ugly trashy Warthog!

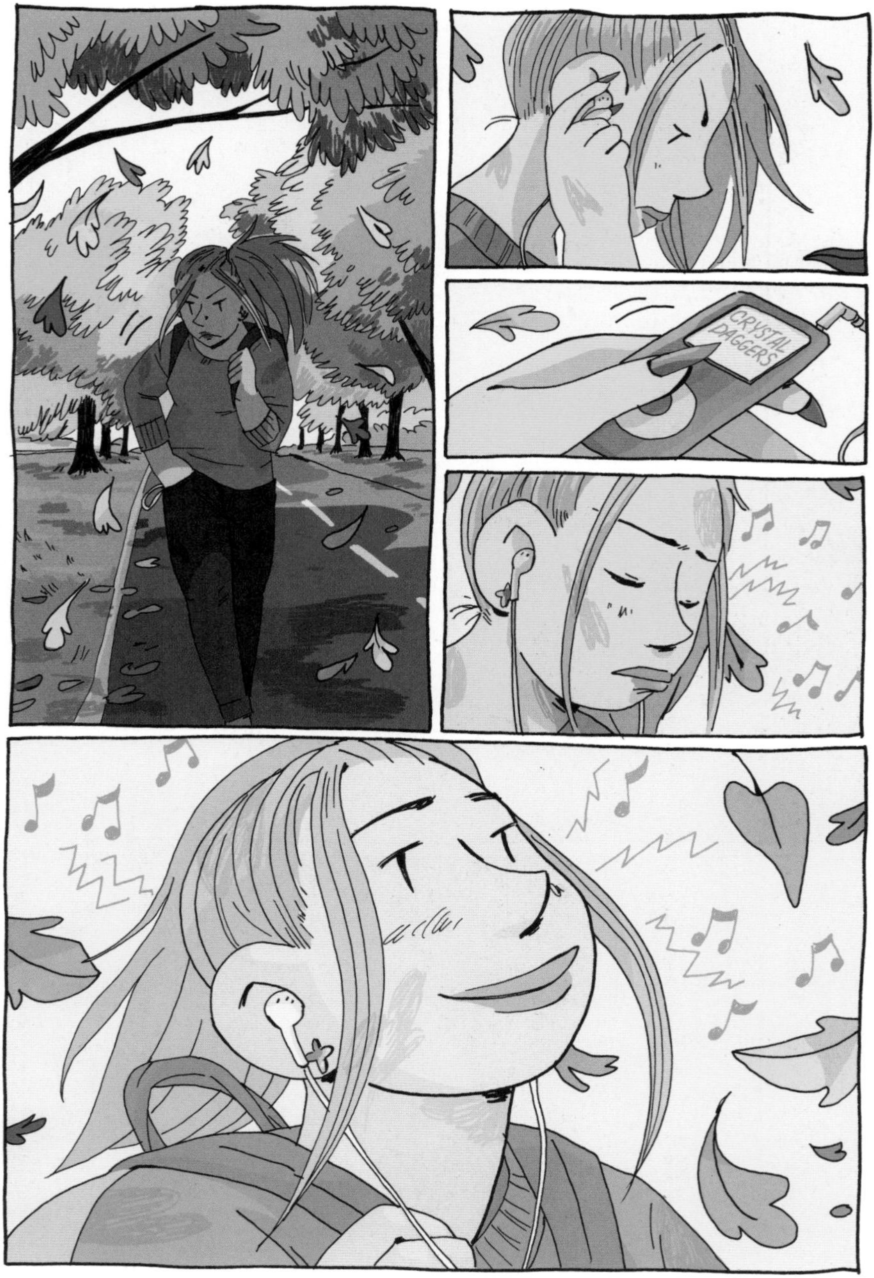
CRYSTAL DAGGERS

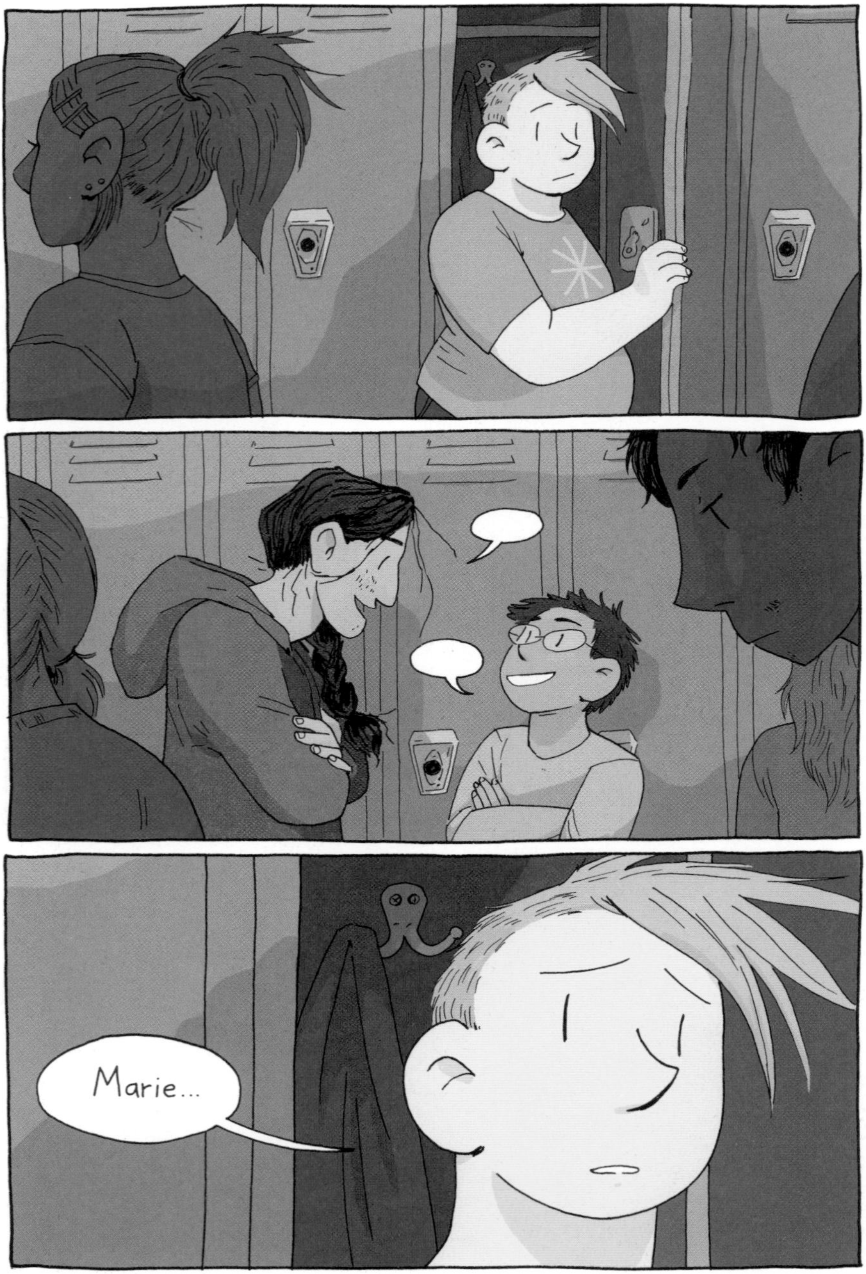
Marie...

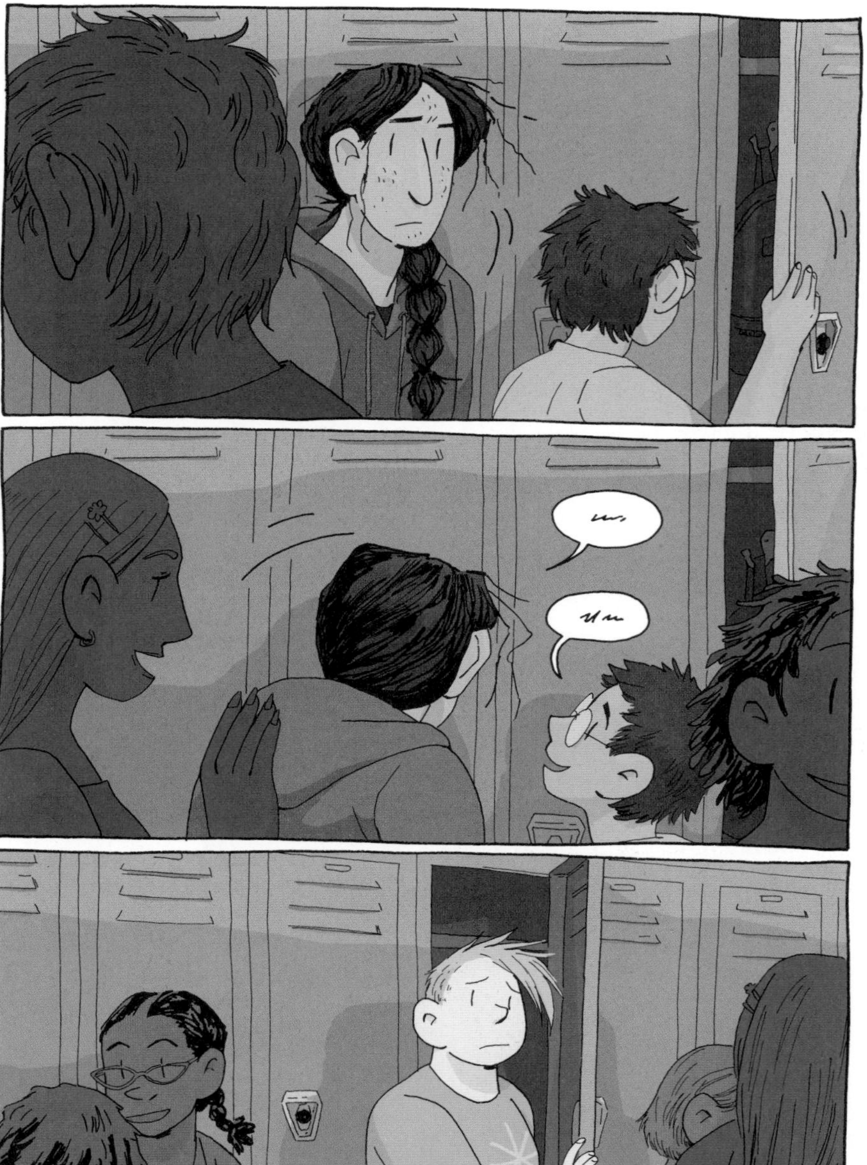

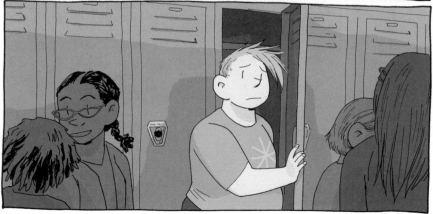

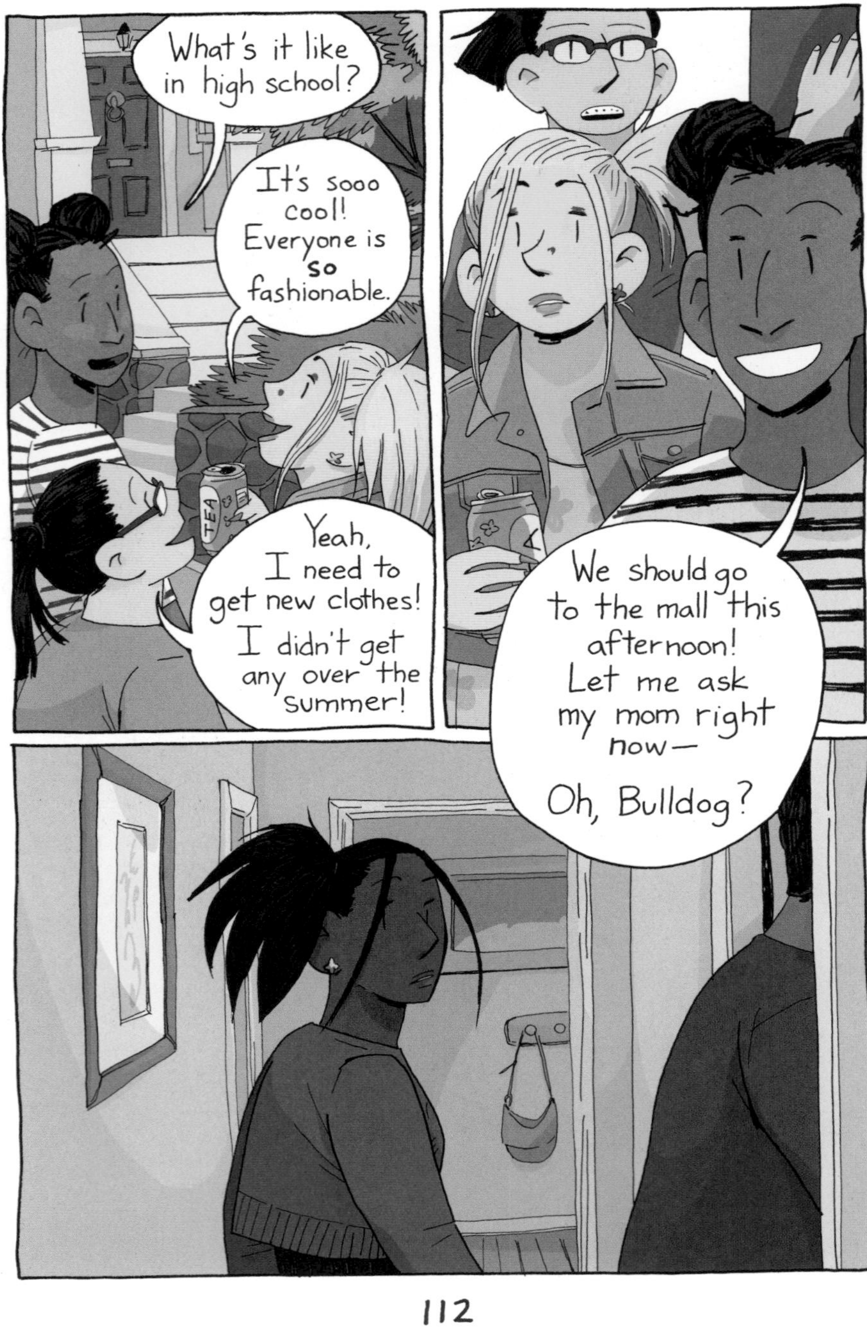
What's it like in high school?
It's sooo cool! Everyone is **so** fashionable.
Yeah, I need to get new clothes! I didn't get any over the summer!
TEA
We should go to the mall this afternoon! Let me ask my mom right now—
Oh, Bulldog?

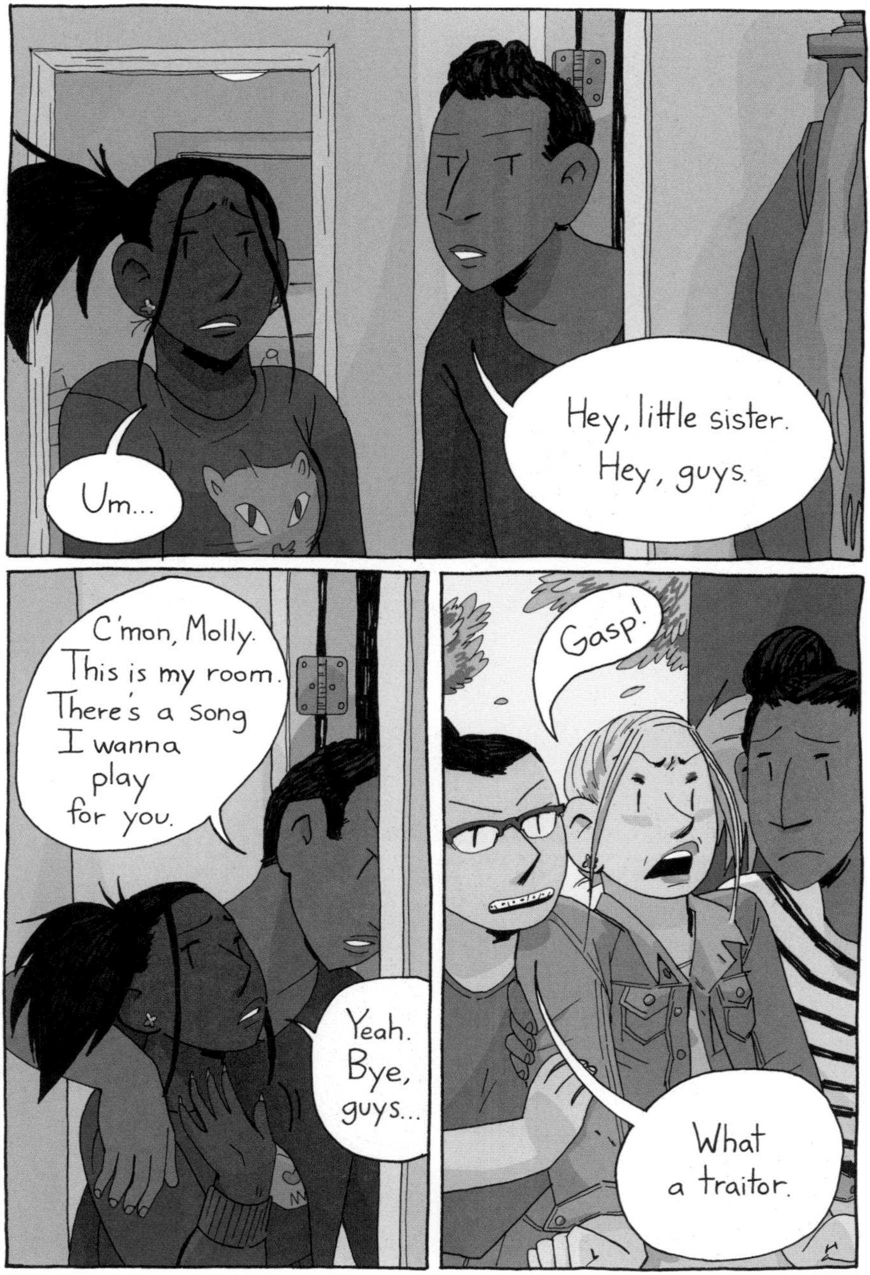
Um...
Hey, little sister. Hey, guys.
C'mon, Molly. This is my room. There's a song I wanna play for you.
Yeah. Bye, guys...
Gasp!
What a traitor.

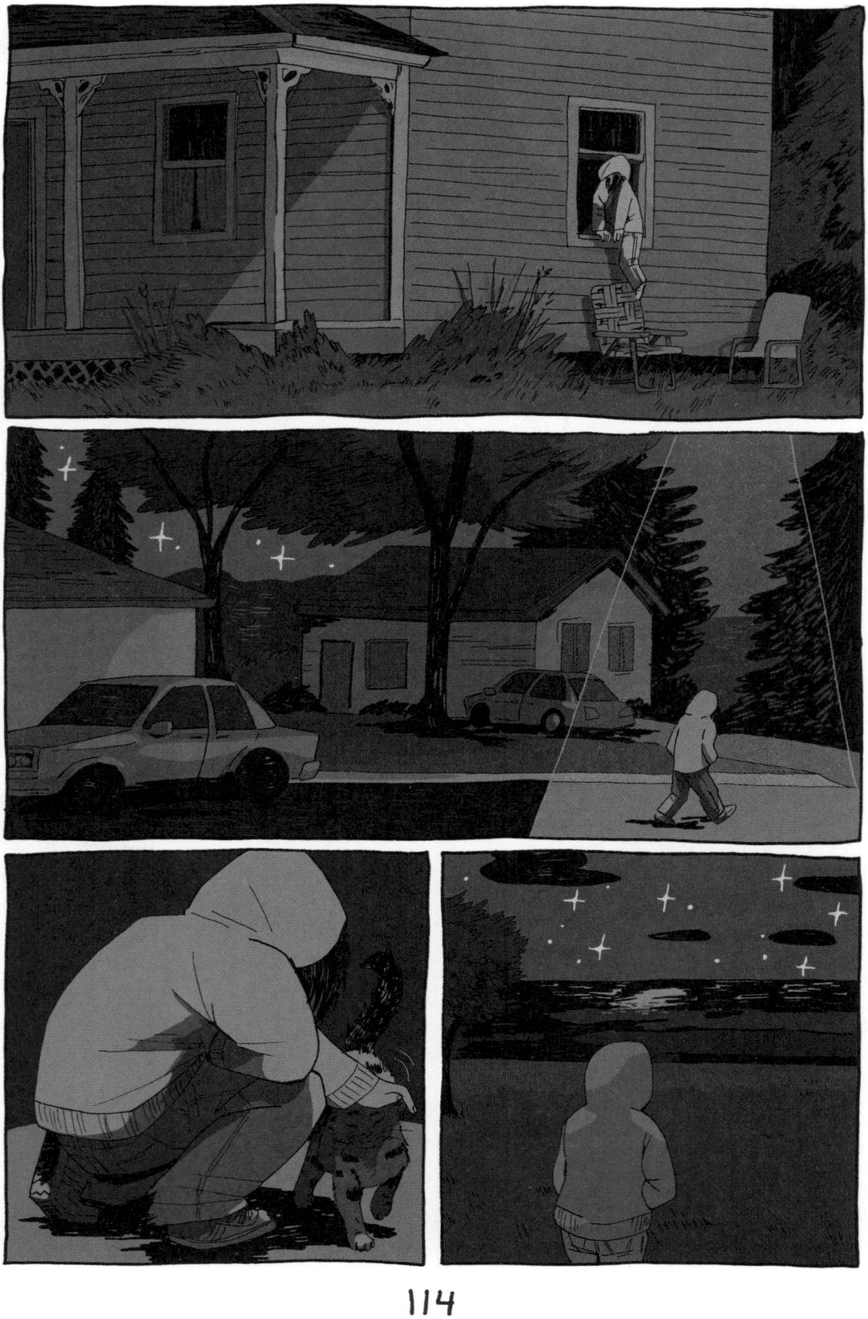

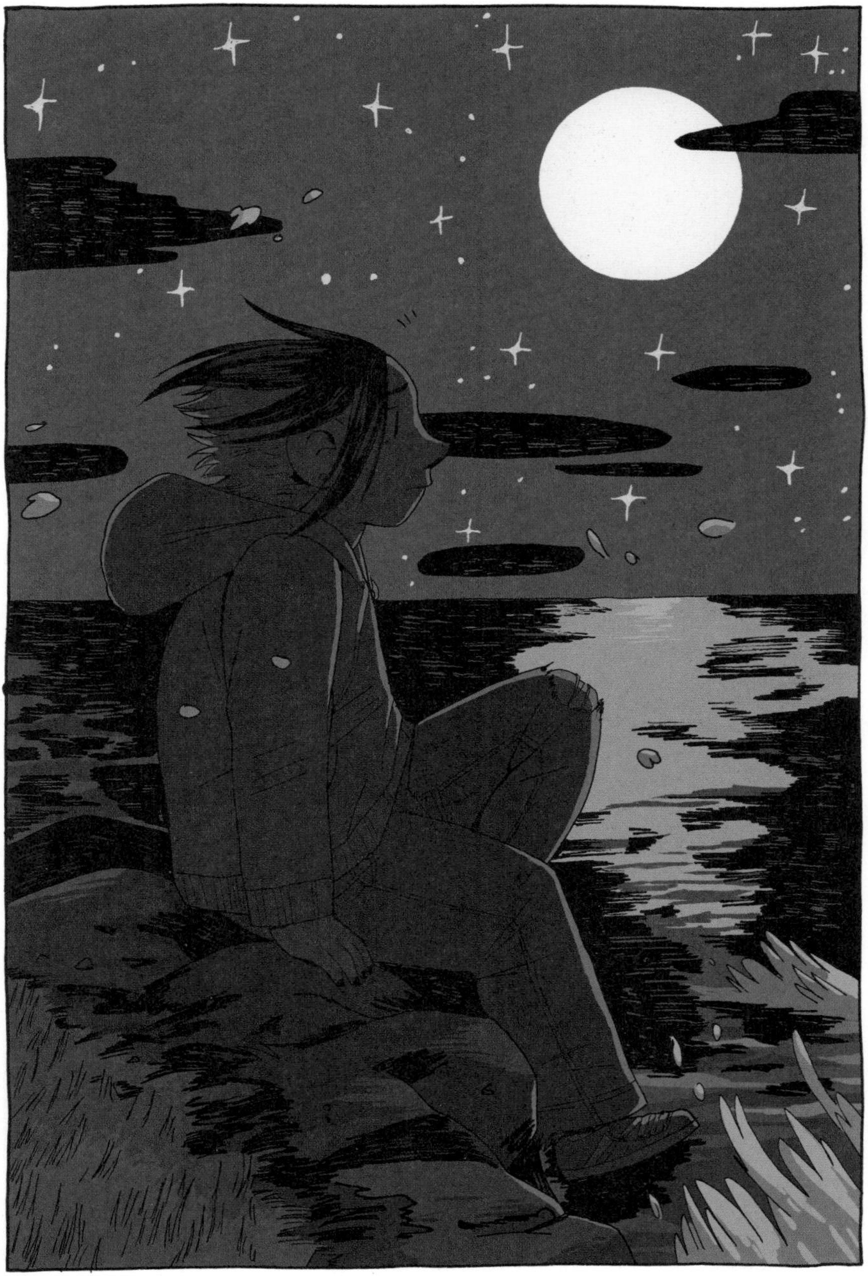

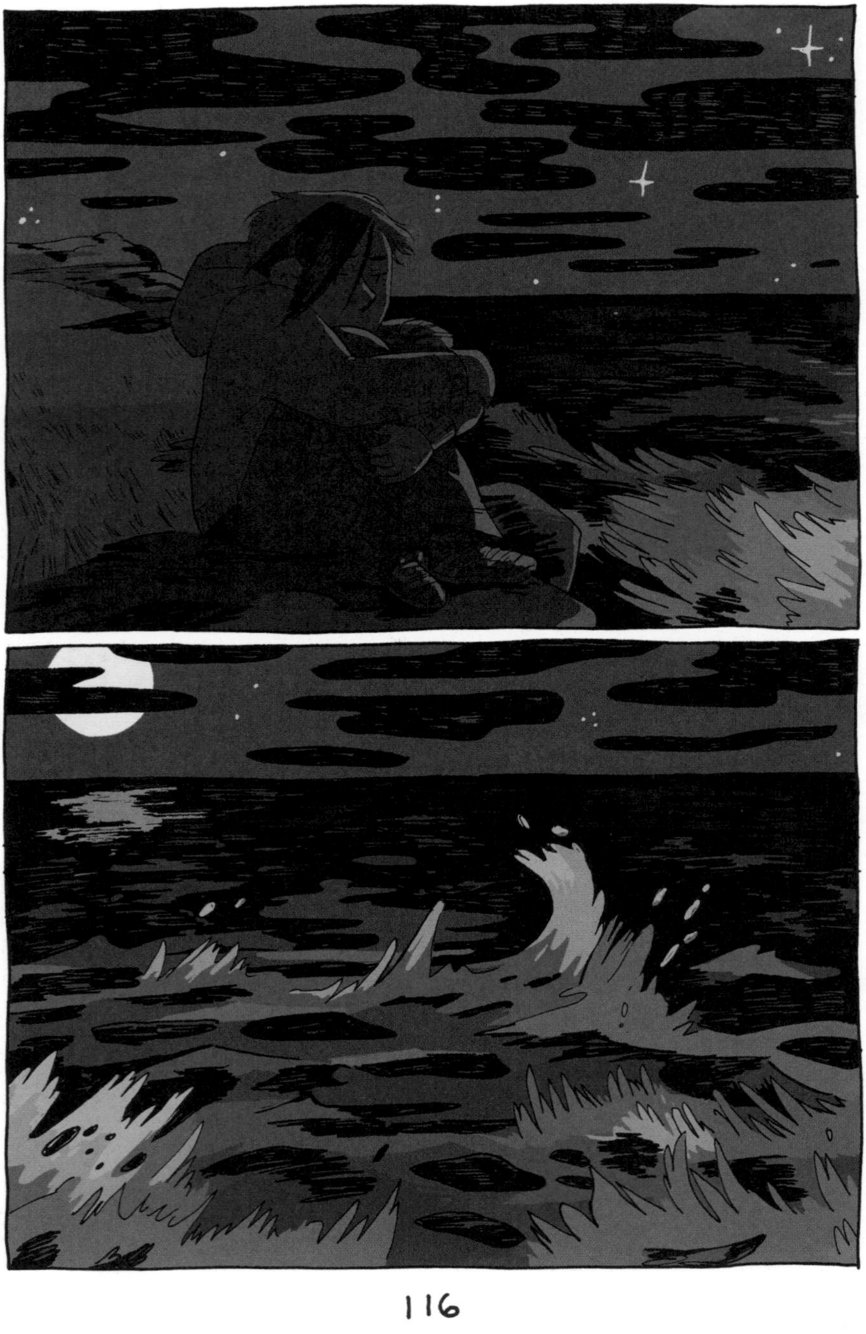

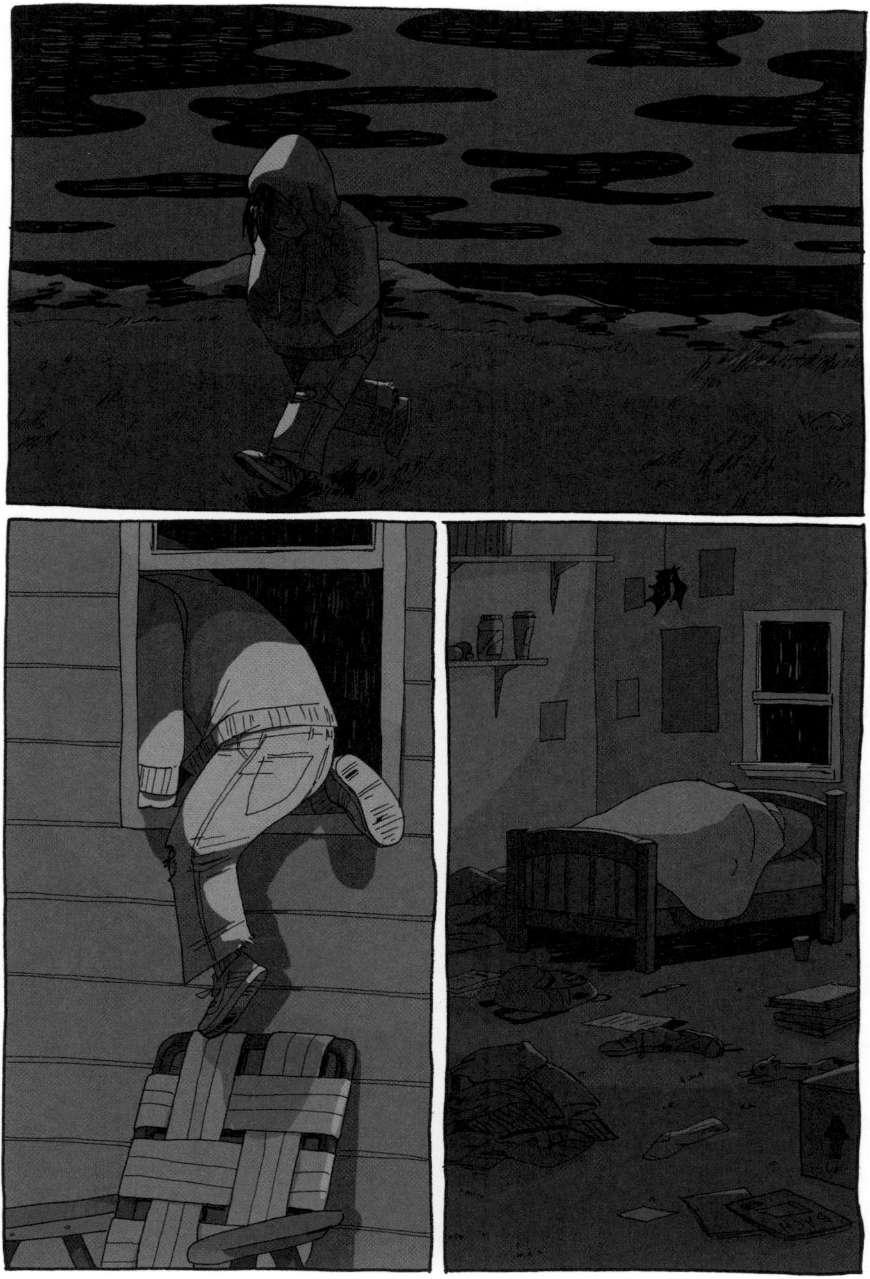

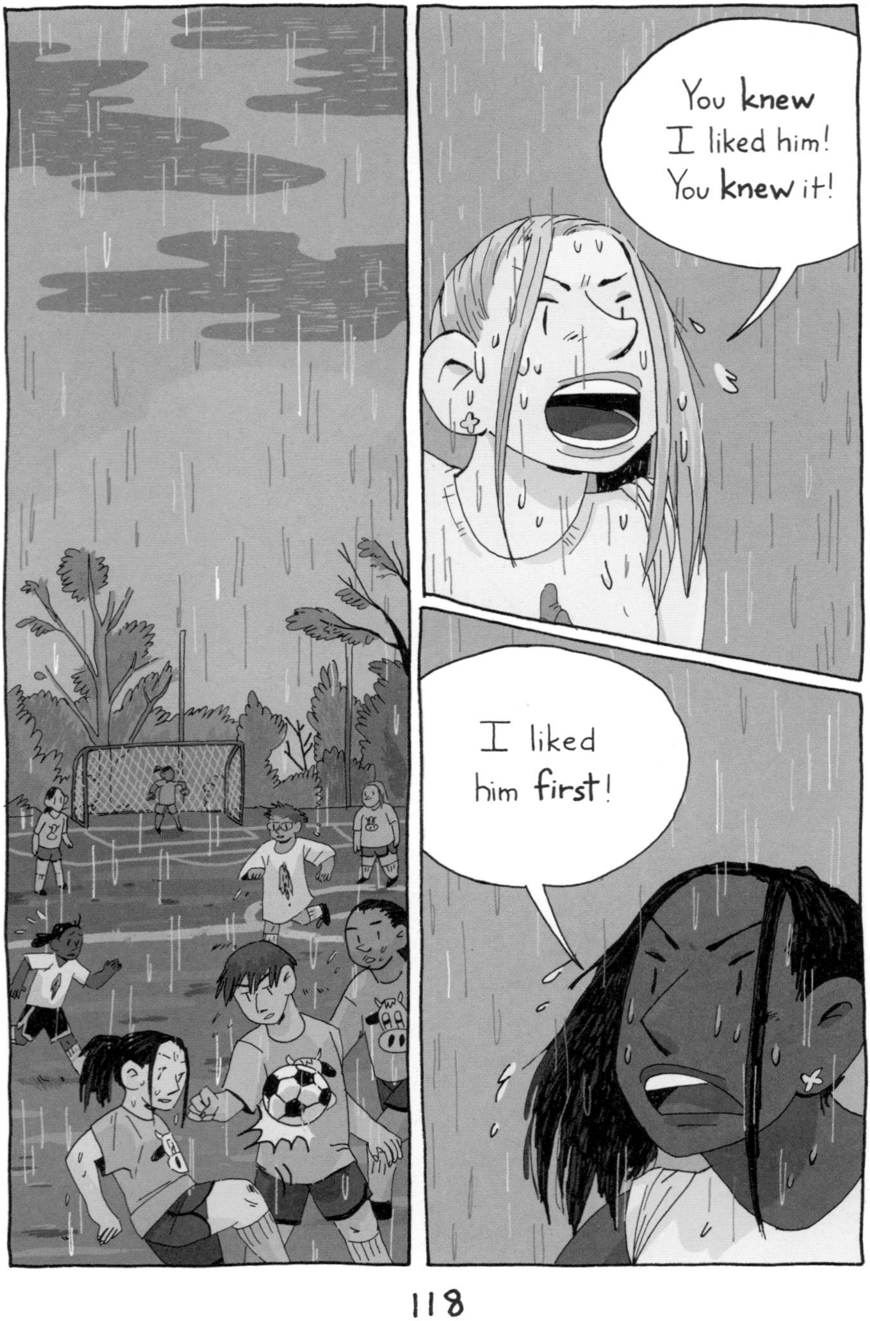
You knew I liked him! You knew it!
I liked him first!

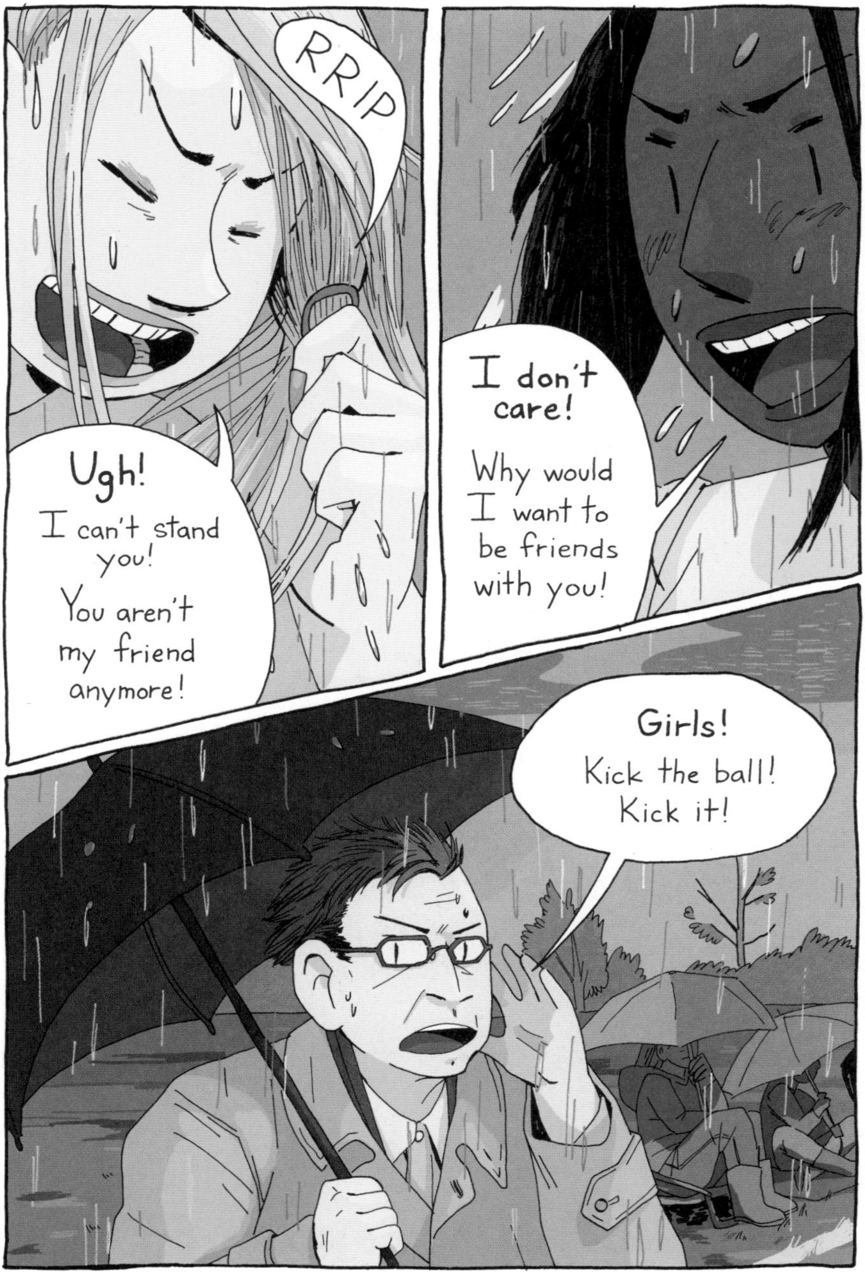
RRIP
Ugh! I can't stand you! You aren't my friend anymore!
I don't care! Why would I want to be friends with you!
Girls! Kick the ball! Kick it!

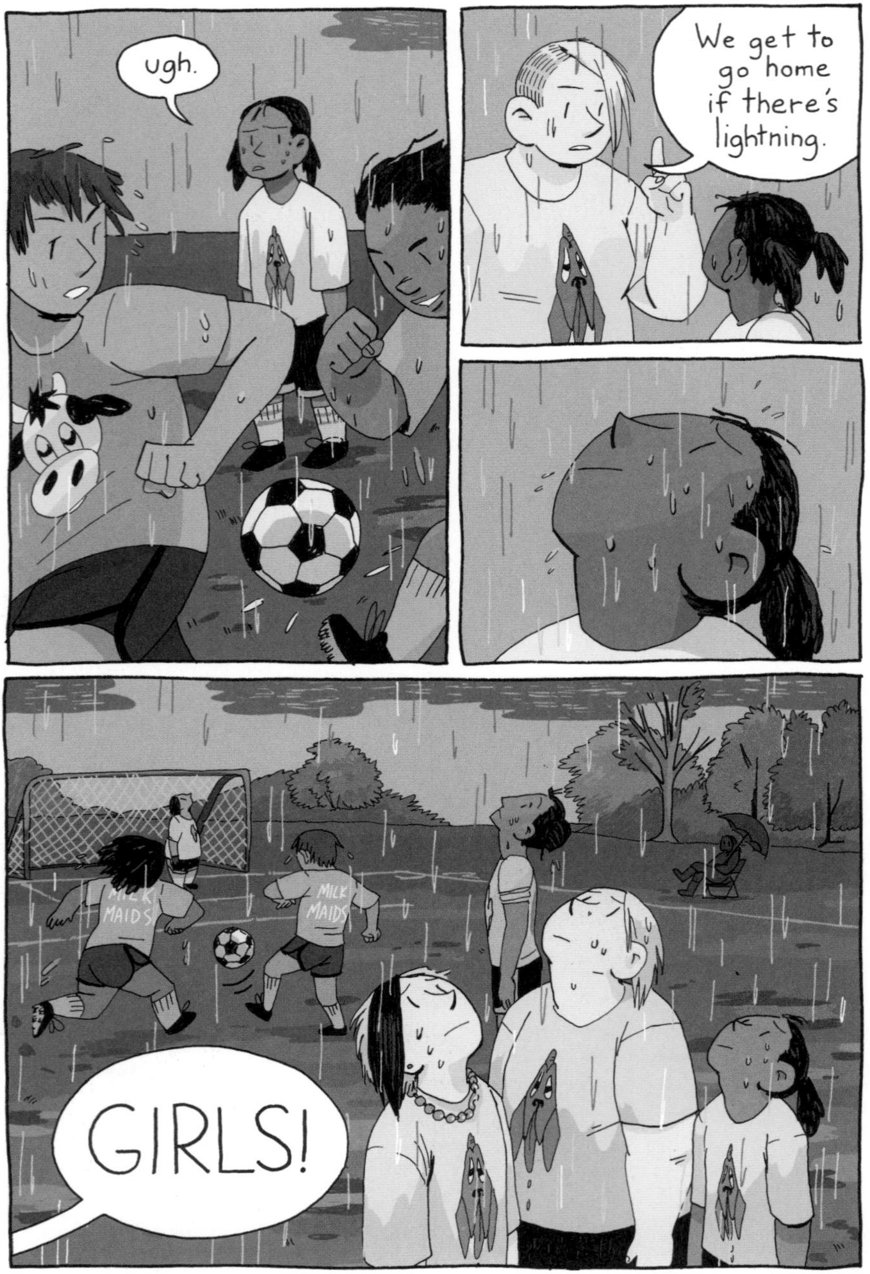

ugh.
We get to go home if there's lightning.
MILK MAIDS
MILK MAIDS
GIRLS!

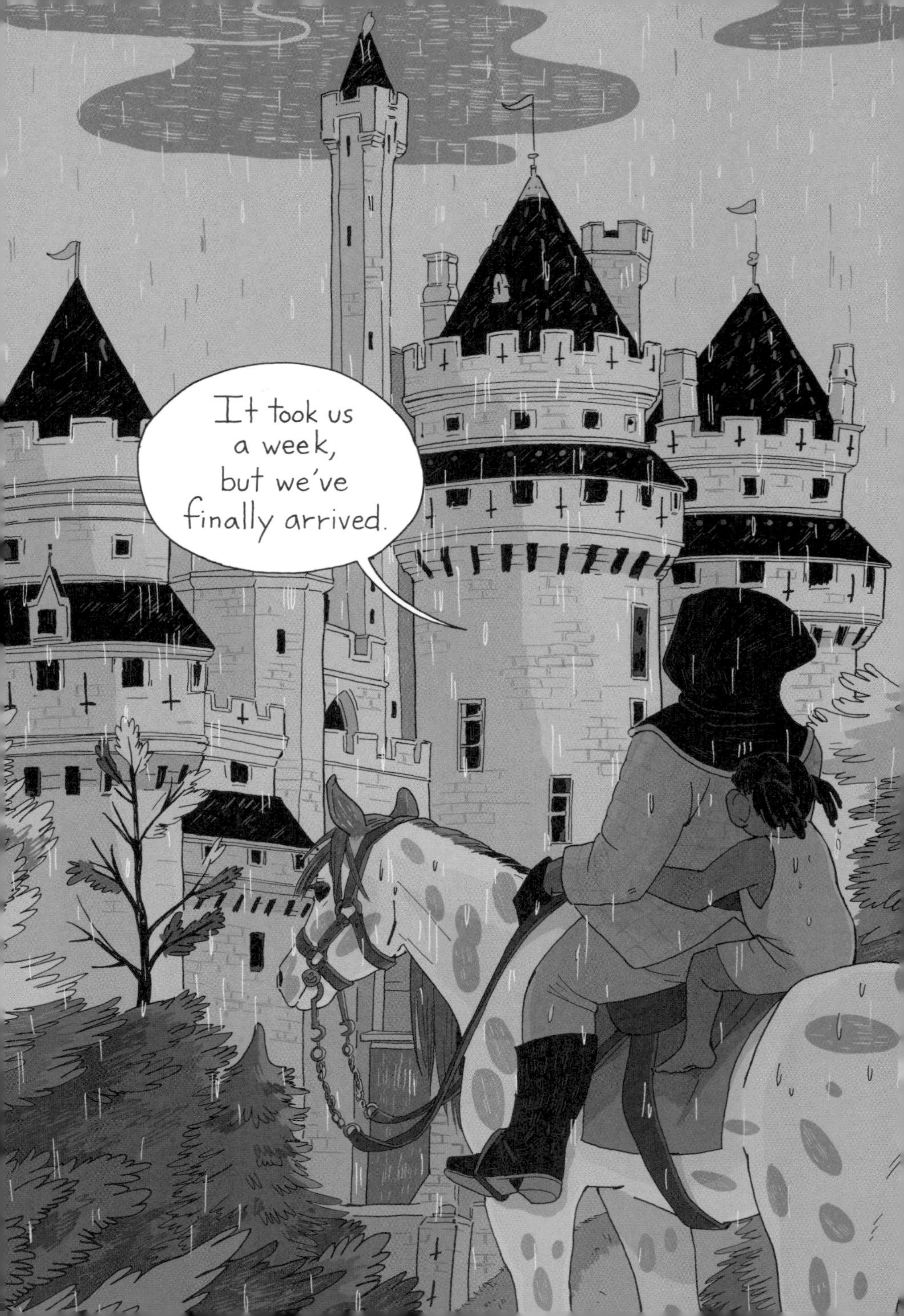
It took us a week, but we've finally arrived.

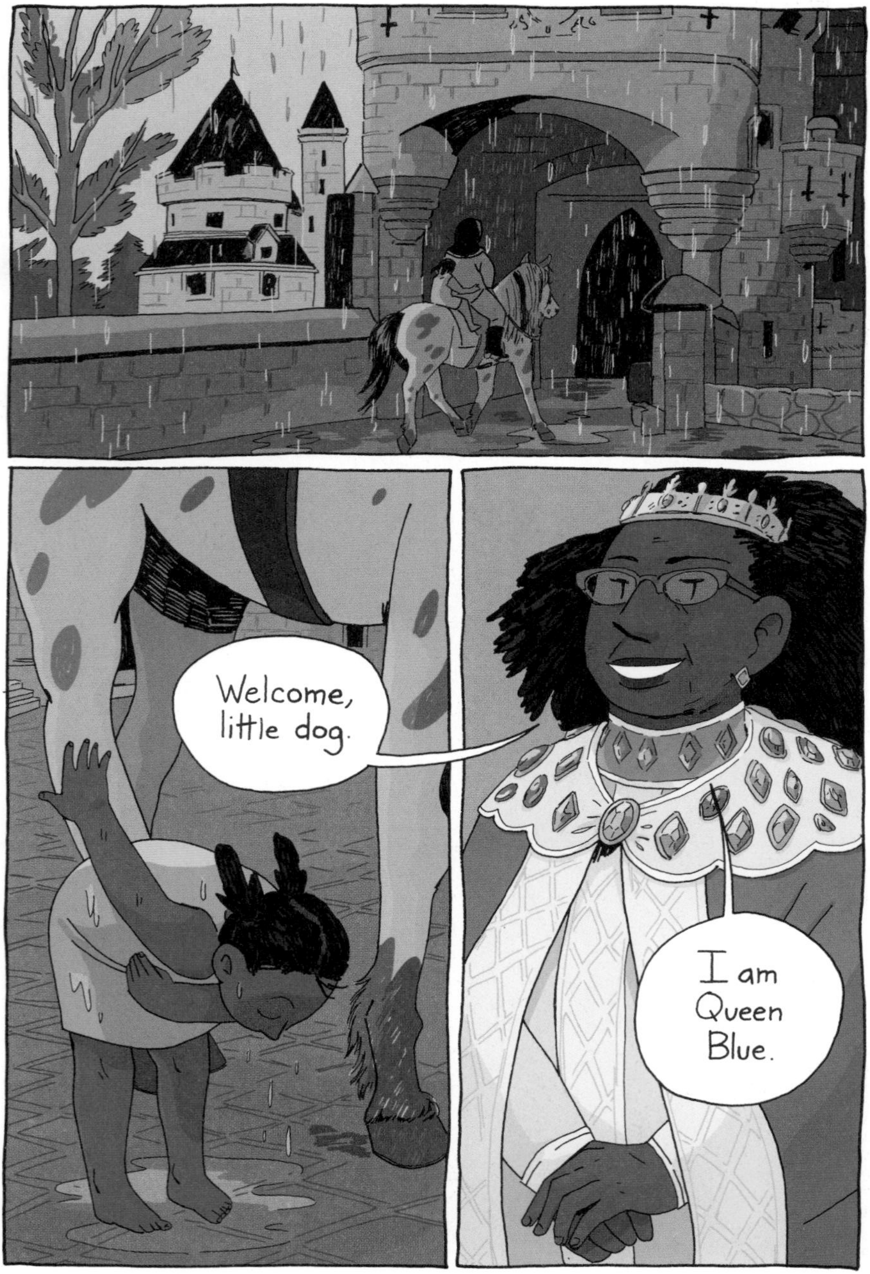
Welcome, little dog.
I am Queen Blue.

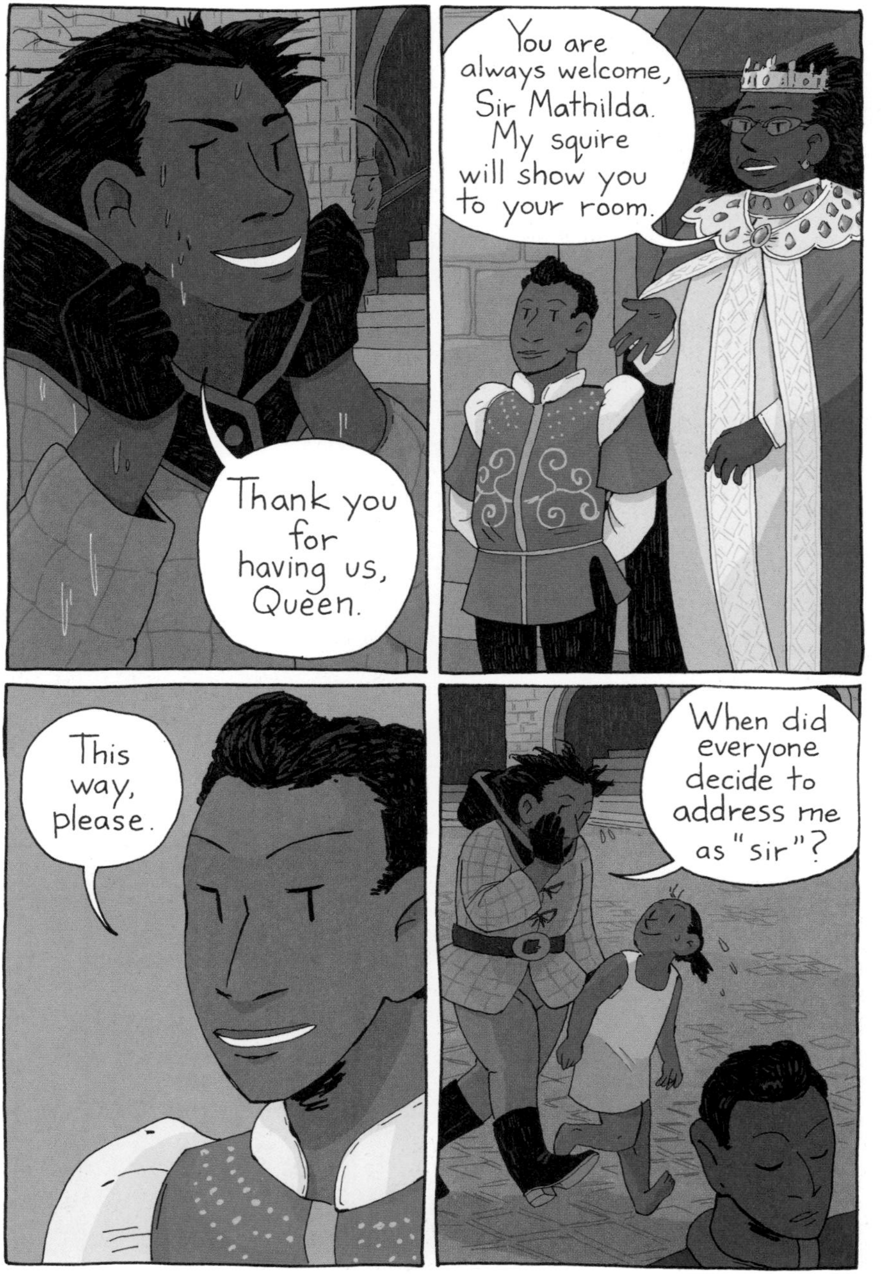
You are always welcome, Sir Mathilda. My squire will show you to your room.
Thank you for having us, Queen.
This way, please.
When did everyone decide to address me as "sir"?

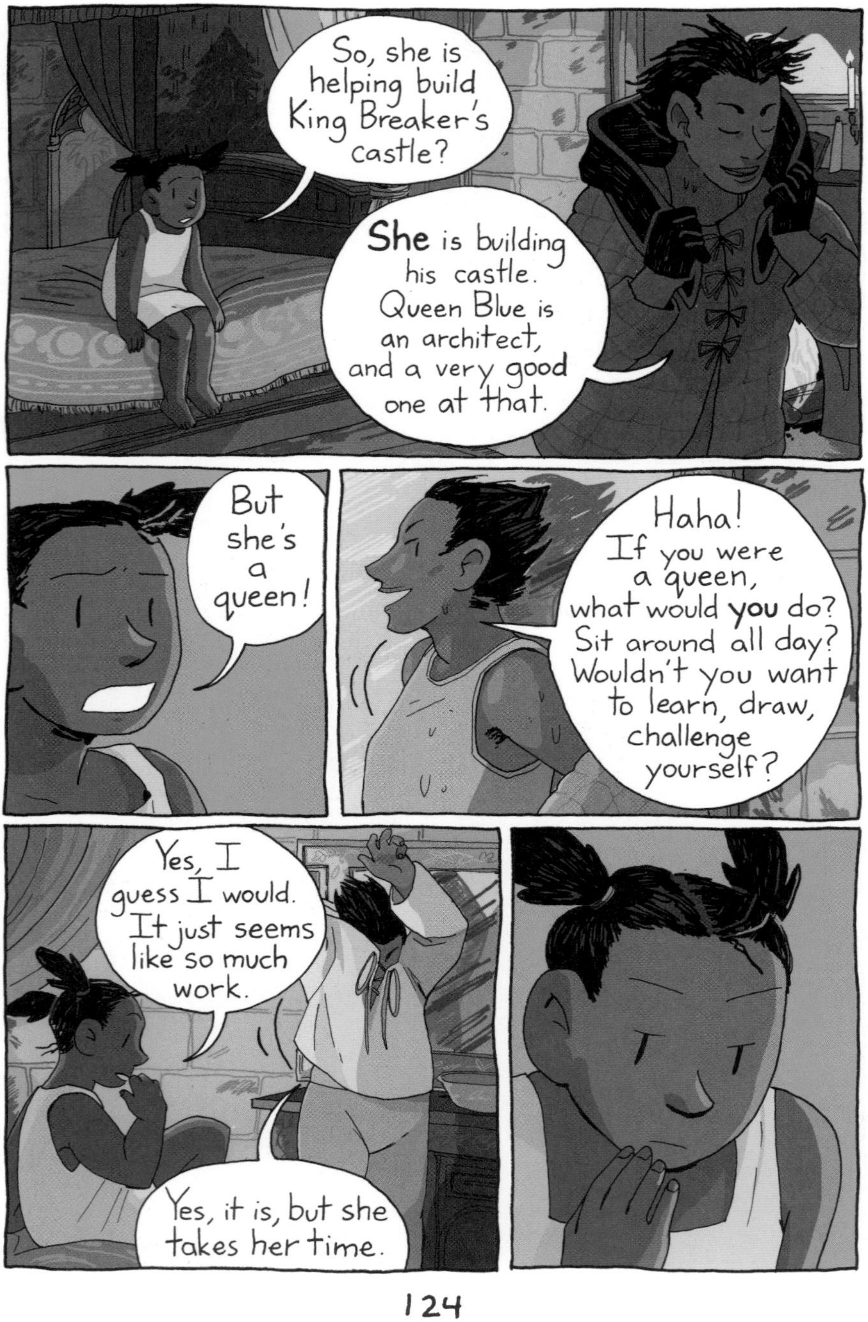
So, she is helping build King Breaker's castle?
She is building his castle. Queen Blue is an architect, and a very good one at that.
But she's a queen!
Haha! If you were a queen, what would you do? Sit around all day? Wouldn't you want to learn, draw, challenge yourself?
Yes, I guess I would. It just seems like so much work.
Yes, it is, but she takes her time.

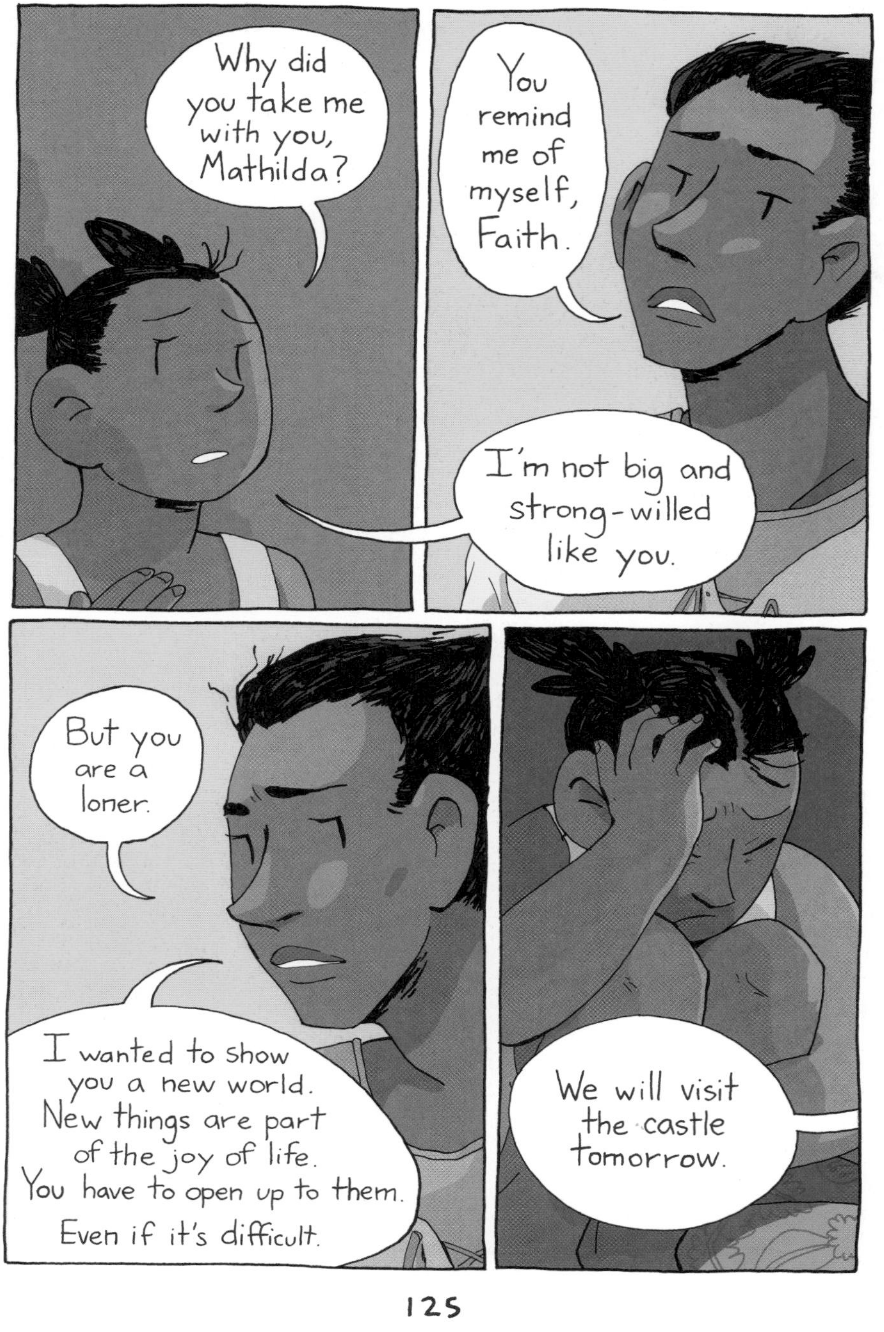
Why did you take me with you, Mathilda?
You remind me of myself, Faith.
I'm not big and strong-willed like you.
But you are a loner.
I wanted to show you a new world. New things are part of the joy of life. You have to open up to them. Even if it's difficult.
We will visit the castle tomorrow.

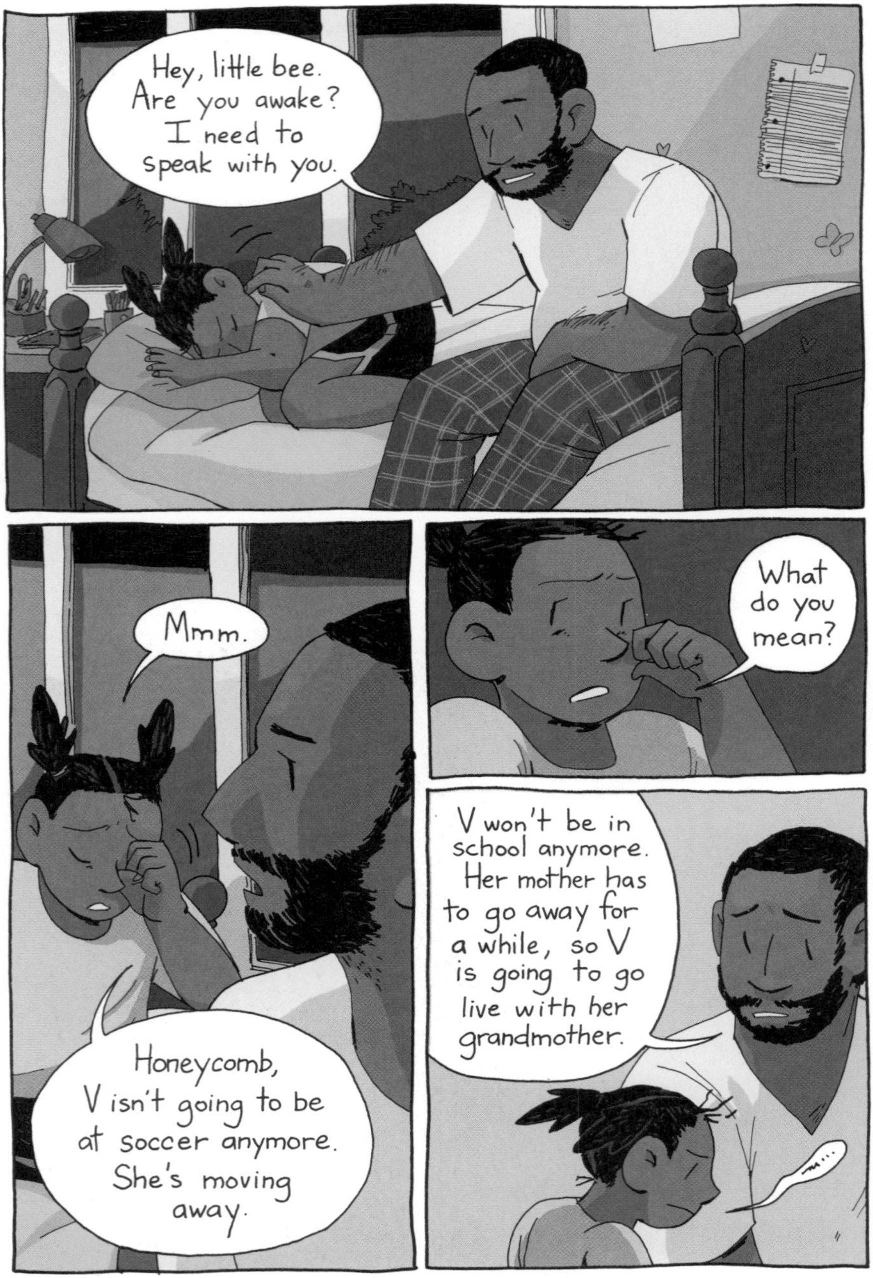
Hey, little bee. Are you awake? I need to speak with you.
Mmm.
What do you mean?
Honeycomb, V isn't going to be at soccer anymore. She's moving away.
V won't be in school anymore. Her mother has to go away for a while, so V is going to go live with her grandmother.
...

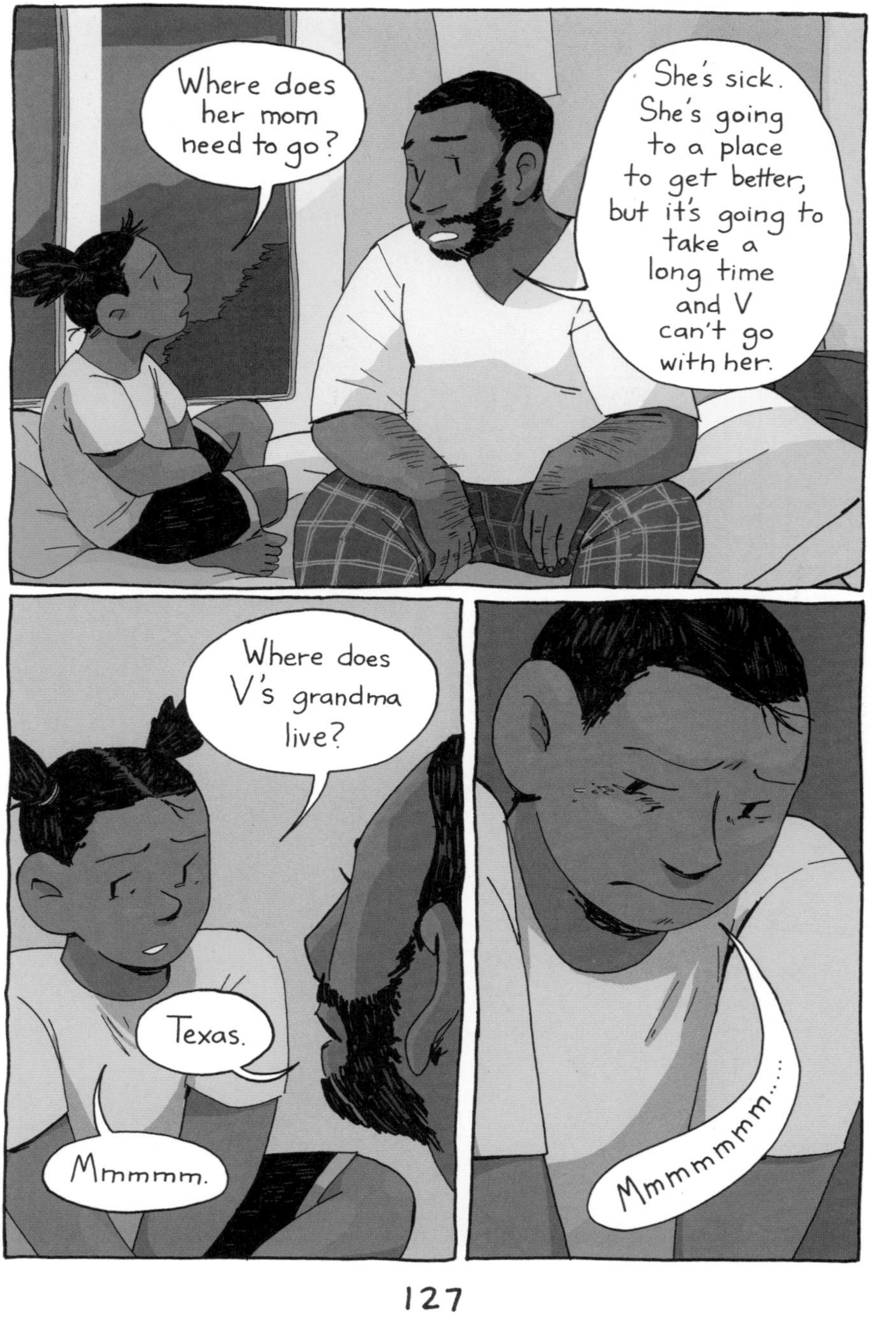
Where does her mom need to go?
She's sick. She's going to a place to get better, but it's going to take a long time and V can't go with her.
Where does V's grandma live?
Texas.
Mmmmm.
Mmmmmm.....

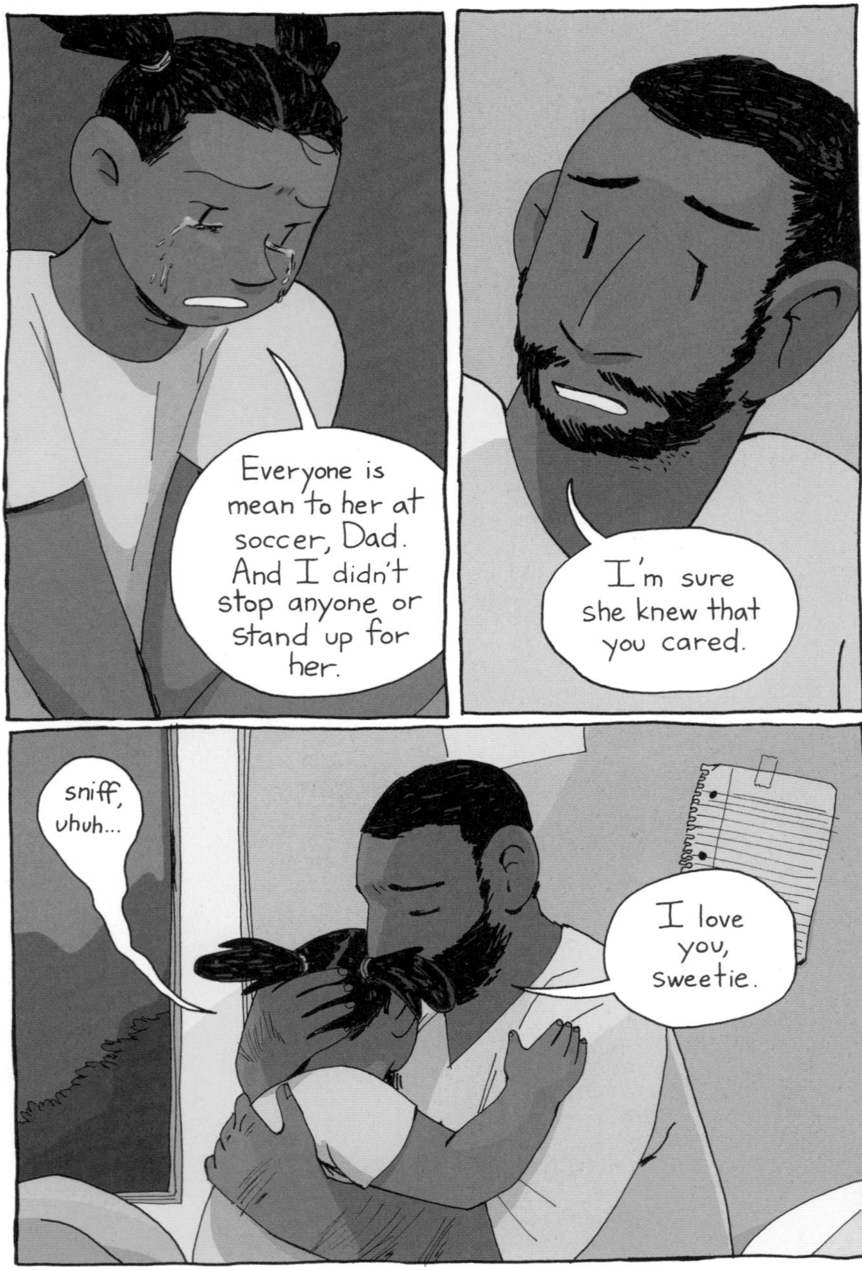
Everyone is mean to her at soccer, Dad. And I didn't stop anyone or stand up for her.
I'm sure she knew that you cared.
sniff, uhuh...
I love you, sweetie.

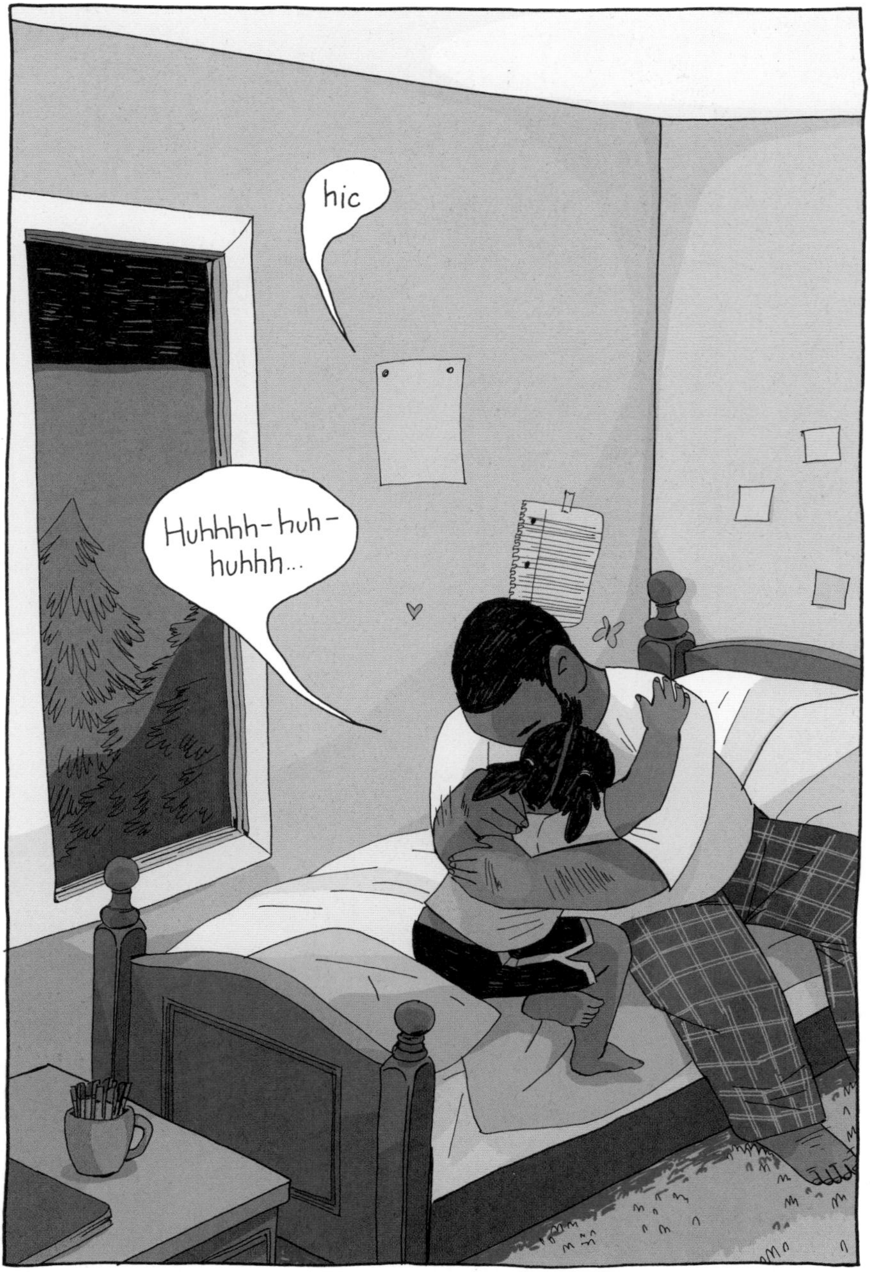
hic
Huhhhh-huh-huhhh...

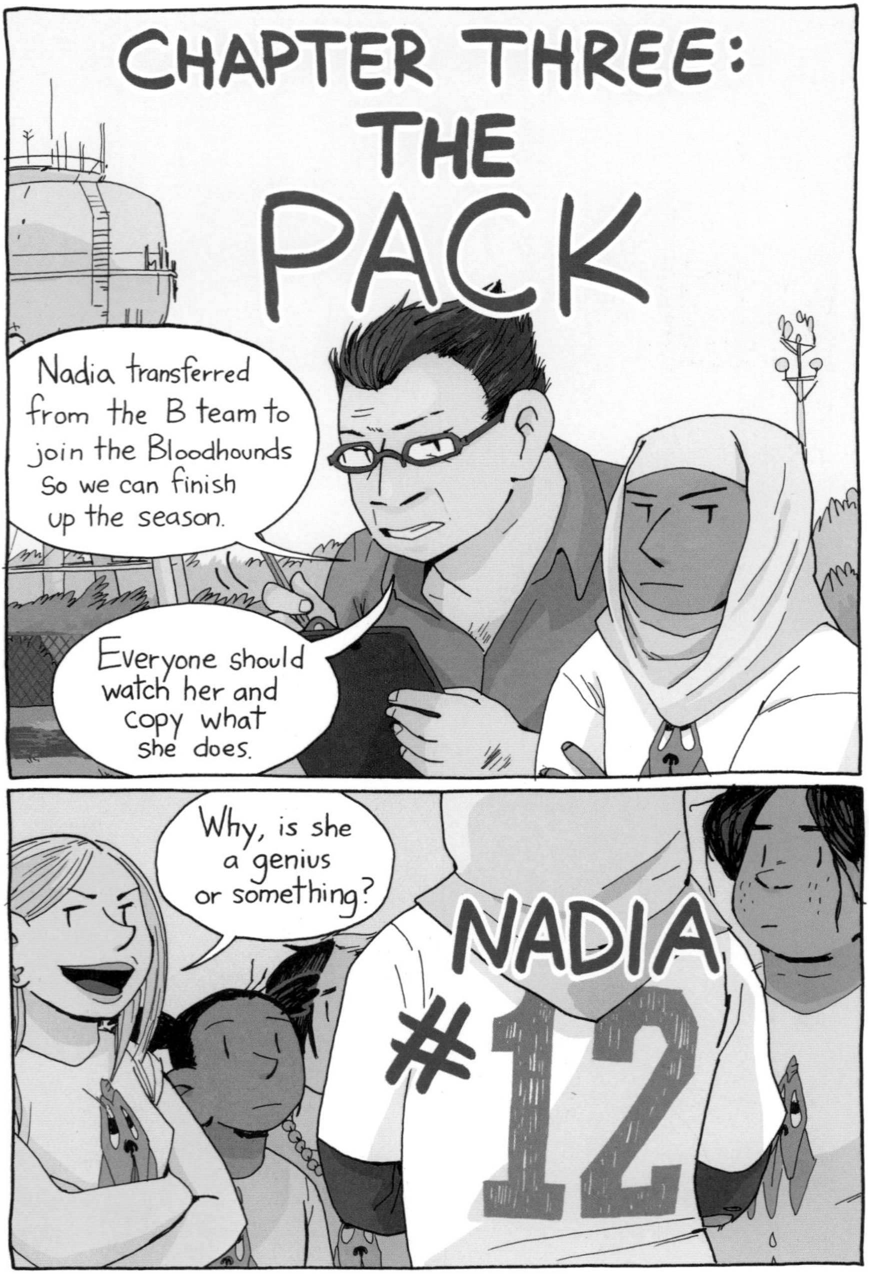
CHAPTER THREE: THE PACK
Nadia transferred from the B team to join the Bloodhounds so we can finish up the season.
Everyone should watch her and copy what she does.
Why, is she a genius or something?
NADIA #12

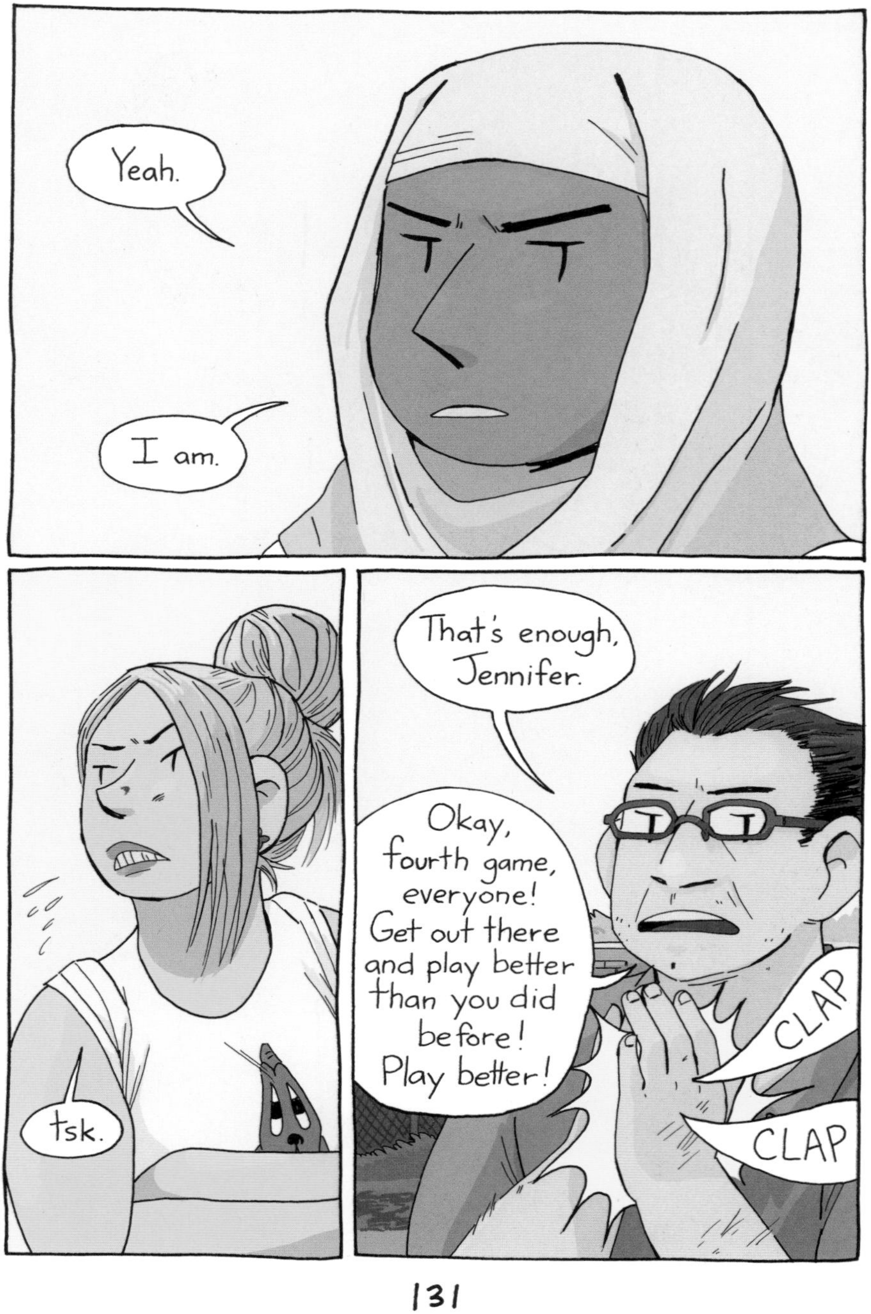

Yeah.
I am.
tsk.
That's enough, Jennifer.
Okay, fourth game, everyone! Get out there and play better than you did before! Play better!
CLAP
CLAP

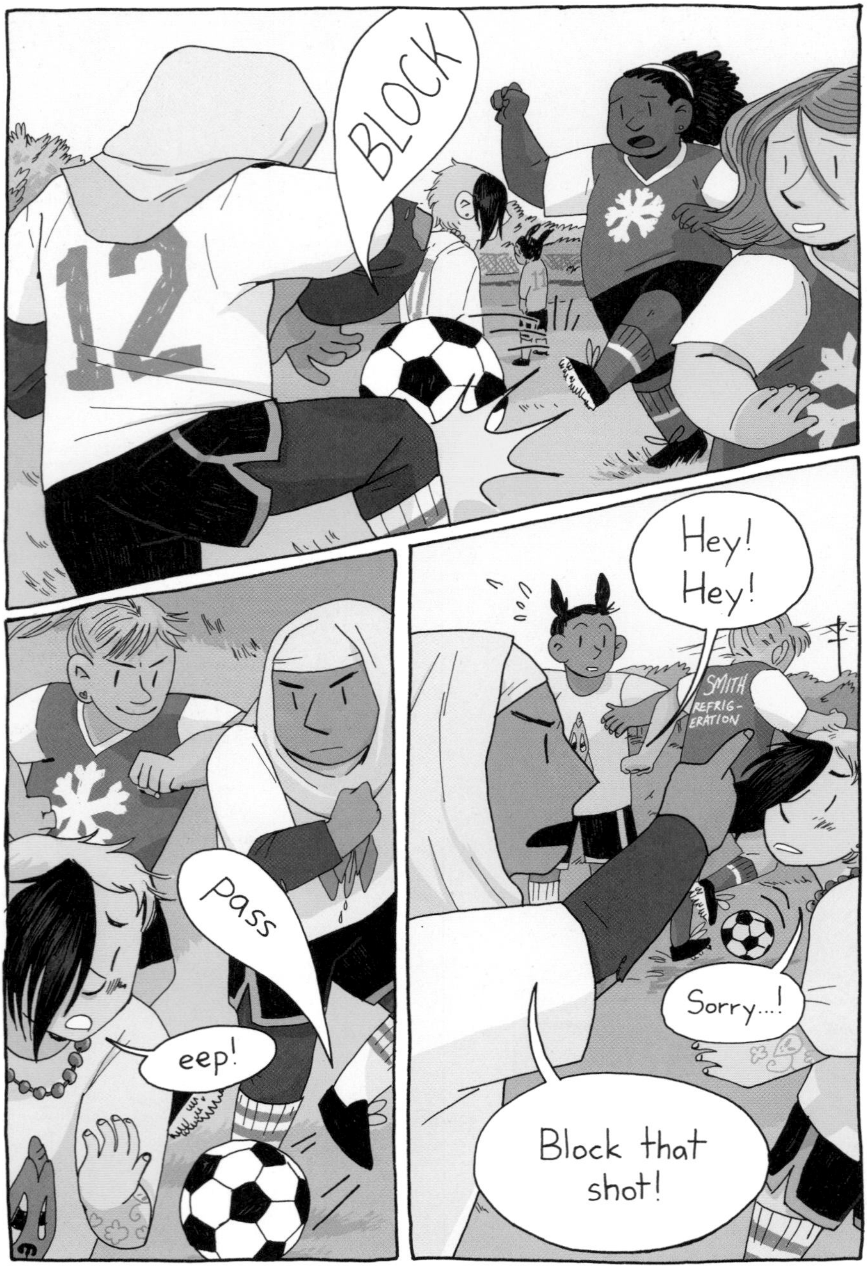
BLOCK
12
pass
eep!
Hey!
Hey!
SMITH
REFRIG-
ERATION
Sorry...!
Block that shot!

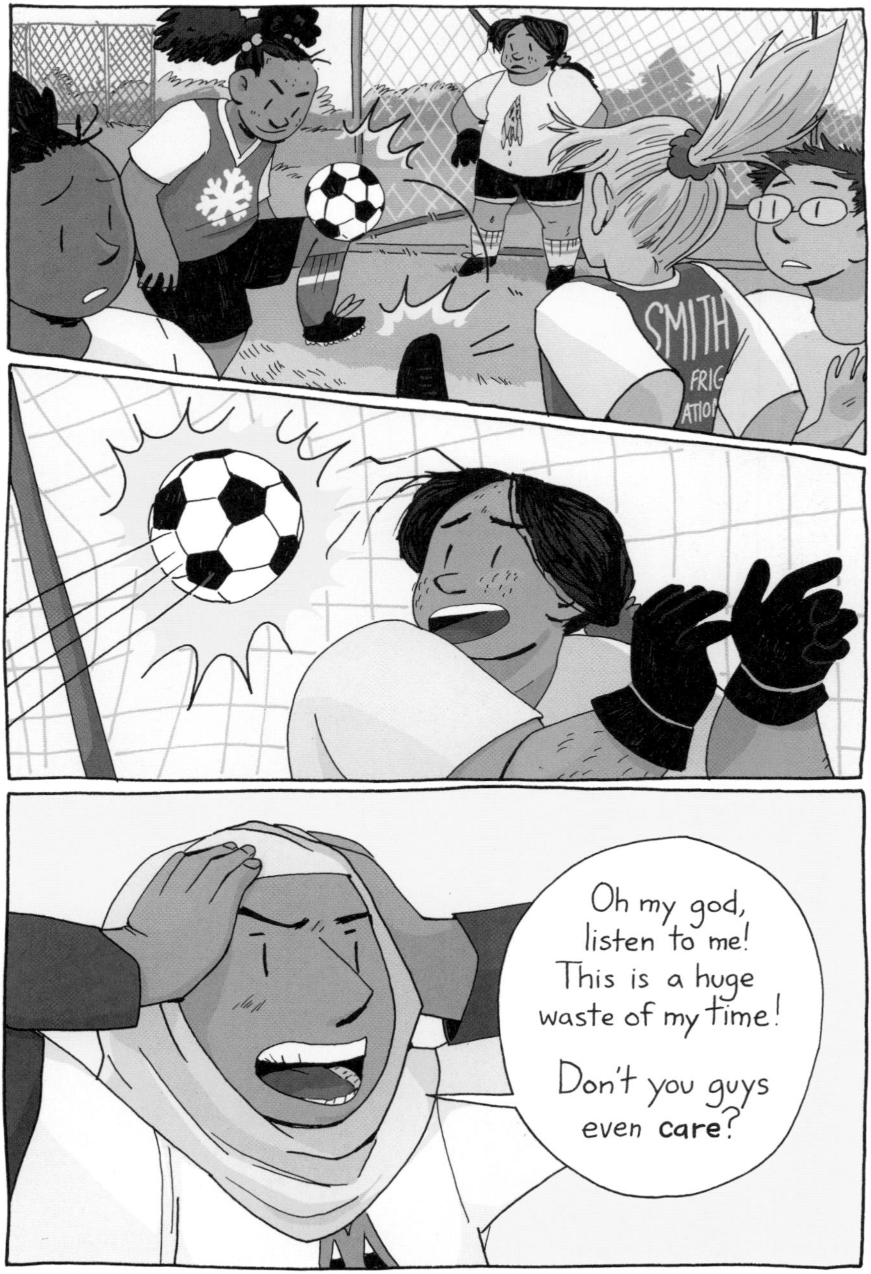
SMITH
FRIG-
ATIO
Oh my god, listen to me! This is a huge waste of my time!
Don't you guys even **care**?

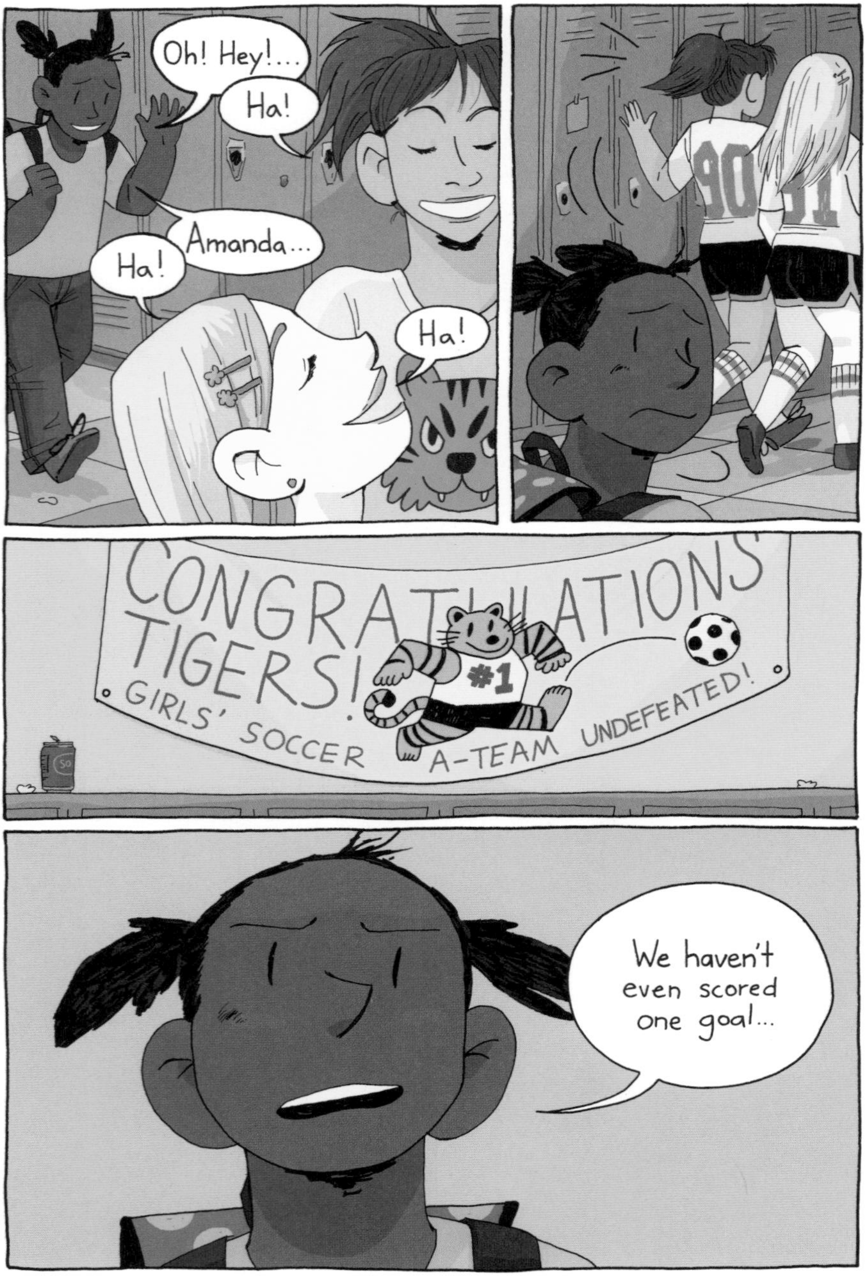
Oh! Hey!...
Ha!
Amanda...
Ha!
Ha!
CONGRATULATIONS TIGERS!
GIRLS' SOCCER A-TEAM UNDEFEATED!
#1
We haven't even scored one goal...

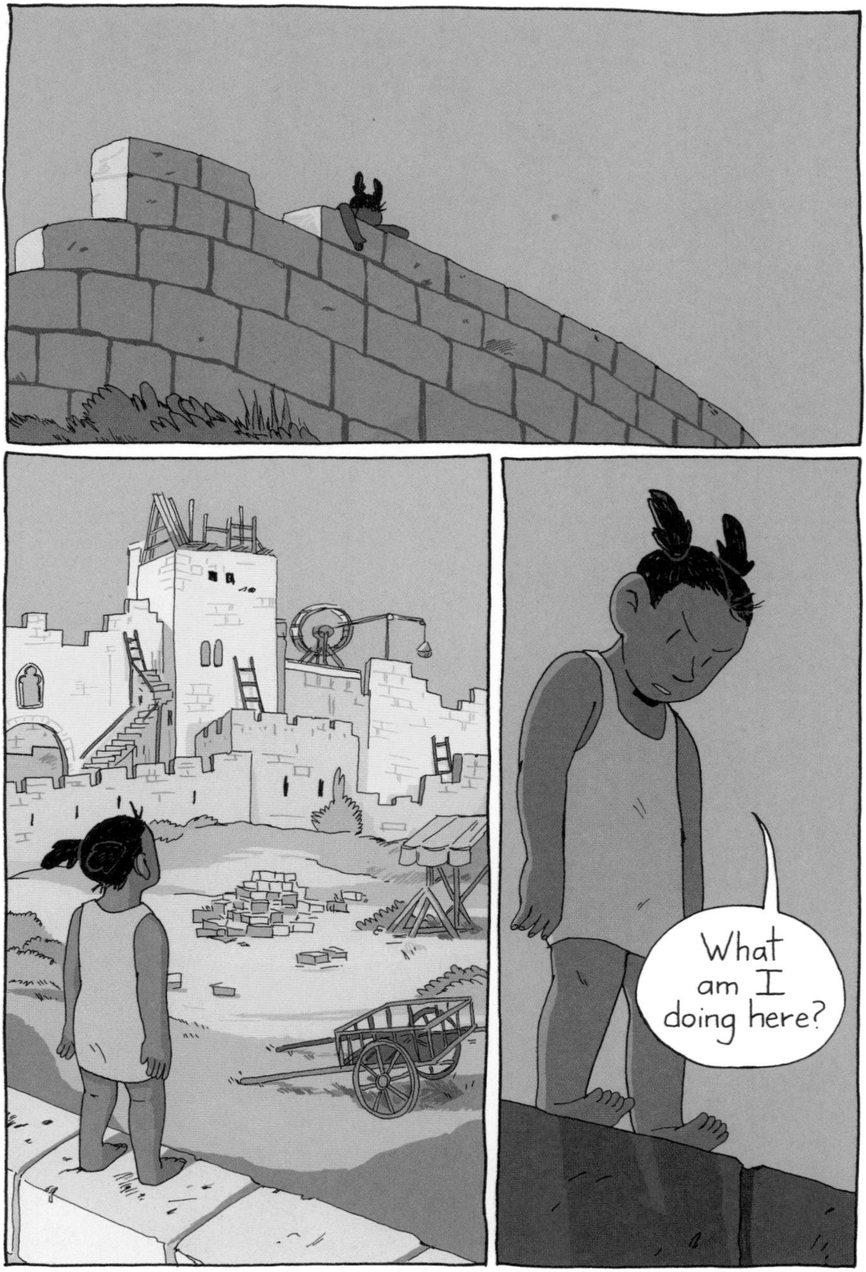
What am I doing here?

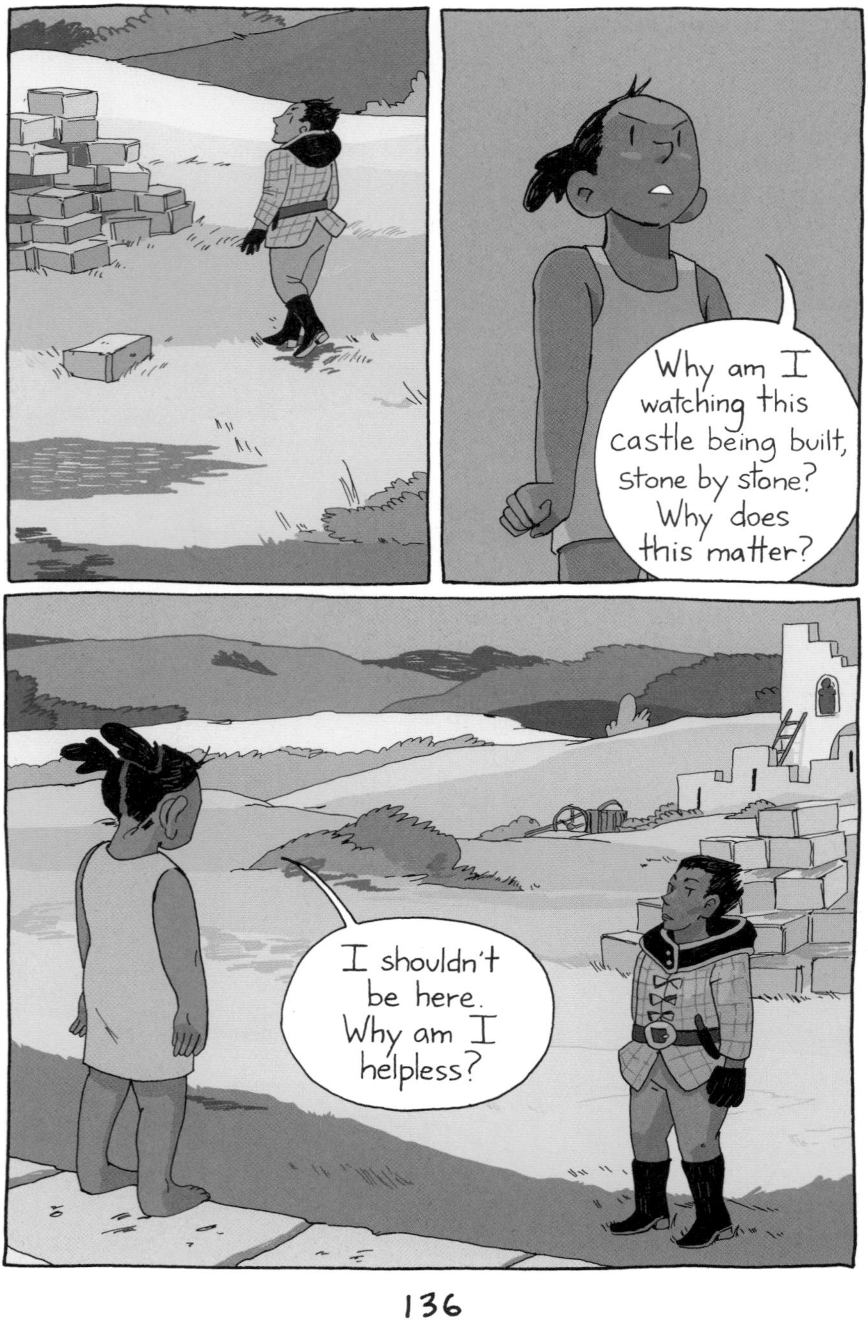
Why am I watching this castle being built, stone by stone? Why does this matter?
I shouldn't be here. Why am I helpless?

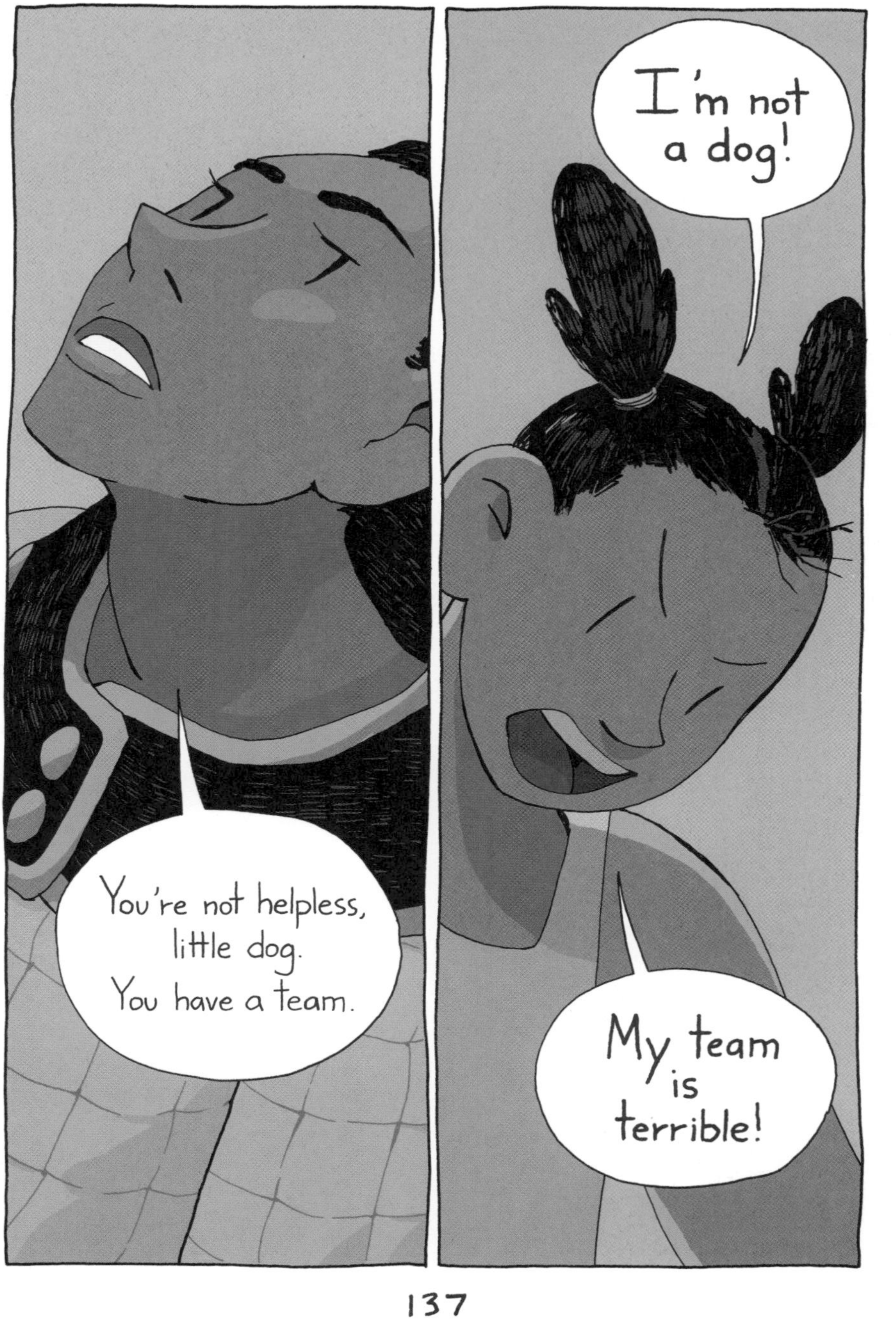
You're not helpless, little dog. You have a team.
I'm not a dog!
My team is terrible!

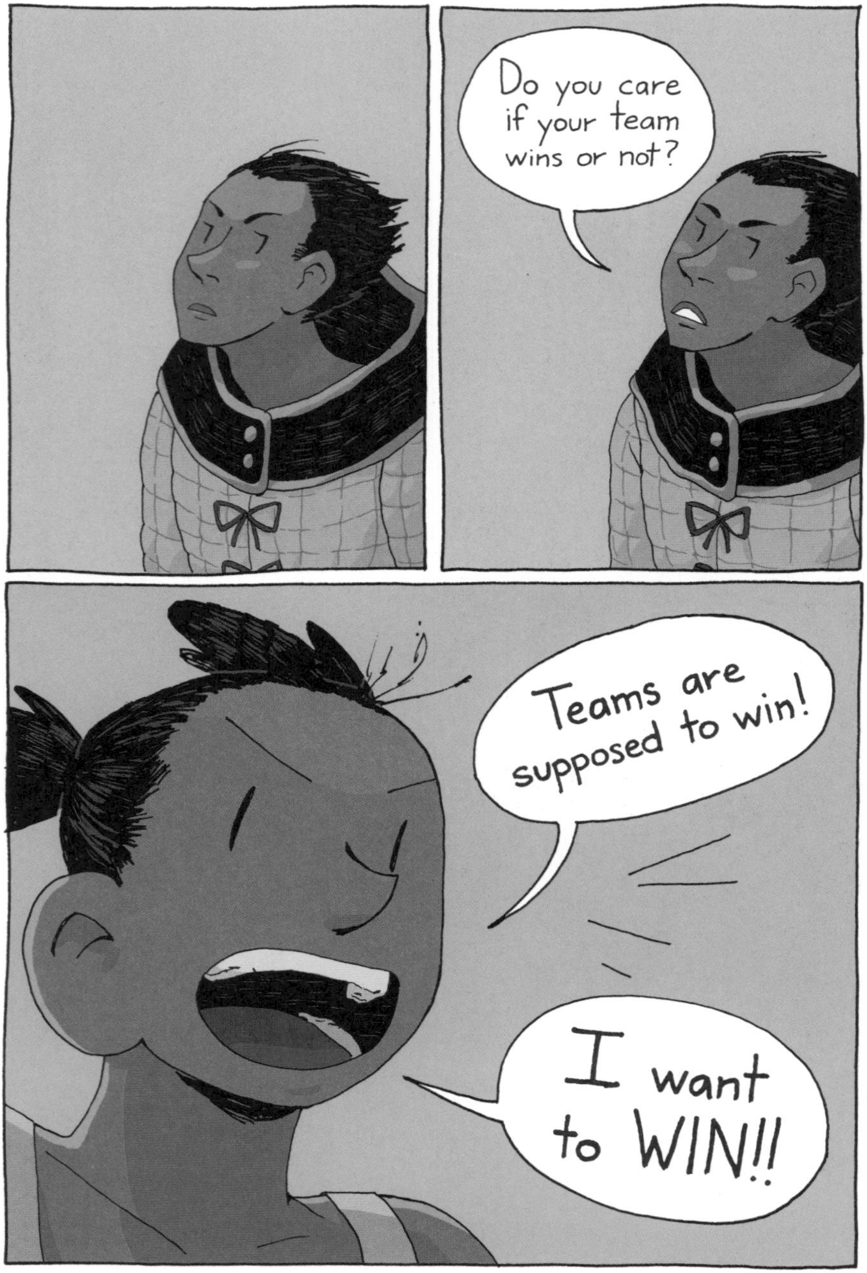
Do you care if your team wins or not?
Teams are supposed to win!
I want to WIN!!

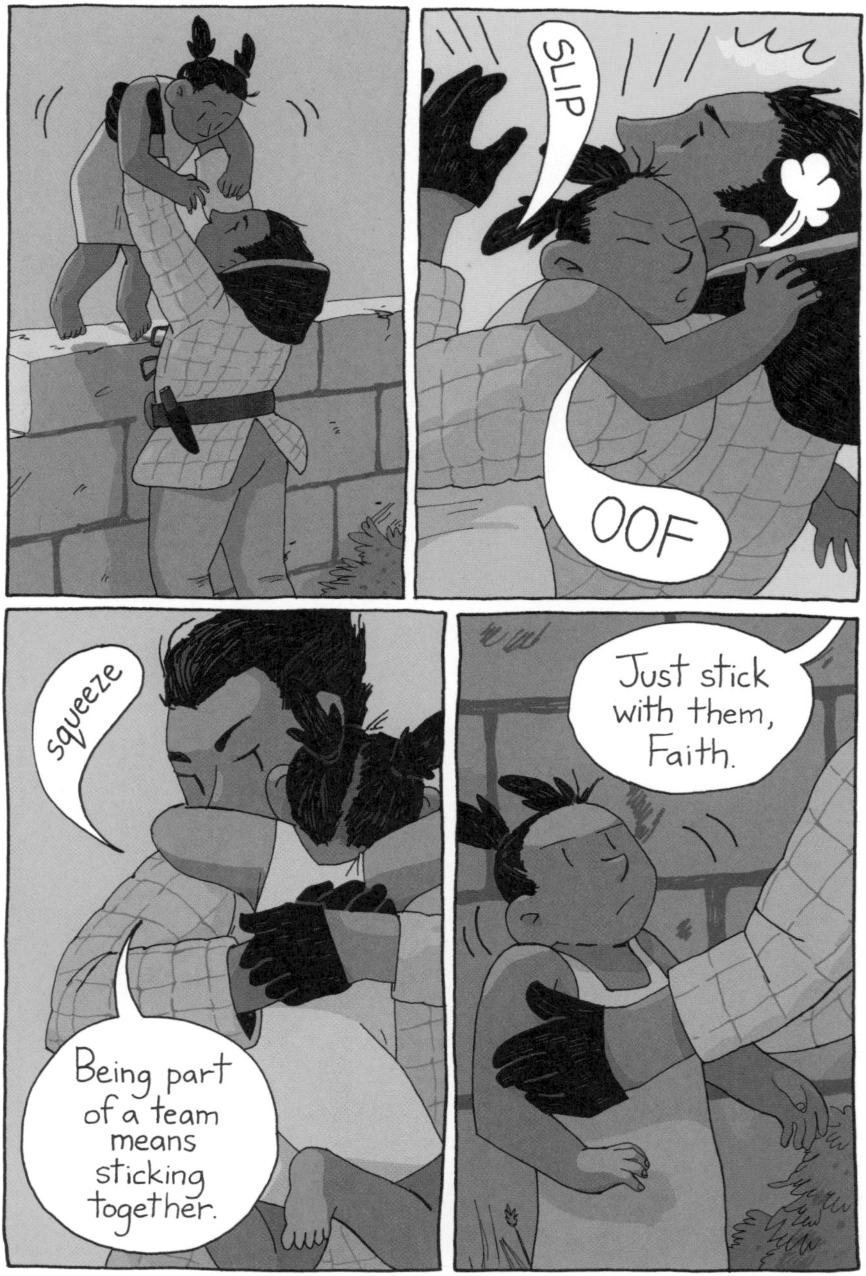
SLIP
OOF
squeeze
Being part of a team means sticking together.
Just stick with them, Faith.

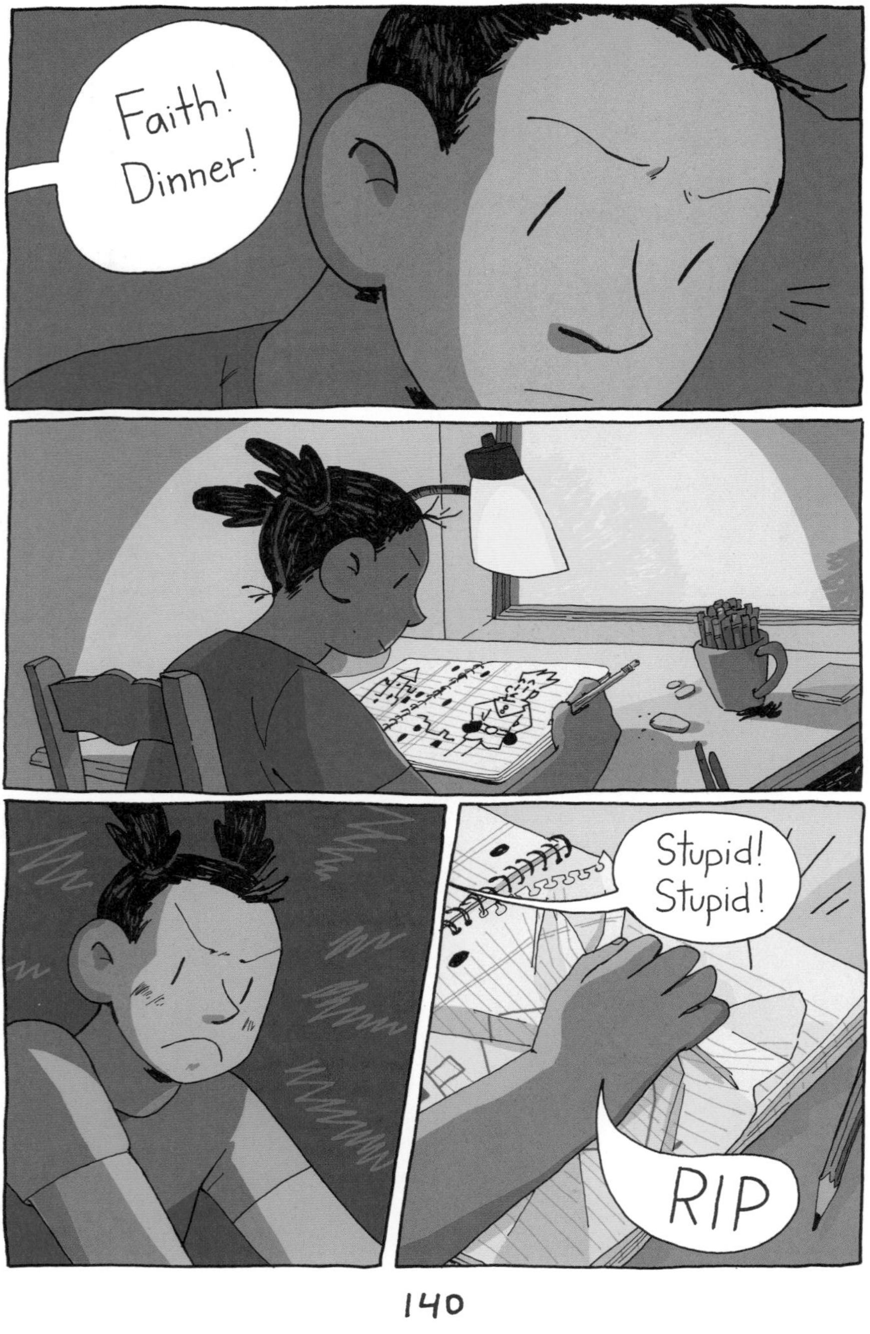
Faith! Dinner!
Stupid! Stupid!
RIP

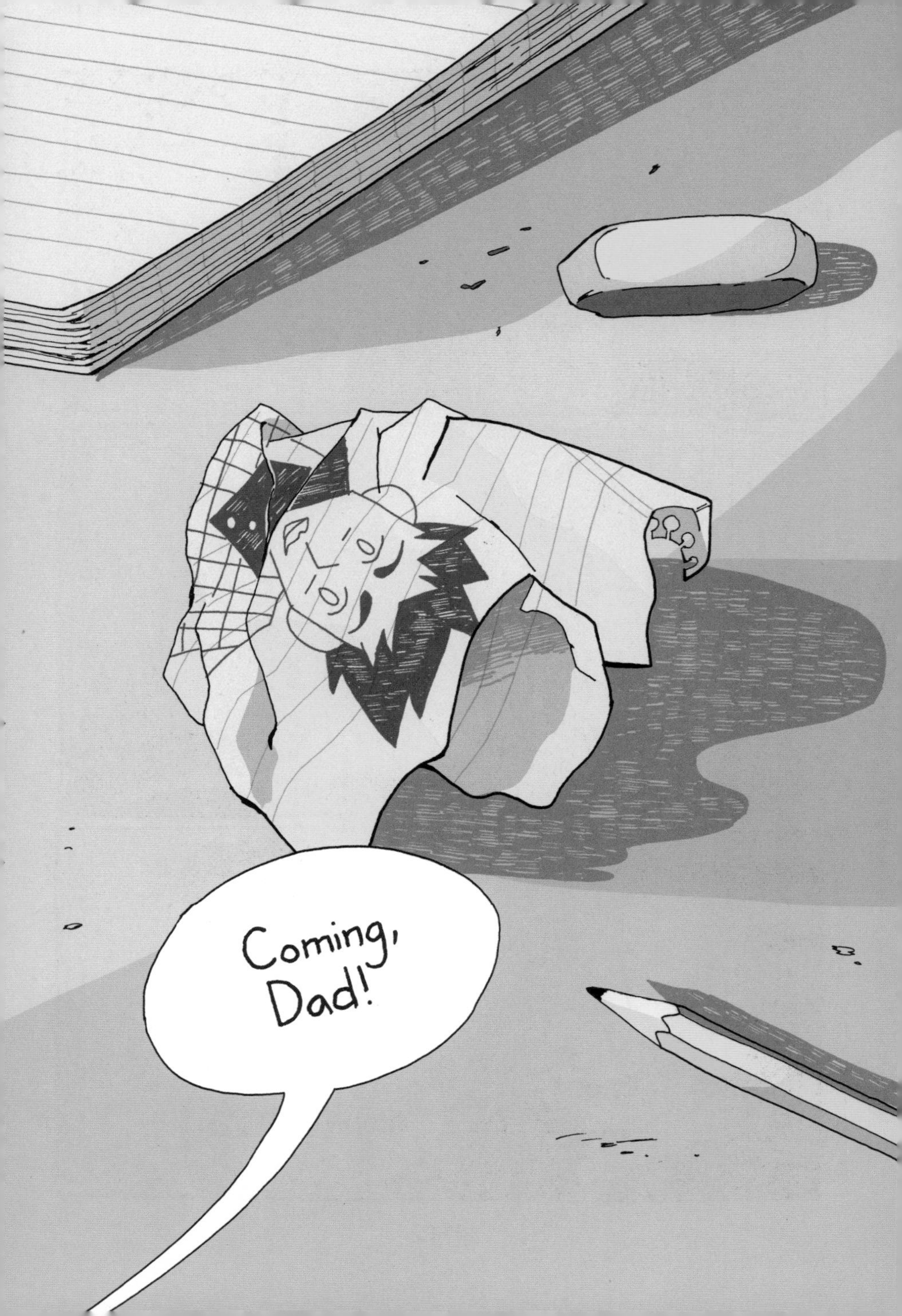
Coming, Dad!

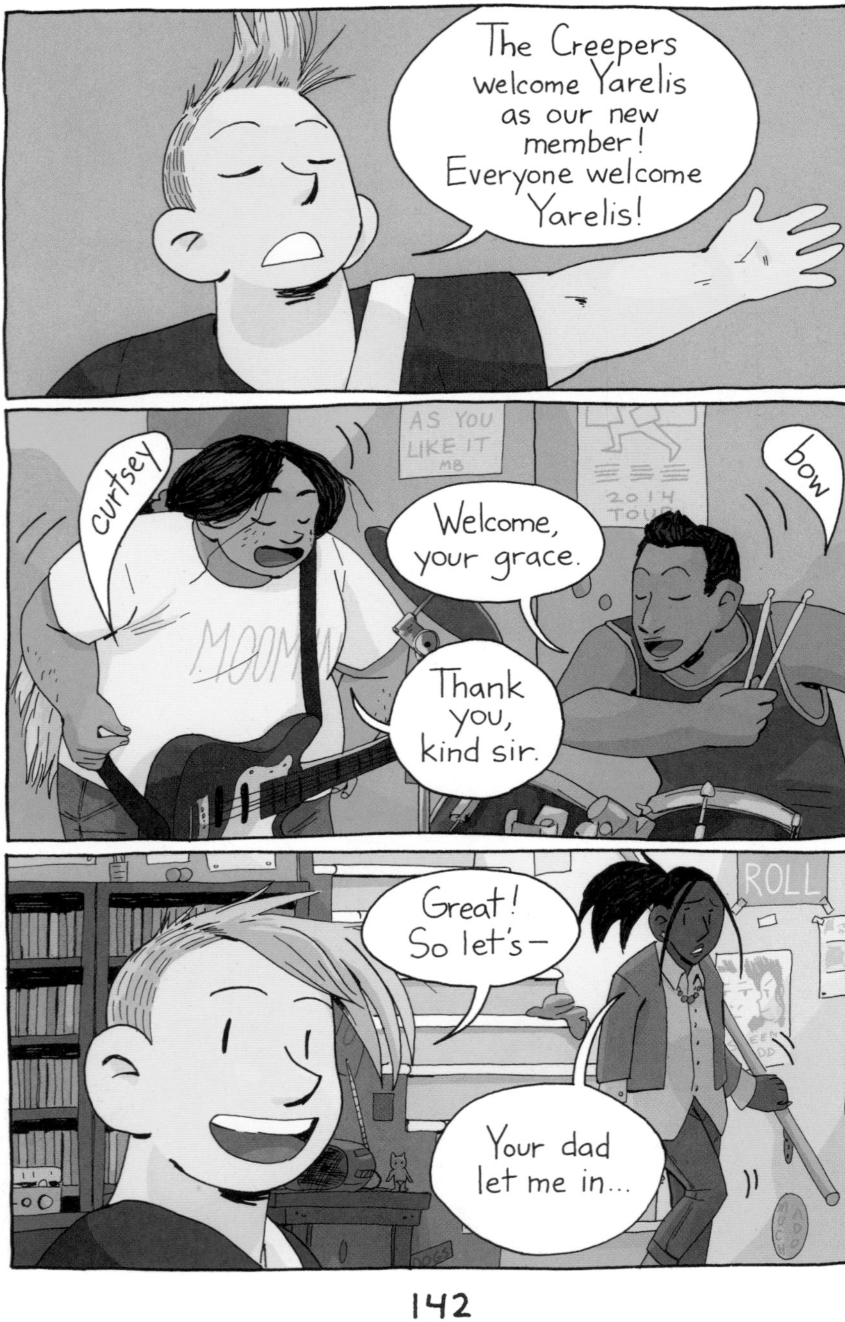
The Creepers welcome Yarelis as our new member! Everyone welcome Yarelis!
AS YOU LIKE IT MB
2014 TOUR
curtsey
bow
Welcome, your grace.
MOOMIN
Thank you, kind sir.
ROLL
Great! So let's–
Your dad let me in...

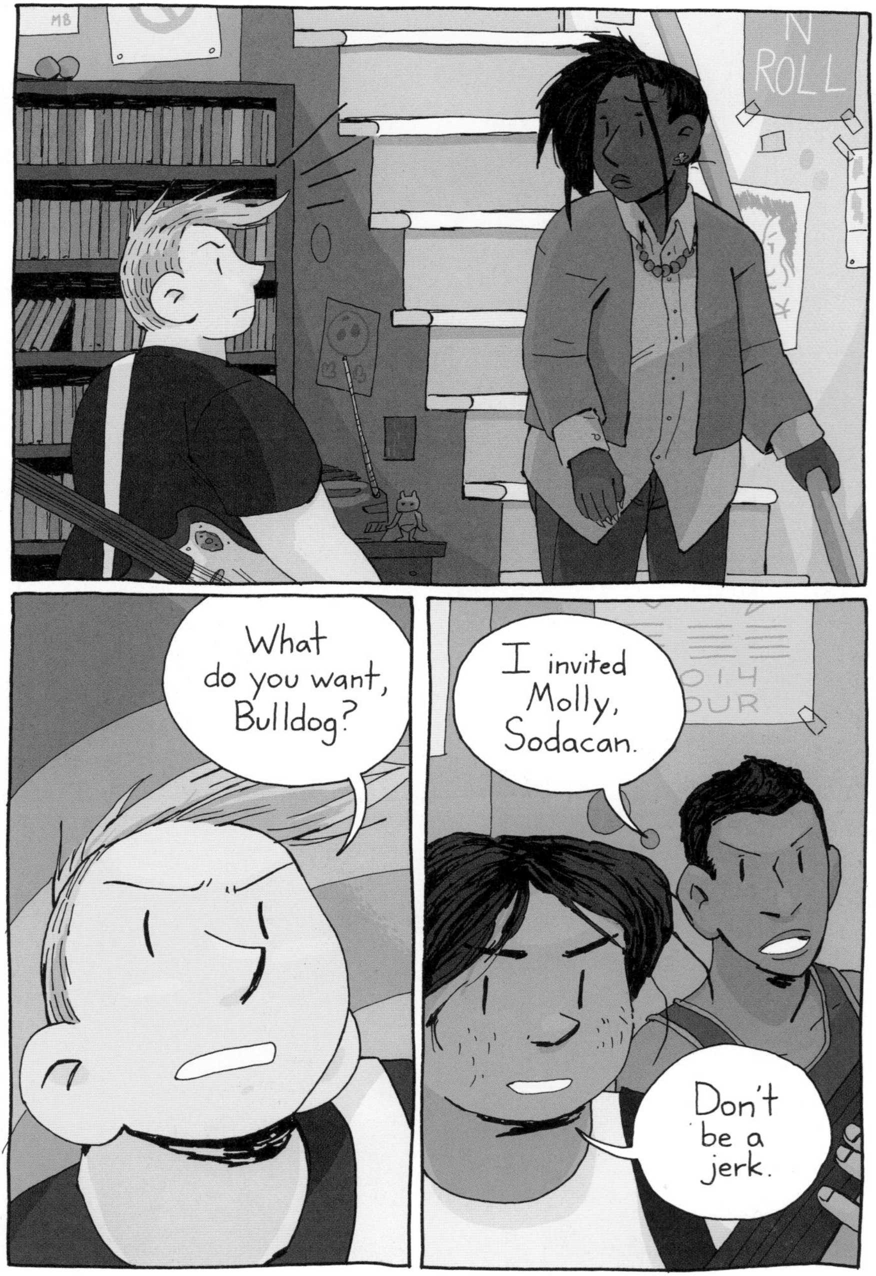
N ROLL
What do you want, Bulldog?
I invited Molly, Sodacan.
Don't be a jerk.

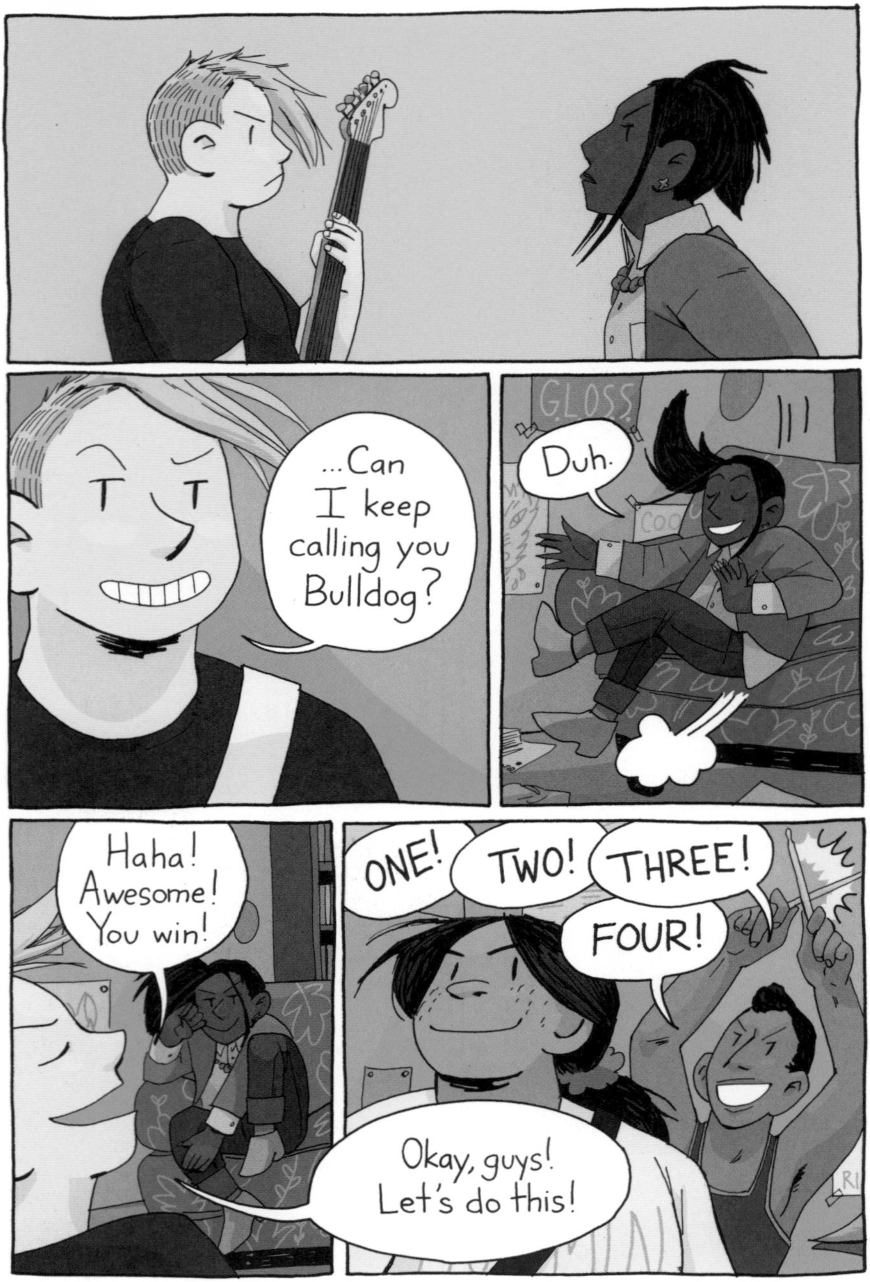
...Can I keep calling you Bulldog?
Duh.
Haha! Awesome! You win!
ONE!
TWO!
THREE!
FOUR!
Okay, guys! Let's do this!

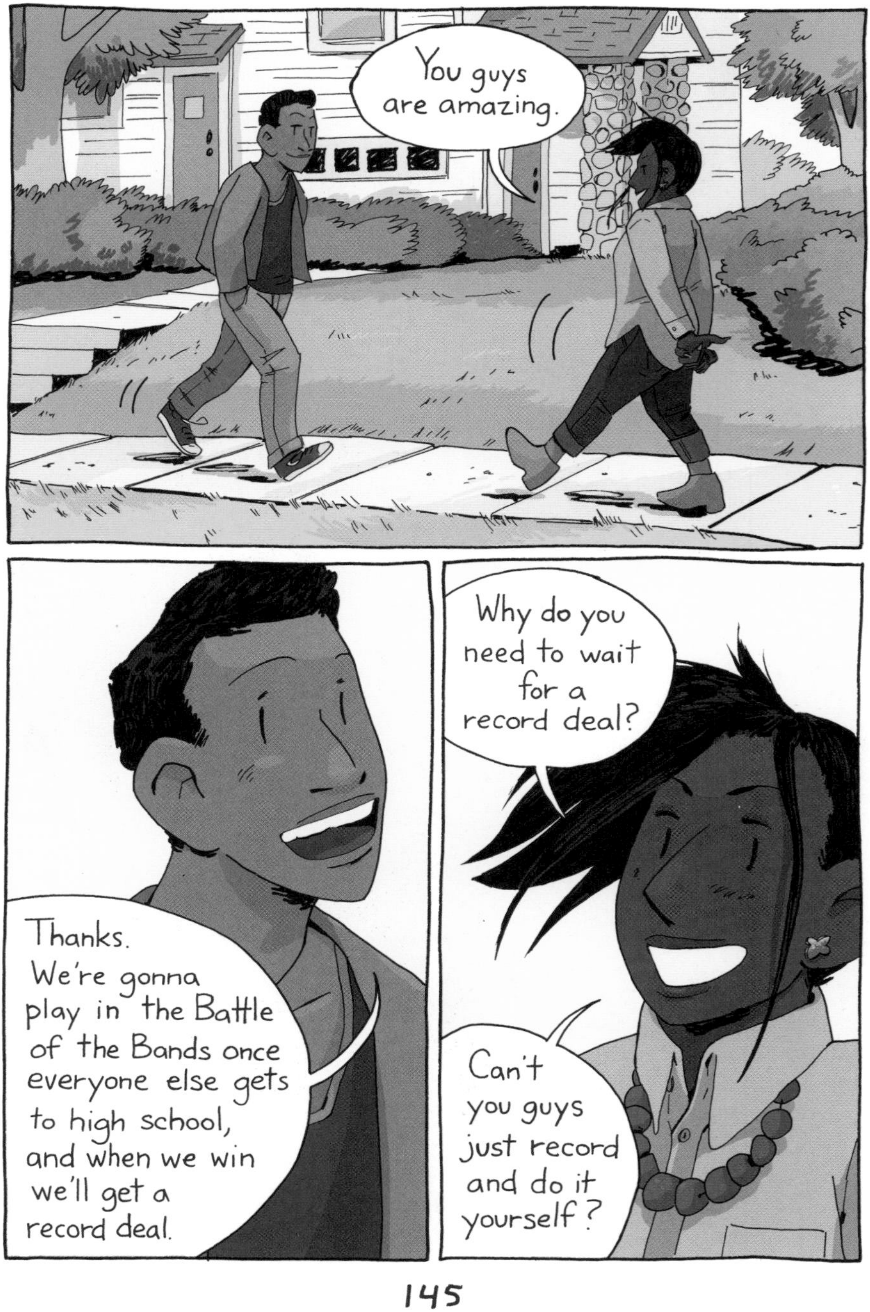
You guys are amazing.
Thanks. We're gonna play in the Battle of the Bands once everyone else gets to high school, and when we win we'll get a record deal.
Why do you need to wait for a record deal?
Can't you guys just record and do it yourself?

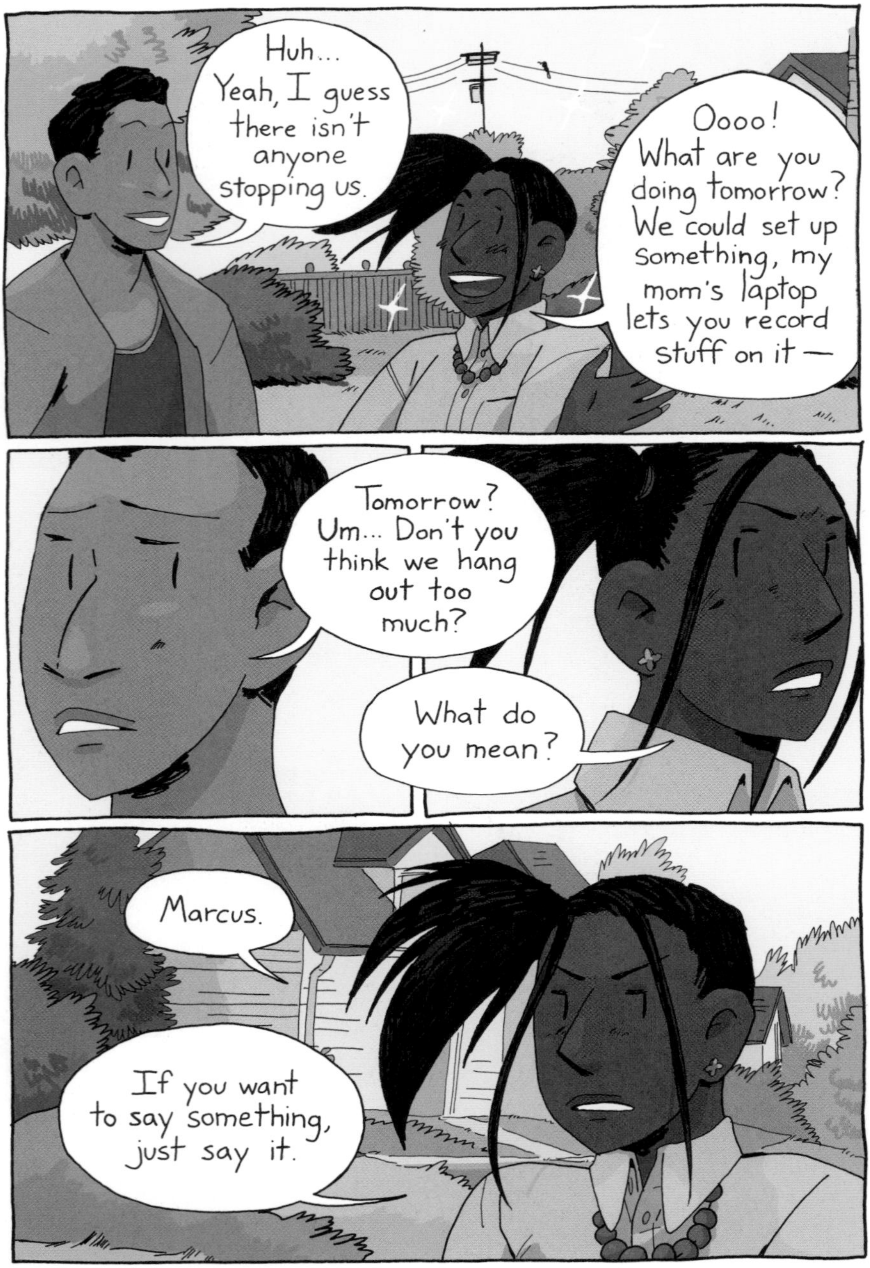
Huh... Yeah, I guess there isn't anyone stopping us.
Oooo! What are you doing tomorrow? We could set up something, my mom's laptop lets you record stuff on it—
Tomorrow? Um... Don't you think we hang out too much?
What do you mean?
Marcus.
If you want to say something, just say it.

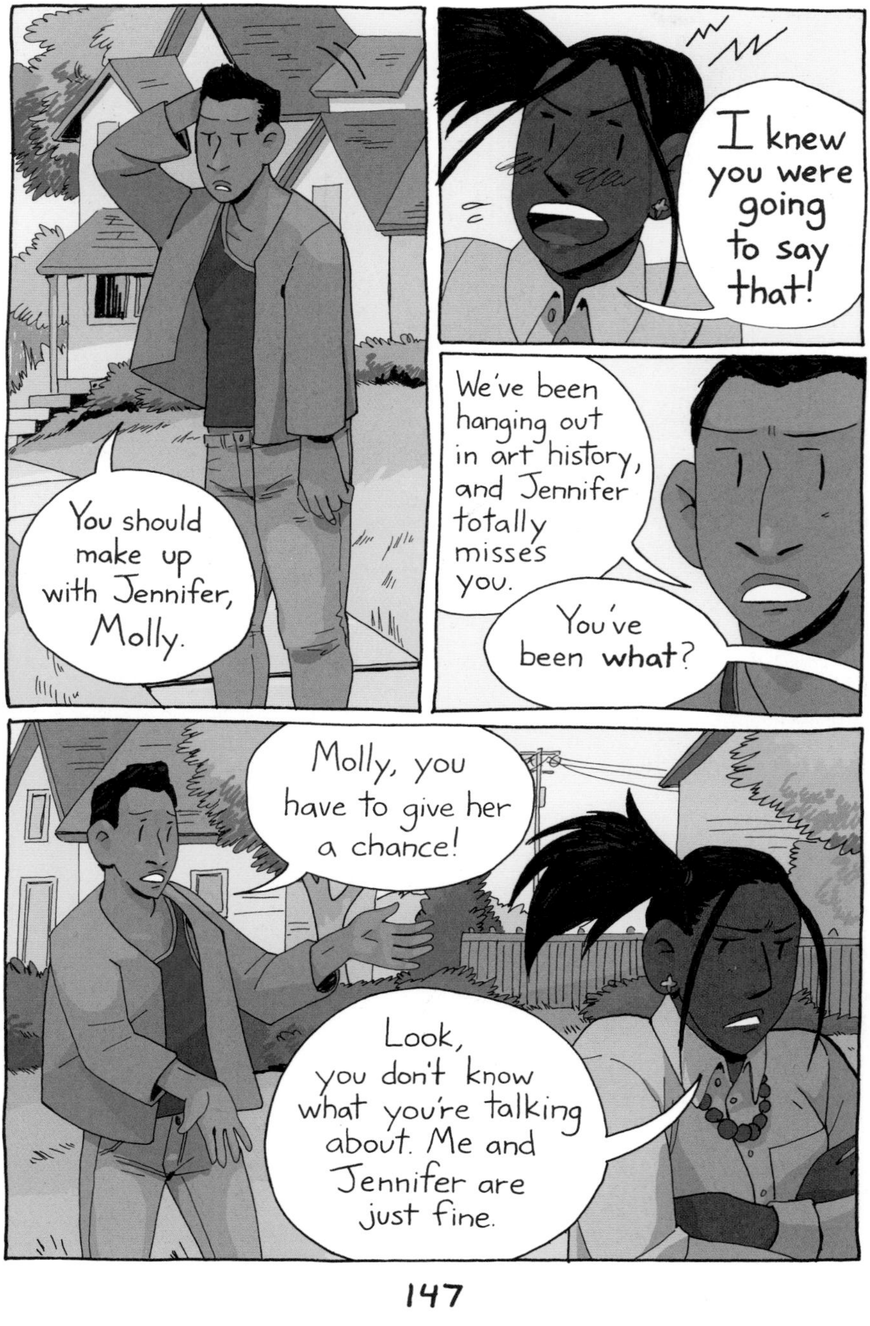
You should make up with Jennifer, Molly.
I knew you were going to say that!
We've been hanging out in art history, and Jennifer totally misses you.
You've been **what**?
Molly, you have to give her a chance!
Look, you don't know what you're talking about. Me and Jennifer are just fine.

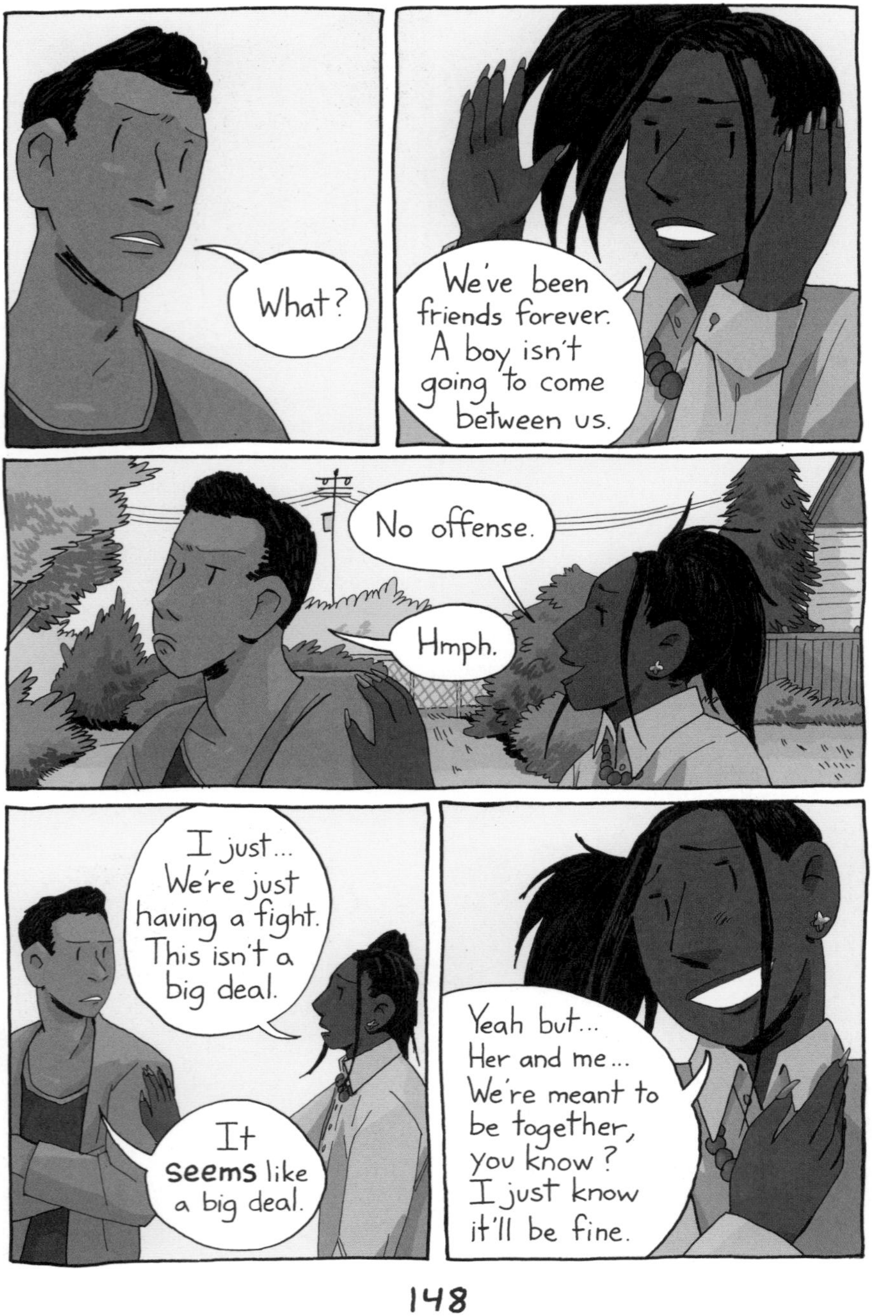
What?
We've been friends forever. A boy isn't going to come between us.
No offense.
Hmph.
I just... We're just having a fight. This isn't a big deal.
It **seems** like a big deal.
Yeah but... Her and me... We're meant to be together, you know? I just know it'll be fine.

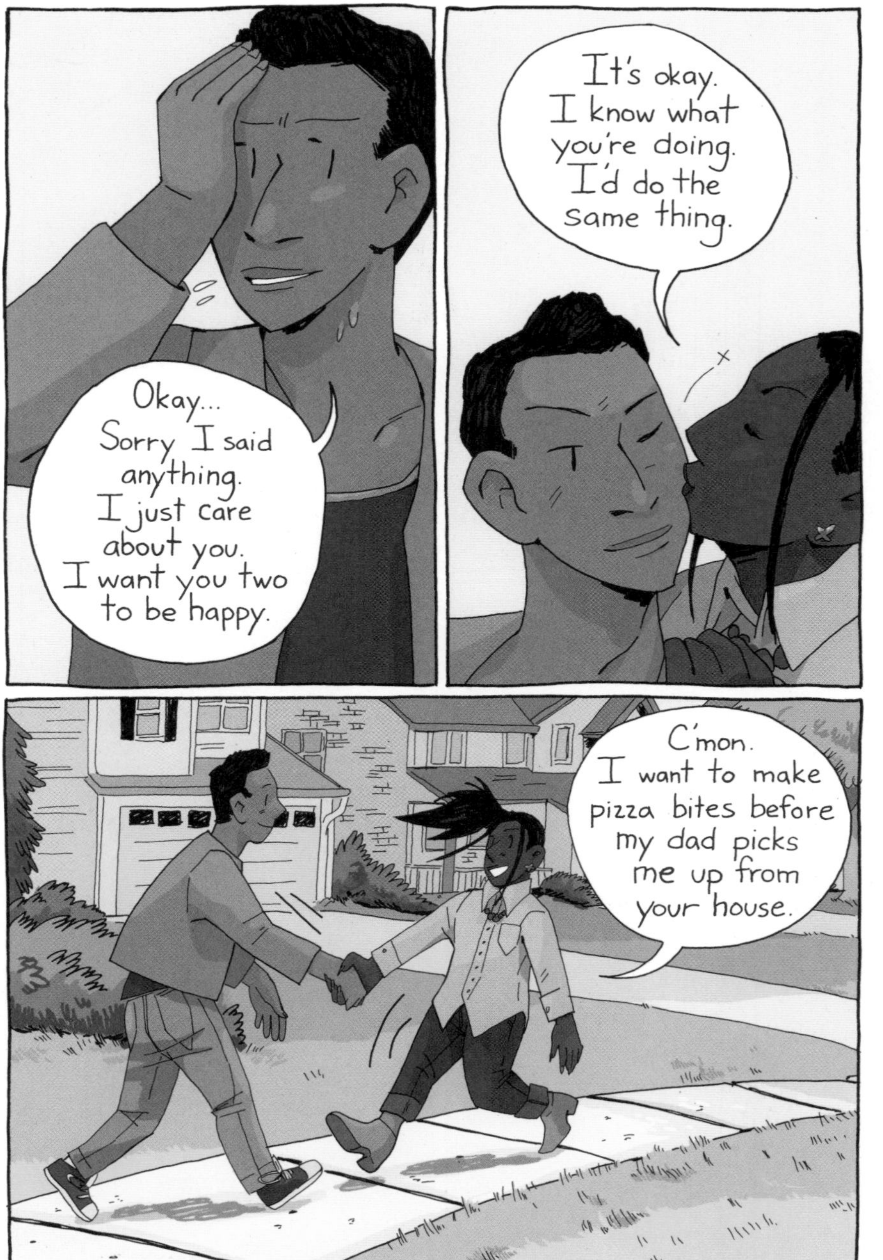
Okay... Sorry I said anything. I just care about you. I want you two to be happy.
It's okay. I know what you're doing. I'd do the same thing.
C'mon. I want to make pizza bites before my dad picks me up from your house.

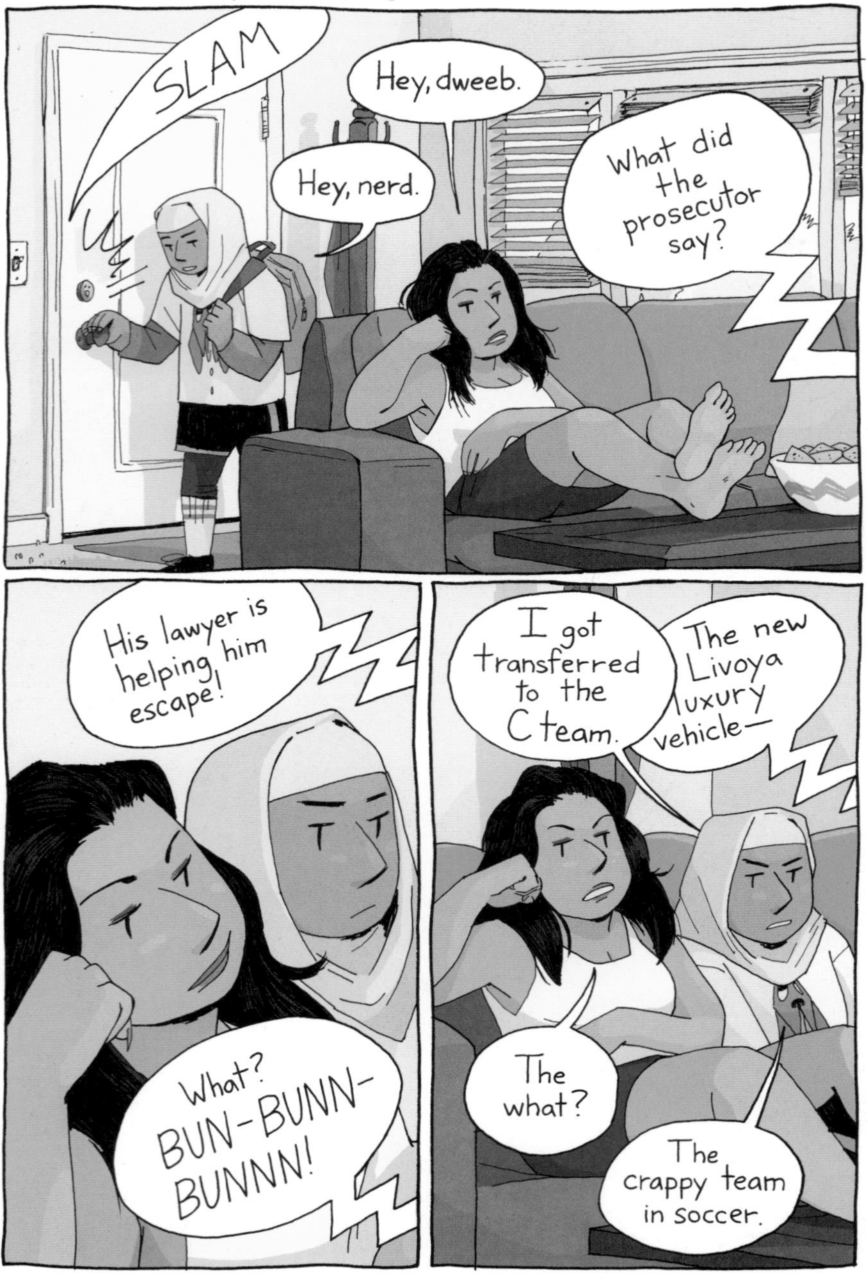
SLAM
Hey, dweeb.
Hey, nerd.
What did the prosecutor say?
His lawyer is helping him escape!
What? BUN-BUNN-BUNNN!
I got transferred to the C team.
The new Livoya luxury vehicle—
The what?
The crappy team in soccer.

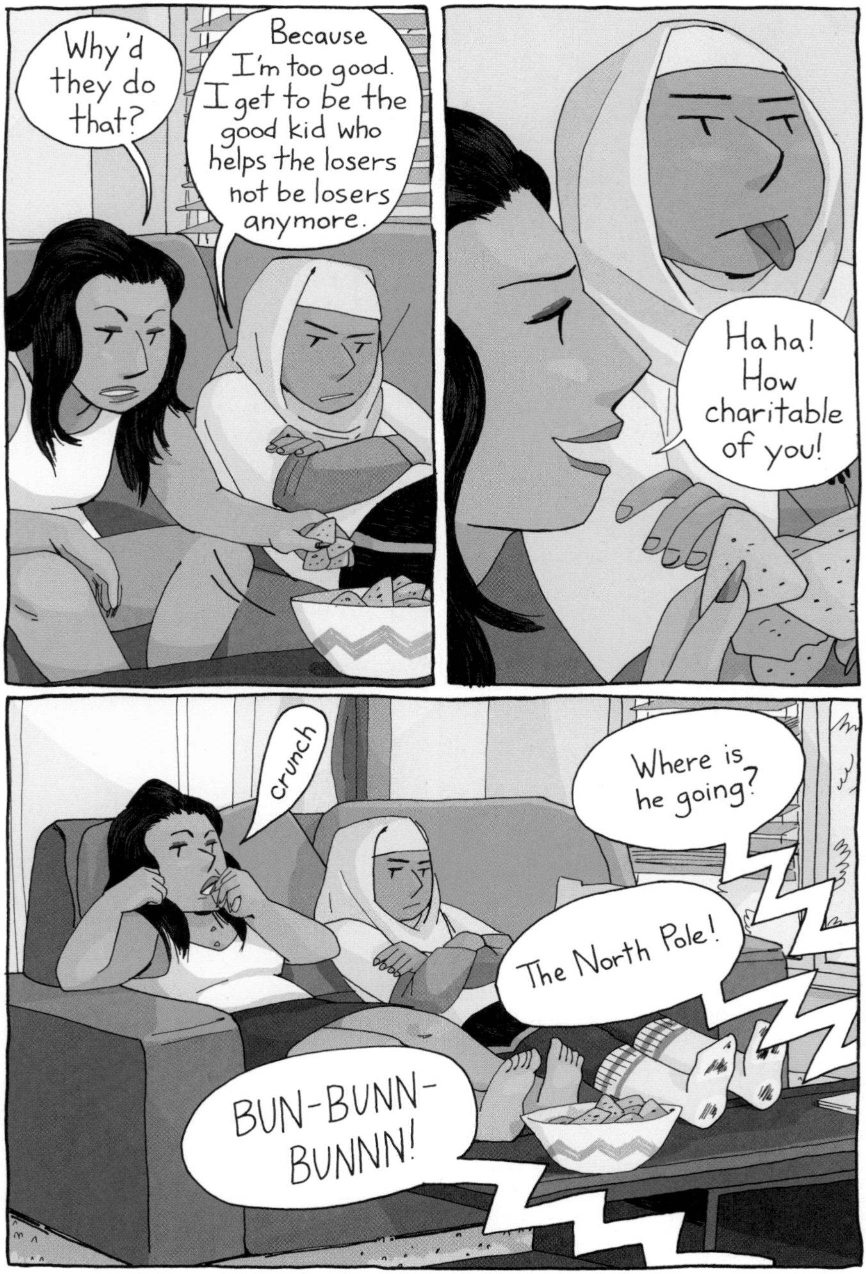
Why'd they do that?
Because I'm too good. I get to be the good kid who helps the losers not be losers anymore.
Ha ha! How charitable of you!
crunch
Where is he going?
The North Pole!
BUN-BUNN-BUNNN!

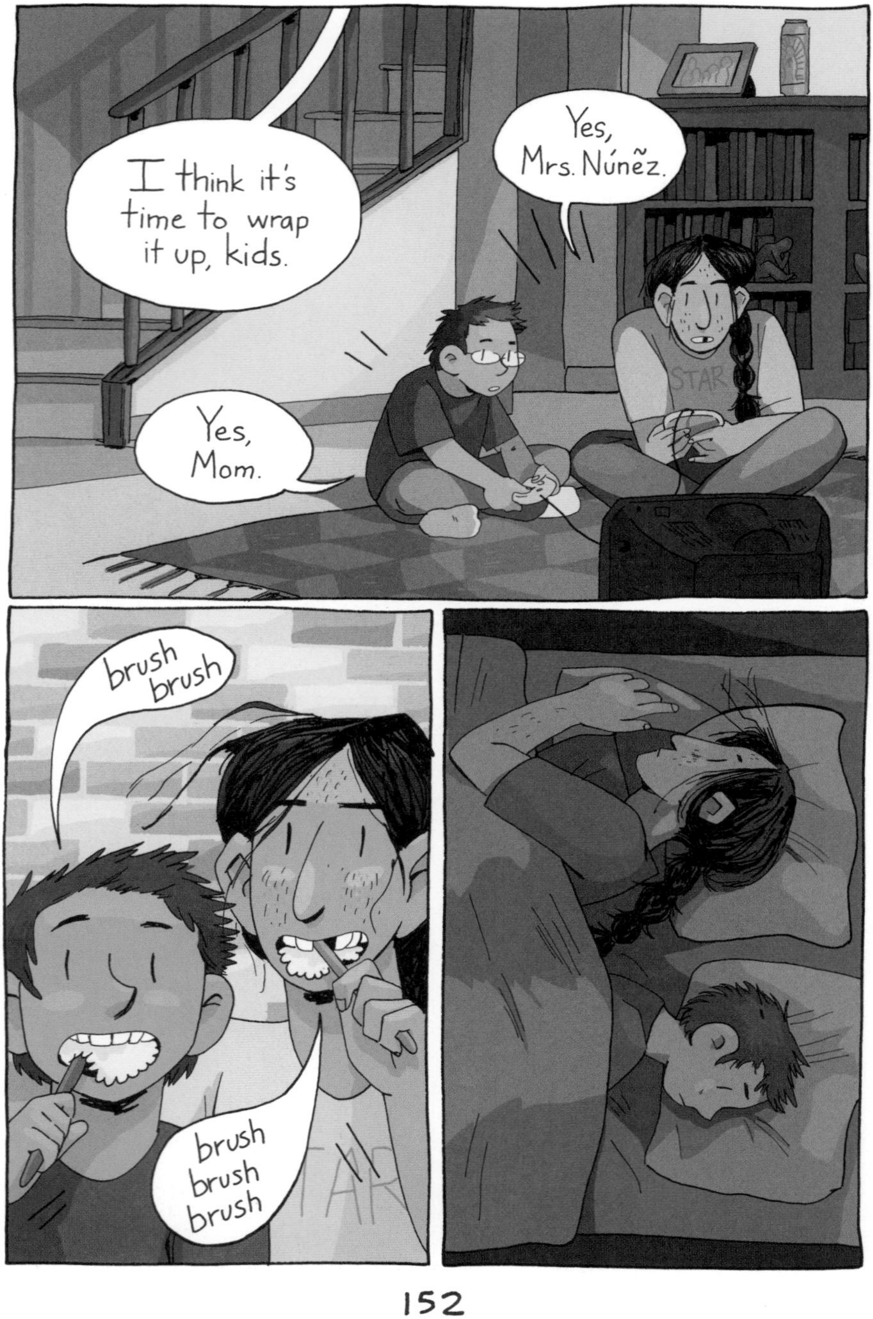
I think it's time to wrap it up, kids.
Yes, Mrs. Núñez.
Yes, Mom.
brush brush
brush brush brush

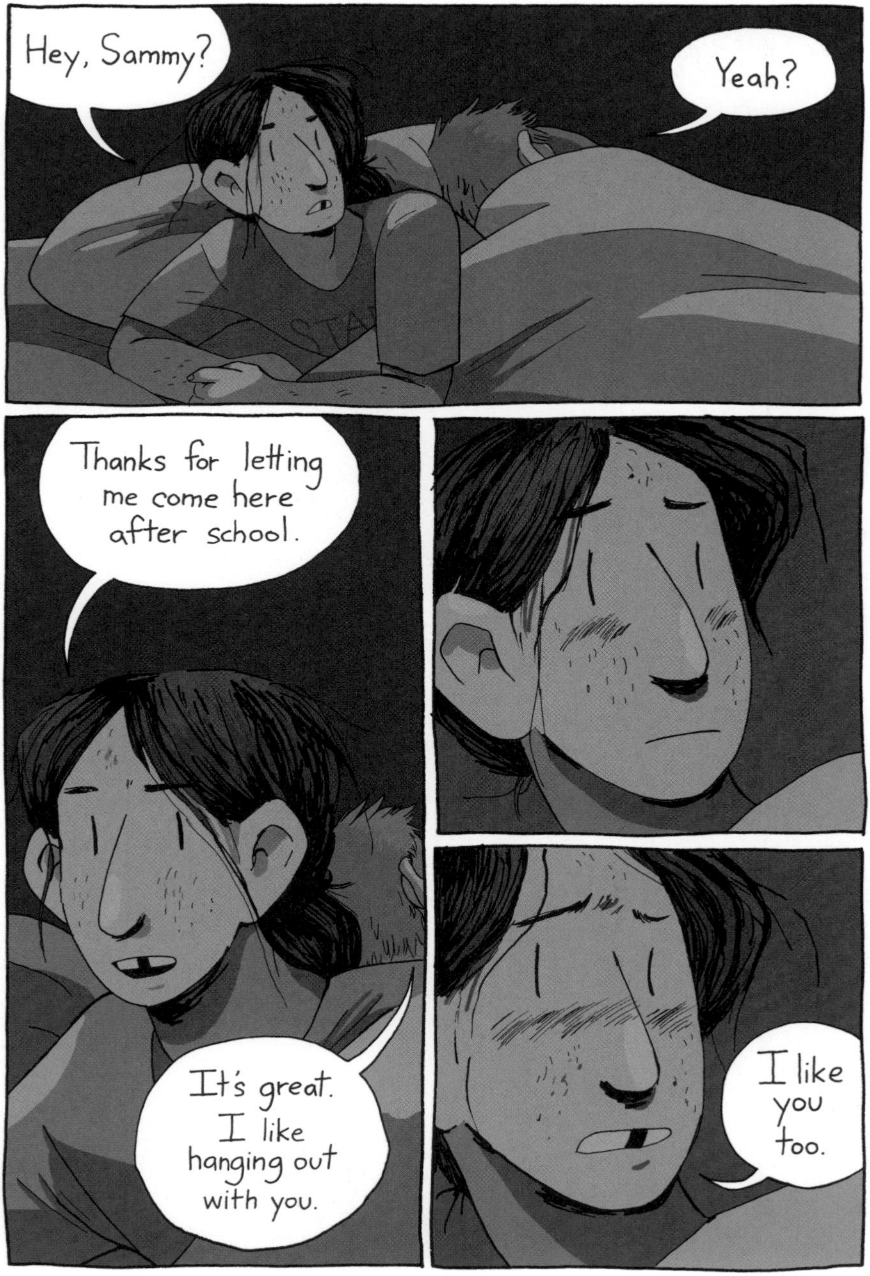
Hey, Sammy?
Yeah?
Thanks for letting me come here after school.
It's great. I like hanging out with you.
I like you too.

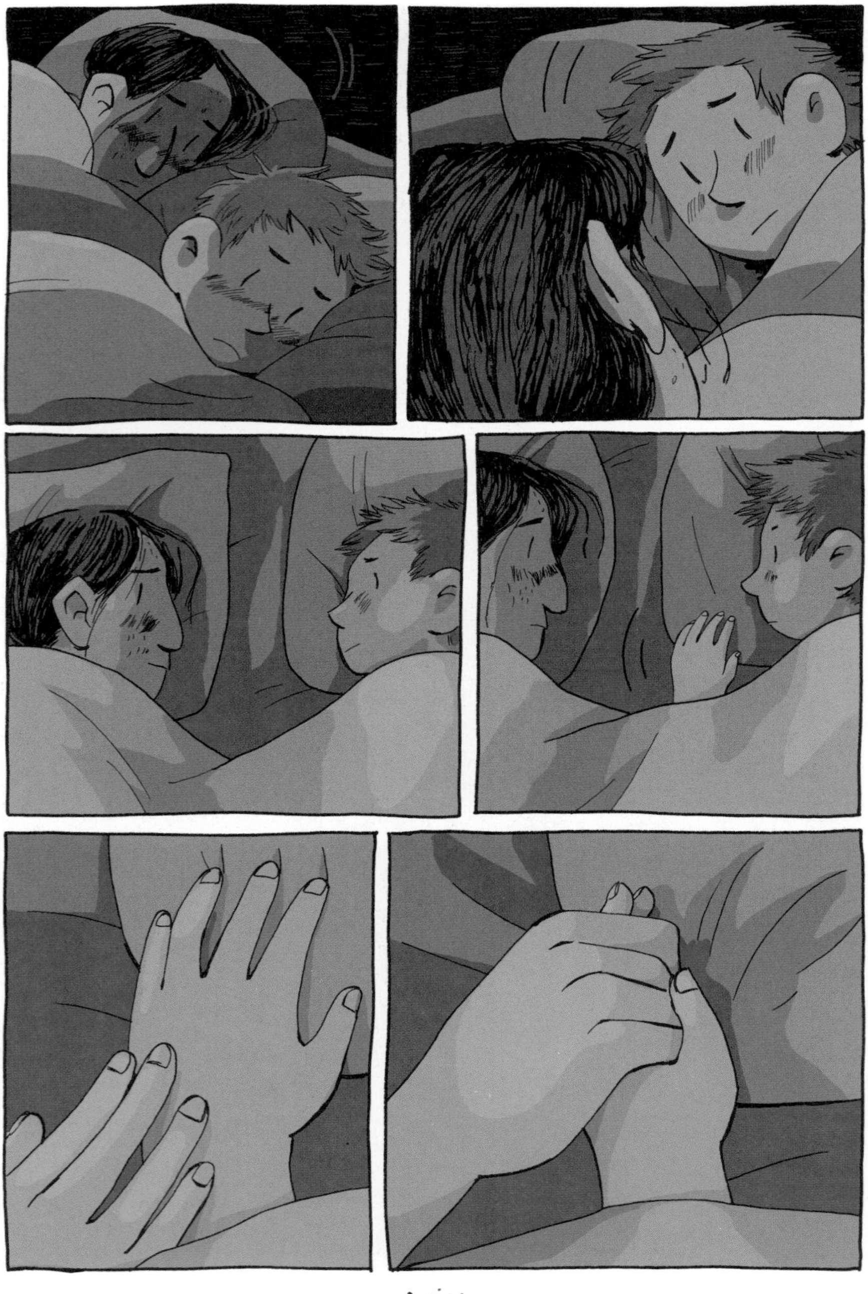

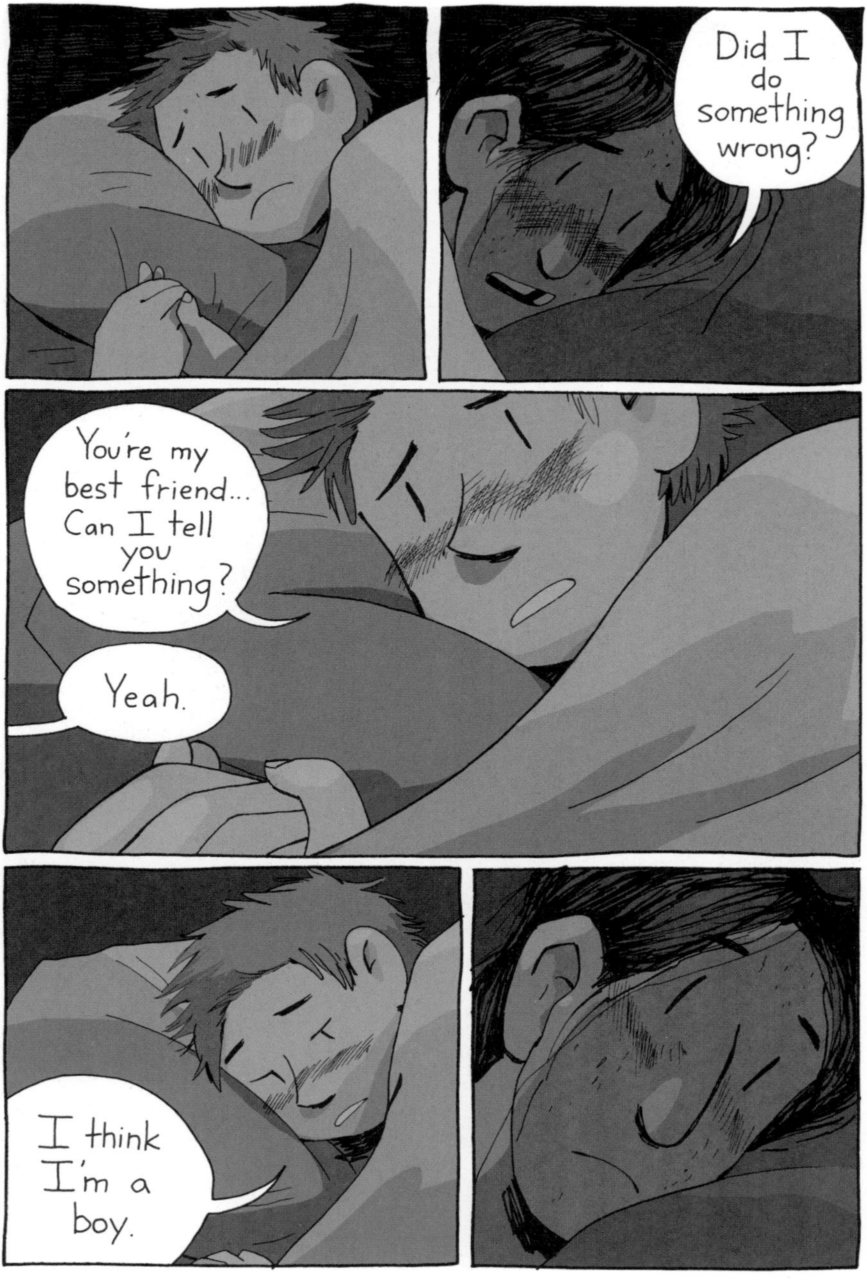
Did I do something wrong?
You're my best friend... Can I tell you something?
Yeah.
I think I'm a boy.

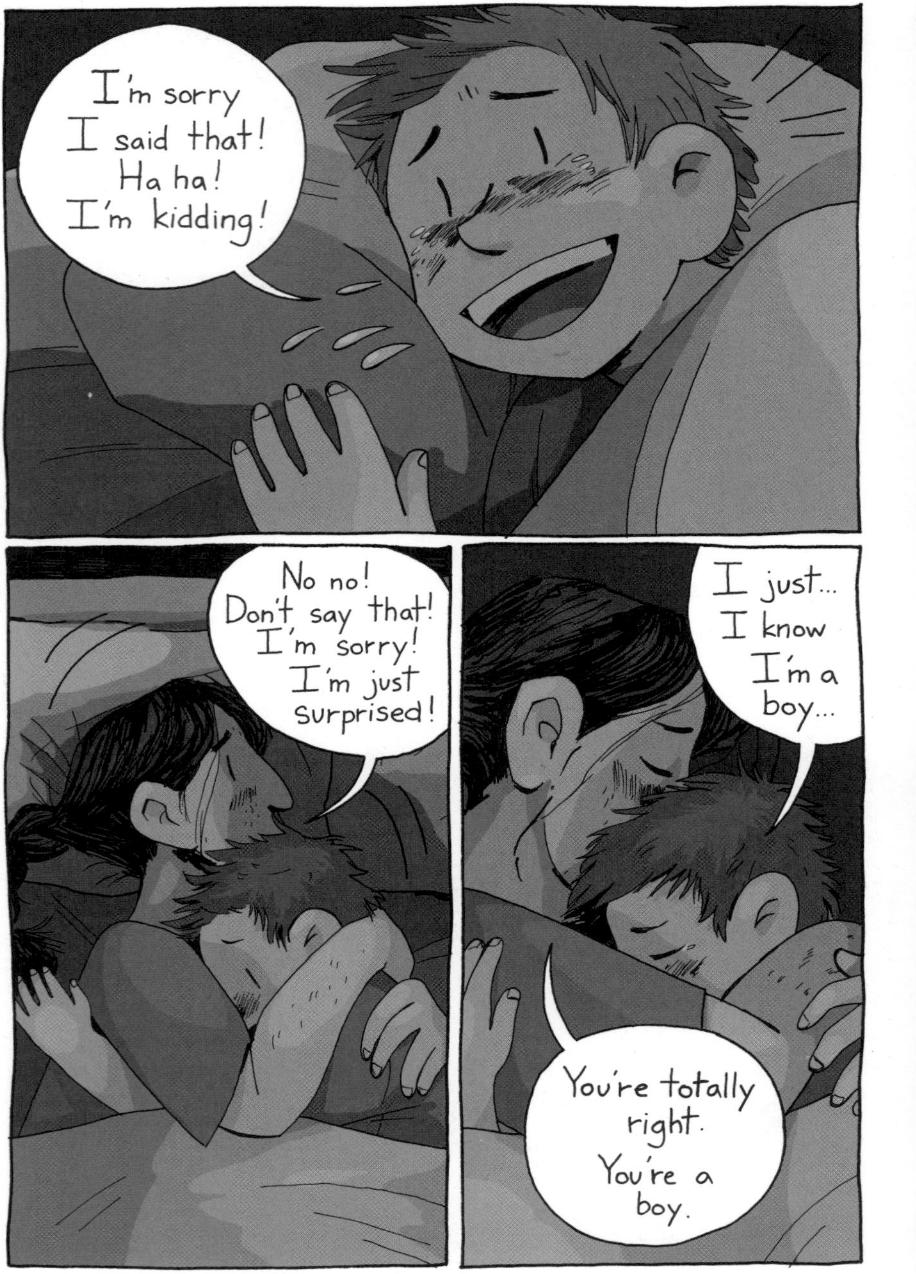
I'm sorry I said that! Ha ha! I'm kidding!
No no! Don't say that! I'm sorry! I'm just surprised!
I just... I know I'm a boy...
You're totally right. You're a boy.

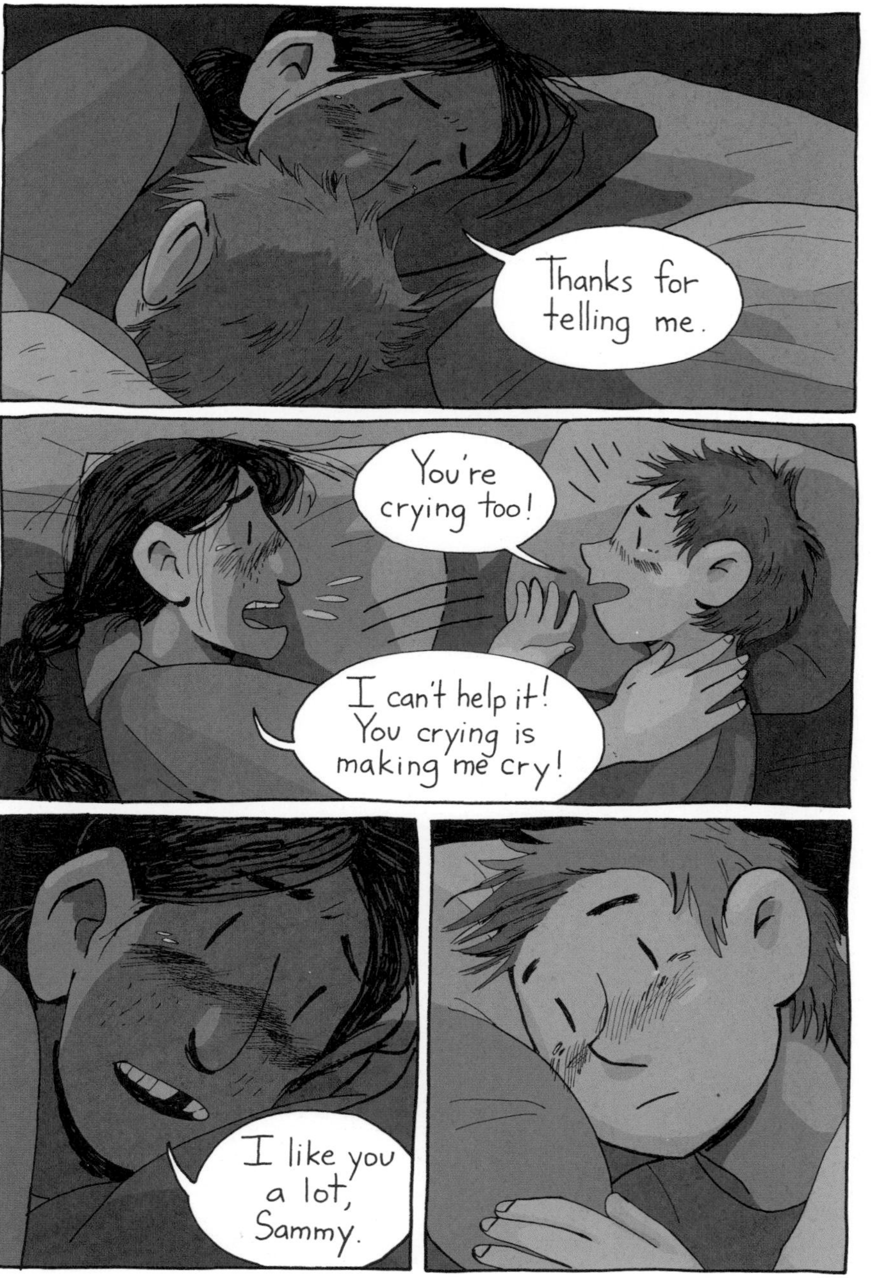
Thanks for telling me.
You're crying too!
I can't help it! You crying is making me cry!
I like you a lot, Sammy.

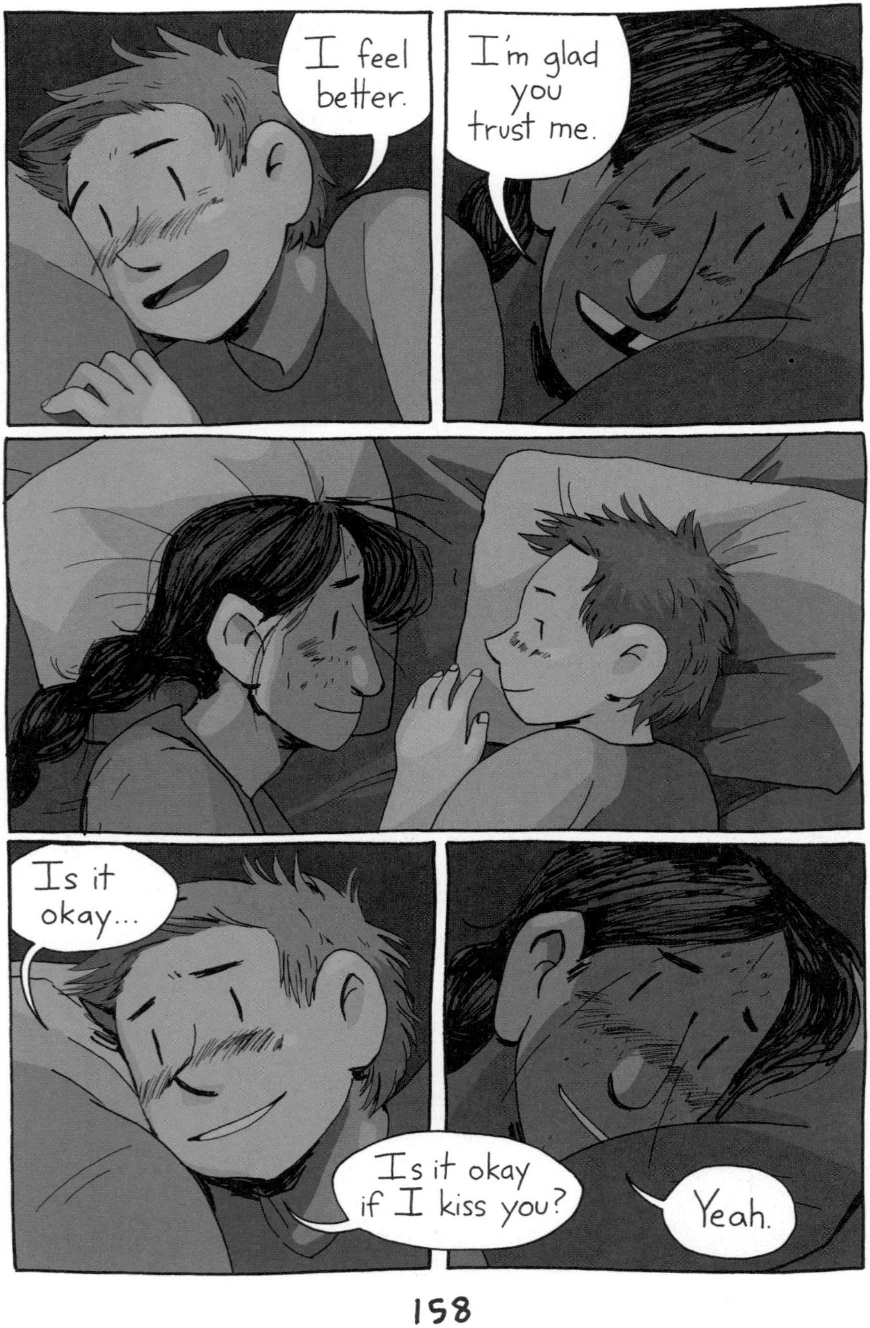
I feel better.
I'm glad you trust me.
Is it okay...
Is it okay if I kiss you?
Yeah.

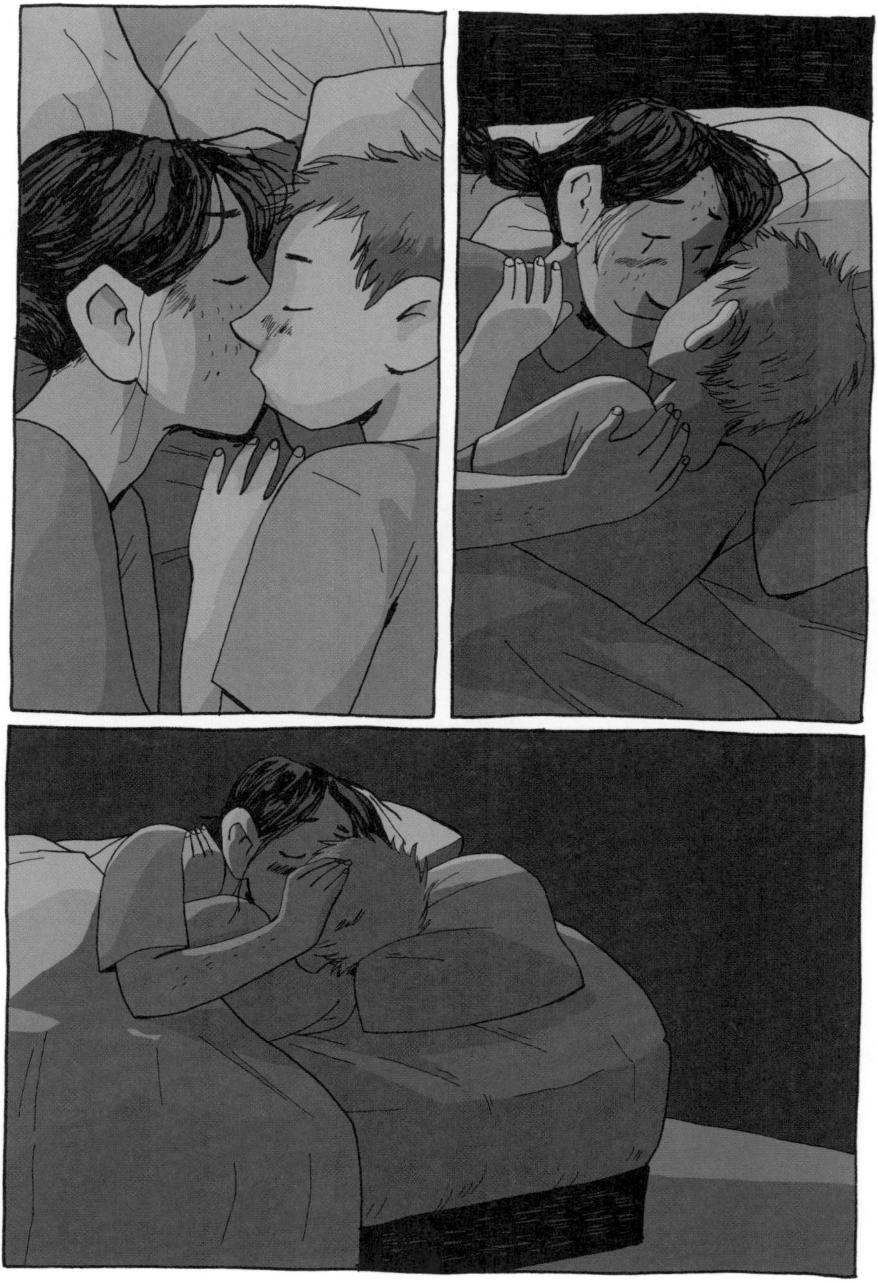

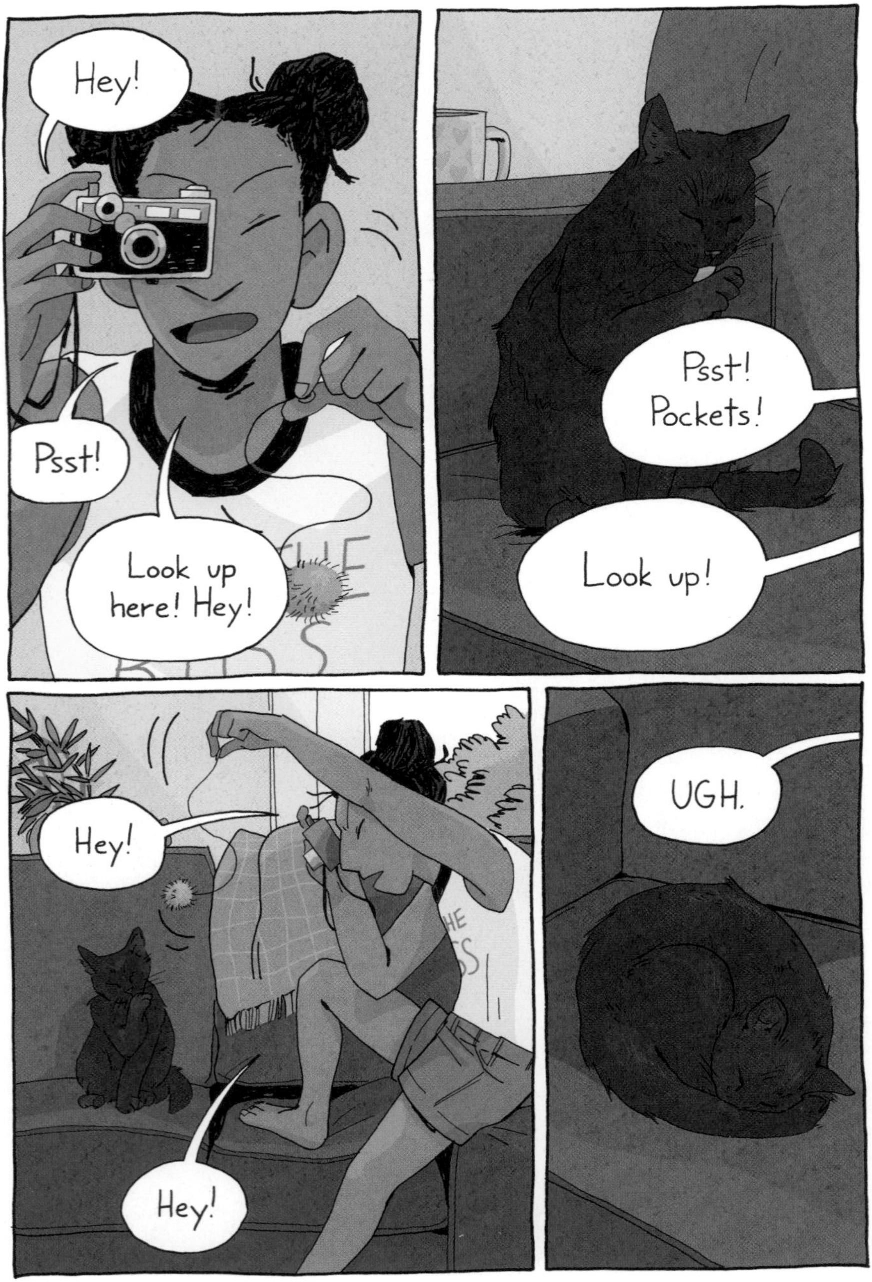
Hey!
Psst!
Look up here! Hey!
Psst! Pockets!
Look up!
Hey!
Hey!
UGH.

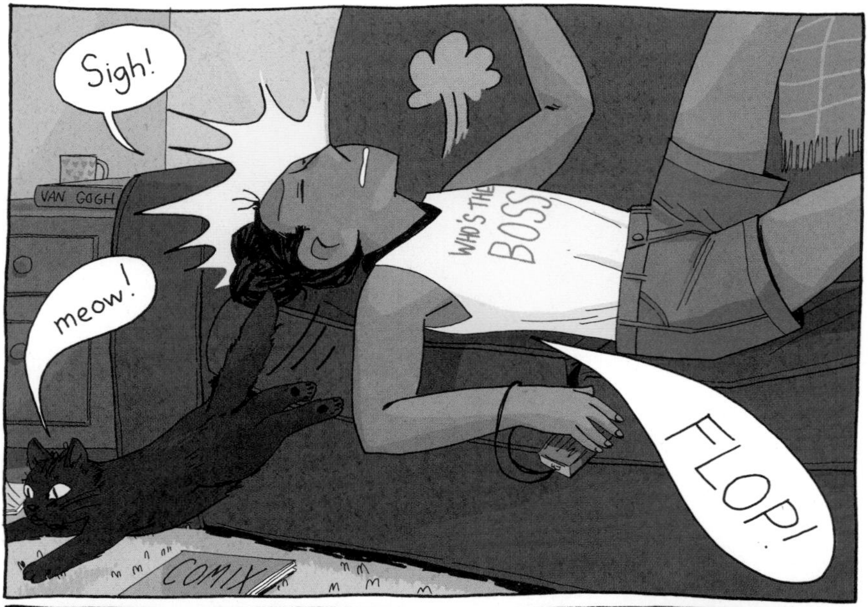
Sigh!
meow!
FLOP!
VAN GOGH
WHO'S THE BOSS
COMIX

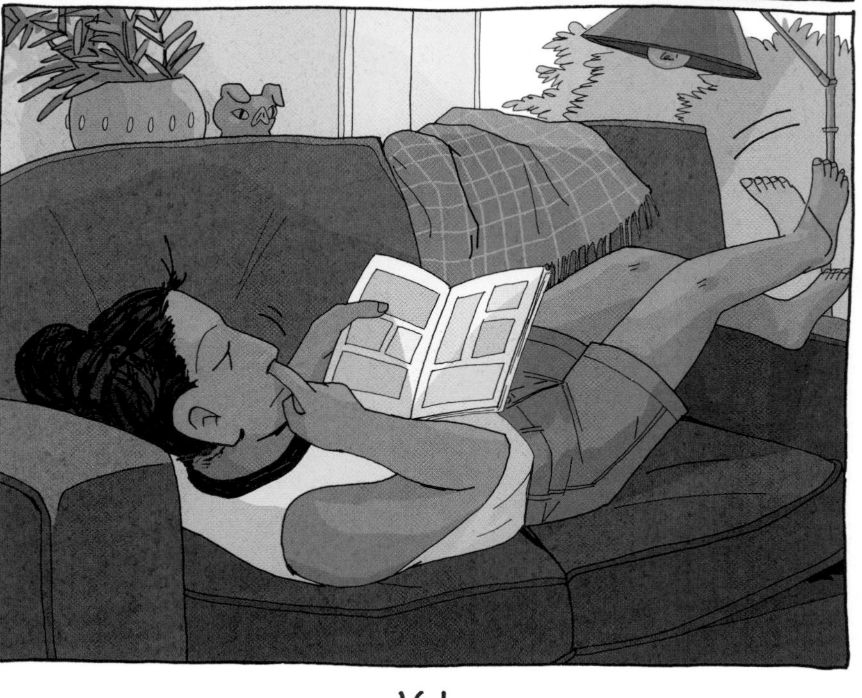

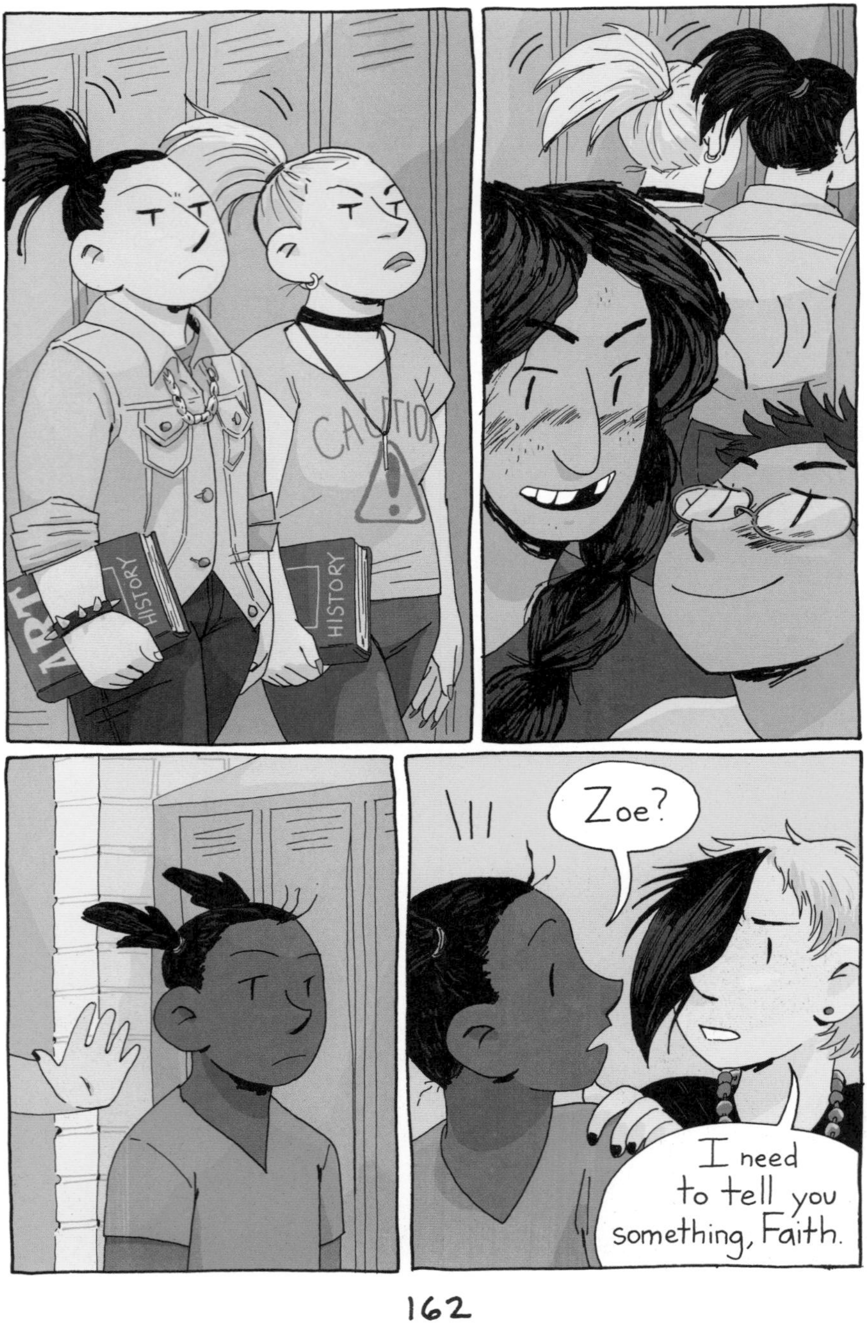
ART
HISTORY
CAUTION
HISTORY
Zoe?
I need to tell you something, Faith.

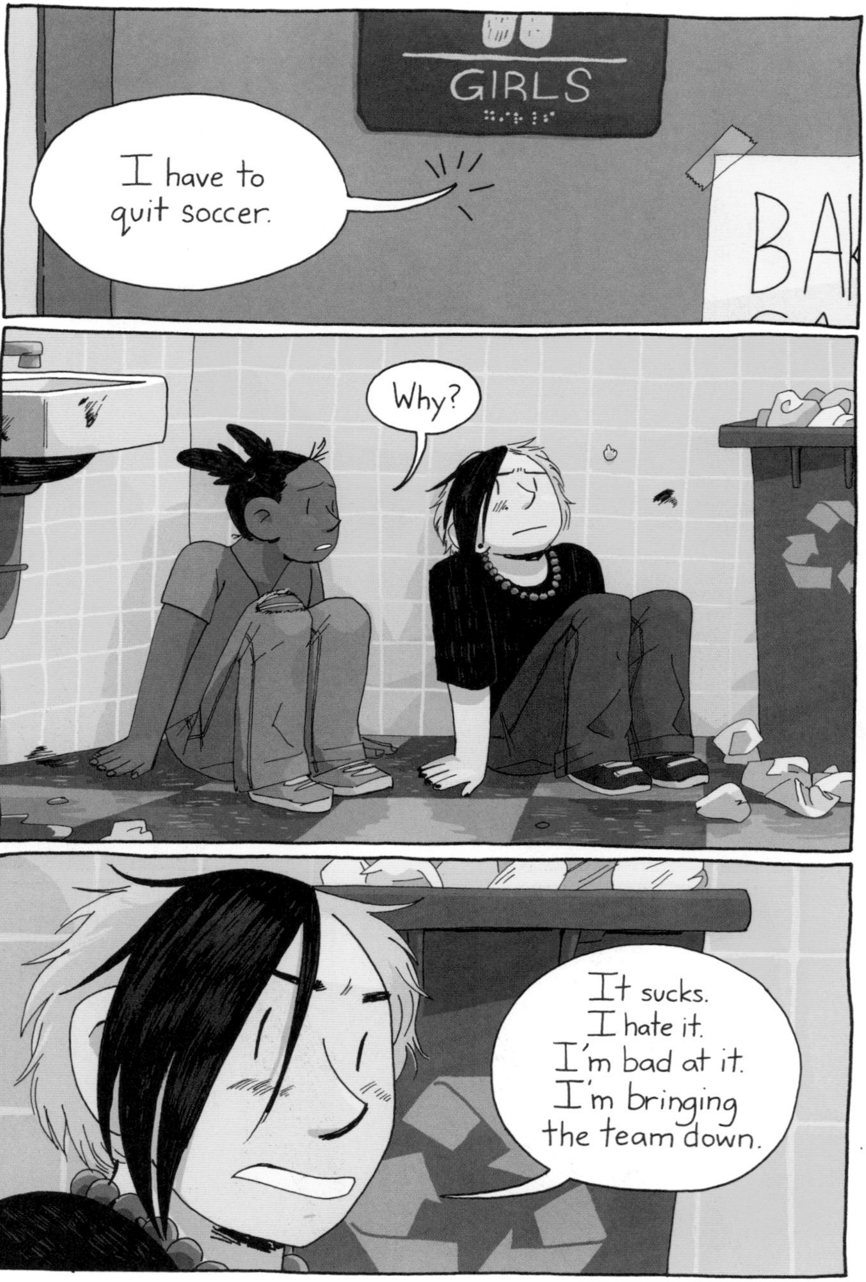
GIRLS
I have to quit soccer.
BAK
Why?
It sucks.
I hate it.
I'm bad at it.
I'm bringing the team down.

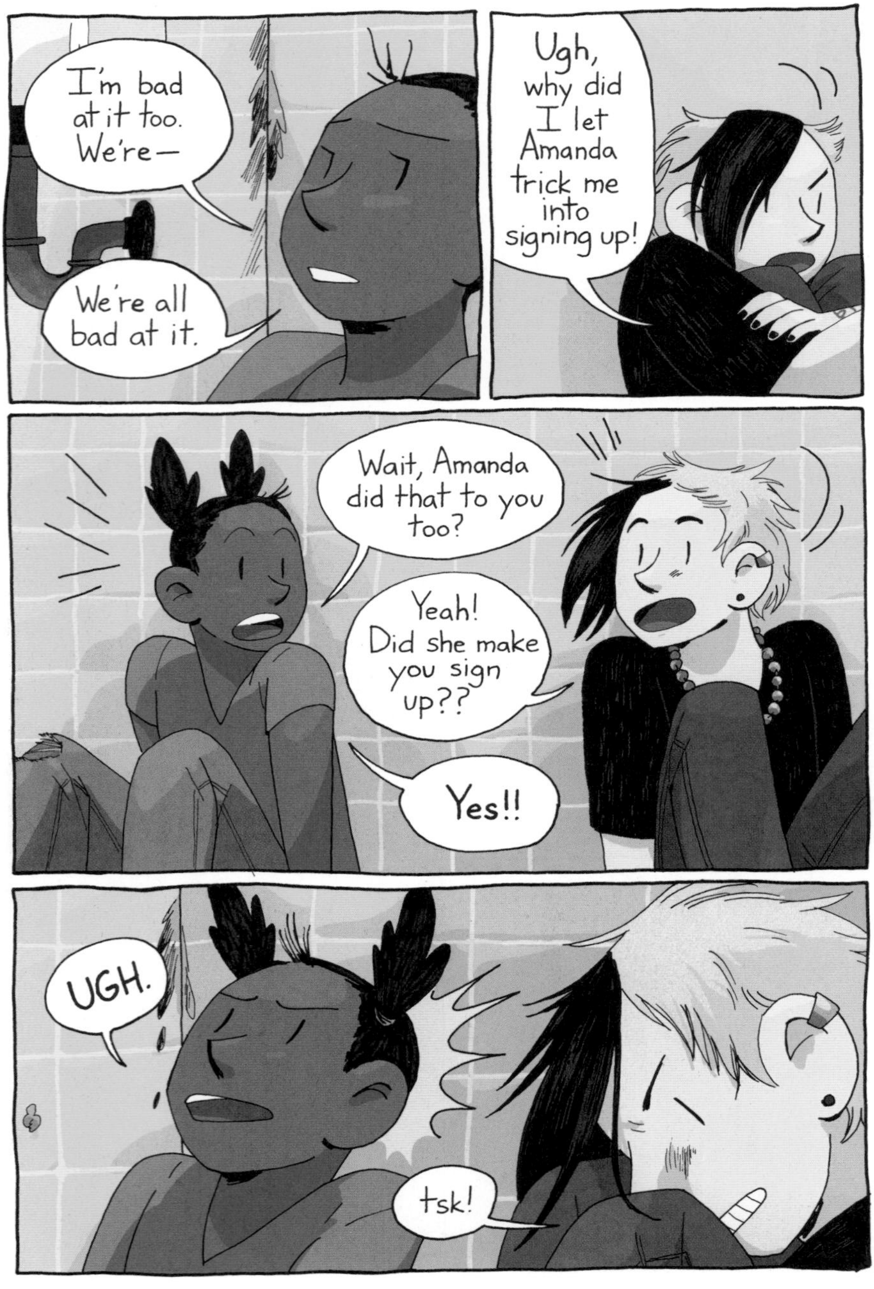
I'm bad at it too. We're—
We're all bad at it.
Ugh, why did I let Amanda trick me into signing up!
Wait, Amanda did that to you too?
Yeah! Did she make you sign up??
Yes!!
UGH.
tsk!

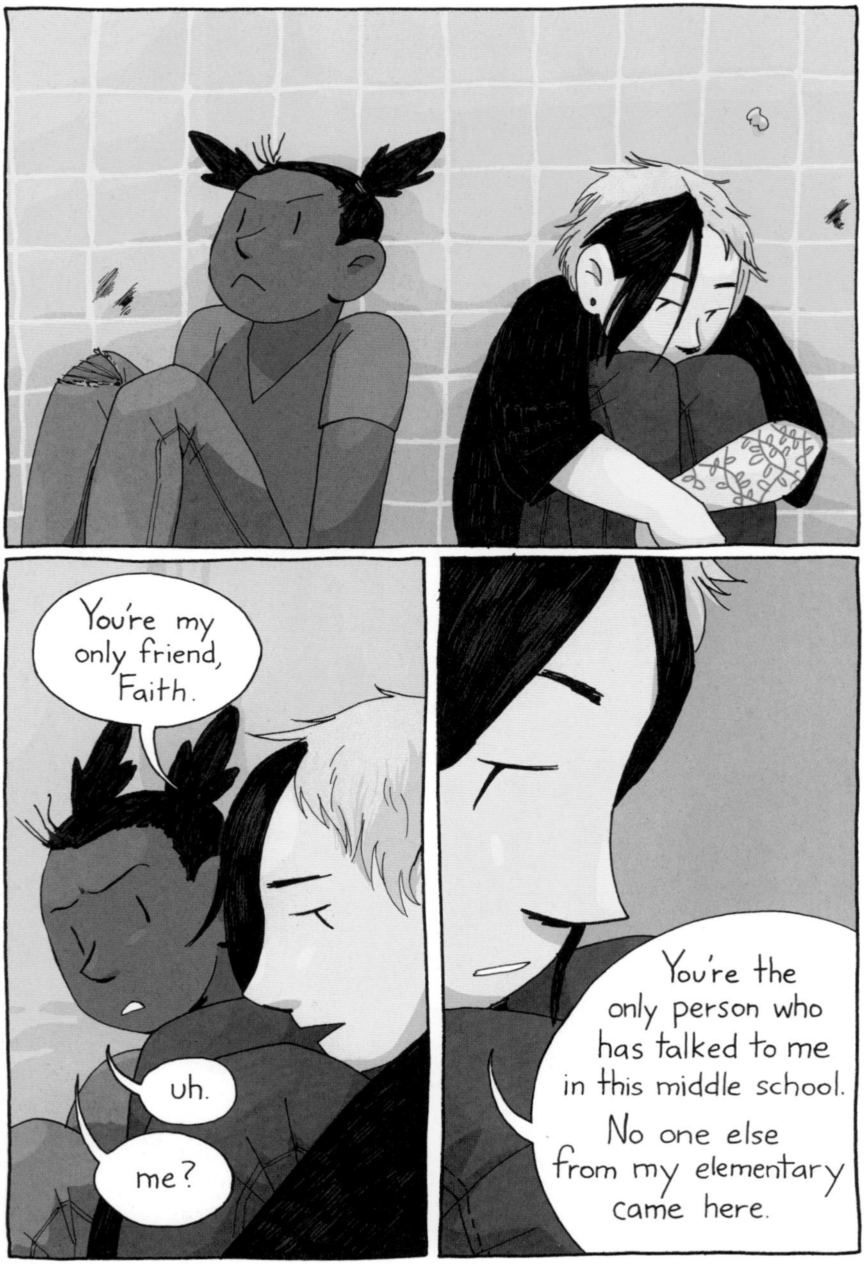
You're my only friend, Faith.
uh.
me?
You're the only person who has talked to me in this middle school.
No one else from my elementary came here.

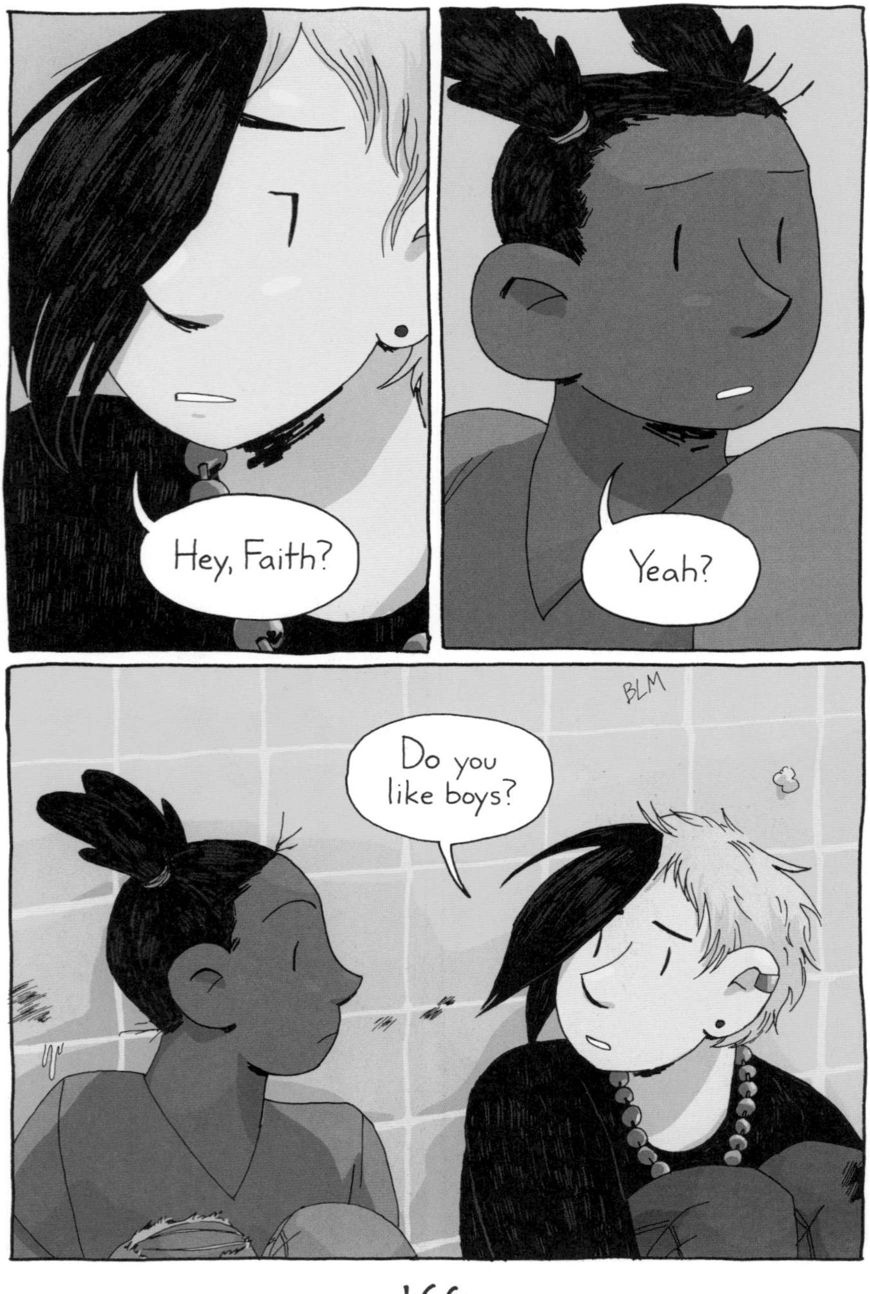
Hey, Faith?
Yeah?
BLM
Do you like boys?

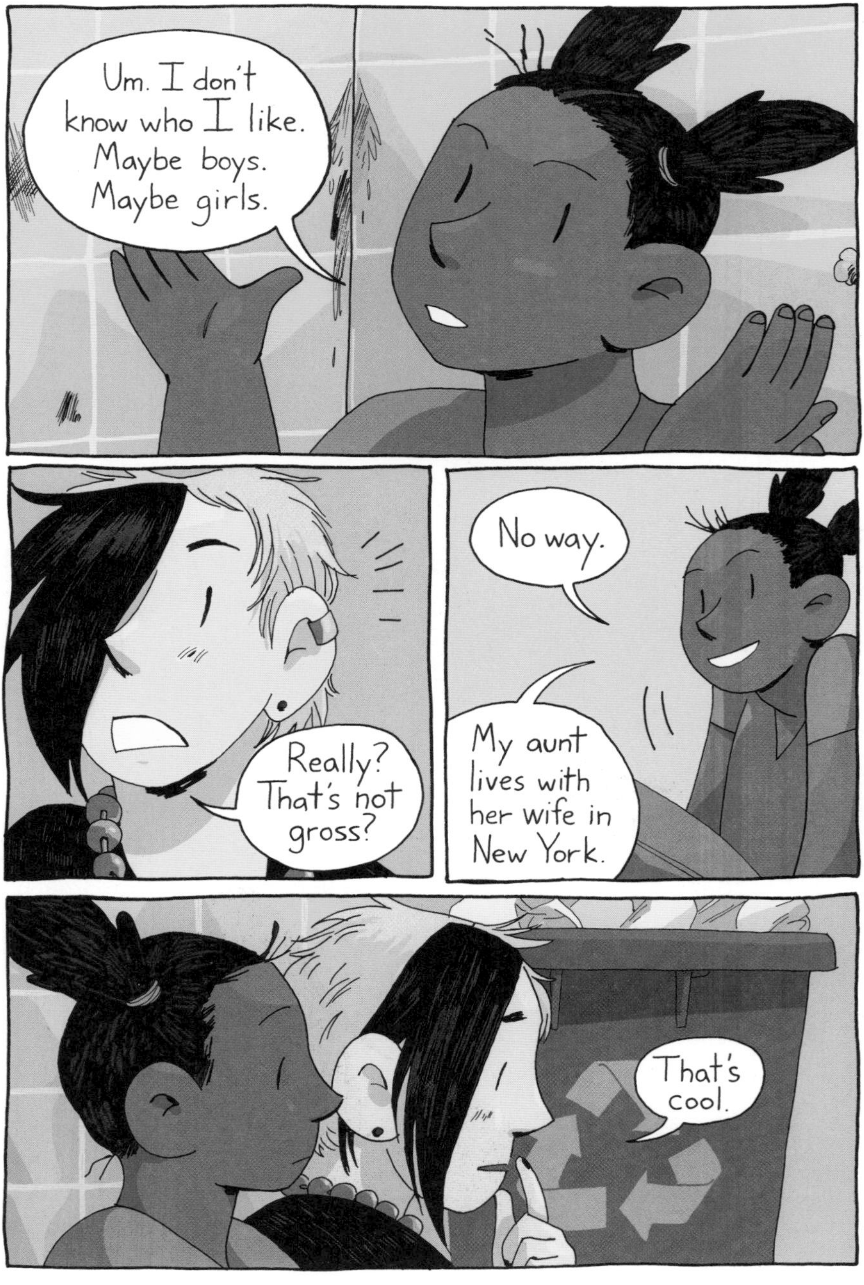
Um. I don't know who I like. Maybe boys. Maybe girls.
Really? That's not gross?
No way.
My aunt lives with her wife in New York.
That's cool.

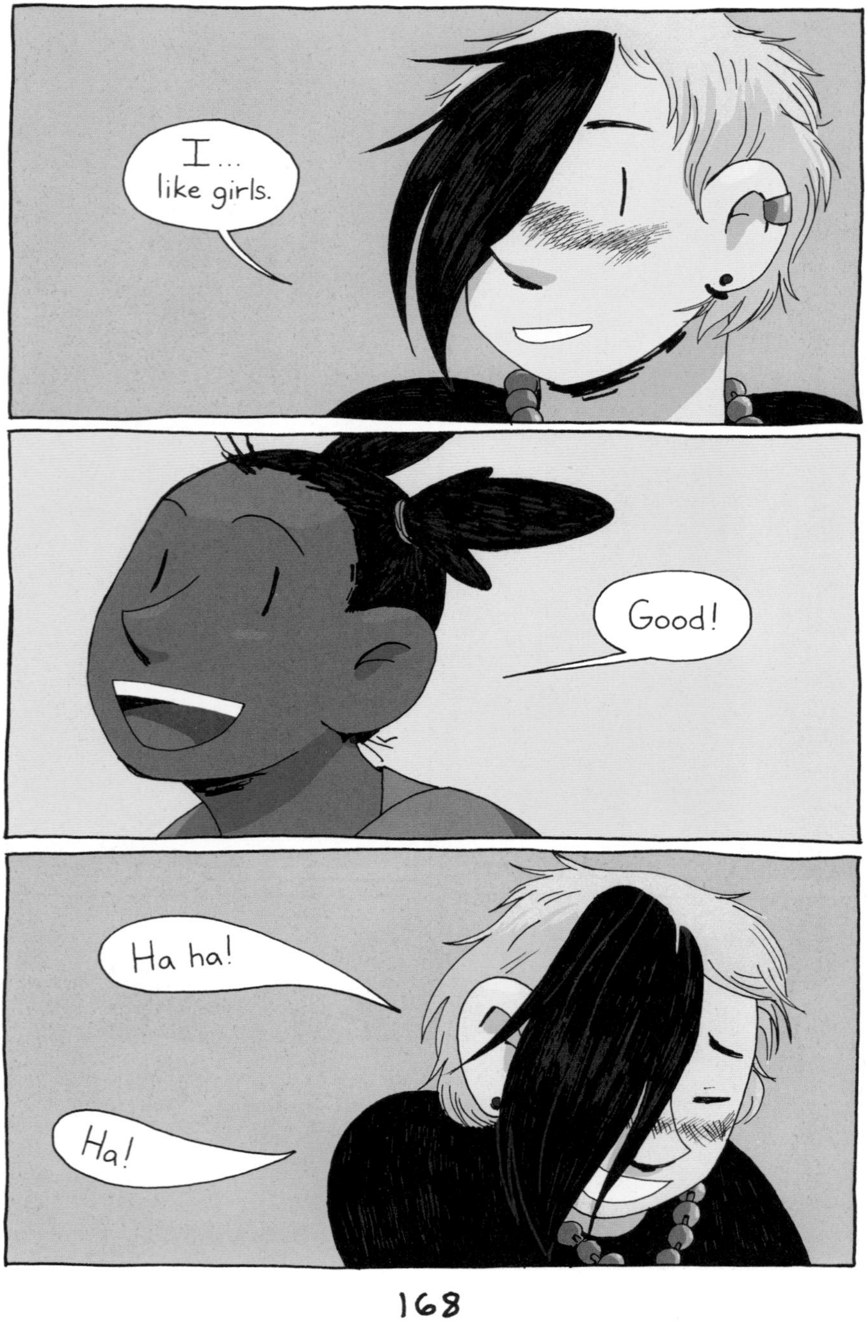
I...
like girls.
Good!
Ha ha!
Ha!

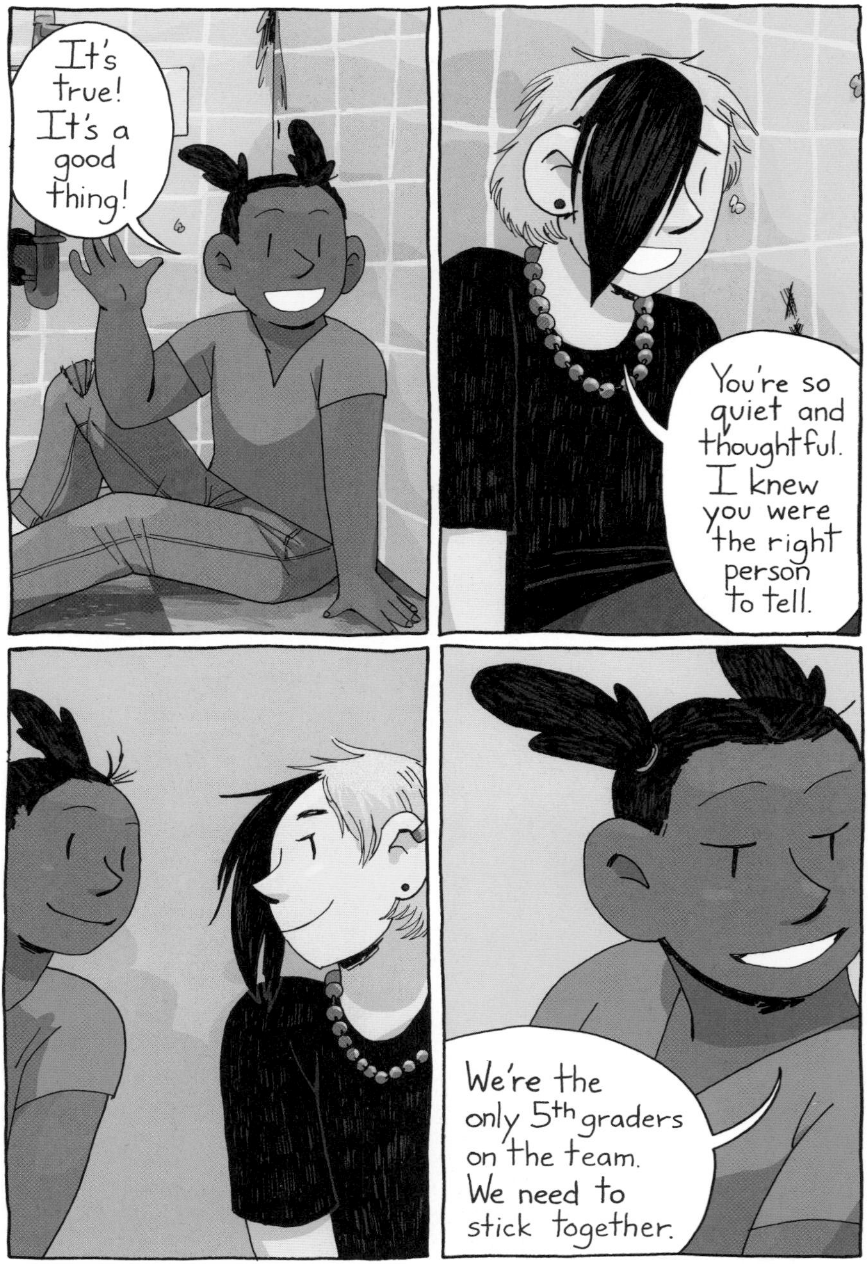
It's true! It's a good thing!
You're so quiet and thoughtful. I knew you were the right person to tell.
We're the only 5th graders on the team. We need to stick together.

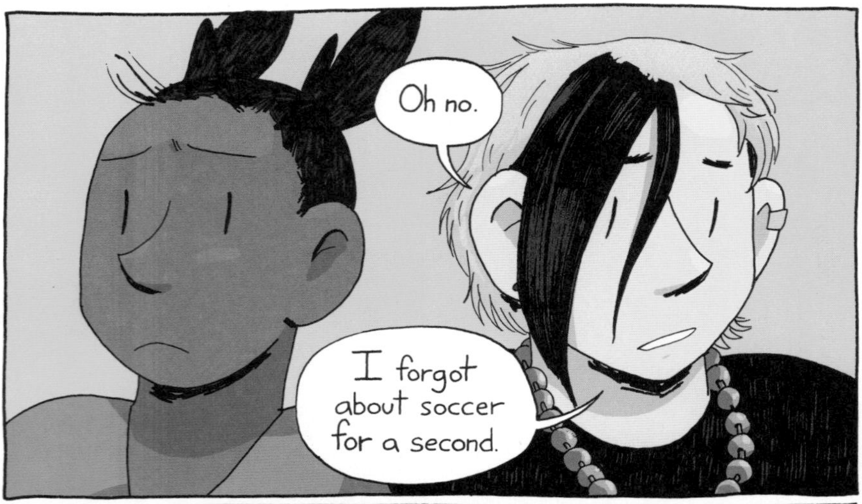
Oh no.
I forgot about soccer for a second.

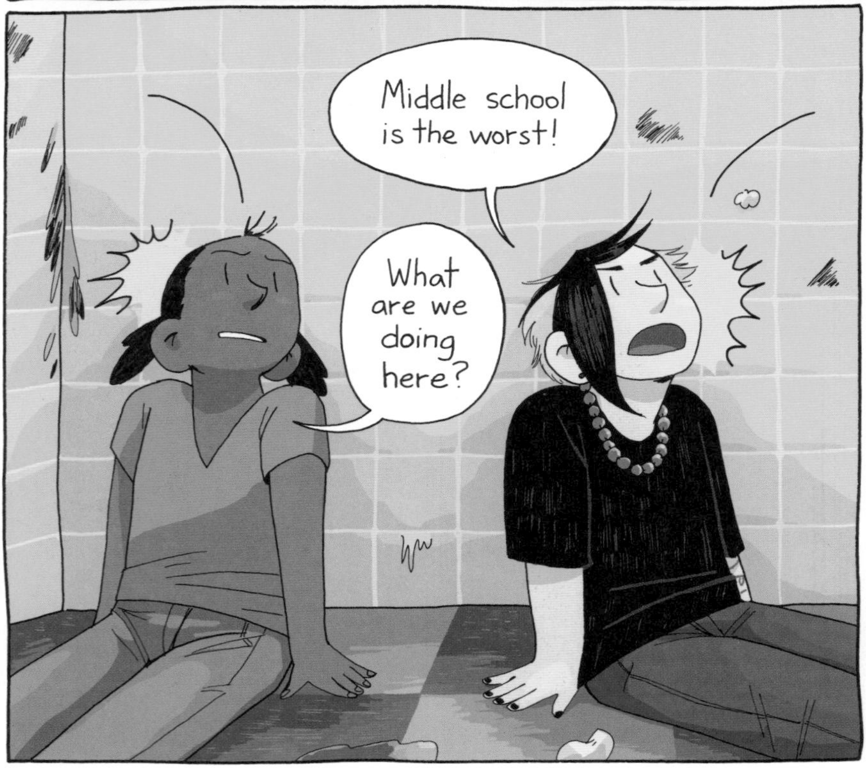
Middle school is the worst!
What are we doing here?

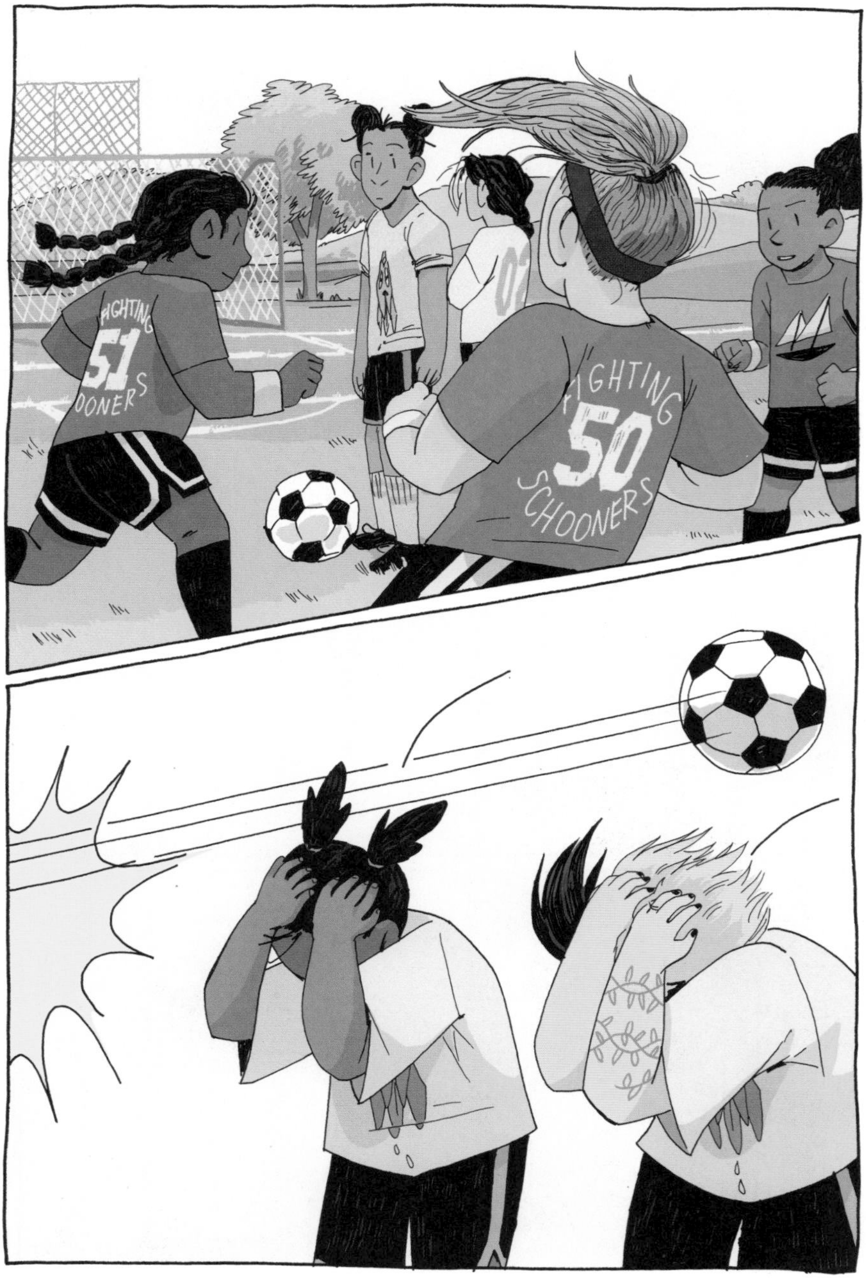
FIGHTING
51
OONERS
FIGHTING
50
SCHOONERS

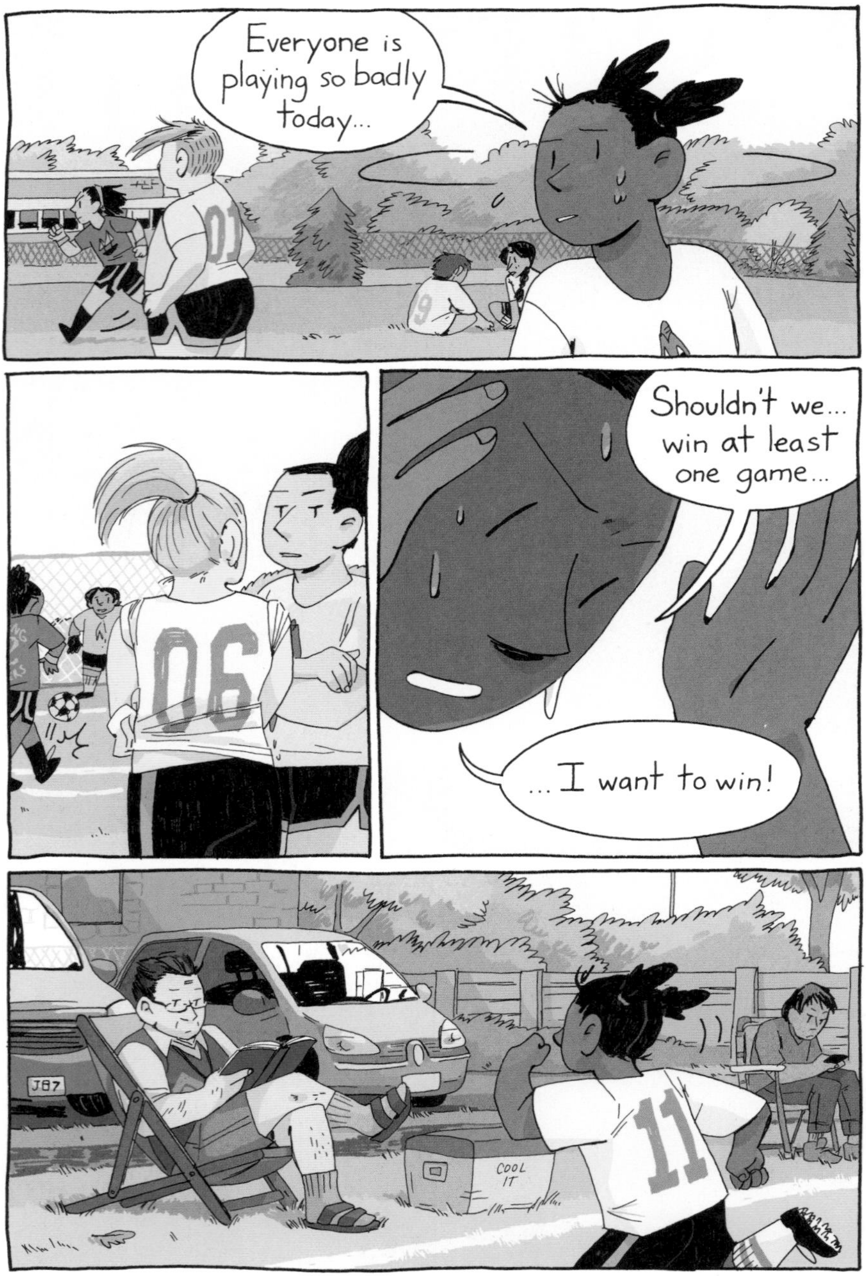

Everyone is playing so badly today...
Shouldn't we... win at least one game...
... I want to win!
COOL IT

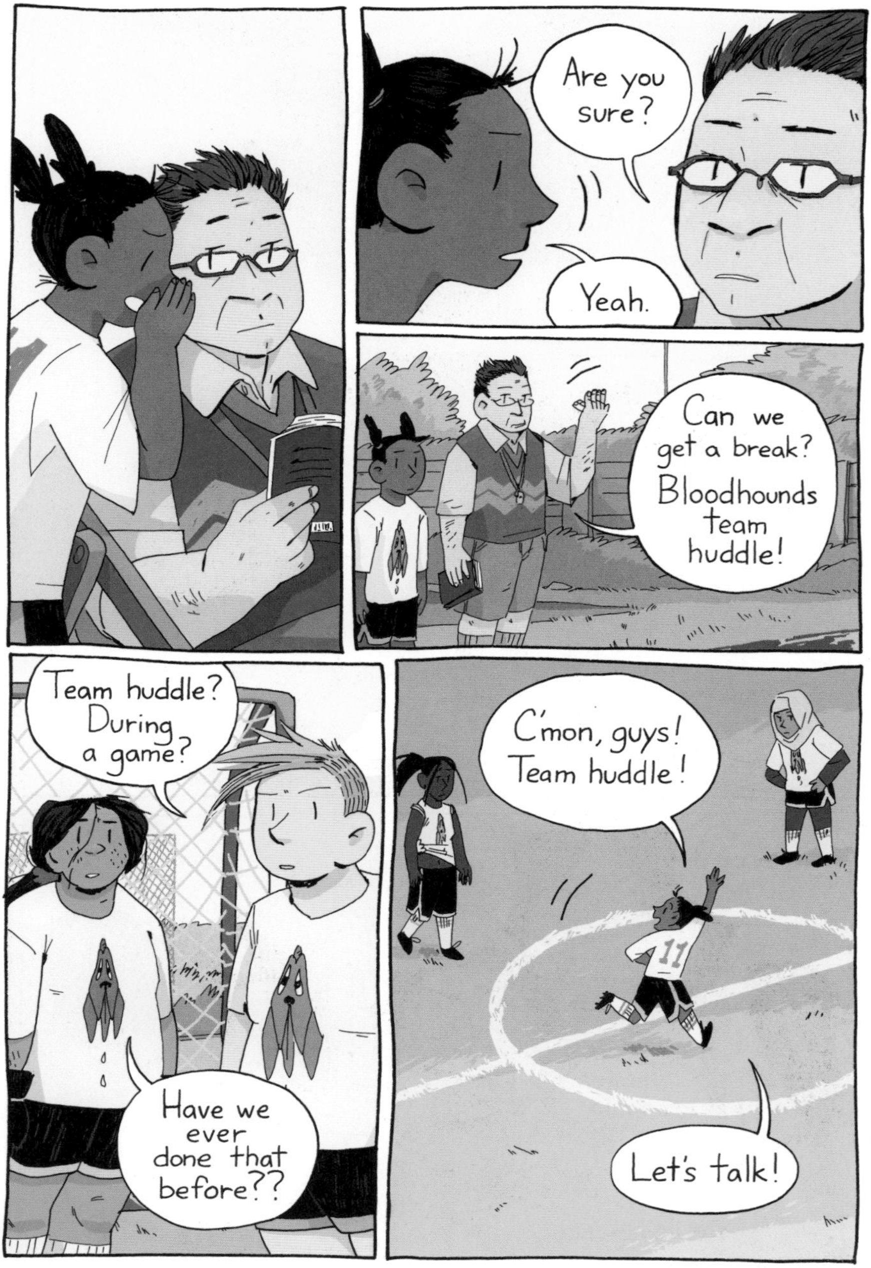
Are you sure?
Yeah.
Can we get a break? Bloodhounds team huddle!
Team huddle? During a game?
Have we ever done that before??
C'mon, guys! Team huddle!
Let's talk!

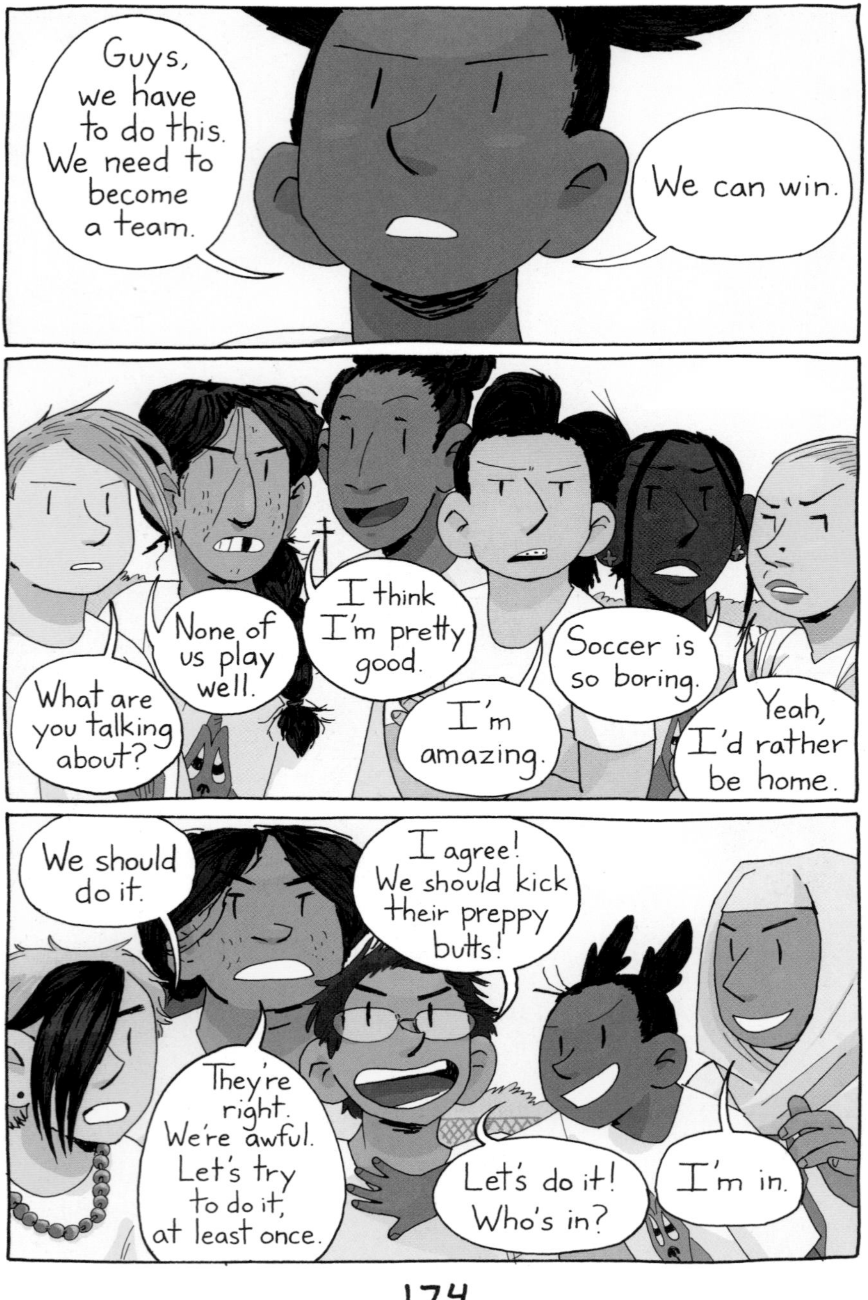
Guys, we have to do this. We need to become a team.
We can win.
What are you talking about?
None of us play well.
I think I'm pretty good.
I'm amazing.
Soccer is so boring.
Yeah, I'd rather be home.
We should do it.
I agree! We should kick their preppy butts!
They're right. We're awful. Let's try to do it, at least once.
Let's do it! Who's in?
I'm in.

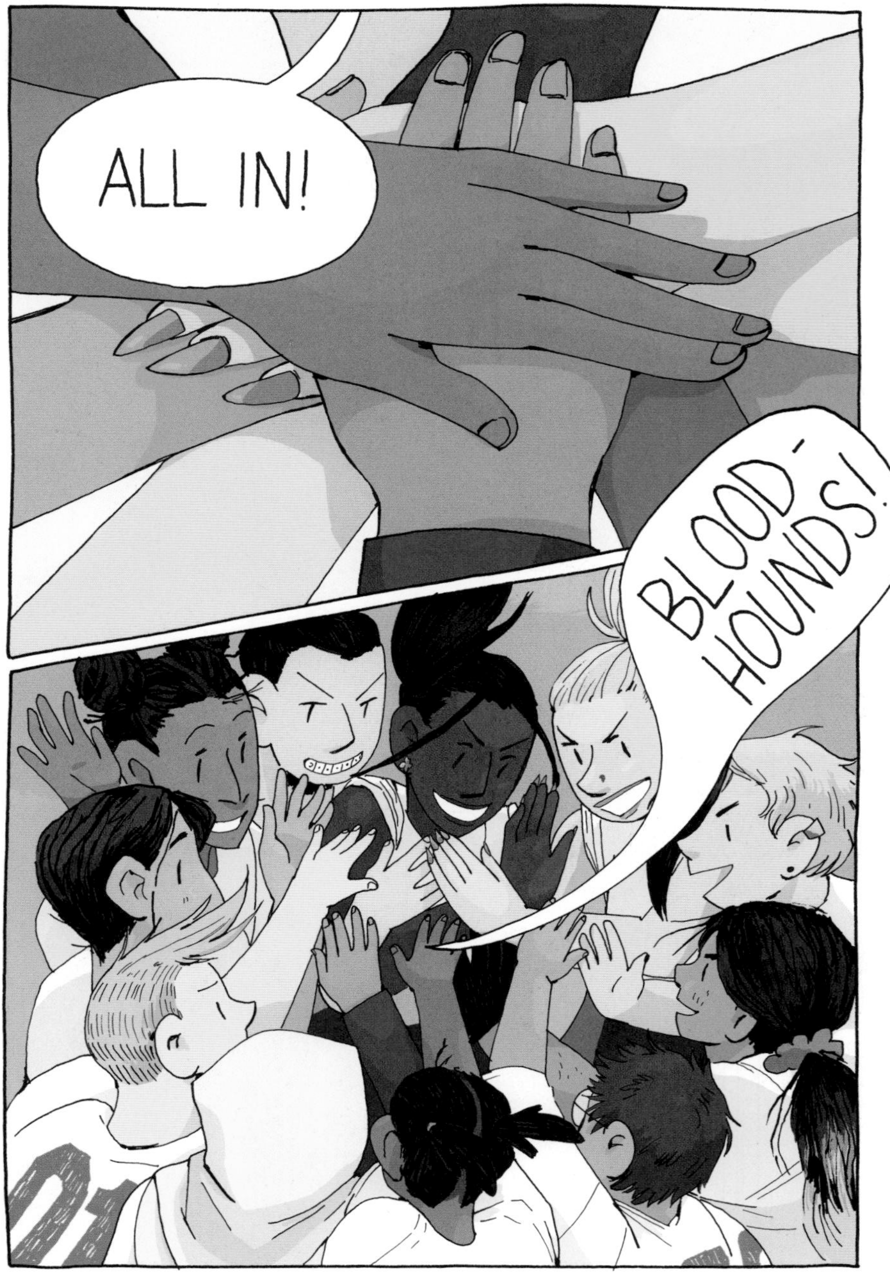
ALL IN!
BLOOD-HOUNDS!

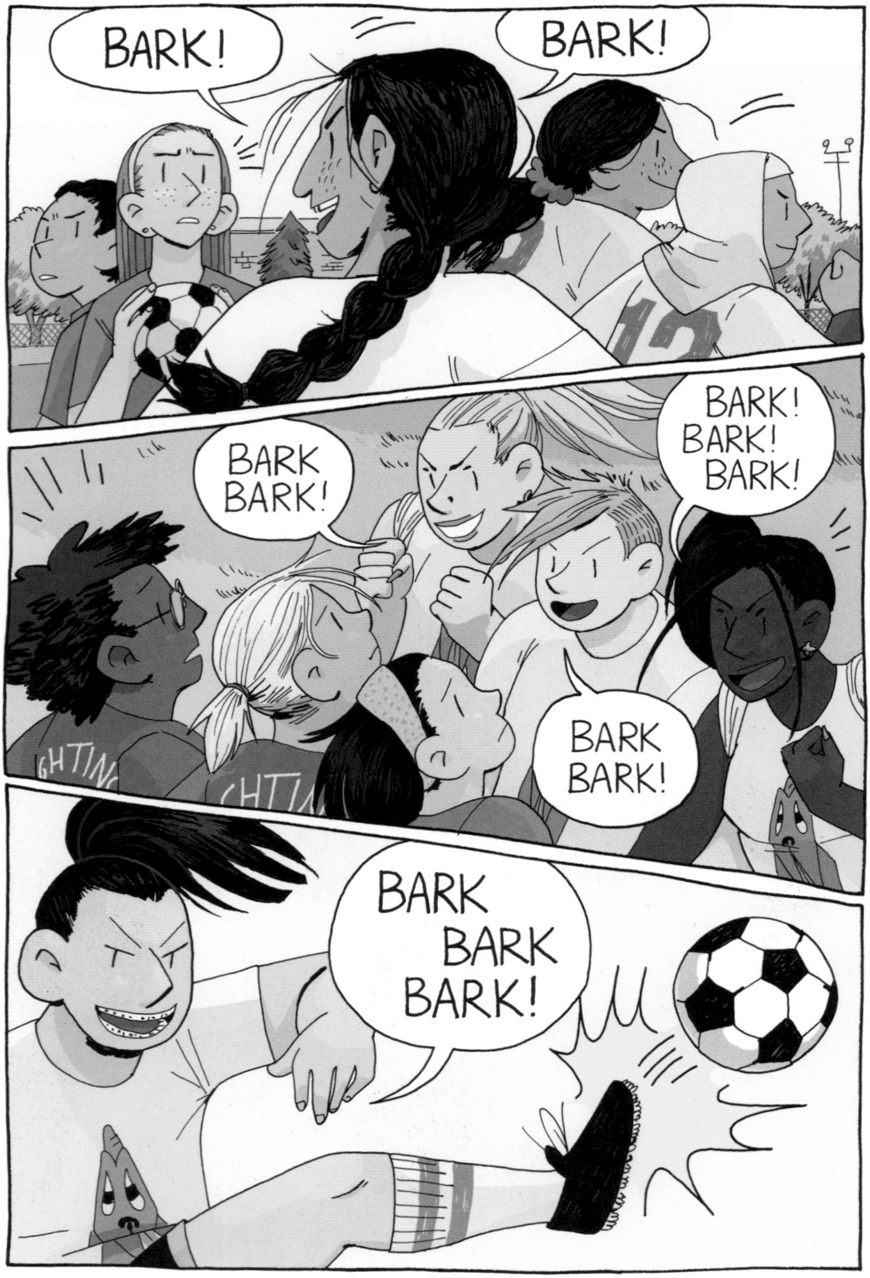
BARK!
BARK!
BARK BARK!
BARK! BARK! BARK!
BARK BARK!
BARK BARK BARK!

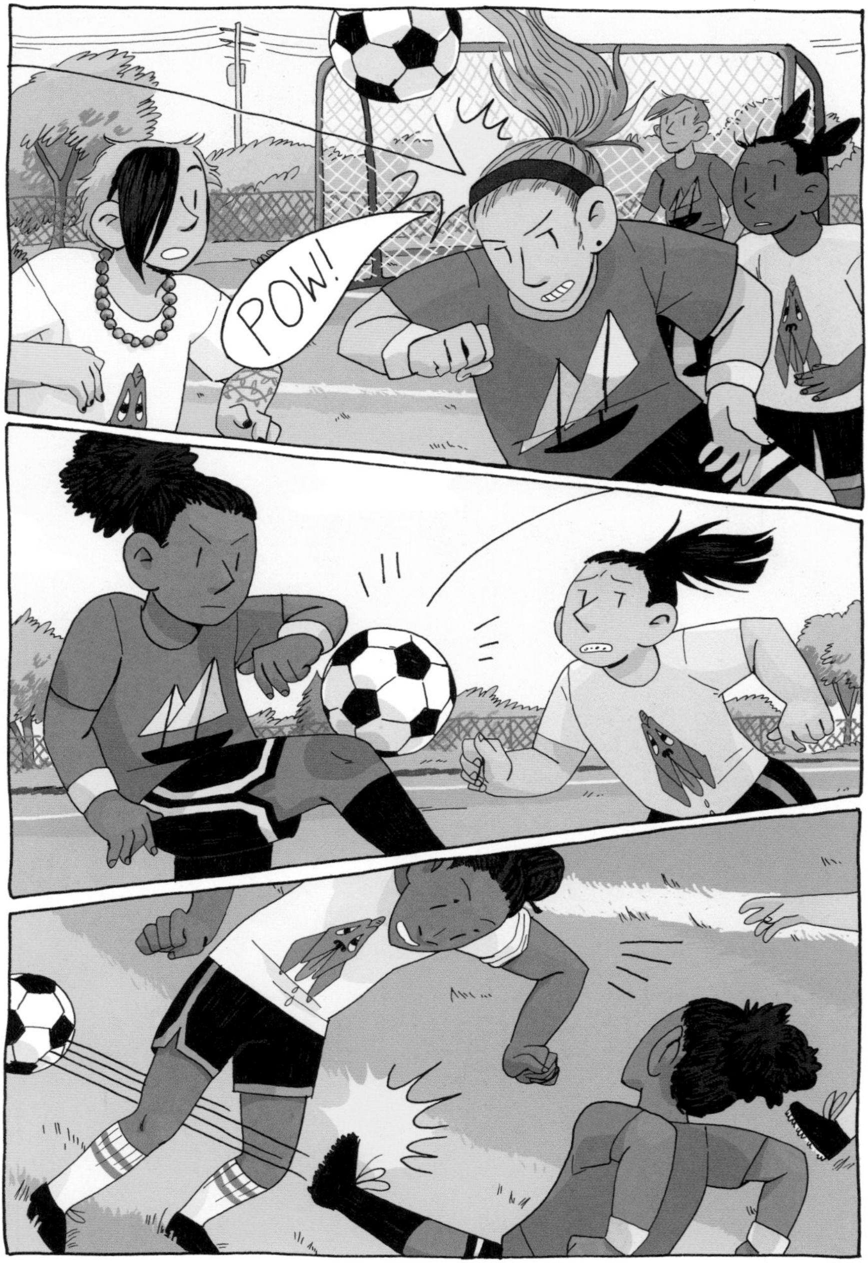
POW!

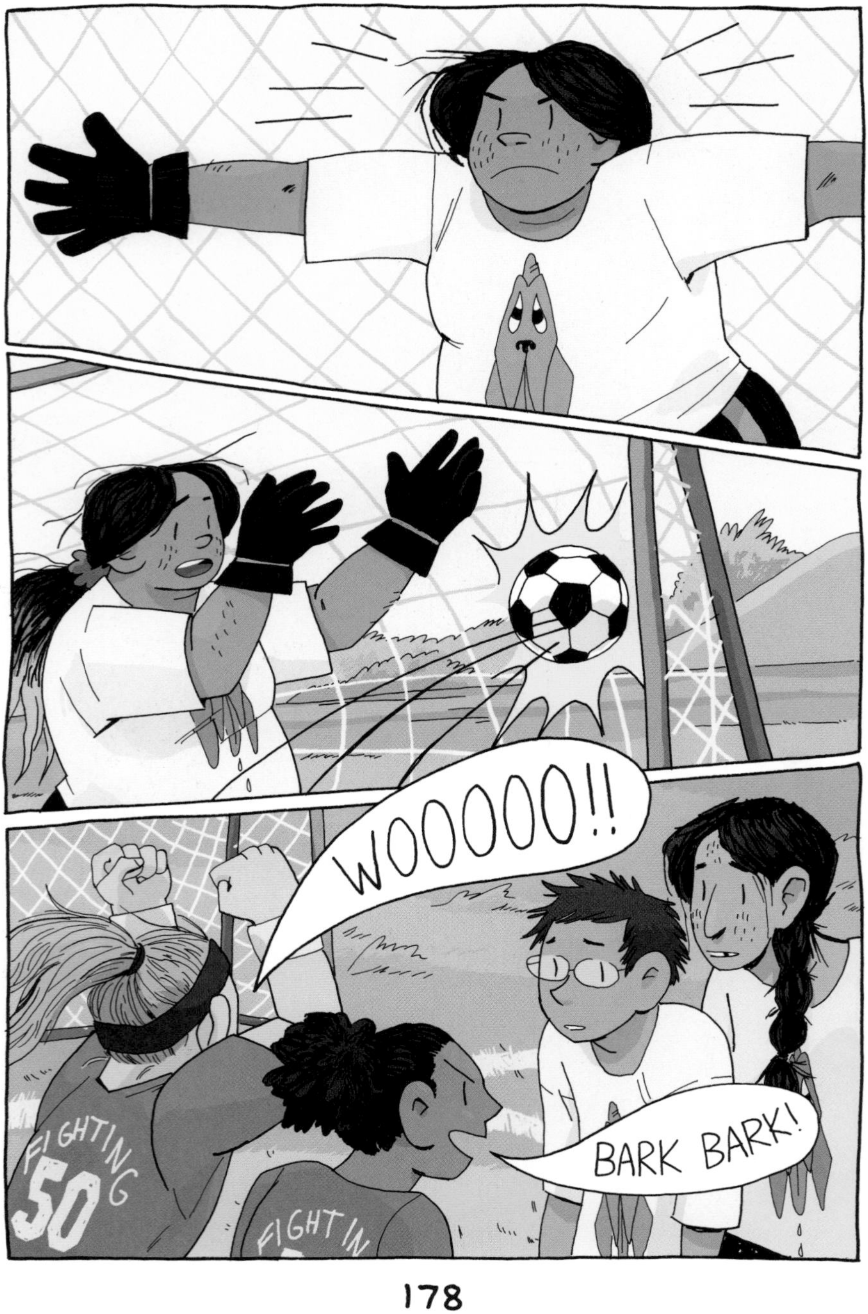
WOOOOO!!
BARK BARK!
FIGHTING 50
FIGHTIN

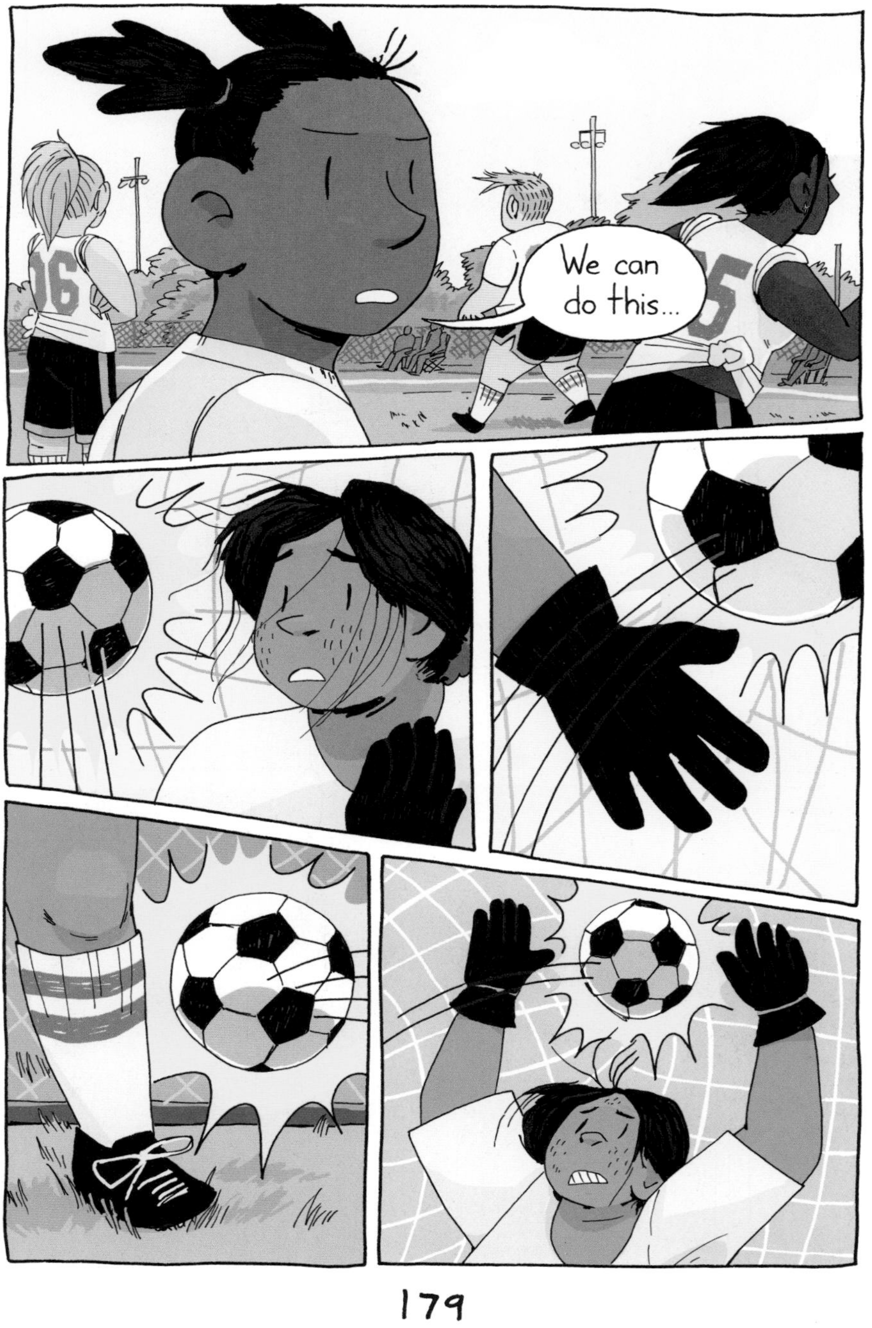
We can do this...

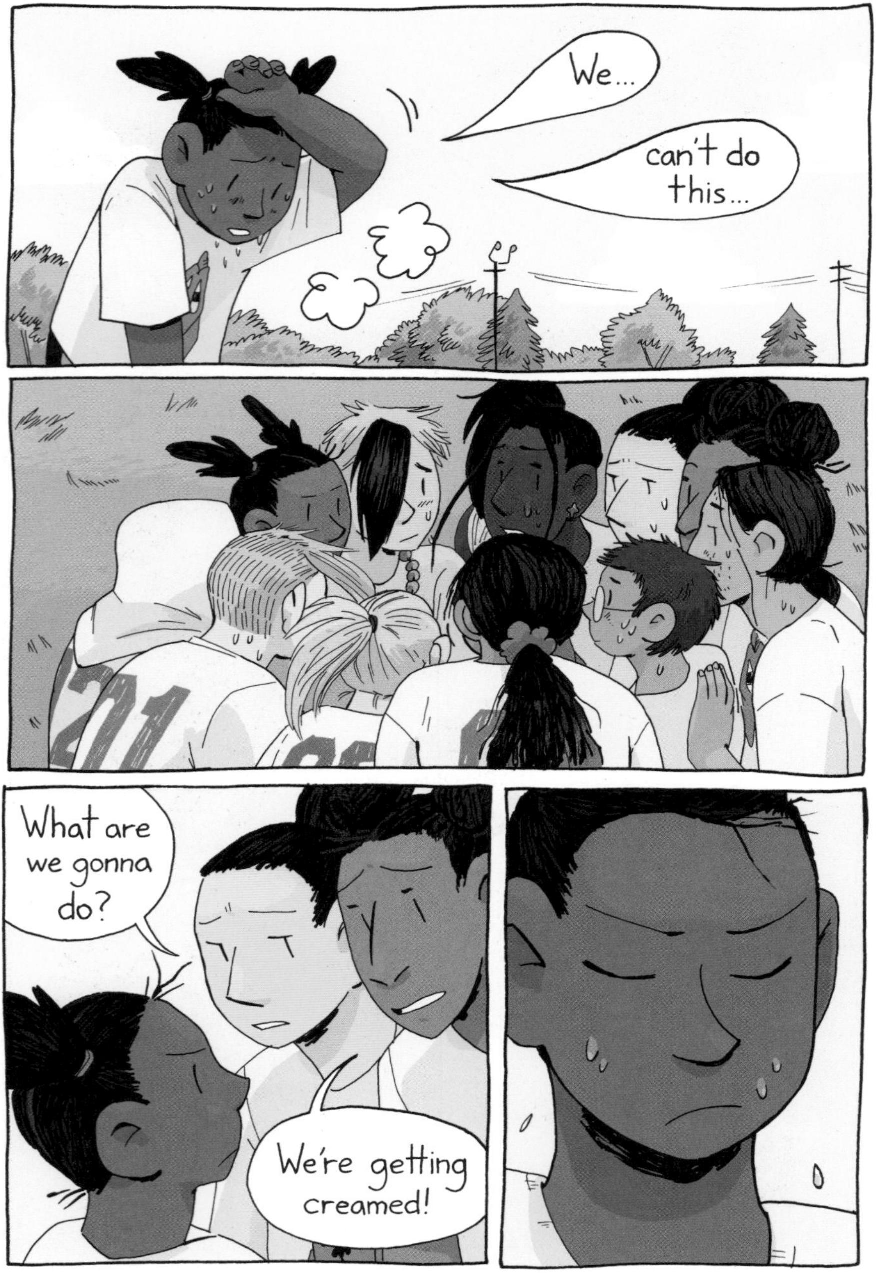
We...
can't do this...
What are we gonna do?
We're getting creamed!

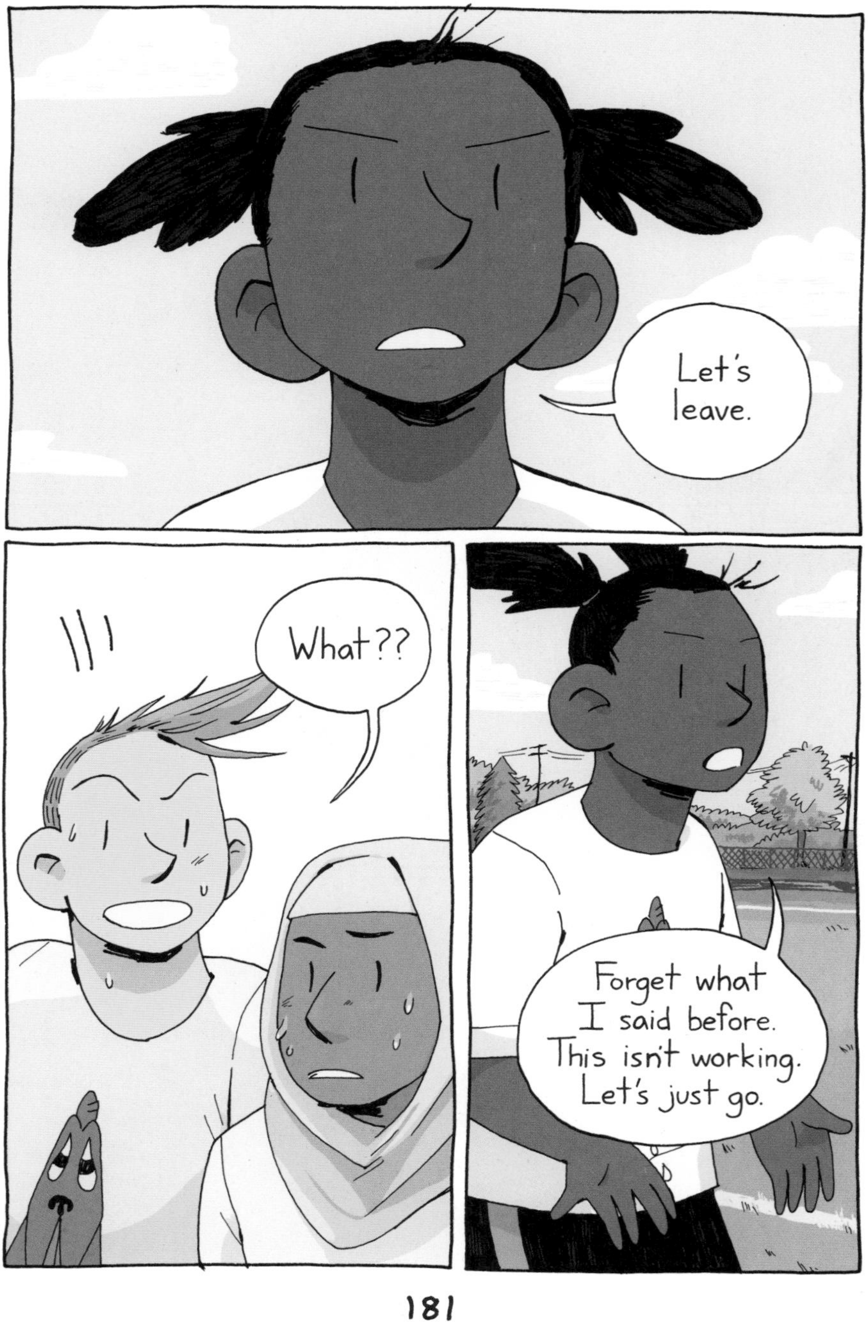
Let's leave.
What??
Forget what I said before. This isn't working. Let's just go.

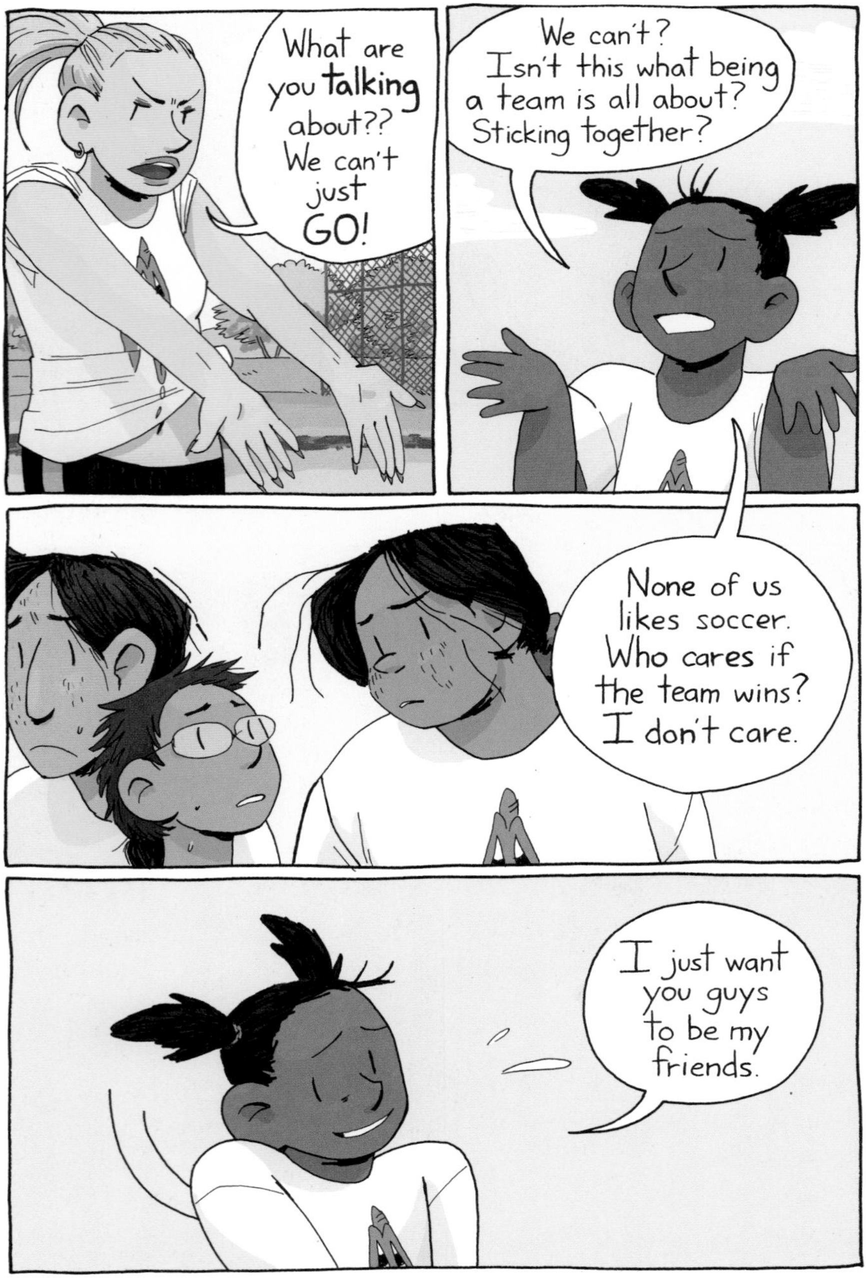
What are you talking about?? We can't just GO!
We can't? Isn't this what being a team is all about? Sticking together?
None of us likes soccer. Who cares if the team wins? I don't care.
I just want you guys to be my friends.

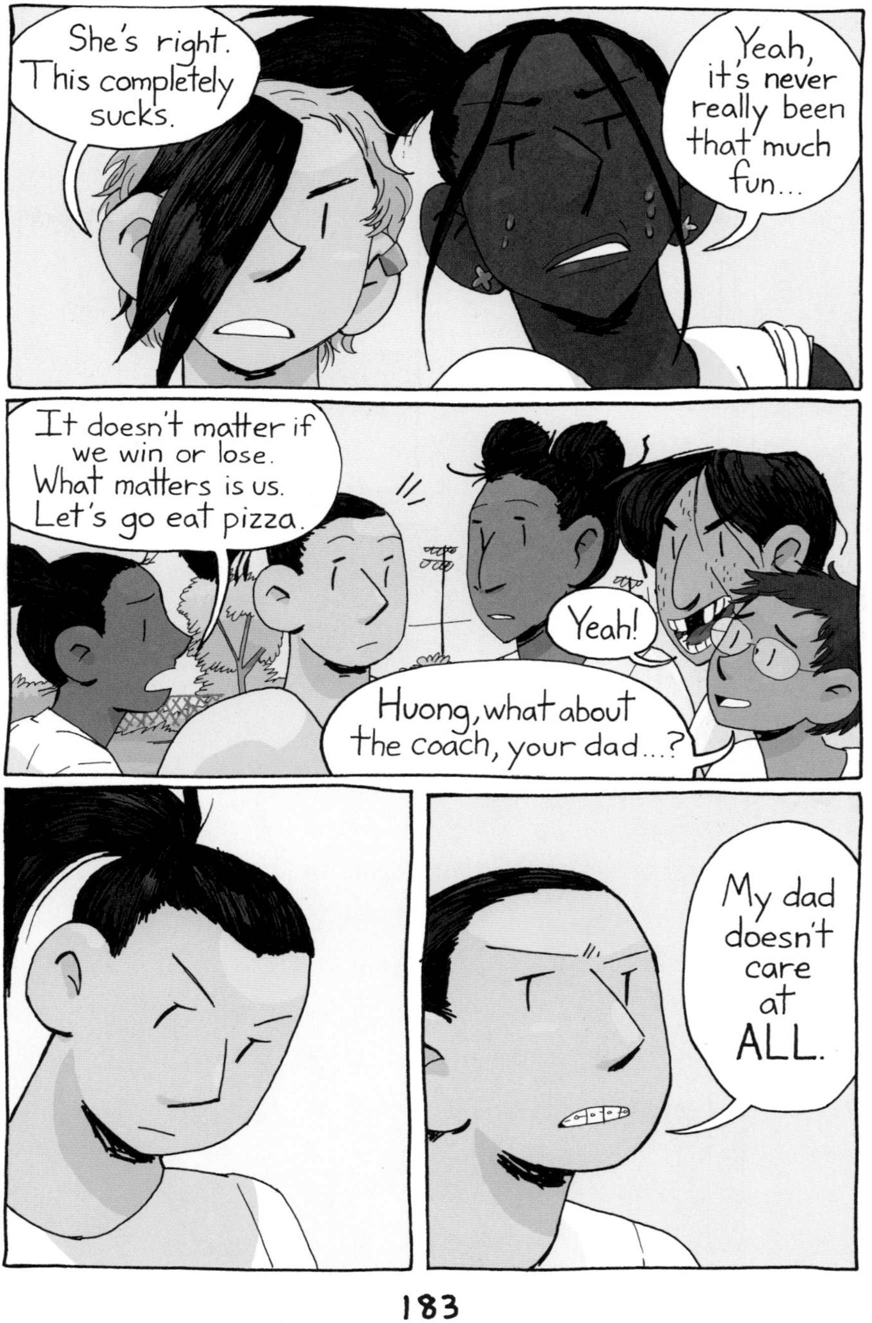
She's right. This completely sucks.
Yeah, it's never really been that much fun...
It doesn't matter if we win or lose. What matters is us. Let's go eat pizza.
Yeah!
Huong, what about the coach, your dad...?
My dad doesn't care at ALL.

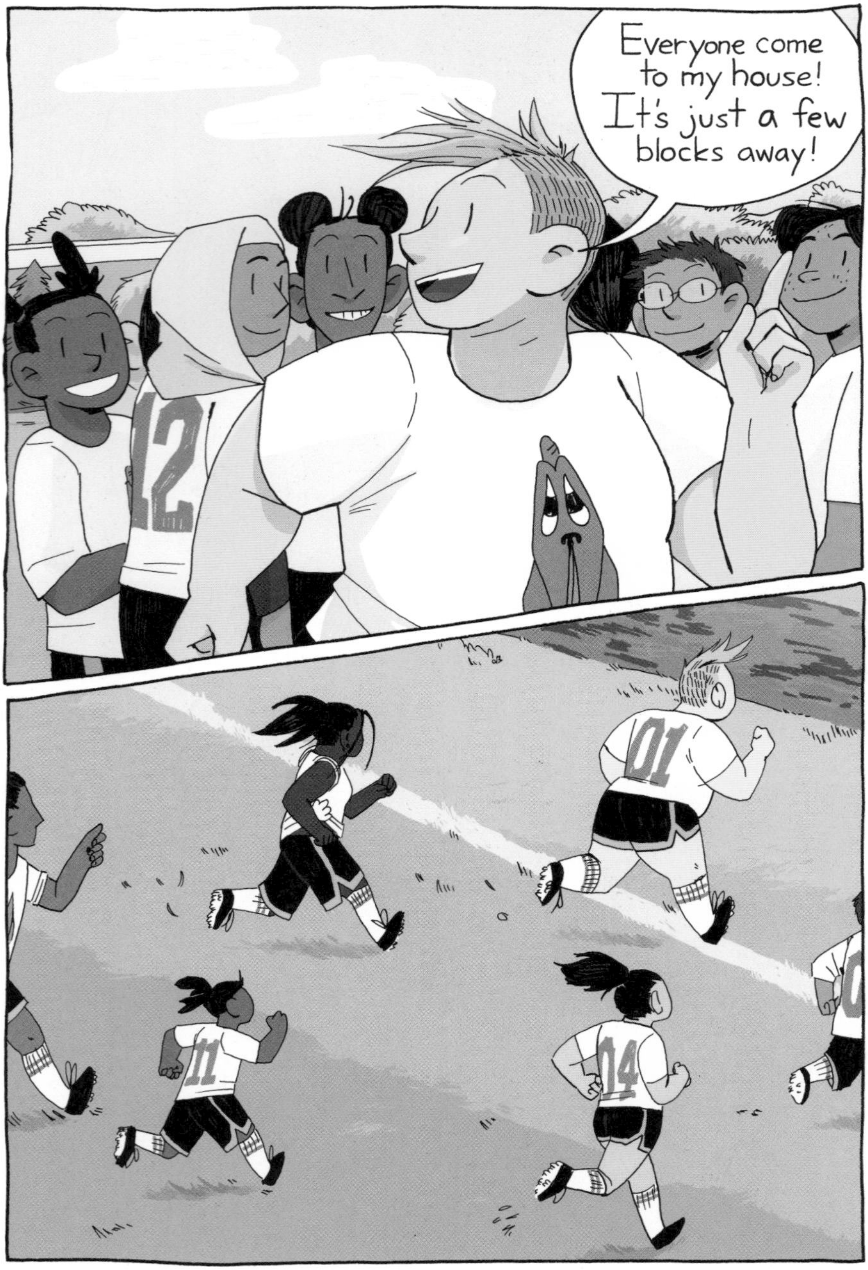
Everyone come to my house! It's just a few blocks away!
12
01
11
14

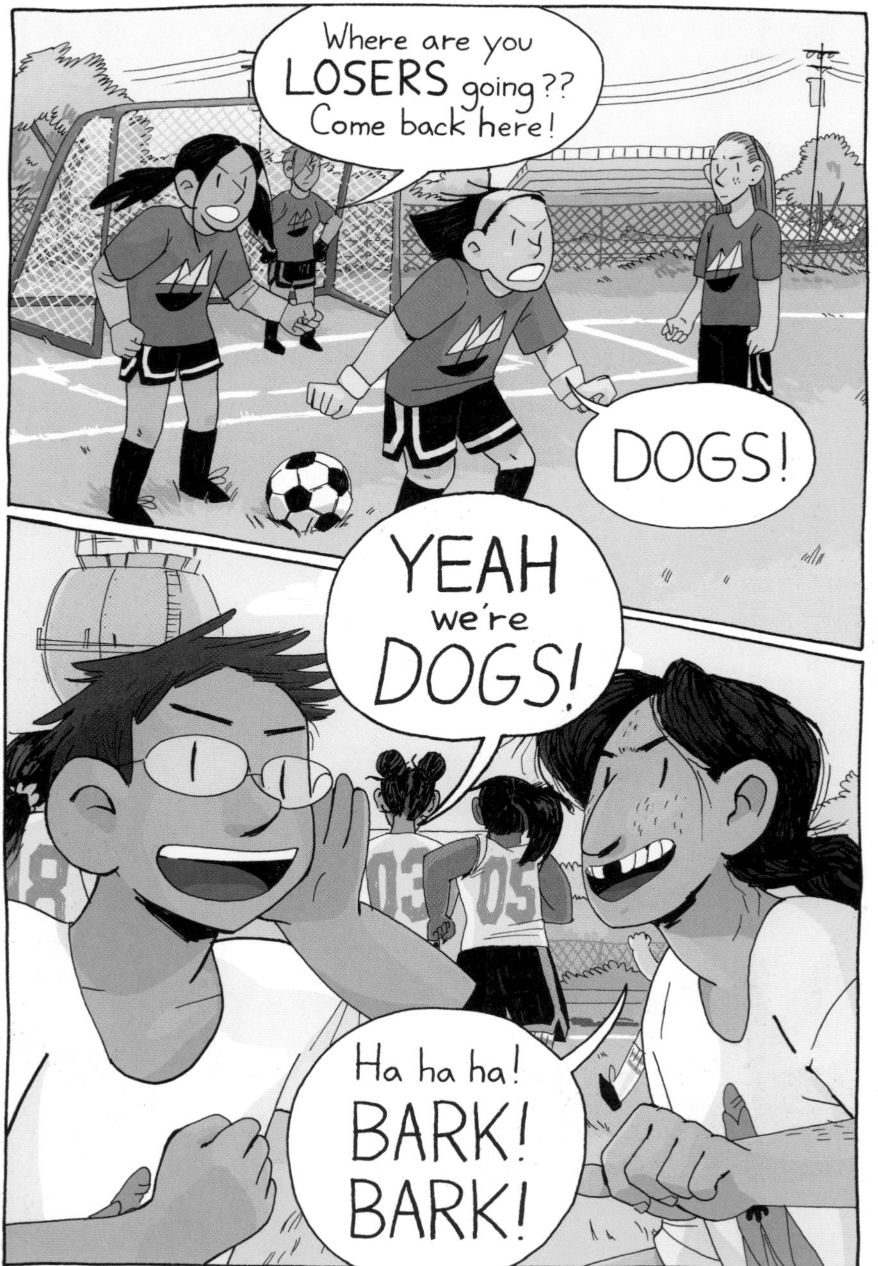
Where are you LOSERS going?? Come back here!
DOGS!
YEAH we're DOGS!
Ha ha ha! BARK! BARK!

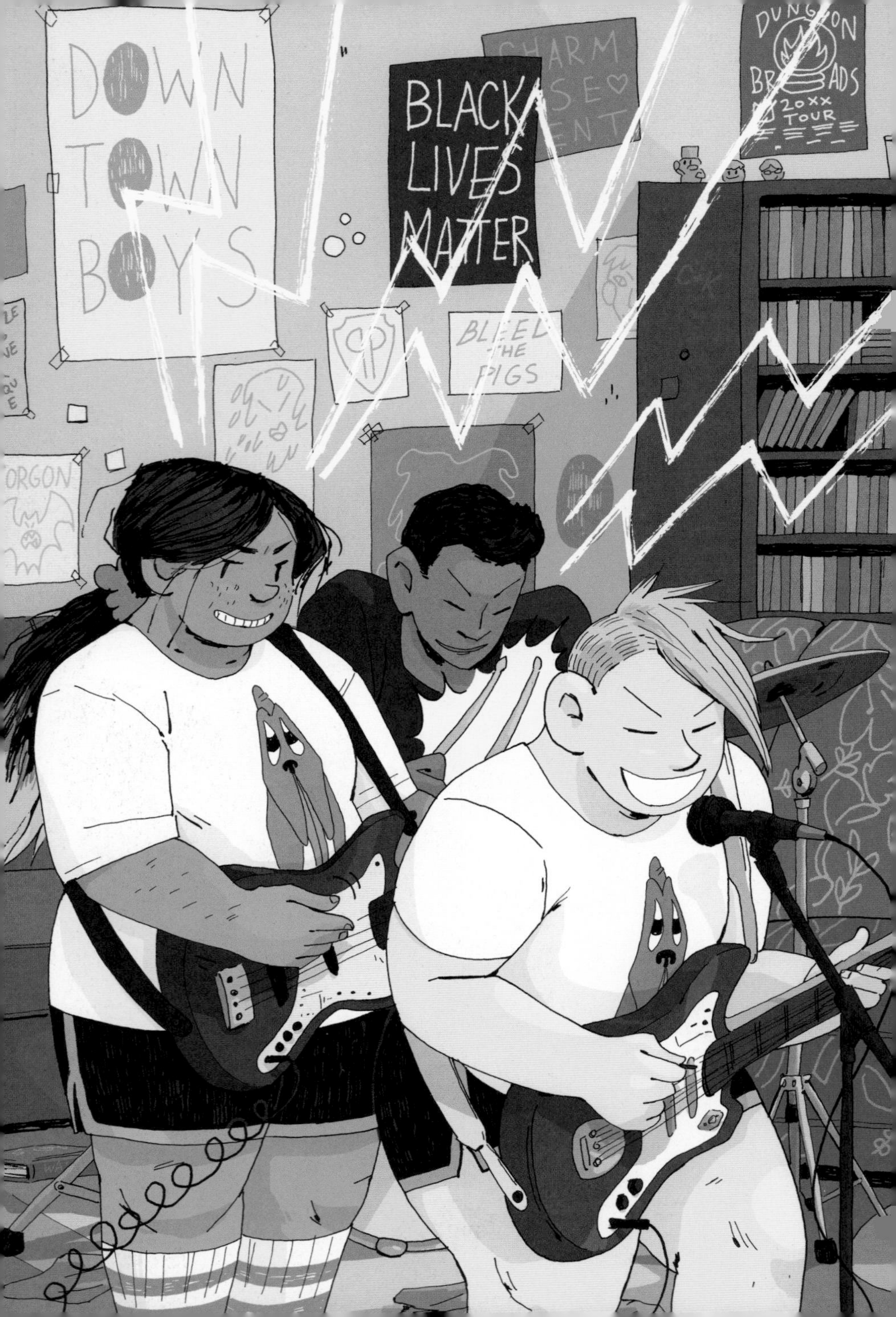
DOWN TOWN BOYS
BLACK LIVES MATTER
BLEED THE PIGS
20XX TOUR

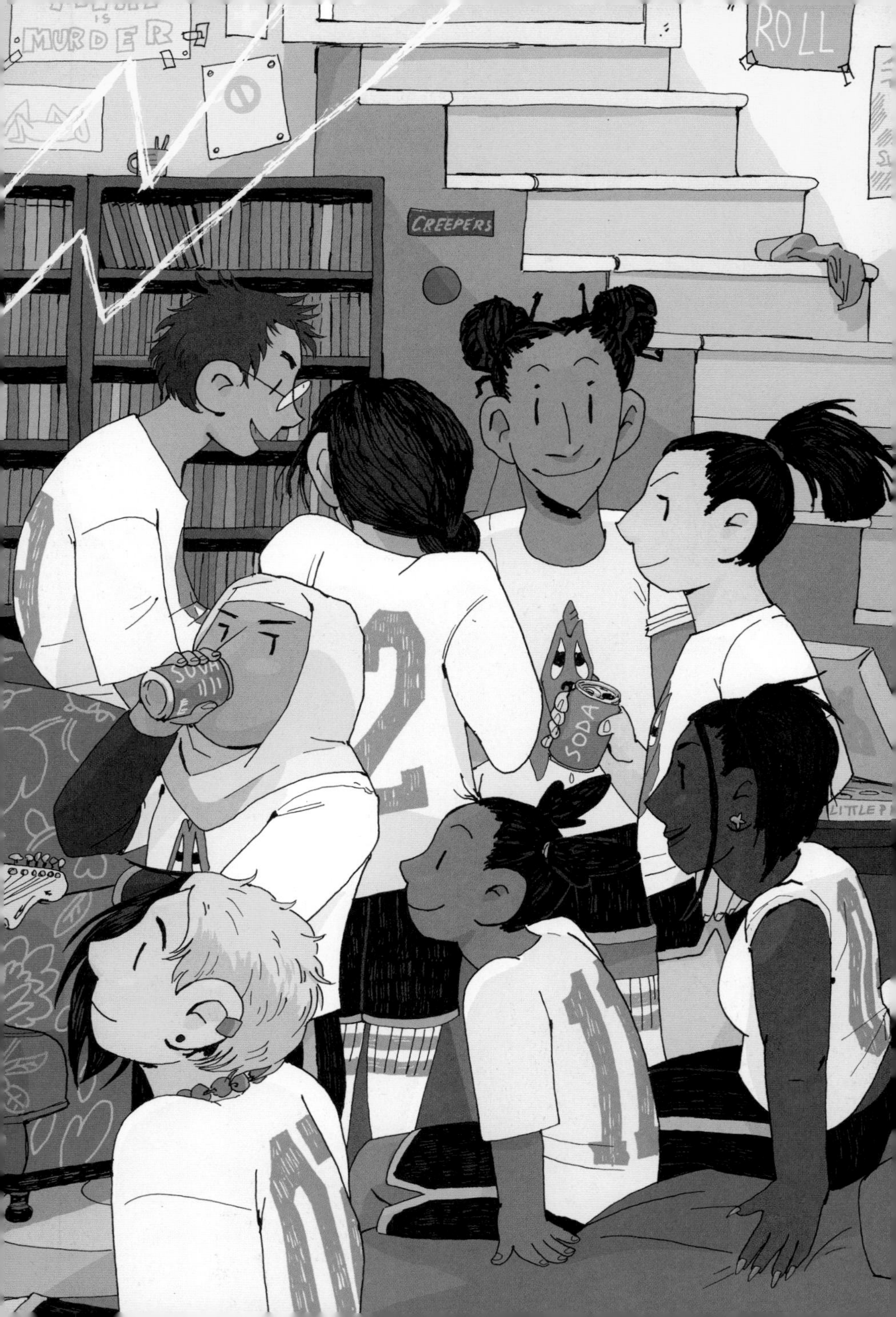

IS
MURDER
ROLL
CREEPERS
SODA

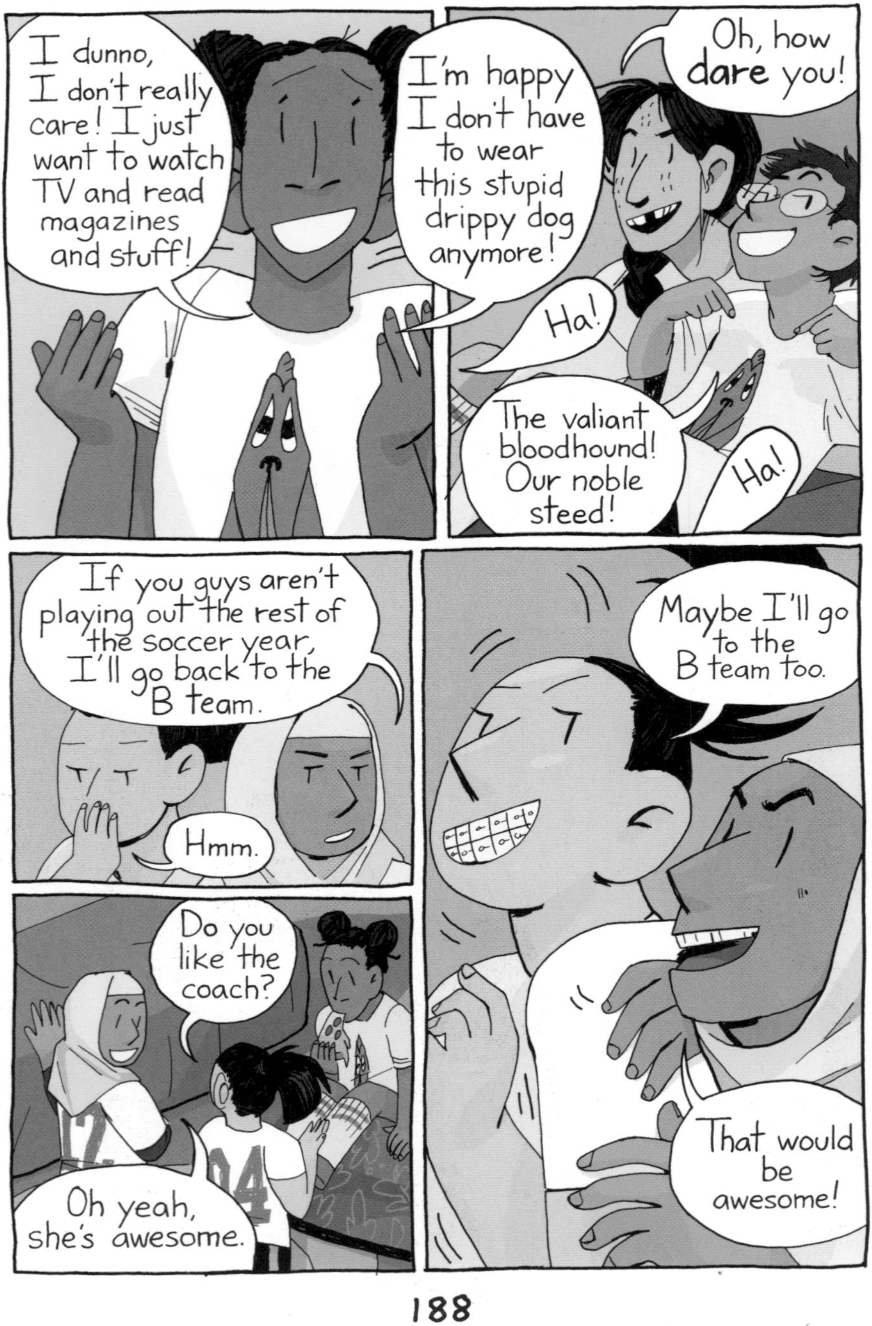
I dunno, I don't really care! I just want to watch TV and read magazines and stuff!
I'm happy I don't have to wear this stupid drippy dog anymore!
Oh, how **dare** you!
Ha!
The valiant bloodhound! Our noble steed!
Ha!
If you guys aren't playing out the rest of the soccer year, I'll go back to the B team.
Hmm.
Maybe I'll go to the B team too.
That would be awesome!
Do you like the coach?
Oh yeah, she's awesome.

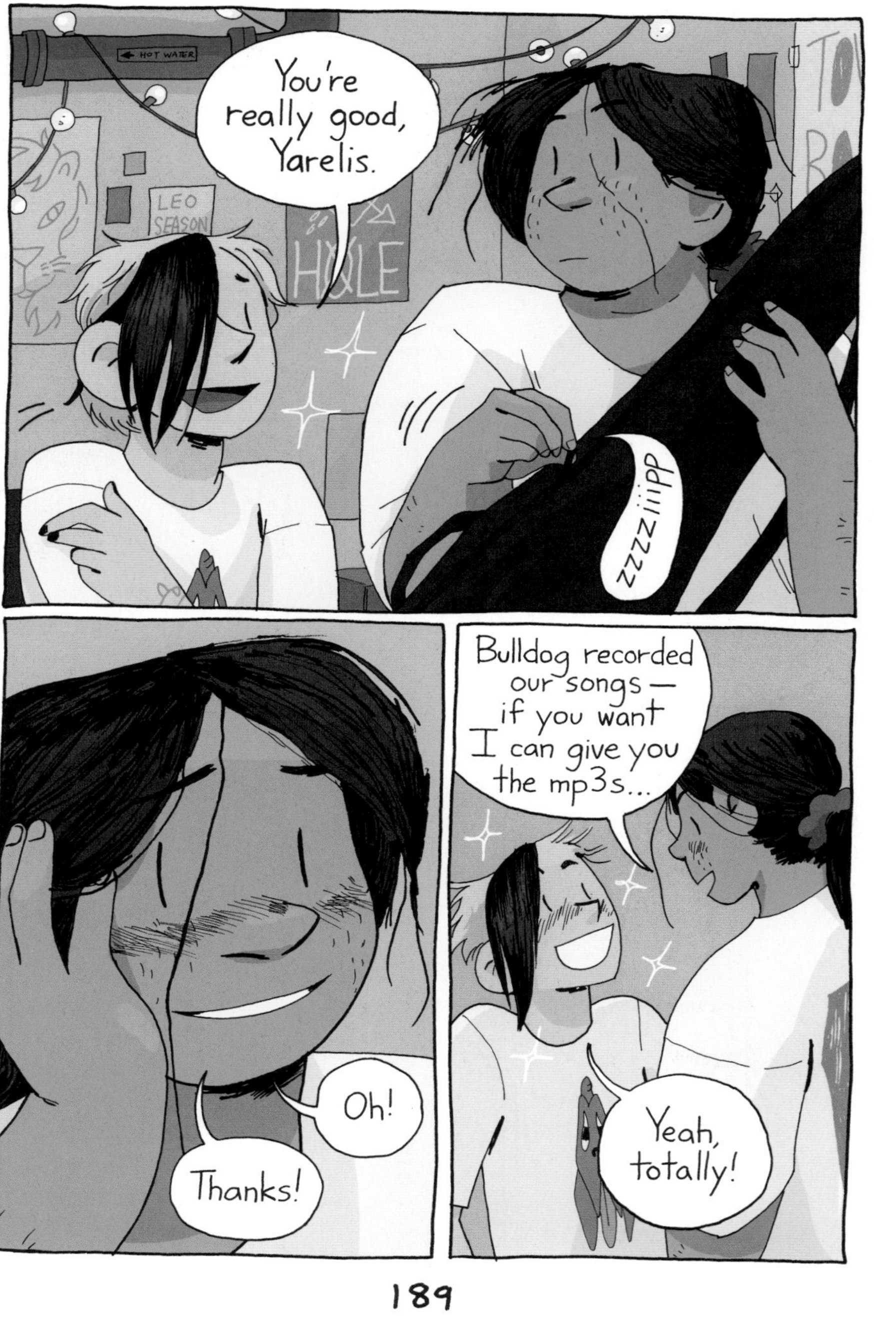

HOT WATER
LEO SEASON
HOLE
You're really good, Yarelis.
zzzziiipp
Bulldog recorded our songs — if you want I can give you the mp3s...
Oh!
Thanks!
Yeah, totally!

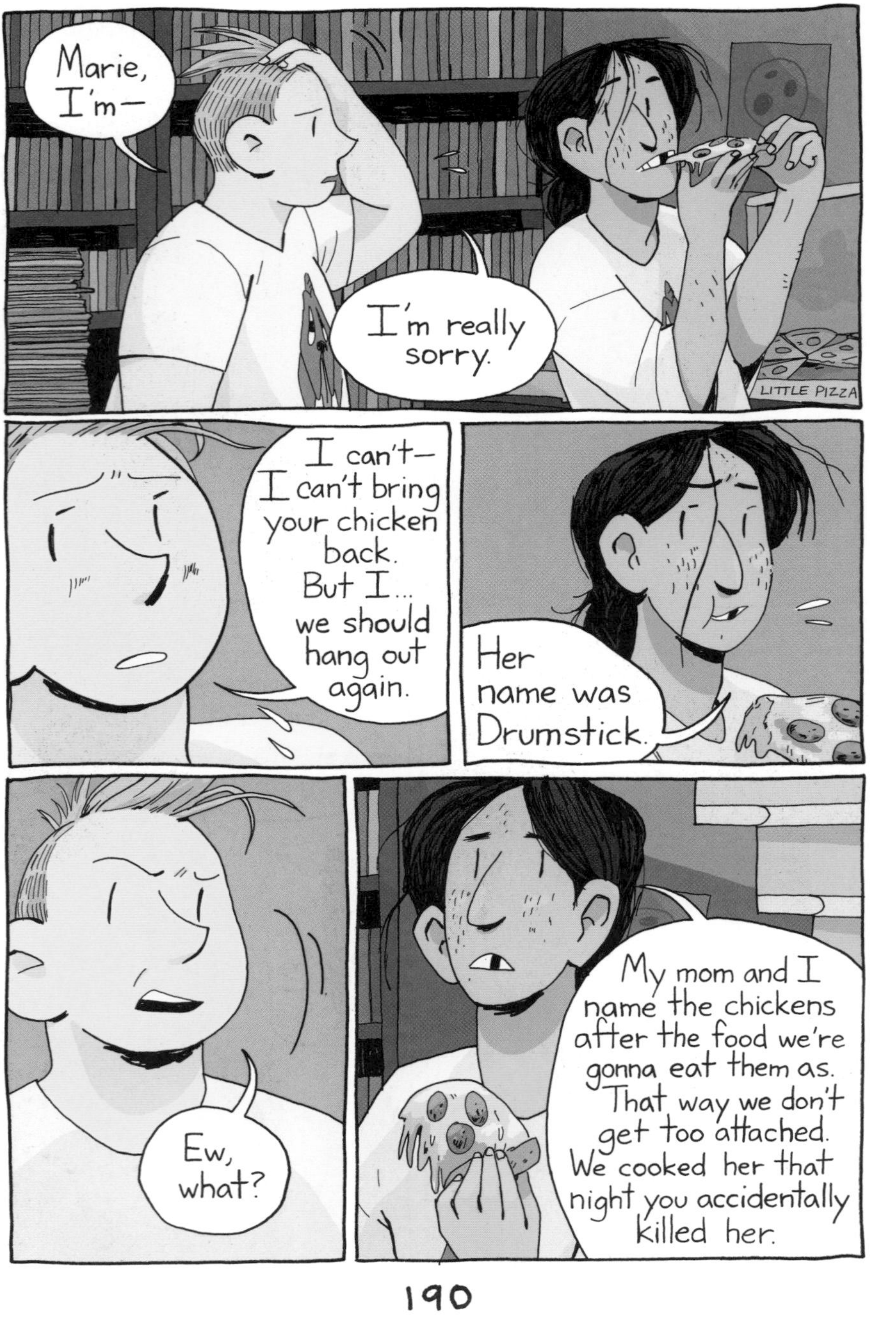
Marie, I'm—
I'm really sorry.
LITTLE PIZZA
I can't— I can't bring your chicken back. But I... we should hang out again.
Her name was Drumstick.
Ew, what?
My mom and I name the chickens after the food we're gonna eat them as. That way we don't get too attached. We cooked her that night you accidentally killed her.

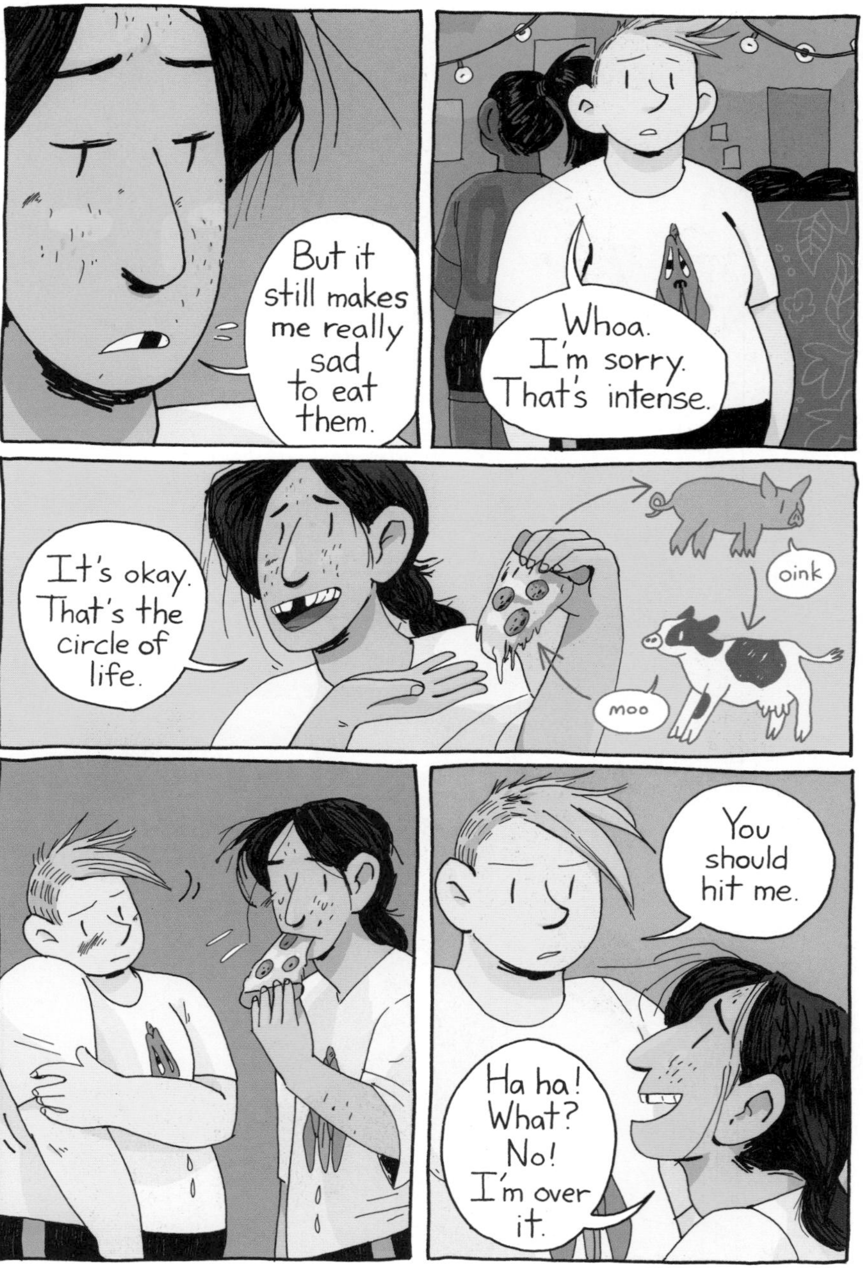
But it still makes me really sad to eat them.
Whoa. I'm sorry. That's intense.
It's okay. That's the circle of life.
oink
moo
You should hit me.
Ha ha! What? No! I'm over it.

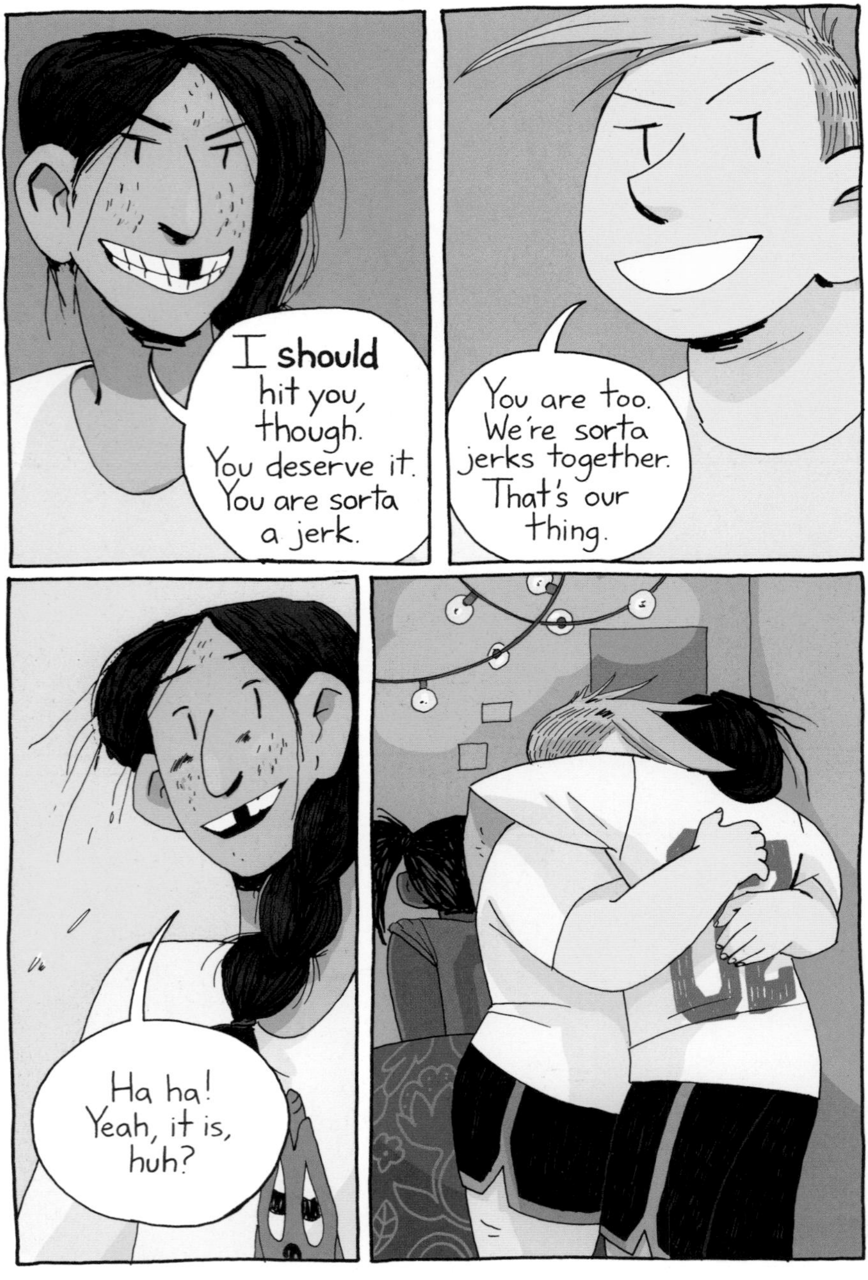
I **should** hit you, though. You deserve it. You are sorta a jerk.
You are too. We're sorta jerks together. That's our thing.
Ha ha! Yeah, it is, huh?

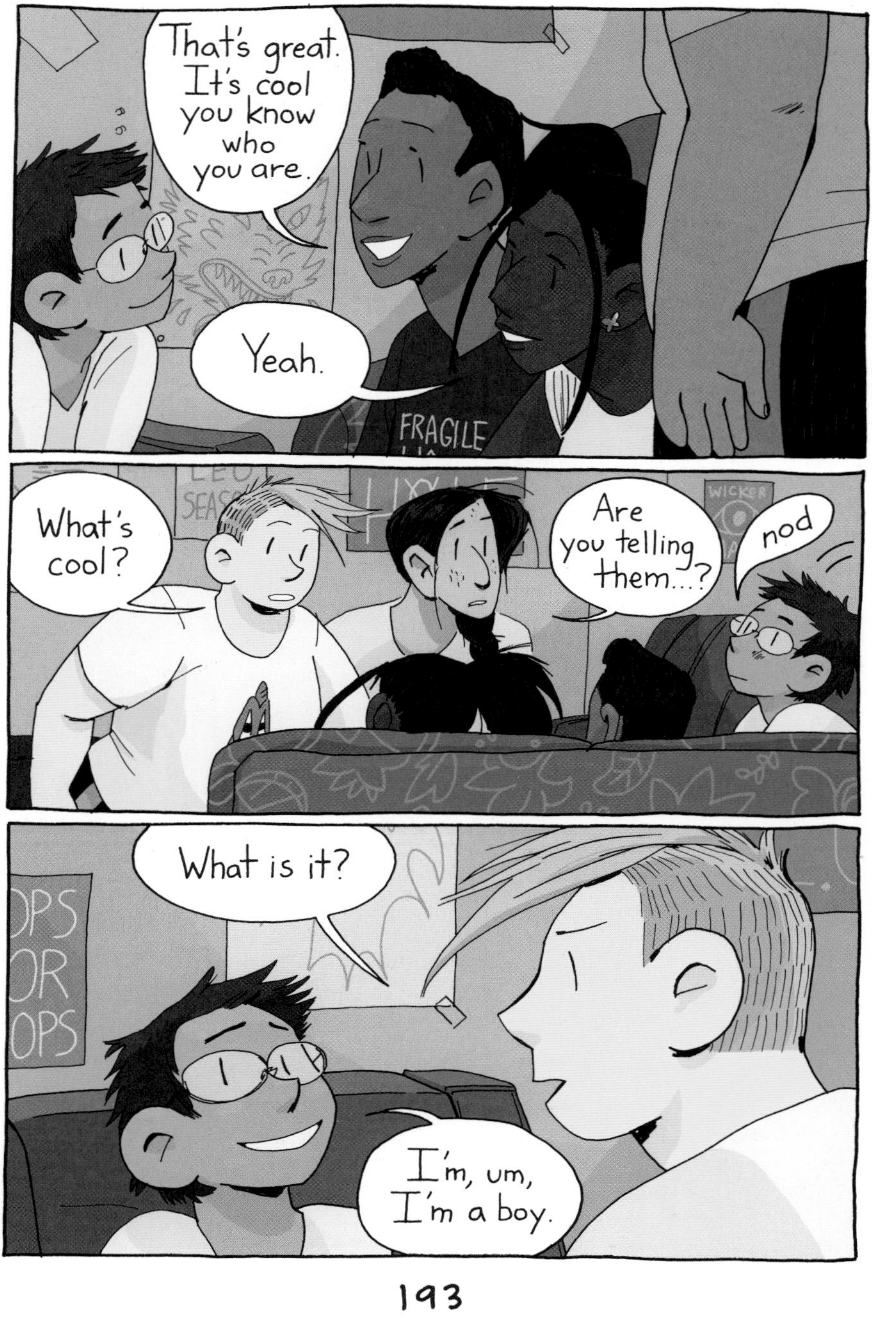
That's great. It's cool you know who you are.
FRAGILE
Yeah.
LEO SEAS
WICKER
What's cool?
Are you telling them...?
nod
What is it?
OPS OR OPS
I'm, um, I'm a boy.

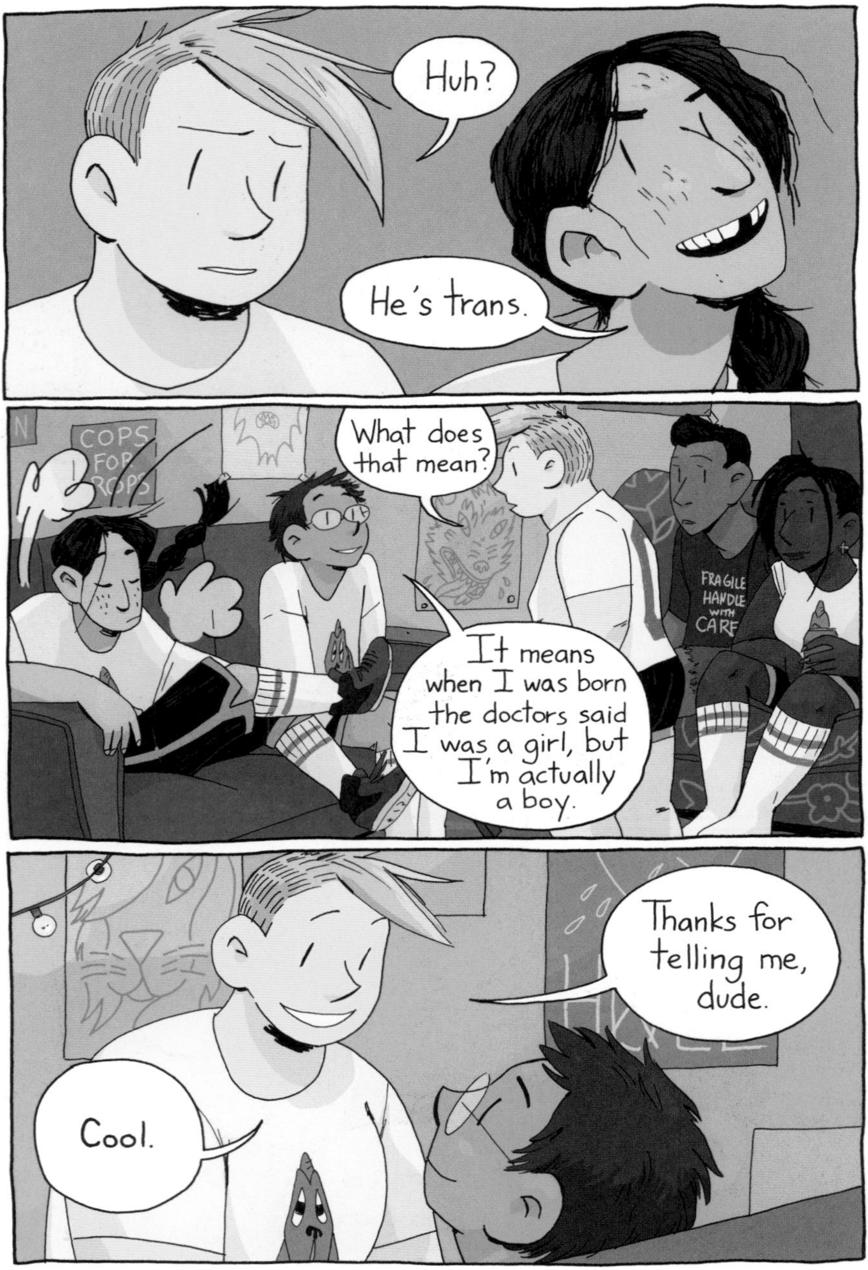
Huh?
He's trans.
COPS FOR CROPS
What does that mean?
FRAGILE HANDLE WITH CARE
It means when I was born the doctors said I was a girl, but I'm actually a boy.
Thanks for telling me, dude.
Cool.

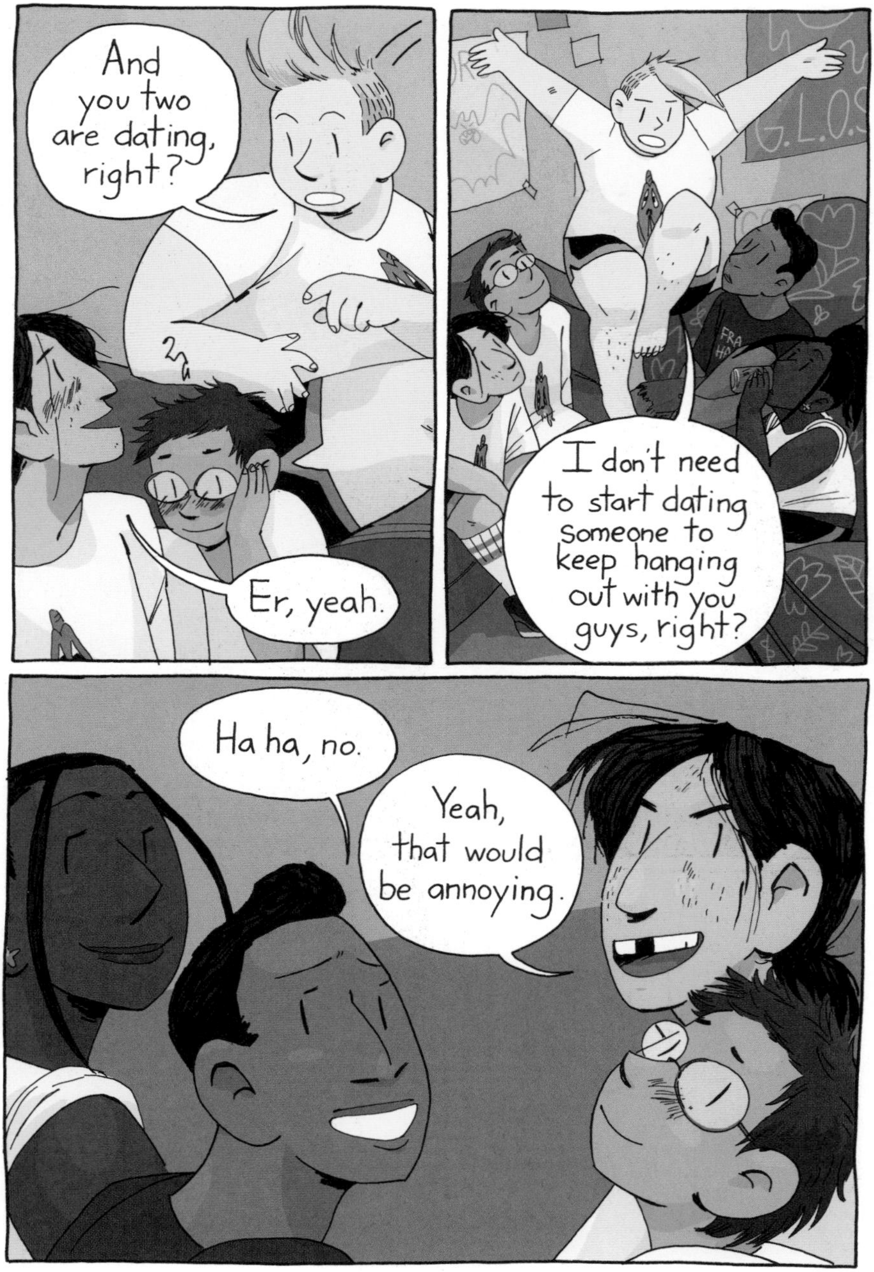
And you two are dating, right?
Er, yeah.
I don't need to start dating someone to keep hanging out with you guys, right?
Ha ha, no.
Yeah, that would be annoying.

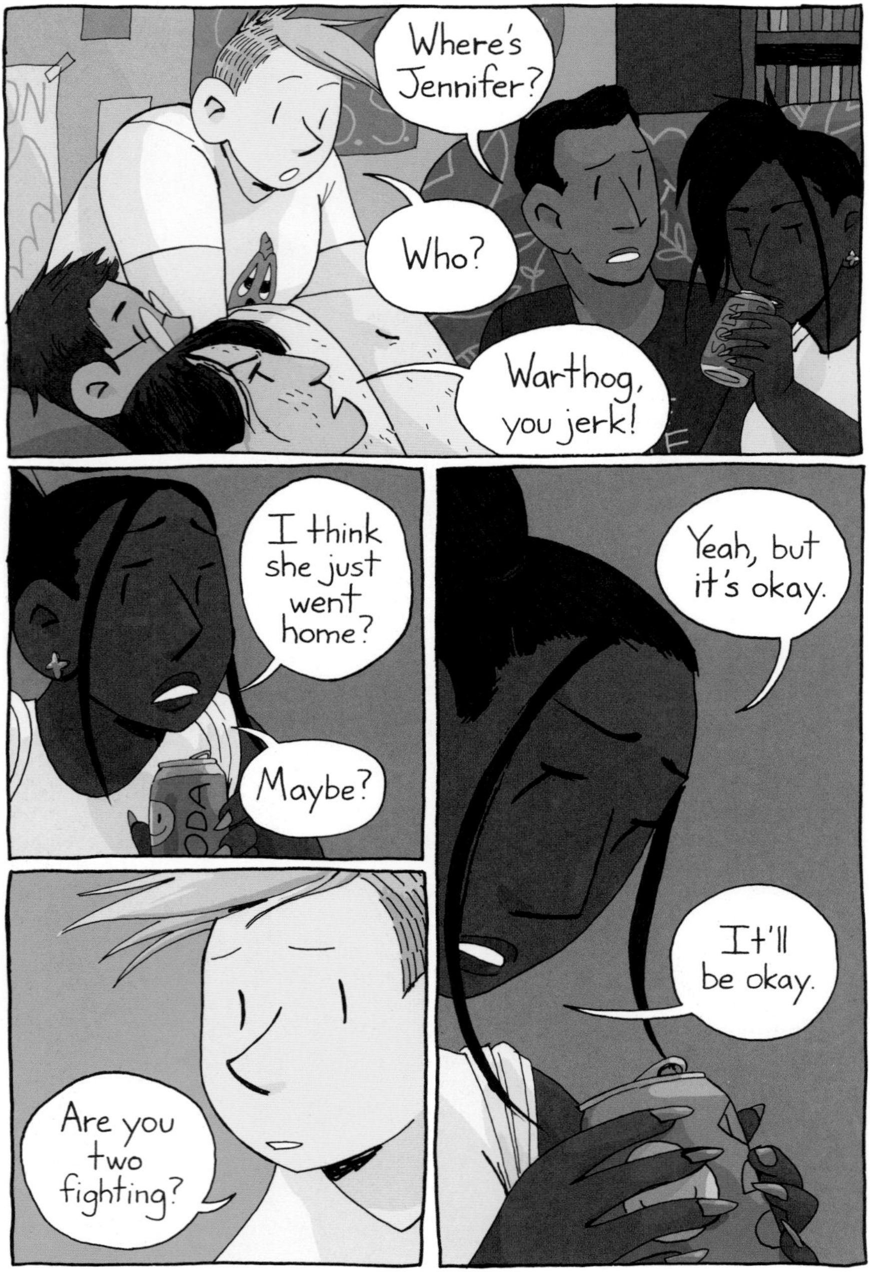
Where's Jennifer?
Who?
Warthog, you jerk!
I think she just went home?
Maybe?
Yeah, but it's okay.
It'll be okay.
Are you two fighting?

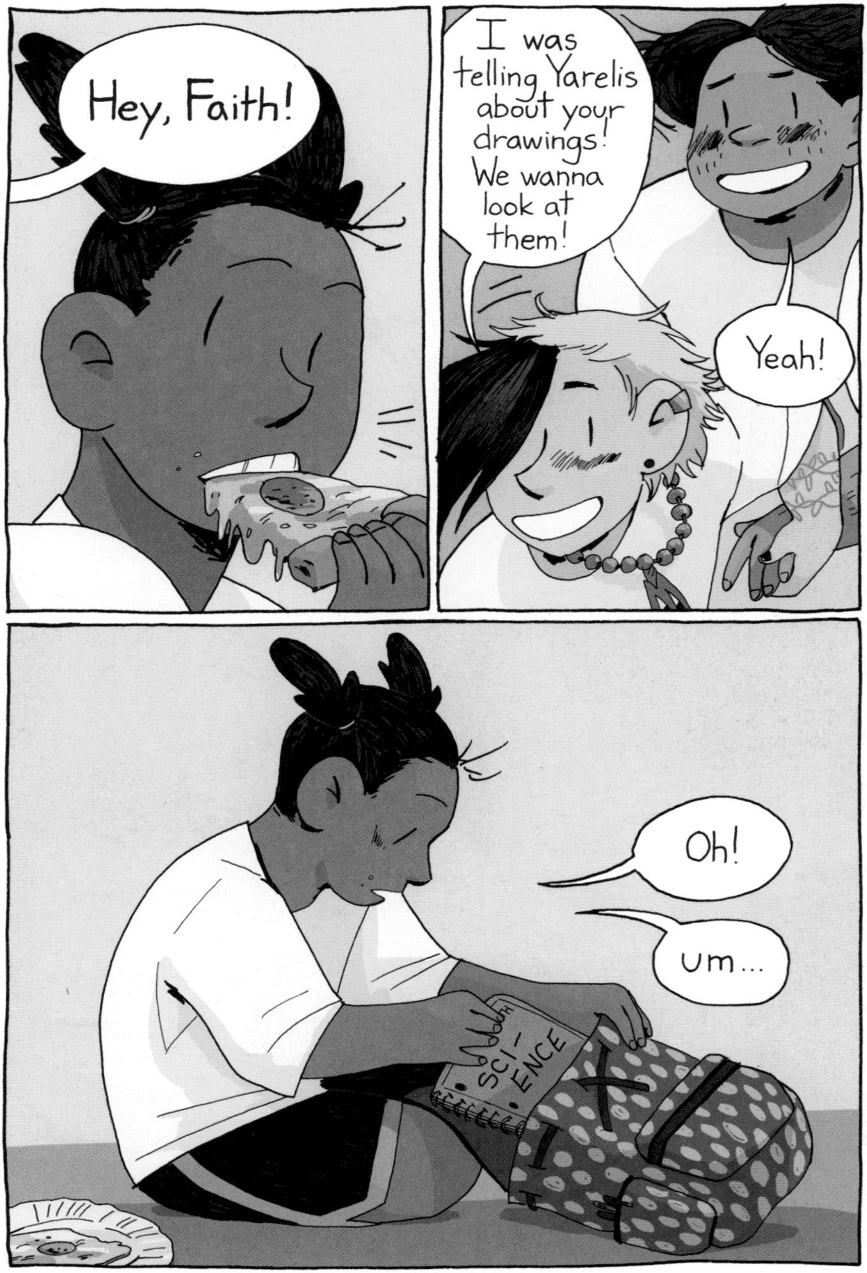
Hey, Faith!
I was telling Yarelis about your drawings! We wanna look at them!
Yeah!
Oh!
um...
SCI-ENCE

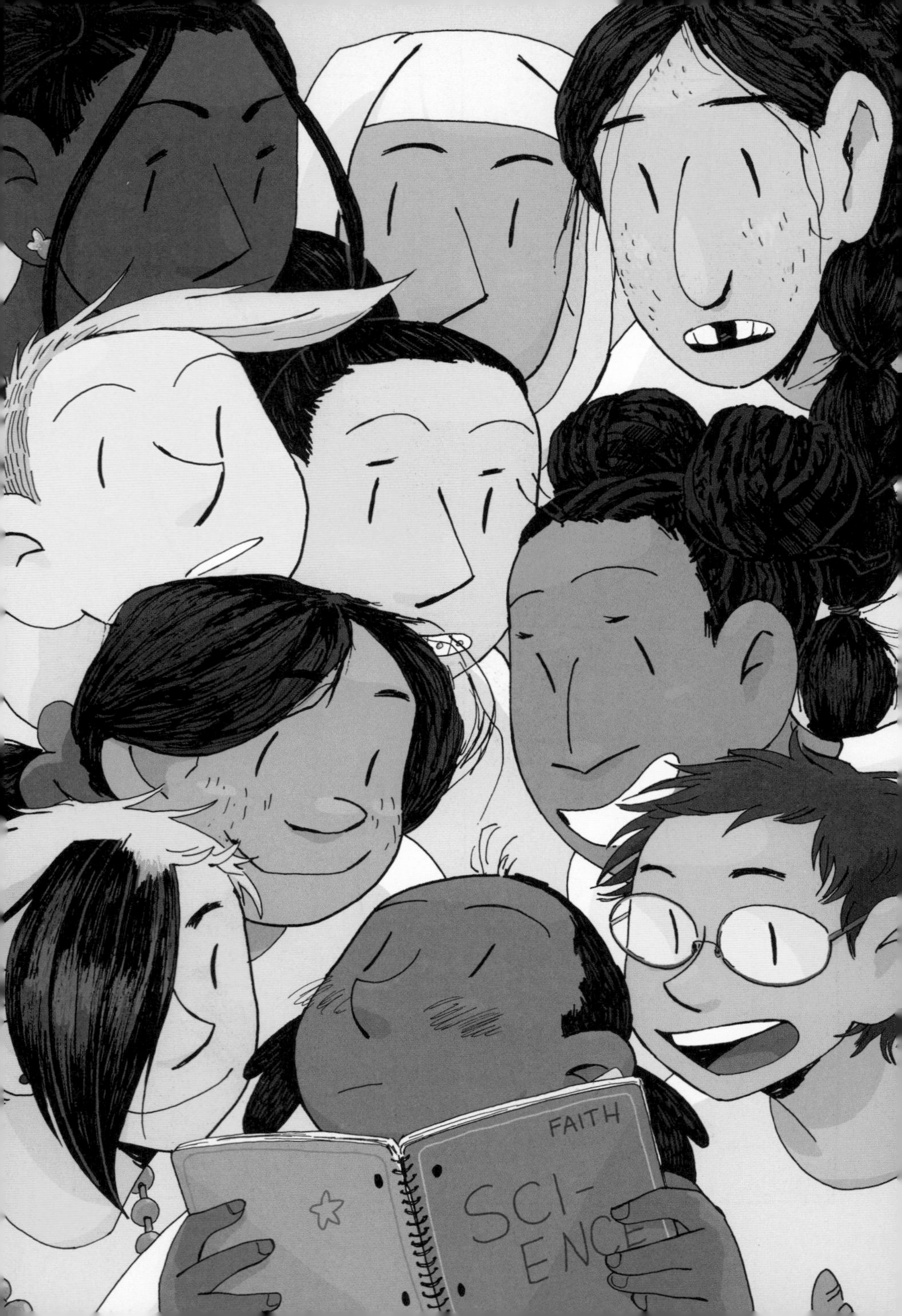
FAITH
SCI-
ENCE

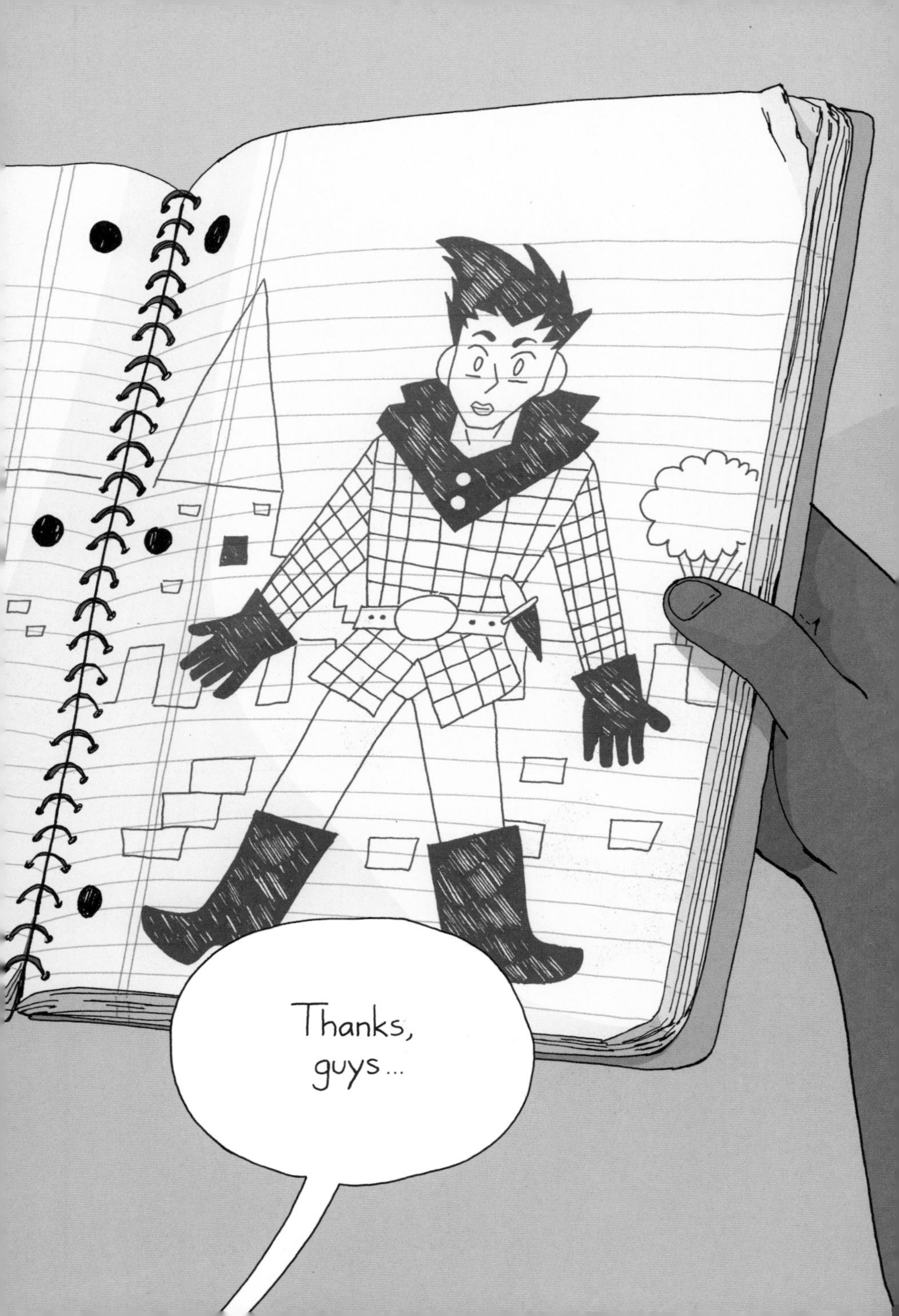
Thanks, guys...

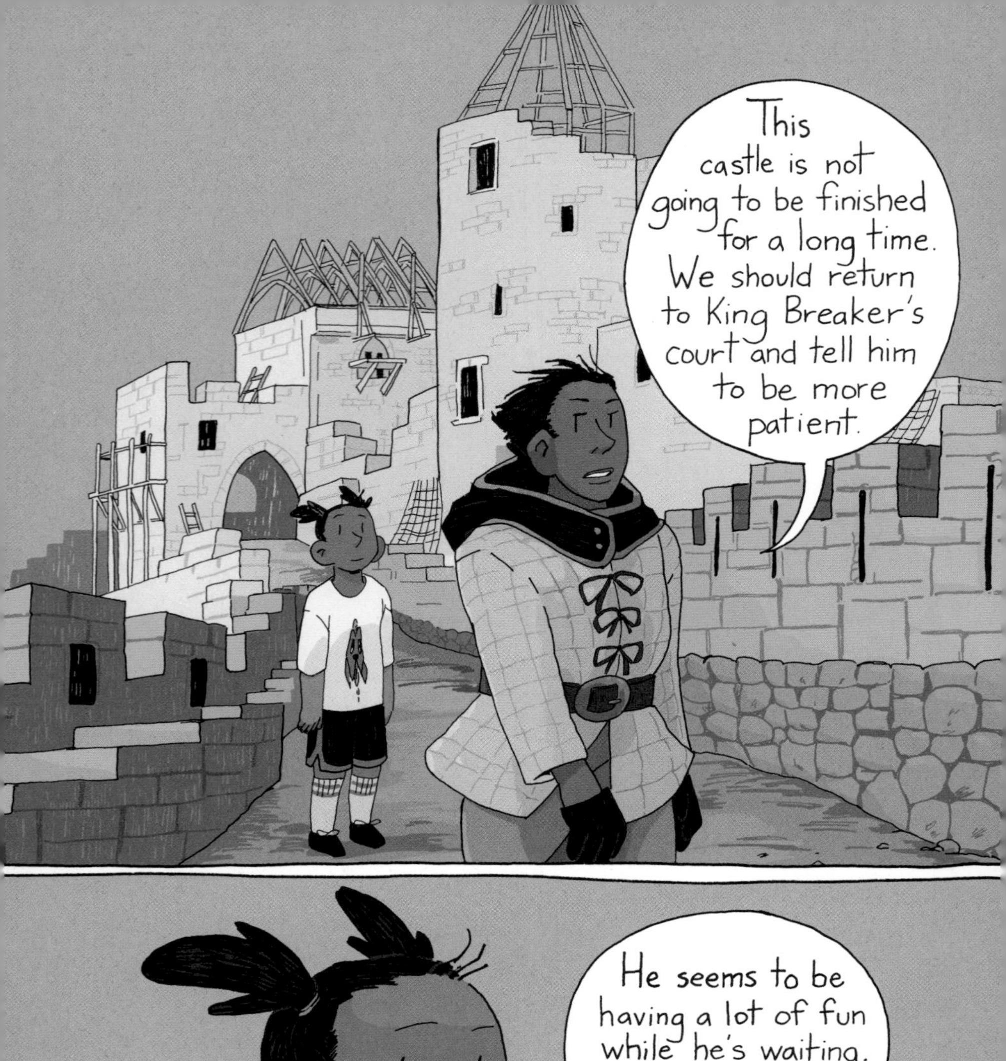
This castle is not going to be finished for a long time. We should return to King Breaker's court and tell him to be more patient.

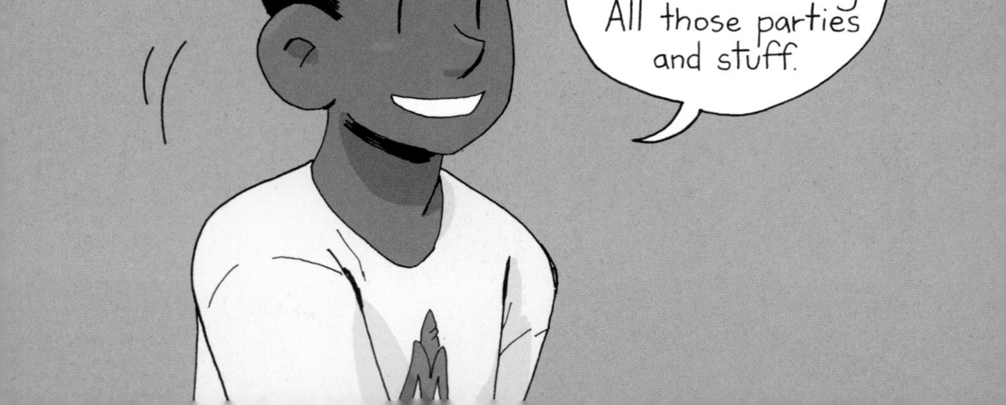
He seems to be having a lot of fun while he's waiting. All those parties and stuff.

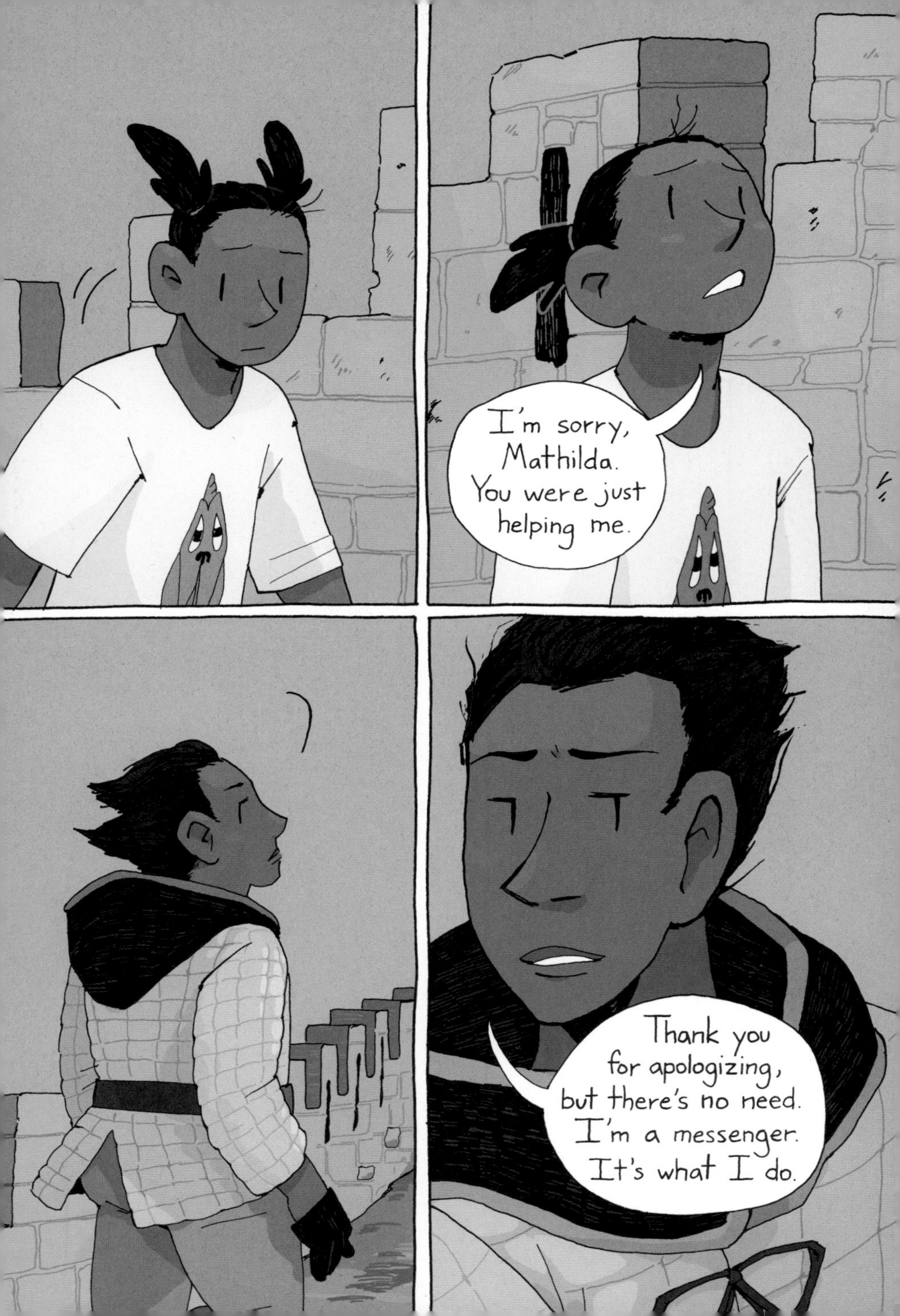
I'm sorry, Mathilda. You were just helping me.
Thank you for apologizing, but there's no need. I'm a messenger. It's what I do.

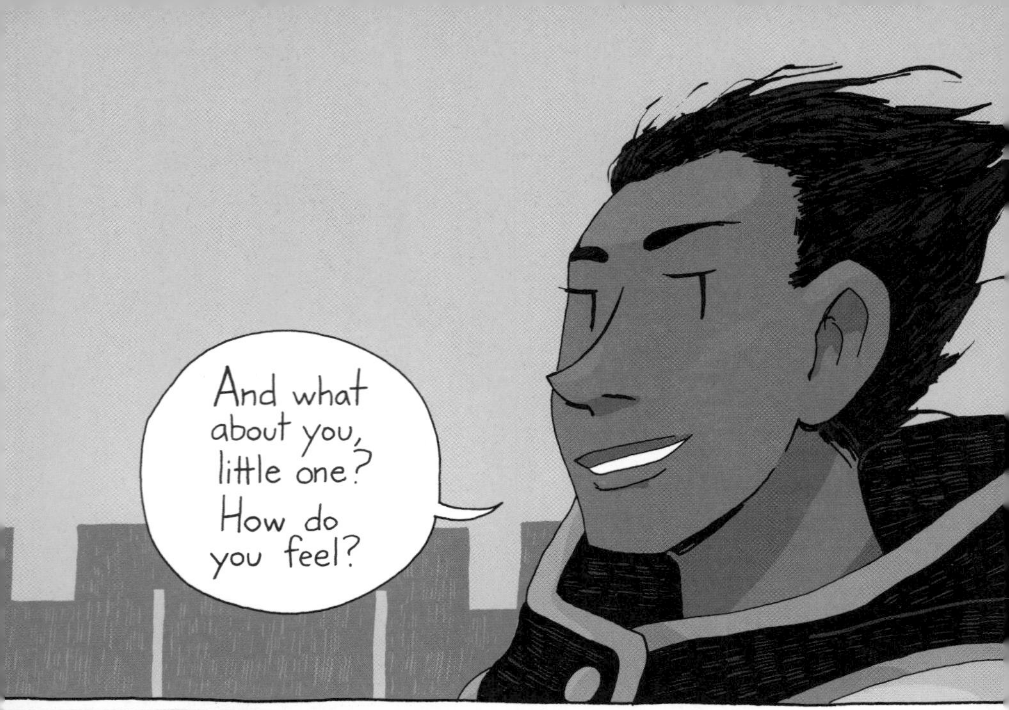
And what about you, little one? How do you feel?
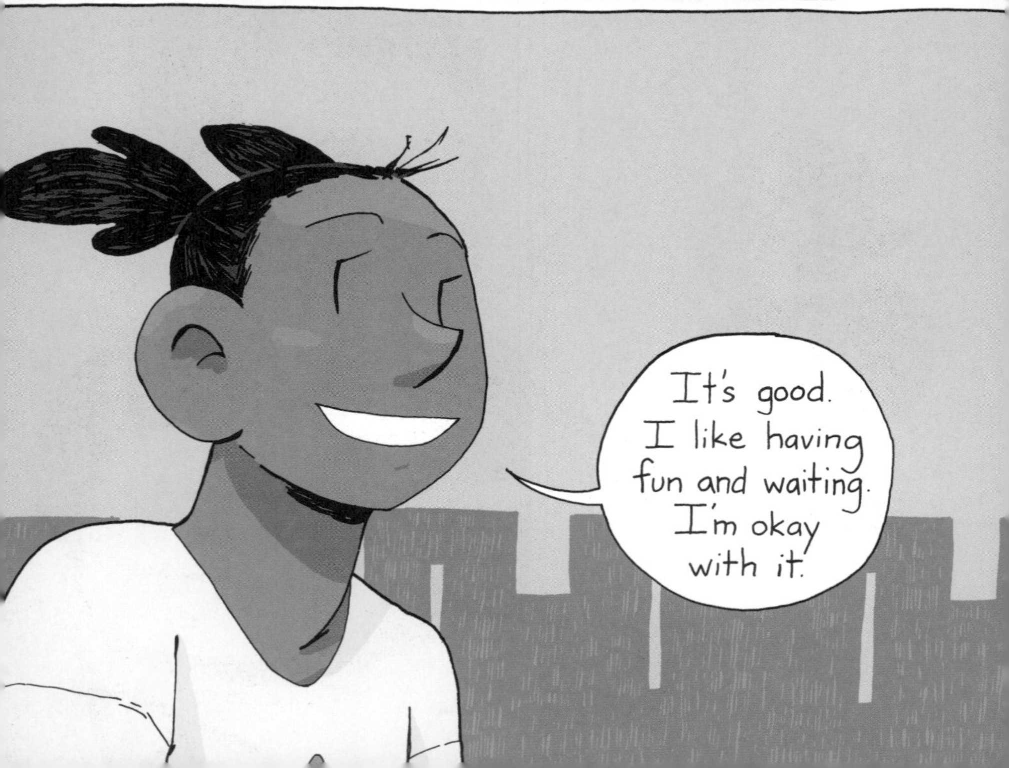
It's good. I like having fun and waiting. I'm okay with it.

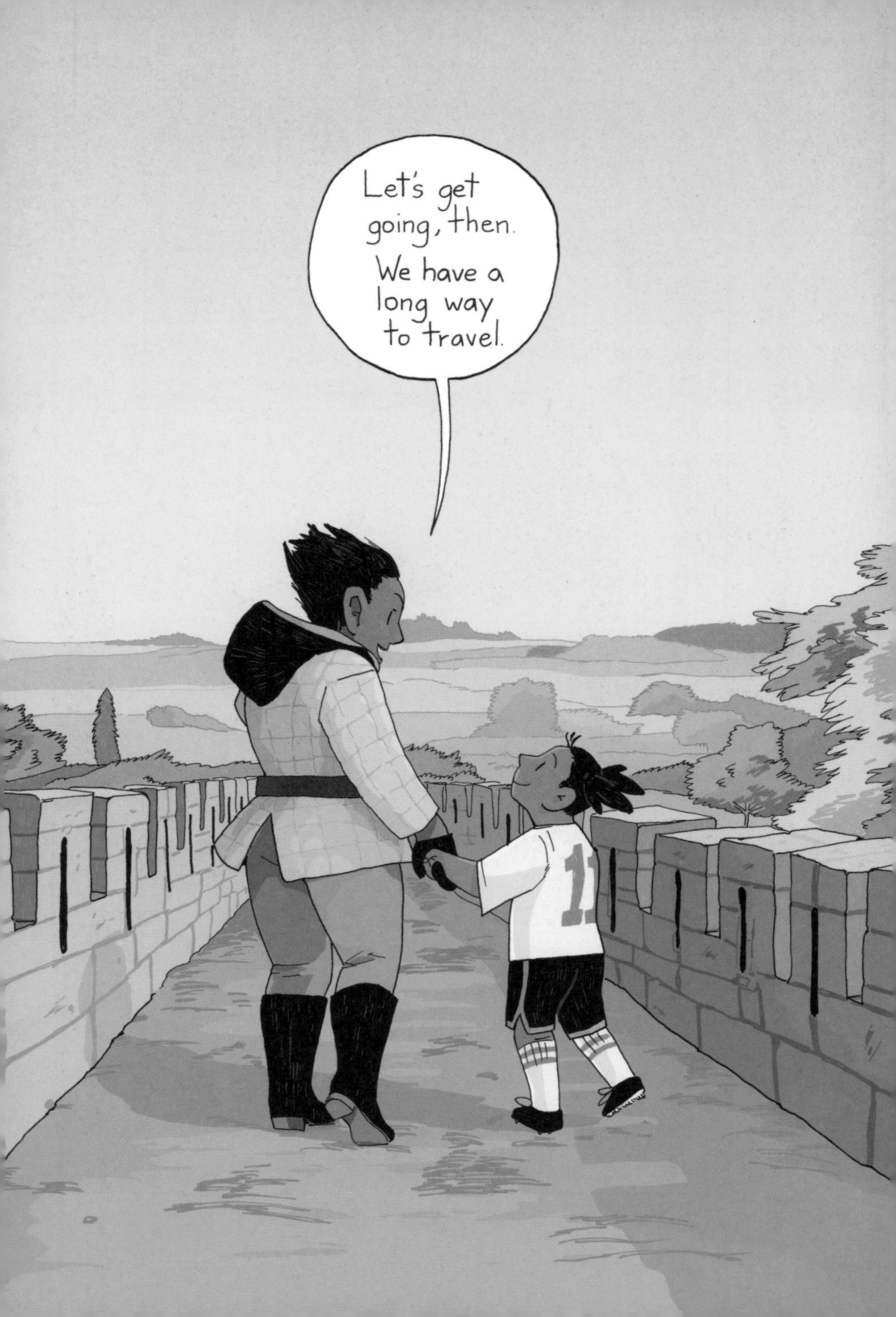
Let's get going, then. We have a long way to travel.

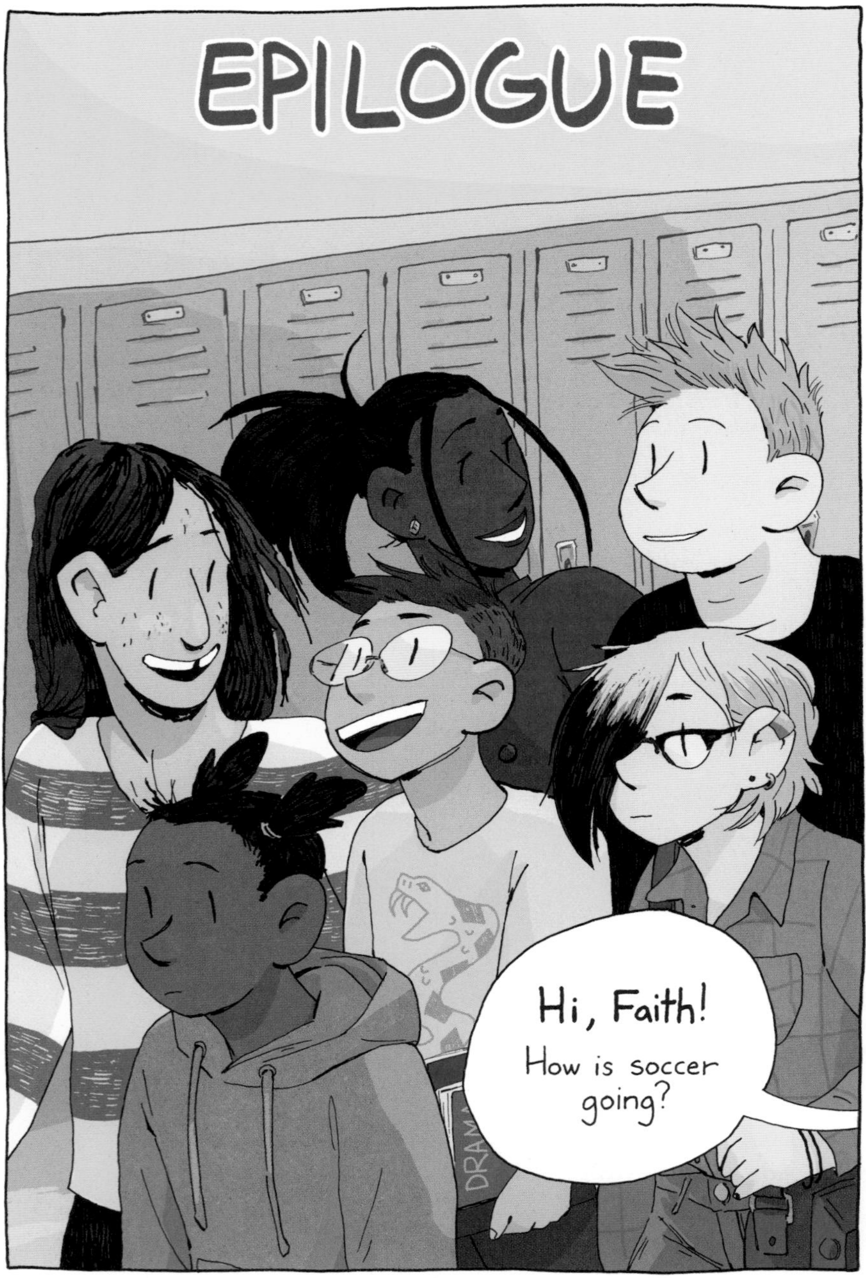
EPILOGUE
Hi, Faith! How is soccer going?

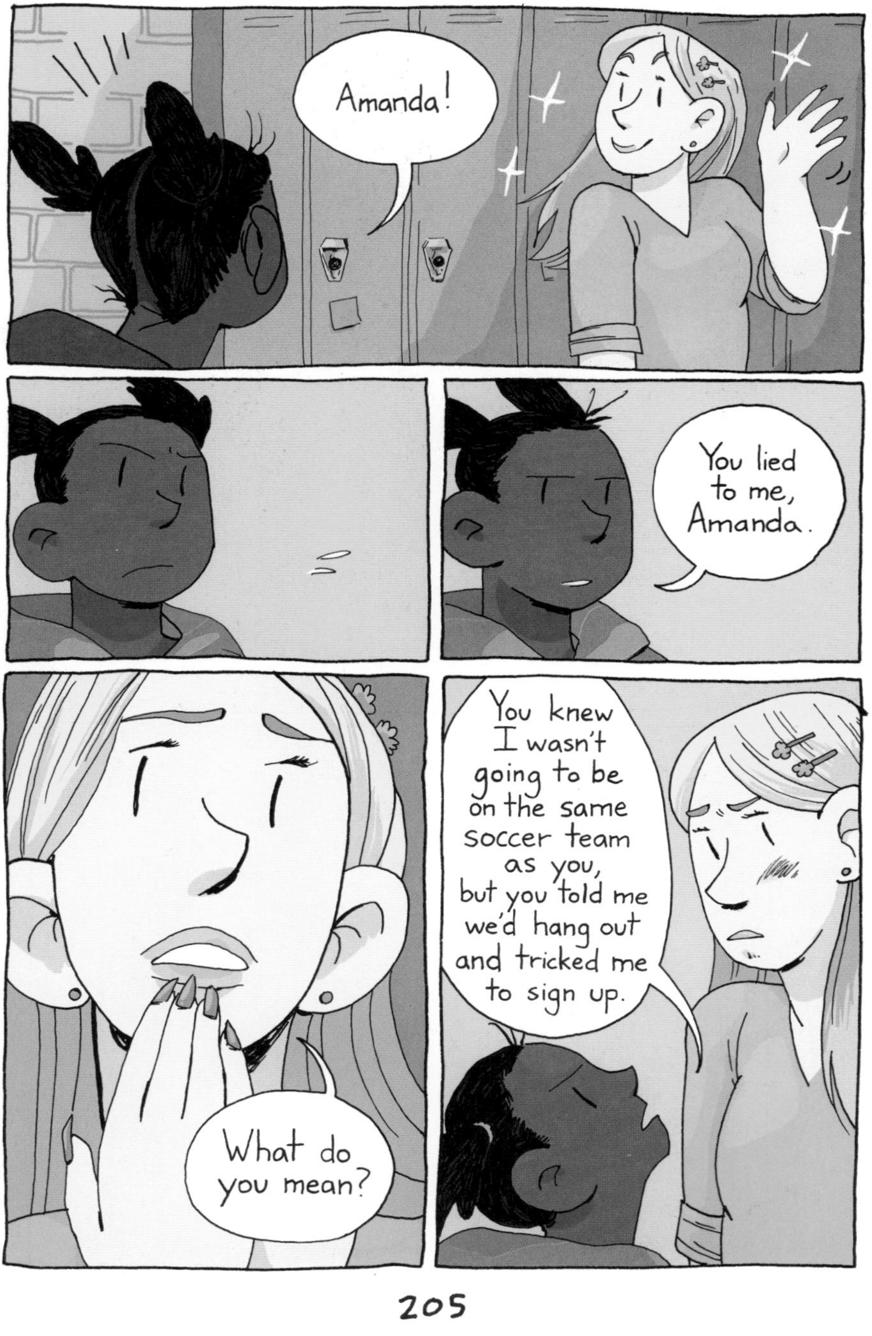
Amanda!
You lied to me, Amanda.
What do you mean?
You knew I wasn't going to be on the same soccer team as you, but you told me we'd hang out and tricked me to sign up.

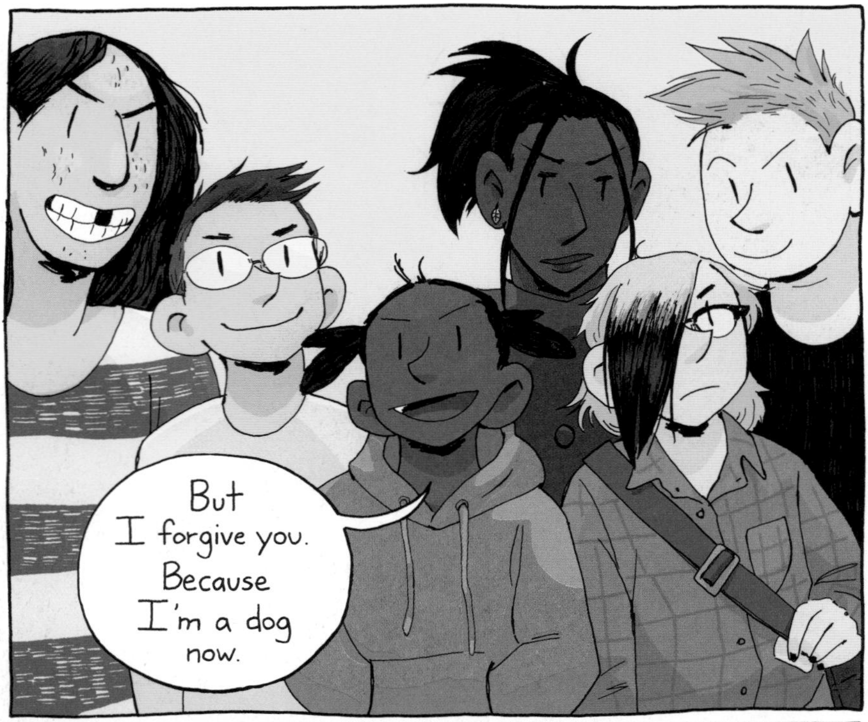
But I forgive you. Because I'm a dog now.

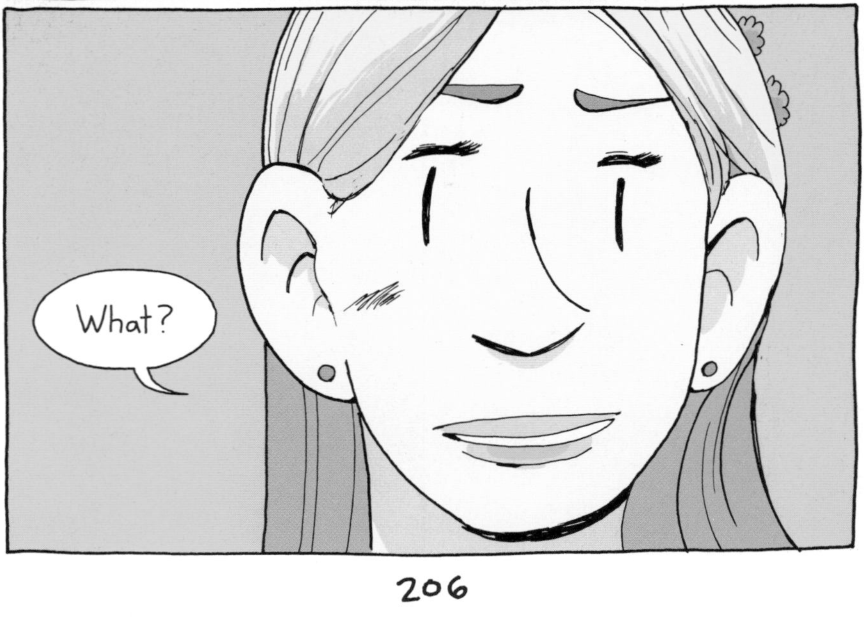
What?

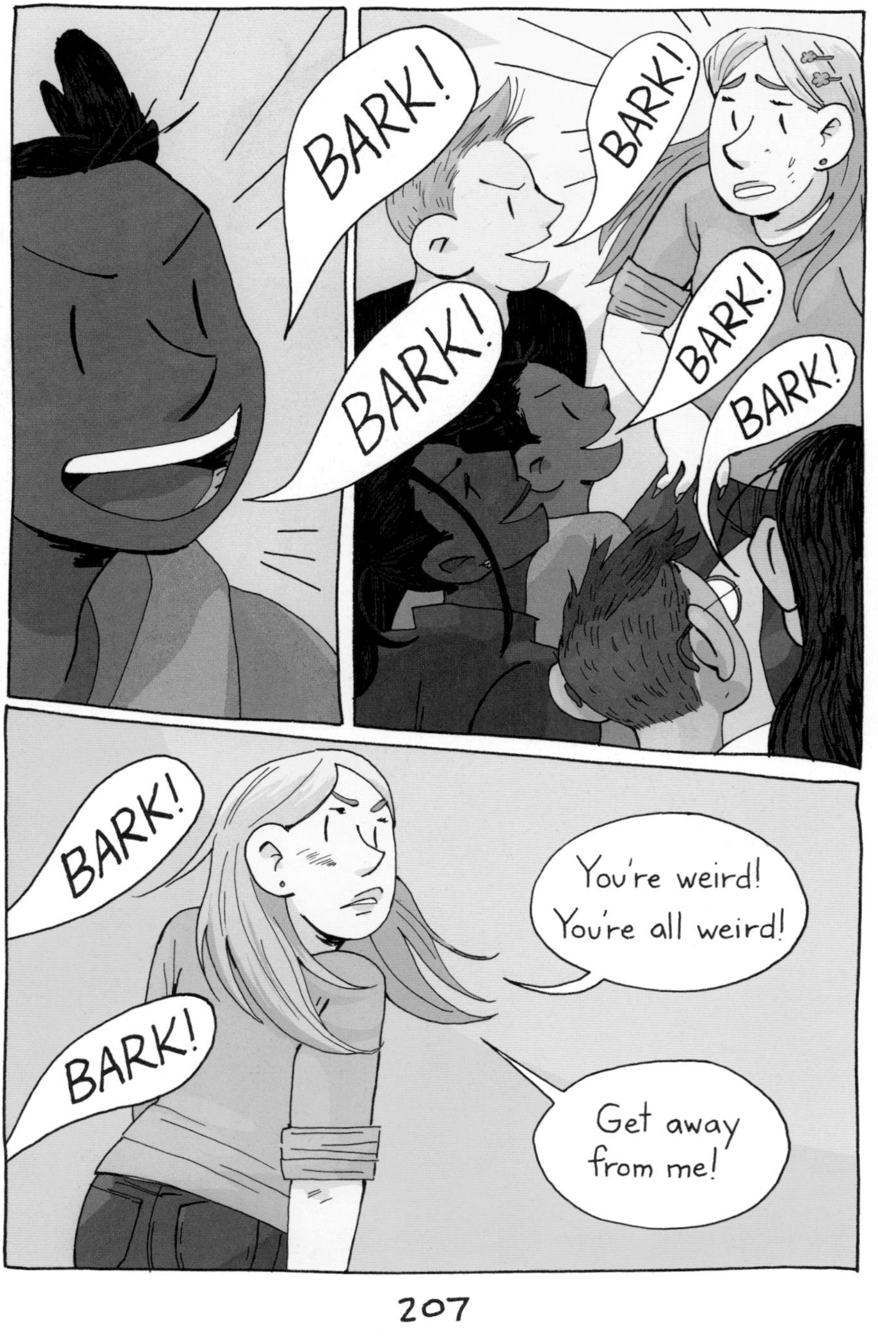
BARK!
BARK!
BARK!
BARK!
BARK!
BARK!
BARK!
You're weird! You're all weird!
Get away from me!

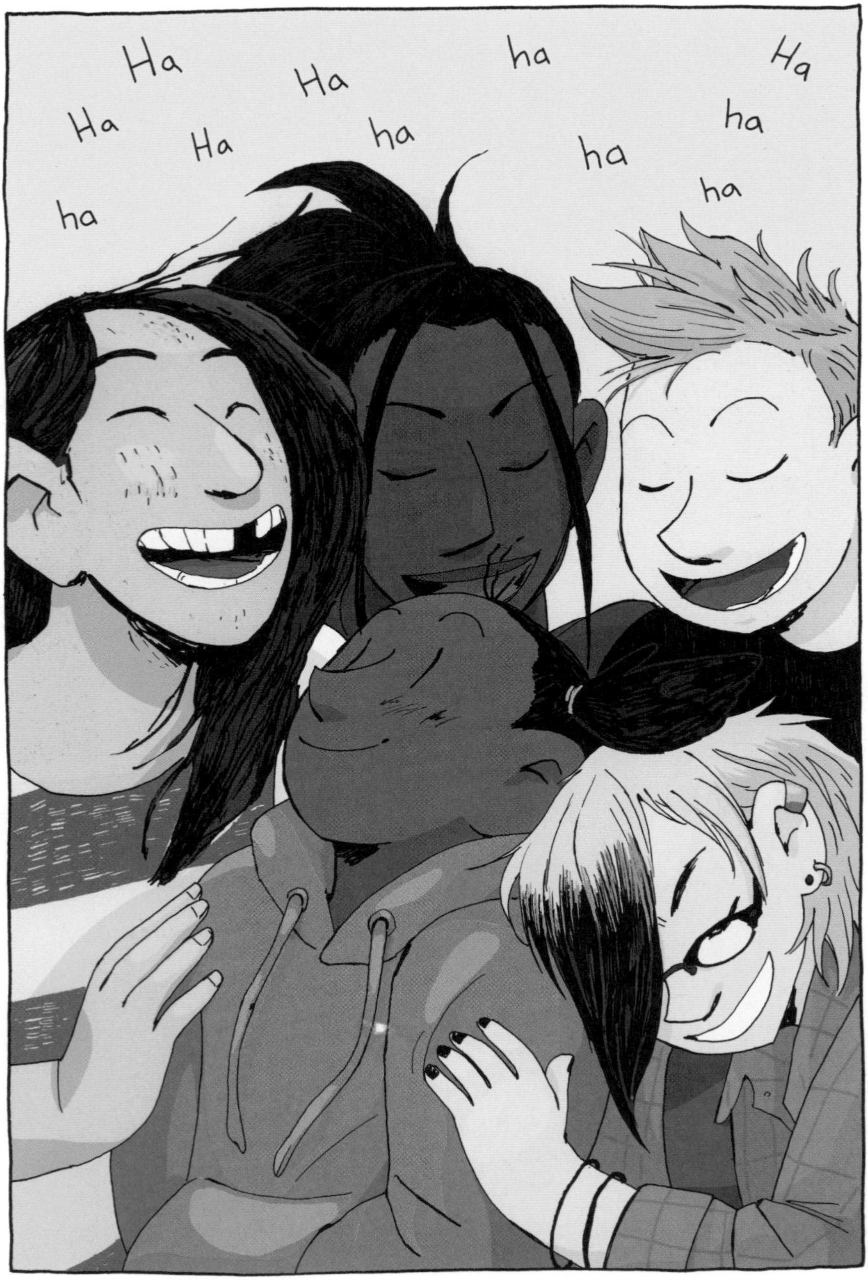
Ha
Ha
Ha
Ha
ha
ha
ha
Ha
ha
ha
ha

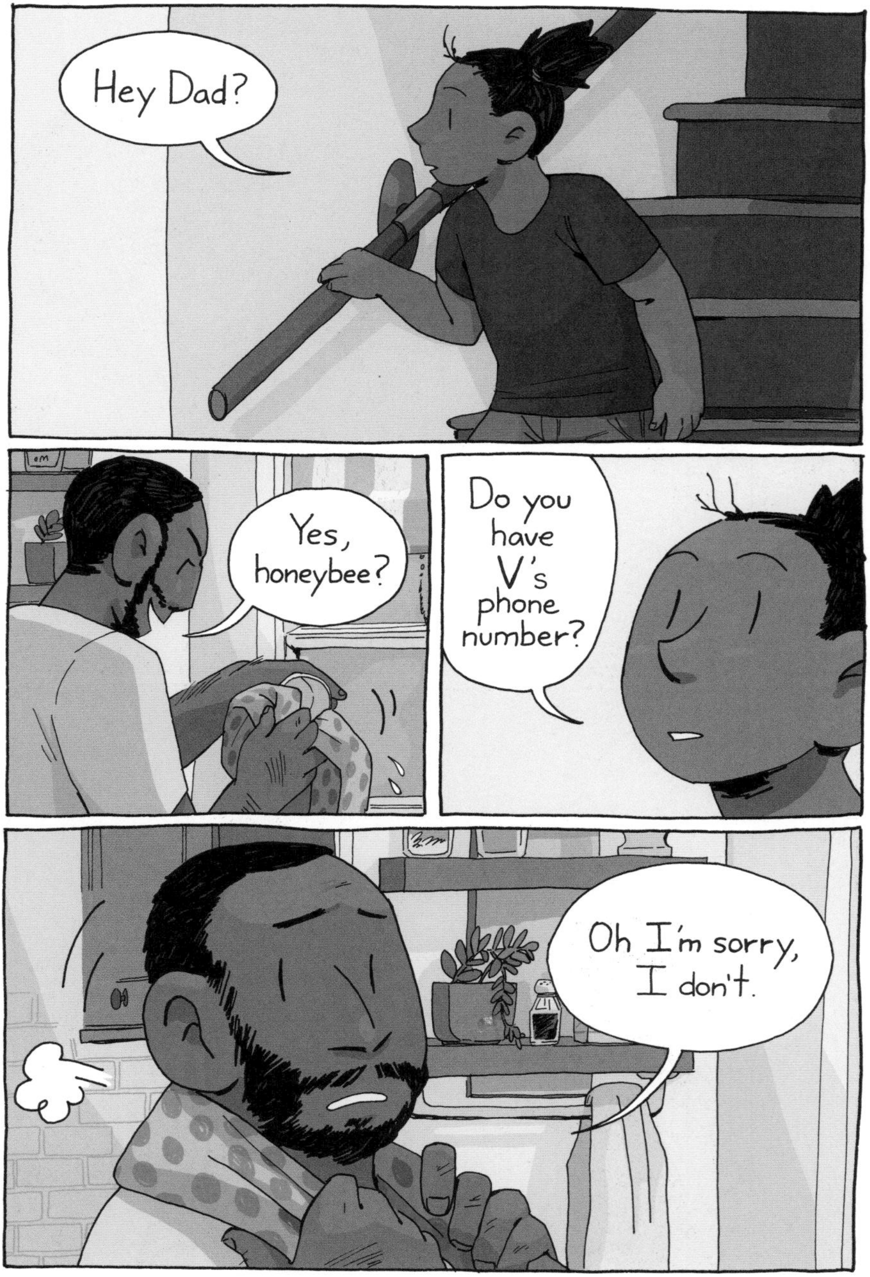
Hey Dad?
Yes, honeybee?
Do you have V's phone number?
Oh I'm sorry, I don't.

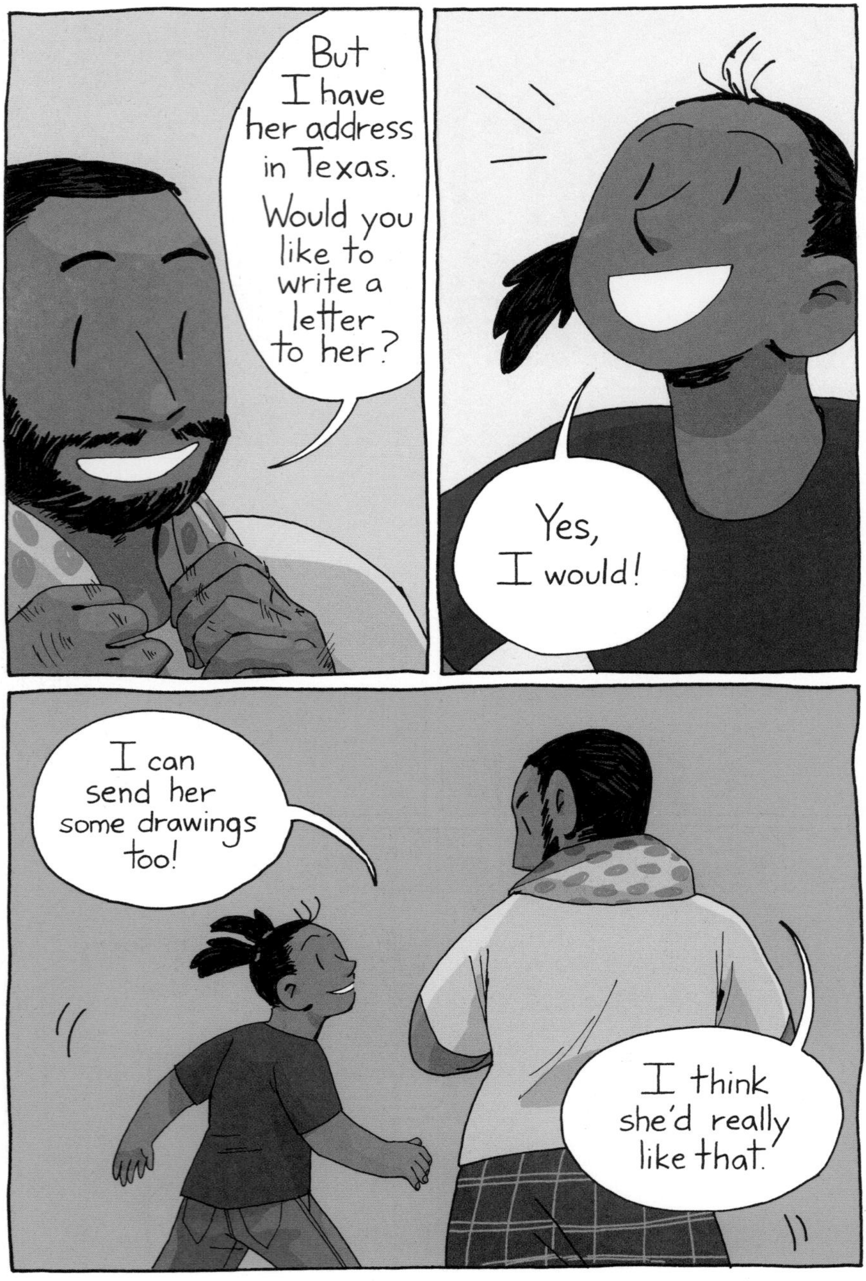
But I have her address in Texas.
Would you like to write a letter to her?
Yes, I would!
I can send her some drawings too!
I think she'd really like that.

THE
END

WHO IS

The Bloodhounds

The Woolly Mammoths

The Fighting
Schooners

YOUR TEAM?

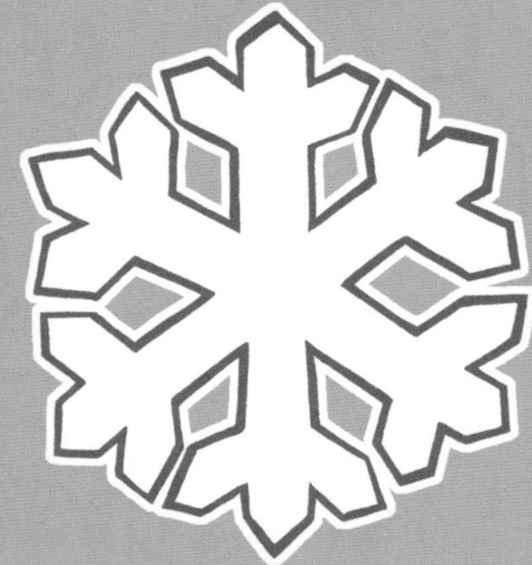

Smith
Refrigeration

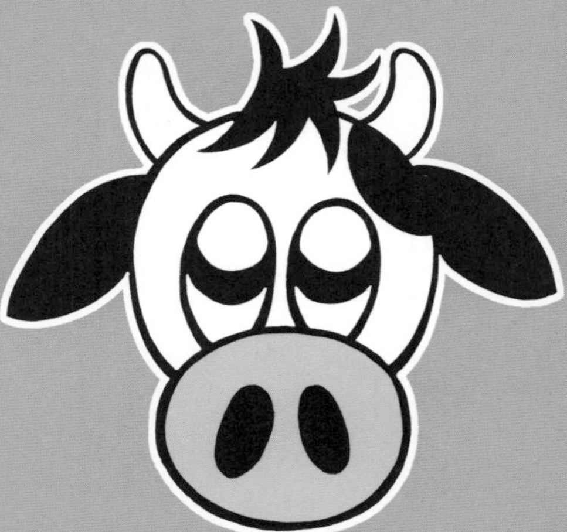

The Milk Maids

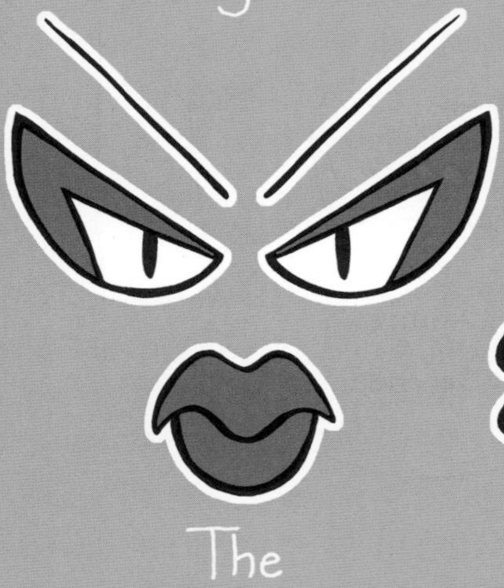

The
Super Models

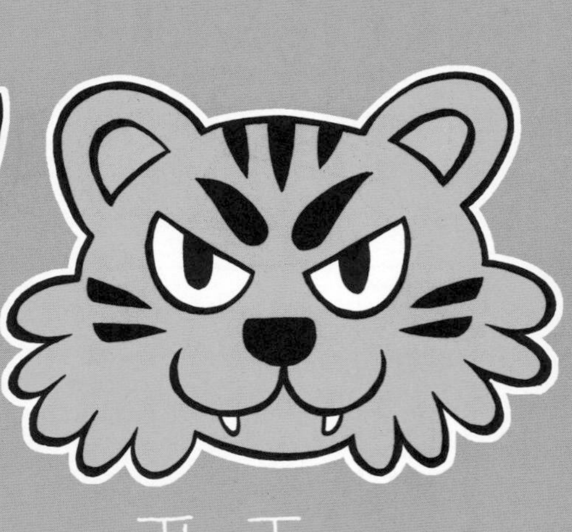

The Tigers

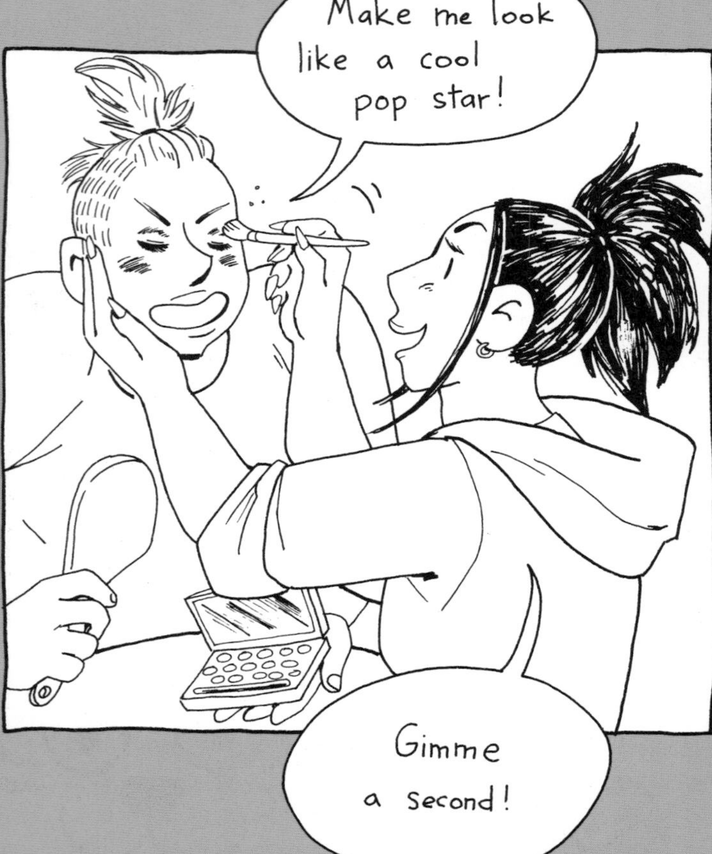
Make me look like a cool pop star!
Gimme a second!

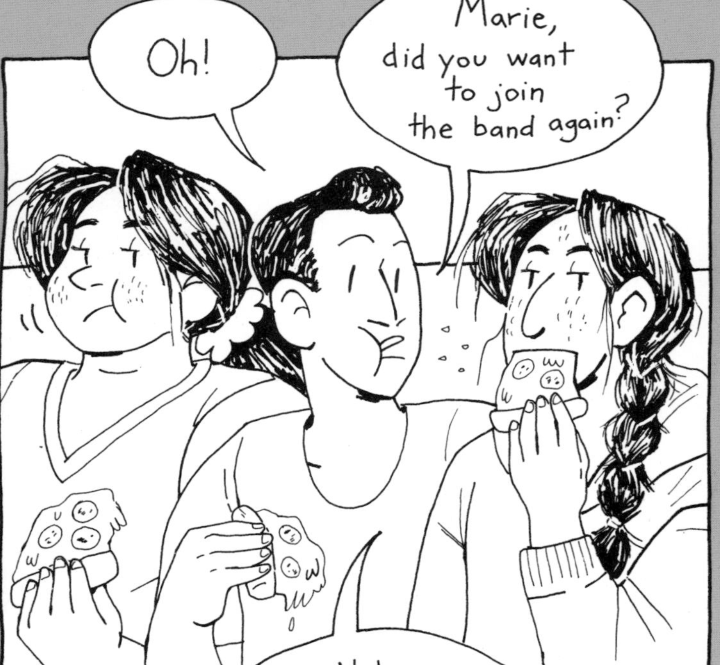
Oh!
Marie, did you want to join the band again?
Nah, the pizza was my favorite part about practice, anyway.

Thank You

To the Girl Scout troops of Rhode Island that I had
the pleasure of leading, thank you. You girls served
as the vibrant spark of inspiration for
the Bloodhounds, and without your energy and
enthusiasm, these characters would not be
who they are. To Fridley Middle School,
which was my middle school, thanks for being
the source of pain, growth, and friendship
that all middle schools tend to be.
To MJ Robinson, Taneka Stotts, and Lauren Brick,
the first few people I got to interview about their
experiences with soccer growing up, thank you.
Thanks to all my roommates, studiomates, and friends
who put up with my nonsense as I worked
on this book, notably O Horvath, Mimi Chrzanowski,
and Dailen Williams. Thank you to my agent,
Jen Linnan, my collaborator and champion.
Everyone at First Second, thanks for your hard work.
To Alexander Roederer and Nick Gomez-Hall
for their assistance with the Spanish. I miss you, Nick.
To my intern of one summer, Connor McCann,
who scanned a lot of this book, thank you.
Thanks to the past and present students, faculty,
and staff of Moses Brown School and
Warwick Center for the Arts.
Special thanks to my loved ones: Caitlin Warner,
Ross Hernandez, Kevin Czap, my parents,
my brother and sister-in-law, my grandparents.
Thank you, I love you, I love you, I love you.

— Cathy G. Johnson
April 2018

Dedicated to the memory of

A.D.
+
Nick Gomez-Hall

Fïrst Second

Published by First Second
First Second is an imprint of Roaring Brook Press,
a division of Holtzbrinck Publishing Holdings Limited Partnership
175 Fifth Avenue, New York, NY 10010

Don't miss your next favorite book from First Second!
Sign up for our enewsletter to get updates at firstsecondnewsletter.com.

Library of Congress Control Number: 2018938078

Paperback ISBN: 978-1-62672-357-3
Hardcover ISBN: 978-1-250-19694-1

Our books may be purchased in bulk for promotional, educational, or business use.
Please contact your local bookseller or the Macmillan Corporate and Premium Sales Department
at (800) 221-7945 ext. 5442 or by e-mail at MacmillanSpecialMarkets@macmillan.com.

FIRST

EDITION

First edition, 2019

Edited by Calista Brill and Whit Taylor
Book design by Chris Dickey
Color by Kevin Czap

Penciled with normal #2 pencils and inked with Rapidograph pens,
colors by Kevin Czap using Photoshop.

Printed in China by 1010 Printing International Limited, North Point, Hong Kong

Paperback: 10 9 8 7 6 5 4 3 2 1
Hardcover: 10 9 8 7 6 5 4 3 2 1

BY ART
WE LIVE